# PARIS in the FALL

# PARIS in the FALL

## Tamsin Hamilton

Seaview Books
NEW YORK

FIRST EDITION

LC: 80-5196
ISBN: 0-87223-617-X

*Designed by M. Franklin-Plympton*

**Library of Congress Cataloging in Publication Data**

Hamilton, Tamsin.
    Paris in the fall.

    1. Paris—History—1940-1944—Fiction.   I. Title.
PZ4.H2197Par  1980  [PR6058.A5539]  823'.914  80-5196
ISBN 0-87223-617-X

# PARIS in the FALL

# PROLOGUE

Suzanne Castel and her mother, Nathalie, walked slowly, reluctantly through the stately streets of the sixteenth district, on their way to have lunch with the Chambords, the mother, stepfather, and stepsister of Suzanne's fiancé, David. They had been invited to the Chambord house only once before, and were well aware that Charles Chambord did not approve of David's liaison with Suzanne, a nightclub singer. The Castels were ill at ease with Charles and Marie-Claude Chambord, though fond of David's mother, Carrie, who they imagined was different because she was American. Visiting the pretentious residence was something of an ordeal, and Nathalie kept straightening her collar and patting her hair nervously. Suzanne was wondering what they would talk about over lunch, if there would be those long silences that made her heart flutter, and if the table would be covered with a display of knives, forks and spoons to be used in a mystifying order. She imagined she had been invited only out of duty, because today was her nineteenth birthday and David was away at the front. Suzanne smiled dreamily, recalling their last meeting and the kisses they had enjoyed, the secret plans they had made about their future. Then she thought again of the sterile rooms of the Chambord house, and prayed she would not spill coffee on the tablecloth. Ahead, the mansion stood between an embassy and the home of a duchess.

Suzanne sighed wearily. "We're almost there, maman."

"I wish we were home drinking a glass of red wine in the garden."

As they continued toward the house, Suzanne tried to comfort her mother.

"Perhaps Madame Chambord will be alone. It's possible, you know. Marie-Claude and Monsieur could have gone out—you know how they hate meeting me."

Nathalie Castel shook her head knowingly.

"No such luck! He'll be there to make sure we don't contaminate his precious carpet!"

Suzanne sighed dispiritedly as she thought of the merry cacophony of sound around their home in Montmartre. In the oppressive silence of the sixteenth district she longed to rush home to enjoy her birthday instead of wasting the next two hours in the company of people she disliked.

As they neared the house, Nathalie whispered coaxingly to her daughter, "Promise me something, Zizi."

"Of course, maman."

"Promise you won't argue with Monsieur as you did last time, and won't hit Marie-Claude when she gets objectionable."

For a moment there was silence. Then Suzanne nodded reassuringly.

They reached the steps, which were scrubbed to pale perfection, and Nathalie rang the bell. A sour-faced butler asked them inside and told them curtly where to leave their coats. Suzanne shook hands with her host, eyed Marie-Claude warily, and kissed Caroline Chambord affectionately on both cheeks. Then she sat near her mother and looked round the sterile room. The Aubusson carpet was pink, cream, and faded blue, patterned with roses and fleurs-de-lis. The occasional tables were inlaid English Sheraton, and a six-frame screen painted in the manner of Watteau matched the insipid tones of the carpet. Stiff-backed tapestry chairs of white and blue were the only seating in the room, and Suzanne fidgeted uncomfortably. The walls were oak-paneled and covered with dark ancestral portraits of disdainful members of the Chambord family. Suzanne yawned nervously, closing her mouth suddenly when her mother nudged her ribs. In the corner of the room there was a grand piano, which Suzanne knew no one in the house could play, and nearby a silver dromedary had been placed

on top of a bureau gilded to vulgarity. Chambord followed Suzanne's mystified glance and explained apologetically that the
bureau belonged to an aunt who was taking the waters and was
unable to return to Paris because of the conflict. Mme. Chambord
rang the bell for drinks, and no one spoke until Marie-Claude
broke the uncomfortable silence:

"I had a card from David this morning."

Suzanne listened without acknowledging the statement. She too
had had a letter from her fiancé, the text so censored with black
ink as to be barely decipherable. The letter had ended: *I'll never
stop loving you, Zizi. The war and the possibility of dying haven't
changed a thing.* . . . She would not mention her letter, because
it was precious and private, not to be soiled by Marie-Claude's
jealous innuendoes. Marie-Claude's high-pitched voice grated on
her ears:

"Papa has agreed that I shall go to finishing school as soon as
this silly war is over."

Suzanne watched apprehensively as the butler and maid appeared with glasses. Chambord took a sherry, his wife the same.
Marie-Claude asked for a cocktail and was admonished until she
accepted a glass of Madeira. Mme Castel ordered a Dubonnet,
though she was longing for a large gin and tonic. Suzanne asked
for pastis, resisting Chambord's disapproving frown. Chambord
took a second sherry and then began to speak in a flat monotone.

"The news from the front is serious. My directors are not at
all happy about our prospects if the Germans continue to circum-
vent the Maginot Line. Things are just not what they were.
Frenchmen have forgotten how to fight. We have become a nation
of shopkeepers, like the British, too soft for our own good."

Suzanne watched his Adam's apple bobbing up and down and
stared unashamedly at the flabby jowls that wobbled as he spoke,
the ponderous stomach that hung over the top of his thighs. *Soft*
was the right word, she thought savagely. Chambord continued,
unaware of her silent disfavor.

"We shall see what General Weygand can do, but in my
opinion they recalled him too late. My directors believe France
is doomed, and that is my opinion, too. Have you heard recently
from your husband, Madame Castel?"

"Nothing, monsieur. Jacques wrote last from Amiens."

"Ah! That was some time ago, I think. The Panzers soon routed us from Amiens."

Suzanne glowered as her mother's hands began to tremble. Why did Chambord have to talk about war? Why could the old fool not take their minds from the torturous thoughts that plagued every waking hour? It was June, a sunny day full of the smell of lilac and orange blossom. Suzanne looked out the window into the garden and calmed herself with the thought that she would soon be home. Chambord droned on, and Suzanne drained her glass, surprising Marie-Claude by asking her reaction to the new hit play, *Le Bel Indifférent*. Marie-Claude blinked, uncertain what to say. She had seen the play but was unsure how to criticize it to such an experienced performer.

"I like Cocteau, of course, but Edith Piaf was *awful*. Every time she came on I closed my eyes."

Suzanne replied quietly, though she was seething with annoyance.

"The critics didn't agree with you."

Marie-Claude ignored the remark. Critics, what did they know about anything! She spoke with authority and disdain.

"A friend told me that Piaf doesn't wash, that she thinks the dirt and fleas on her body protect her from disease. Isn't that horrible? I can't watch her without shivering, she's so primitive, so ignorant."

"Can you listen to her sing, Marie-Claude?"

"Of course I can't! The gutter calls only to the gutter, my dear Suzanne."

"Lunch is served, mesdames, monsieur."

Nathalie Castel breathed a sigh of relief. Suzanne had a fierce temper and controlled it only with those she loved. One of these days she would surely tell Marie-Claude what she really thought of her pretensions. In the far distance guns sounded, and Nathalie watched a shiver of apprehension on her daughter's shoulders. She walked to the dining room, cowed by its grandeur and irritated by the same anemic paleness that ruined the entire house. A white damask cloth lay on a circular table that had as a centerpiece an ornate arrangement of green grapes and white lilies. Suzanne and her mother looked at each other, knowing that lilies reminded them of funerals.

At fifty, Carrie's once lively face was deeply lined, drawn and tired. Suzanne longed to comfort her, but her observations were interrupted by Chambord saying grace. Suzanne looked down at the pale carpet, frowning in disapproval of the lifeless gray walls and faded beige tapestries. She had decided never to come to lunch with the Chambords again. It was too much of an ordeal, unnecessary and unnerving. It was David she loved, David she had always loved ever since that first meeting at a picnic in the Montmartre vineyard in the summer of '34. It was David she would marry, not his family.

They ate a watery consommé, then quenelles de brochet, insubstantial white dumplings of ground pike. The main course was veal in a creamy sauce, with button onions, carrots, and potatoes on the side of the dish like objects in a still life too perfect to touch. Suzanne glared at Nathalie Castel. Then, as her mother winked mischievously, she shrugged her shoulders and smiled. She must make the time pass as quickly as possible and rush home to the hustle and bustle of Montmartre to enjoy the rest of the day. Apricot sorbet completed the meal, along with coffee that was too bitter for the Castels' taste. Chambord spoke infrequently, and was answered dutifully on each occasion by his daughter. His wife tried to carry on a conversation with Suzanne, but each time she spoke her husband raised his voice imperceptibly as though determined to overrule her. Suzanne finished her coffee and looked up at the ceiling, and, sensing her apprehension, Carrie asked her gently about her work.

"Tell me about your new job, Suzanne."

"I'm about to start rehearsals at the Bal Tabarin. The show will be called *Monocle*."

"What's your part in the show?"

"I will sing a ten-minute spot to close the first half of the program."

"The Bal Tabarin's pretty close to your home, isn't it?"

"It is, madame. I only have to walk a little way through Pigalle and then up to Montmartre by the steps."

"That's sensible. Last week one of my best friends was run down by a truck during the blackout."

"Did she die?"

"She certainly did. The truck was on its way to les Halles with a load of potatoes. They had to scrape her remains off the sidewalk."

Suzanne grinned at Chambord's frown of disapproval. She was sure he loathed every one of his wife's American friends, and probably everything she said into the bargain. She leaned toward Carrie and said confidentially:

"There's going to be a benefit to aid the army injured, Madame Chambord. Will you be attending? It's to be on the eighteenth, and Maurice Chevalier has agreed to appear."

Madame hesitated, her husband looked displeased, and Marie-Claude answered before her stepmother could reply.

"Papa and Madame don't go to nightclubs, Suzanne."

"They don't hold benefits in nightclubs, Marie-Claude. This one will be held at the Empire in the avenue Wagram."

Marie-Claude raised a condescending eyebrow.

"Perhaps that would be all right. The avenue Wagram, that's in the seizième, isn't it, papa?"

Suzanne's eyes narrowed as Chambord shrugged his shoulders disinterestedly.

"The avenue Wagram is in the seventeenth arrondissement, Marie-Claude. But must you always worry about staying inside your own area in case you catch fleas!"

"Suzanne!" Mme. Castel was shocked by her daughter's outburst.

"I'm sorry, maman."

Marie-Claude stared in disbelief at Suzanne, amazed that a poor chanteuse from Montmartre should dare defy her in her own home. She looked over at Suzanne's cheap sandals and smirked.

"Don't you find that your feet become terribly dirty in those shoes, Suzanne?"

Suzanne sighed, weary of the confrontation.

"Dirt can easily be washed off my feet Marie-Claude. It's much more difficult to wash it out of the mind."

"Come, come, children, stop bickering at once." Charles Chambord rose impatiently and left the table. His wife ordered more coffee to be brought to the terrace, and the party adjourned to sit overlooking a garden of geometric rose beds.

Chambord was proud of his roses. Each year he entered them for the Prix Foch competition, and each year he gave such a generous contribution to the committee funds that they felt obliged to award him first prize. This year, for the first time, there would be no rose show. Every fit man was at the front, at least those of suitable age, and Paris had become a city of women, with only very young boys and very old men to look after them.

Chambord turned his back on his guests and bent down to turn on the radio. Then he took out his fob watch and checked the second hand with the chimes of Big Ben. This he did every day, and he was proud of the fact that his watch had never lost a second in years.

"I always listen to the BBC. Do you have a radio, Madame Castel?"

Nathalie nodded, bored to death by her host's patronizing attitude. Marie-Claude was picking lavender in the garden, and Suzanne wondered why, in such a small space, they had paved, formal walks and a pretentious gazebo of white treillage. The announcer's voice shattered the calm of the afternoon.

"This is London and here is the BBC news for today, June tenth, at two P.M. Greenwich Mean Time, Alvar Lidell speaking. It has been reported that General Rommel's Seventh Panzer Division has broken through the British defense at Bethune and is proceeding through Forges-les-Eaux toward the river Seine. The Paris military government has been ordered to become the Paris army. The army will be commanded by General Herring and will defend the city and the Paris advanced position. The west flank of the French Tenth Army has surrendered. The British Fifty-first Division has withdrawn from Abbeville to Bresle. General Hoth's Armored Corps has liquidated strategic opposition from the French Tenth Army and has proceeded to Hornoy. There will be a special bulletin at four P.M. Greenwich Mean Time, and the next news will be at six P.M."

Suzanne felt suddenly cold, and Chambord looked warily at his wife as though needing her reassurance. Nathalie put down her cup, and Marie-Claude the lavender she had picked. *General Hoth's Armored Corps has liquidated strategic opposition from the French Tenth Army . . .* that meant that the "hedgehogs" were dead, that the new way of fighting so admired by the French people had proved ineffective against the almighty Panzers. Suzanne thought of the brave men who had spent weeks hiding in small operational bases in woods and villages, demolishing unwary Germans with 75-mm. antitank guns. They were gone, never to return to their shops and their homes and their children. She thought of David, far away in Picardy, and wished he had loved her as she wanted to be loved—*really* loved, like a wife— but he had kissed her longingly and then returned to his unit, unwilling to risk the possibility of leaving her pregnant. If the Germans invaded Paris she would die unloved and untried, a foolish virgin who had never tasted passion. Tears of frustration poured down her cheeks, and she blew her nose loudly.

Charles Chambord frowned at the interruption of his thoughts. If there was to be a German occupation, the enemy would take over his bank, all the banks, and he would face financial ruin and even death. The Chambords had been presidents of the Banque de Lyon for five generations. Would they now be forced to accept orders from an enemy determined to undermine French currency? Chambord thought of the gold bars hoarded in his safe, and decided to bury them in the garden as soon as it was dark. In the final analysis, stocks and shares, bank notes and currency of any denomination meant nothing. Only gold would keep its value.

Nathalie was thinking that as soon as she got home she would bury all her best wines under the apple tree. They were fine wines, some of them left her by a rich relative. Lovingly she thought of the ruby and tawny liquids, of the Château Laroise and the Château Lafite and the Château d'Yquem, some of the bottles more than twenty years old. She had never in the past found an occasion important enough to warrant opening a bottle, but tonight she would open the first. Then in the darkness she would bury the rest. It would also be wise to buy seeds and bedding plants and to get rid of the flowers in the back garden and plant vegetables instead. Then, whatever happened they would have food and a way to stay alive.

Marie-Claude busied herself writing a list: ten pairs of summer shoes, ten pairs of winter shoes, boots for snow, a new umbrella, a silk parasol for garden parties, a fur coat, six sets of silk underwear, an organdy petticoat, and two dozen pairs of silk stockings—the old twenty-gram ones, not the new, economy eight-to ten-gram type. Then a dozen lipsticks, powder, and the biggest

possible bottle of Guerlain's Shalimar, to be obtained somehow
or other. Without perfume she would be ashamed to go out into
the street, so she must find someone who knew how to obtain such
things. Marie-Claude schemed how to get the money out of her
father the next morning. She would ask his advice on how to
choose a finishing school, writing down everything he said because Papa loved being learned. She thought that if the Germans
came to Paris they would surely bother the residents of the
seizième least. Money counted, after all, even during a war. Still,
her heart fluttered excitedly. She had heard unpleasant stories
about Germans and their ways of dealing with their enemies.
Marie-Claude glanced at her stepmother, annoyed that Carrie's
eyes held only a misty, faraway longing.

Carrie was thinking of her childhood, shrimping with her
brother among the rock pools on the sandy shores of Cape Cod.
She had adored summer vacations and every minute of the wild,
carefree days of childhood that always pass too soon. Her mind
wandered to thoughts of her first husband and how she had loved
him. She had grumbled at his footloose, disorganized way of life
and wandered with him all over the world, always longing for a
secure and stable home. Fifteen years after his death, she had
her stable, silent home, and each day was predictable, exactly the
same as the previous day, and all of them bored her to death.
Carrie thought defiantly that if the Germans came to Paris at
least things would be different. She had come to the point where
she thought she would rather starve than shrivel in the prison of
present routine. She made a mental note to buy as much fruit as
she could find and to go to the country, if that was possible, to
buy potatoes, carrots, onions, and zucchini. Then she would order
the staff out of the steel kitchen Charles had designed and make
vast jars of jam, pickles, bottled fruits and vegetables, just as she
had long ago in her youth. Carrie wondered if she should suggest
to her husband that they have the gardener remove the roses
and plant potatoes instead. In bad times roses could not be eaten—
indeed nothing in their garden was of the slightest use to the
larder. Charles had even refused to grow herbs because he thought
it déclassé to grow food like a peasant. If she suggested uprooting
his precious roses, he would raise his eyes to the ceiling in exasperation and ask, "Whatever will the neighbors think?" Chambord's

life had always been lived according to what the neighbors would think, and it would take more than Germans to change him.

Before leaving, Suzanne went to the bathroom. On her way back to the lounge she paused on the landing, thinking how strange it was that David's mother and stepfather slept in separate bedrooms. Chambord's door was open because he insisted on having a through draft for the good of his health. Suzanne thought that he would be healthier if he learned to drink less claret after dinner. From the color of his cheeks, the banker had been pickling his liver for years. The next room, Suzanne knew, was Carrie's bedroom. She looked around to check that no one was watching and then opened the door a fraction, staring at the interior in amazement. Toile-de-jouy walls of pink and saffron framed a bed draped with bright yellow silk. The chairs were covered with rose brocade that matched an exotic Chinese carpet of the eighteenth century. The furniture was Charles X bois-claire, and a trompe l'oeil painting on the wall showed steps leading to a secret garden of delight. Suzanne closed the door nervously, shocked that Carrie's taste did not run like her husband's to clinical emptiness. She was halfway across the landing when she saw Carrie coming upstairs carrying an exotic gold orchid in a pink pot. Suzanne thought guiltily that the flower and pot matched precisely the colors in the bedroom she had just seen. As Carrie drew near, Suzanne admired the orchid.

"I never saw such a strange flower before."

"One of my friends brought it back from South America. I hope I can keep it alive come the winter, but I'm not too optimistic. If you like plants, come and see my collection."

Suzanne followed Carrie back to her bedroom, watching as she put the orchid on her bedside table. Carrie opened the door of the bathroom, and inside Suzanne saw a profusion of greenery— ferns with feathery leaves, cacti with spiky pink blooms, and flowers with fleshy liplike apertures that Carrie told her ate flies. As Carrie watered the "garden," Suzanne talked of her fiancé.

"David told me you were once married to a famous writer."

"That's right. Jack wrote novels about America in the early pioneer days."

"Do you think David will inherit his father's talent?"

"He's creative, there's not much doubt of that. Maybe he'll

write when he's older, but right now he's only interested in fighting Germans and marrying you."

Suzanne teased her gently about David's accent. "Will he write in French or in English?"

Carrie's face crinkled into a smile. "I tease David that he dreams in French and talks in English."

"How old was he when you first came to Paris? He never talks about his early days in the city."

"I think he hates to think of those days because they were sad ones for us. David was twelve. His father had just died at thirty-seven, and I figured we both needed a complete change of scene to help us get over the shock. I didn't like Paris much when I first arrived, but David loved it, so we stayed for a month and then two. It was through him that I met Charles."

"Where did you meet Monsieur?"

"I met him in the Bois de Boulogne. David insisted on kicking his football to Charles, and when they'd played awhile he brought Charles over. Hélène Chambord had just died in a car crash, leaving Charles alone with Marie-Claude, who was only two. I suppose you could say unhappiness brought us together."

"And so you settled in Paris and became a 'femme française.'"

Carrie put down her water jug abruptly, and Suzanne saw that her face was resigned and sad.

"I've remained resolutely American, Suzanne, that's my problem—but I don't think we should talk about that, do you? Let's go join the others."

Back in the living room, Suzanne thanked her host and kissed Carrie's cheeks, thinking happily that there was still half a day left to enjoy. Nathalie held her daughter's arm, and together they made their way from the house to the Champs-Elysées. Each was thinking of the broadcast that had signified disaster. If the Germans came to Paris, how many of their friends would survive? Would the rich buy favors and the poor suffering? Or would resilience bred on poverty outlast softness fed with plenty? Nathalie looked affectionately at her daughter's strong brown limbs and the heart-shaped face that was thoughtful and still. Sounds of far distant gunfire came to their ears, and the horizon was full of smoke from villages burned in the German advance. Suzanne thought apprehensively that the golden days were almost over. Soon darkness would fall on the sunlit boulevards of Paris.

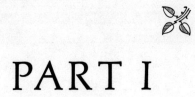

# PART I

# CHAPTER ONE

*June, 1940*

Suzanne and her mother caught the bus down the Champs-Elysées to the place de la Concorde. From there they would walk home, past Maxim's in the rue Royale and the Madeleine church, pausing for a cool drink in the place Diaghilev before contemplating the steep climb. As they drank, they discussed the Chambords.

"I don't think we'll go to lunch there again, maman."

"I agree, it's too much of a strain."

"I looked in Carrie's bedroom and it was all pink and yellow and full of pictures and photographs. Monsieur Chambord sleeps next door, not with her."

"I thought there was something wrong. She should never have married that man. Did you see how he dusted the chairs before he sat down—as if there could be any dirt in that mortuary! And he kept telling me there were germs everywhere. When he tends his roses he wears a surgical mask!"

They dissolved into peals of irreverent laughter and continued on their way. As they neared Montmartre, familiar sounds made them smile—hens crowing, distant cars honking, children screaming as they chased each other past the Bateau Lavoir. Old men were playing boule in a nearby square, and the lace maker was at her window, looking down. Suzanne thought approvingly that everything was the same as it had been the previous week and the month and year before that. When she saw their own peach-painted house, she ran ahead to open the door, waving to their next-door neighbors, the Marchands, and rejoicing that she was back in the area she loved. Like everyone else in Montmartre, the Marchands were digging up their flowers and planting vegetables.

Suzanne ran through the living room, throwing open the windows and looking out on the iron lampposts and flagstone steps of the rue Foyatier. Father Valery, the elderly priest from St. Pierre, was toiling up the steps with his new assistant, Father Chanson. Suzanne waved and then went to the kitchen to heat water for coffee. For a moment she stood looking out on the garden and thinking that she never wanted to live anywhere else because the house was perfection and Montmartre the only area in the city where she could be content.

Nathalie lingered for a few minutes in the front garden, inspecting her bird feeders and having a word with Vivienne Marchand. Then she entered the house, closing the door, turning the lock, and breathing a sigh of relief that they were home. Nathalie frowned, aware that something urgent would have to be done to raise money so she could buy food to store for the bad days. She looked around the living room with its fat chintz sofas, art nouveau tiled fireplace, and mahogany tables. Dozens of books lined the walls, and the coffee tables were full of bric-a-brac. On the far wall there was a faded portrait of herself when young, in the pink tights she had worn for her trapeze act. For a moment Nathalie remembered with great pleasure her days in the Music Hall and her first meeting with Jacques Castel, then one of the most popular dancing stars in Paris. She had loved Jacques from the moment of first meeting, and they had married three months later. Romantic memories flickered through her mind as she looked at the photographs on the wall, the dresser, the coffee tables. Then she patted her ample waist and thought ruefully that at forty-eight she was putting on weight. She had lost her figure with her taste for performing in the Music Hall, but she had never lost her adoration of Jacques.

She walked around the room looking at her mementos and trying to assess which, if any, would sell. On one wall photographs and gaudy theatrical posters reminded her of the happy days when she had been a minor star. The screen had no value except to the family. Scattered about the room were Negro masks from Africa, cased butterflies from her husband's collection, Gothic crucifixes, model ships, shells, pebbles collected on holidays long past, porcelain owls, Chinese brush paintings, and a selection of silver-framed sepia photographs of the family.

Suzanne entered with a tray of bright red cups and a yellow coffeepot, a far cry from the pale austerity of the Chambord mausoleum. She listened as her mother explained her thoughts.

"I'm trying to think how to raise money. We need cash, Zizi, so we can buy food before everything disappears from the shops."

"I have my holiday money—five thousand francs, I think. Shall I go and get it? We could go to the shops as soon as we've finished our coffee."

"The sooner the better. Everyone's going to have had the same idea."

Nathalie began to make a list as Suzanne disappeared to her bedroom. Minutes later she returned carrying a china pig filled with small coins. Nathalie emptied the pig and counted the coins.

"There's five thousand, one hundred and fifty francs."

"Take it all, maman."

"I have ten thousand, which I've always kept for emergencies."

"Is this a real emergency?"

"I think it is, Zizi."

Suzanne's face fell, and her hands twitched nervously as she tried to control her agitation. The Germans were coming. Whatever was going to happen to them without Papa?

"When will Papa be coming home?"

Nathalie did not answer, because she did not know. They had no idea where Jacques Castel was, if he was a prisoner of the Germans, if he was even still alive. Nathalie thought of the day when Jacques had arrived home with the news that he had volunteered for service. At first she had not believed that he had been accepted, protesting that he was too old. They had had a row, which she had regretted ever since, but Jacques had been adamant in his desire to fight for France. First he had been sent as a clerk to the army offices in Fontainebleau. He had been able to return home every weekend, and things had seemed little altered. Then Jacques had been posted to the front, and now all Nathalie received were censored letters long out-of-date, with the postmarks removed so she could never find out where her husband was stationed.

Determined to keep from dwelling on such thoughts, Nathalie put some of the money in her purse and looked again around the room. Still nothing of real value caught her eye. Dealers would not buy rubbish, and even valuable antiques were lying unsold in the shops because the people of Paris were concerned only with acquiring food.

Suzanne followed her mother from the living room with its homely clutter to the yellow kitchen full of pots and pans, whisks and pestles. They proceeded upstairs, checking every item in Suzanne's bedroom, but there was nothing but a double bed covered in pink patchwork, a wardrobe, a rocking chair, and a table covered with makeup and fancy boxes bought in local flea markets. In her own bedroom Nathalie pounced on her husband's silver-backed hairbrushes, and she picked up a small gilt clock in the spare room.

"This clock belonged to my rich Aunt Berthe. It's worth money for sure."

"Let's go, maman, it's getting late. I think I know who will buy your things."

"Who?"

"Monsieur Rosenberg might. He has the antique shop next to the pest-control store in the rue St. Rustique. You know the one, maman, the window with the steel traps and stuffed foxes and rats."

"I don't like that place!"

"They're all dead, maman."

"I know they are, but sometimes as I pass I think they move. I easily have nightmares about rodents, as you know, Zizi. I shall keep my eyes shut as I go past."

They went downstairs to the living room, where Nathalie wrapped the brushes and clock in newspaper before putting them in her string bag. Suzanne washed the coffee cups. As she worked she sang contentedly, and her mother asked herself where Suzanne's talent for music came from. Jacques Castel's family had all been dancers in the ballet, hers trapeze artists in the circus, for as long as anyone could remember. Nathalie decided the crystal-clear voice was a gift from God.

Suzanne went out to the garden. She picked gypsophila, burying her face in clouds of tiny white flowers. Again, she paused to look over the wall at old folk toiling up the steps of the rue Foyatier, clutching the iron railing at the center and panting. In the kitchen, Suzanne put the flowers in a green vase. She carried them into the hall, pleased by the pretty contrast of color—pink, white, and emerald against the pistachio and violet of the flowery wallpaper.

The house in which the two women lived was called la maison Fleuri because in times long past, when the village of Montmartre had been inhabited by quarry workers, flour millers, and market gardeners, it had belonged to a florist. Suzanne looked around the hall and at the rickety wooden stairs, believing their house the finest in Paris. Nathalie was taking baskets and a jacket from the hall cupboard. Suzanne gathered a wrap from the chair and followed her mother out into the street.

As they walked down the rue Gabrielle they chattered happily and tried to avoid M. Laval's inquisitive eyes. As always he was in his attic bedroom, looking down on the world, and Nathalie whispered to her daughter, "Thank God Laval doesn't live next door to us, we would not know a moment's privacy. No one can have any secrets from that old goat!"

"How old is Monsieur Laval?"

"God knows—fifty-five, I should imagine. He was a tax collector in his younger days, but they retired him prematurely because of his health. Now he spends his time looking for someone to report. When and if the Germans come, he'll be the first collaborator in Montmartre, I tell you, and you know what happens to those people."

Suzanne shook her head, and Nathalie continued, unaware of her daughter's increasing unease.

"Vivienne Marchand told me that a friend of her sister's was killed by people in her own street in Alsace for giving a jug of lemonade to a German officer who called to question her about her husband. The neighbors must have thought the German was her lover."

"And what did they do?"

"They stabbed her with her own bread knife, thirty times, until she was good and dead, then they set fire to her body. The poor soul had lived in the street for years, so you would have thought they could have trusted her."

Suzanne thought of their own neighbors and wondered if they too would turn into enemies under the stress of German oppression. Her mother's words had touched her, and she felt insecure and apprehensive. Nathalie continued her story without realizing how much it had upset Suzanne.

"The French feel strongly about collaborators. They suspect everyone, Zizi, even their best friends. It's our history, I suppose. We've been hating the Germans for centuries."

Nathalie closed her eyes as she passed the pest-control shop. Suzanne loitered behind, peering through the window at the stuffed fox and upended rodents hanging in mute testimony to the taxidermist's art and the efficacy of the traps the owner sold. She heard her mother call, and watched as she disappeared into the antique dealer's shop. Maman, Suzanne reflected, was forty-eight and suddenly looking older. Her hair had turned white and she was overweight. Suzanne reflected that if the Germans came to occupy Paris they would all starve, so there would be no point in suggesting that Maman diet. She watched as her mother showed M. Rosenberg the clock and the silver-backed brushes. The old man turned them this way and that, revolving the hour hand twelve full circles until the room was filled with the sound of brittle chimes. Then he began to make excuses.

"Times are hard, madame. I can't sell brushes like these, people want only onions and potatoes. As for the clock, well, it's a fine clock. My mother, God rest her soul, had one just like it. . . ."

"How much will you pay, monsieur?"

Nathalie tried hard not to seem too anxious. Rosenberg thought what a handsome pair they were, though the girl's face was somewhat strained and the mother's dress was old and worn. Were they desperate for money? He did not want the clock or the brushes, but he felt inclined to do someone a favor. With the Germans marching on Paris, who could tell when he might need a friend? Rosenberg was alone in the world, happy and settled— or so he had thought until the ominous radio broadcast earlier in the day. At last he made his decision and the best offer he could afford.

"I'll pay twenty thousand for the lot, not a sou more."

"I'll take it."

Nathalie sighed with relief. The till opened with a tinkling sound. The money changed hands, and M. Rosenberg walked to the door to see his clients out. The two women linked arms and went quickly down the street. Rosenberg watched until they turned the corner into the rue Norvins. The girl's wide gold-green eyes haunted him, her long, cloudy black hair and heart-shaped face reminding him of young Jewish girls in Cracow walking with their parents along the Slawkowska in the June evenings of his youth. The dealer sighed. He had lived in Germany, Poland, Belgium, and France. Would the next stop be a German camp for "undesirables"? He locked the shop and shuffled back to the living room. If the Germans came to Paris, he would tell all his neighbors he was leaving. Then he woud hide in the cellar with enough food to withstand a siege. He took all the cash he had in the house and went out to buy food.


Suzanne and her mother walked through the place du Tertre to the rue St.-Eleuthère. First they visited the grocer, where Nathalie bought two sacks of brown flour, two of sugar, two of white flour, and a sack each of dried haricots, peas, and lentils. Then they called at M. Thomas's garden center to buy planting potatoes, onion sets, and seeds. Nathalie loved gardening and, fired with enthusiasm and newfound wealth, she bought everything she thought necessary for a vegetable garden par excellence. Nathalie was confident that she and Suzanne could stay alive by eating what they grew long after meat and fish had vanished from local shops.

They walked on, through narrow, curved lanes, some unchanged from the days when the village of Montmartre had been the garden of Paris. An old man sweeping the cobblestones raised his cap, a child scampered by carrying a long loaf from the nearby bakery, and a choir of voices echoed from the village hall, practicing for the summer festival. Each block of houses and apartments in the quarter had its own bakery, butcher, crémerie, café, and general store, and the scene on each street was similar. Concierges sat outside their buildings, knitting furiously and missing nothing. Housewives were retrieving quilts thrown over windowsills to catch the sun. Children in blue smocks were returning home from school, and in leafy squares old men in black berets sat smoking their pipes and recalling the days when they were young and strong and given to chasing women.

Suzanne followed her mother from one shop to the next, enjoying the familiarity and camaraderie of their contacts in the area. Increasingly there were notices in shop windows saying REGULARS ONLY. Soon, she reflected, what little food there was would be gone and she and Maman would be glad they had spent all their lives in Montmartre. Suzanne's feet hurt, and she turned to her mother and complained, "I'm tired, maman."

"I don't know what's the matter with you. You're so listless lately."

"I'm thirsty, too."

"We'll have a glass at Rostand's."

They stood at the bar, one foot raised on the brass rail, drinking a long, cooling glass of beer. A butcher, his apron stained with blood, was regaling the barman with stories about his experiences in Algeria. A glazier appeared, carrying a sheet of plate glass in a frame on his back. He ordered a vin rouge, drank it down in a swig, paid, and edged carefully outside. Suzanne's feet were blistered, and she felt jaded. She decided to try not to think of David, because she was sure that worrying about his safety and longing for his body were responsible for most of her problems. She must force herself to think only of her safety, of Maman's health, and of keeping their precious home intact. She applied pressure to the largest blister, wiping the escaping liquid on her handkerchief. Then, finishing her drink, she turned resolutely to her mother.

"Where shall we go next, maman?"

"I want to buy some tins of tongue, the ones Madame Argentan uses at the Hôtel des Abbesses. Then we should try to get fertilizer for the garden and some barrels of wine and a side or two of ham."

Suzanne sighed. Normally her mother tired quickly and they returned home around five to make dinner of stewed hare or pig's trotters in vinegar. Tonight they were going to open one of Maman's precious bottles of wine, and they would eat cassoulet made with goose fat hoarded since Christmas. Suzanne's mouth watered at the thought of the luxurious heaviness of the dish, and she wondered if her longing for it was the reason her body was determined to feel tired.

It was seven when they arrived home. Nathalie put on the radio and then went to the kitchen to heat up the meal. The goods she had bought that day had already been delivered, and as Suzanne carried them into the stone-shelved pantry she was surprised to see how little space they occupied. Supplies that had seemed so lavish would not even last them a year.

"We'll need more than this if there's to be an occupation, maman. Have you any of the money left?"

"Of course I have, plenty. We'll go out again tomorrow, and the next day, too, if the shops are still open."

"I don't suppose the Germans will stay long if they come, will they?"

"Who knows what they'd do? You can never tell with Germans, they're not like other people."

While Suzanne set the table, her mother went to the cellar, reappearing with a dusty bottle that she wiped, opened, and set in the center of the cloth. Suzanne took soup bowls from the dresser, long-stemmed wineglasses from a cabinet and placed them at either side of the table. She was pretending that it was David with whom she would be dining, David who would toast their future. The radio announcer's voice broke into her thoughts as she was about to take the tureen through to her mother in the kitchen: "The German army is crossing the lower Seine to the west of Paris. . . ." Suzanne turned the dial and tuned in to the music of Joe Bouillon. In the kitchen, Suzanne gave her mother the tureen, helped make an endive salad, sniffed the wine cork, and lit some pink candles for the table. Nathalie carried the cassoulet to the table, and the two women sat facing each other, pretending valiantly that they had something to celebrate.

"What shall we toast, maman?"

"We'll toast Papa's safety."

"And David's."

"Of course."

Suzanne savored the perfection of a topaz Yquem, accepting a second and third glass and another helping of the tasty cassoulet. Soon the wine made her head light, her body warm, her heart eager for love, and she forgot everything that had ever troubled her. When the meal was over, Nathalie carried the dishes to the kitchen. She was tired, but the thought of a German drinking her long-hoarded wine compelled her to action, and at ten o'clock, when it was dark, she wrapped the bottles in cotton wool and wedged them into a box. Then she dug a hole at the bottom of the garden, shaded from the sun by the apple tree, and placed her precious bottles under the soil. She trod down the earth, put the spade away in the potting shed, and reminded herself to plant some lettuce over the newly turned soil.

Four houses down the street, M. Laval was at his attic bedroom window, cursing the fact that it was a moonless night. Surely he had seen someone in the Castels' garden? He dashed to the dresser to find his binoculars, but it was too late. Madame was locking the kitchen door and drawing the bolts, well satisfied with her work.


All night distant guns sounded, preventing the two women from sleeping. Nathalie tried to imagine what would happen if the Germans came, how it would be in Paris and whether life would change irreparably, forever. Most important of all, how long would the alien presence have to be tolerated? Suzanne had said they would stay for only a short time. Nathalie did not agree. If the Germans ever got a foothold in Paris, it was likely they would stay for years. As the clock chimed three she turned away from the window, pulled the bedclothes over her head, and resolved to sleep.

Suzanne had tidied her cupboards, read David's letters for the tenth time, and then leaped into bed. She thought how proud she had been on the day when she had first seen David in his army uniform, thrilled by his looks and touched that he was willing to fight for a country that was not his own. But already Suzanne had changed her mind, and as the Germans approached she wished fervently that David could be far away from the conflict. Husbands and sons of many of her friends had already been killed, and few women knew where their men were fighting. The mail they got was heavily censored, often indecipherable. Suzanne thought again of a line in one of David's letters . . . *We have to get the Germans off French soil or you and I shall never be able to live happily in our own home. Don't worry about me, Zizi, I'll be back, I promise.* . . . Suzanne's eyes filled with tears, and she was tormented by the fear that David might already have been killed.

It was a humid night, with the heavy atmosphere that often precedes a storm. She threw back her blankets, looking anxiously through the window and wondering if there would soon be thunder. Somewhere two tomcats were serenading, and from the vineyard at the corner of the rue des Saules she could hear the eerie sound of owls hooting. The gunfire seemed much nearer than on previous nights, louder and more insistent, with frequent violent explosions.

Suzanne lay on her back, her eyes accustoming themselves to the darkness. If the Germans came to Paris there would be terrible times ahead. All Germans were crude, violent murderers, willing to do anything to accomplish their ambitions. They had conquered wherever they went, goose-stepping into one country after another. Soon they would try to be masters of the world.

She wondered if she would lose her job at the Bal Tabarin if the Germans occupied the city. If so, how would she and her mother live when they had had nothing from her father for over six weeks? And if the Germans came, where would they live, those thousands of steel-helmeted men? Would they be billeted in houses with spare rooms?

Suddenly Suzanne thought of the Chambord family with their fifteen-room mansion and she laughed out loud at the thought of Monsieur having to share his precious residence with the enemy. Then she thought of David, examining in her mind's eye his face, his body, every characteristic movement of his hands. His hair was brown and soft, slightly curly, and worn rather long. His eyes were gray—sometimes dark and solemn, sometimes light and mercurial. He was neither tall nor short but thickset and strong, with broad, powerful shoulders and arms like steel.

She remembered his kisses and the secret things David had told her they would do when they were married. Sweat covered her brow, and she leaped up and opened the windows wider to let in some air. Then she lay under the sheet, wishing her body were not so full, so hot, so ripe for love it felt as if it would burst. Angry for allowing longing to torment her, Suzanne turned on the bedside light and read a chapter from *Mes Apprentissages*. Then she told herself firmly that she would have to learn to control her temper, her need, and wanton, shameless thoughts, or be a very unhappy woman. Having chastised herself, she dropped the book on the floor and fell asleep until dawn.

Far away in the sixteenth arrondissement, the Chambords were entertaining the Swedish ambassador at dinner. Marie-Claude had made plans for a visit to Balenciaga with the ambassador's daughter, and Carrie was in her room having a fortifying drink. As darkness fell, German aircraft droned overhead. After a phone call, the ambassador was obliged to excuse himself so he could return home. The streets of Paris were empty, and only a few cars were on the roads. These were the vehicles and trucks of market gardeners, food producers, office administrators, and club owners en route to high-walled country residences far away from the acrid cigar smoke of their tawdry cabarets. Paris looked forlorn and hopeless, and the ambassador thought himself unlucky to have been posted to this magnificent city at such an inopportune time.

In the Chambord residence, Marie-Claude was sound asleep, Carrie was wandering the garden and watching the flashes in the sky, and Chambord was in the cellar counting money he had withdrawn from the bank that day. As he counted he smiled, because the touch of money was a sensuous pleasure. Some men adored women, some wine or a fine cigar. The only truly important things in Charles Chambord's life were gold and the love of his daughter.

The following morning a cockerel crowed in M. Roger's garden and Nathalie turned on the radio. On the steps at the side of the house, a child was singing a nursery rhyme. The cockerel crowed again, insistently, waking the neighbors. Nathalie sipped coffee and ate a croissant covered with apricot jam. The news on the radio semed no worse than the previous day's, so she rose with a yawn, took her tray down to the kitchen, and went for a walk around the garden in her negligee. M. Laval, who had just risen, watched from his window, frowning at her déshabillé. Theatricals were all loose women. He pulled a face and looked again.

Seeing his disapproving face, Nathalie bowed mockingly and waved a regal greeting to annoy him. Then she tucked herself back in her robe, stuck her head in the air, and returned to the kitchen to make breakfast. Today was going to be a busy day. She would send Suzanne to do some of the remaining shopping while she dug over the flower garden, at least those parts of the garden that had enough soil to grow vegetables. After lunch they would plant seeds and arrange the beds as advantageously as possible. Nathalie heard her daughter stirring, and called from the hall, "Hurry and come down, Zizi, there's so much to do today. The coffee is ready, and I am grilling ham."

Suzanne lay in bed smelling the smoky fragrance of the ham, the pungent odor of coffee flavored with figs which her mother favored. These smells were the smells of home and the clatter of pans in the kitchen the familiar sounds of morning. Suzanne washed and dressed, presenting herself for breakfast and chatting eagerly about the future until Nathalie silenced her with an account of all that had to be accomplished before nightfall.

"I've made you a list, Zizi. While you're out at the shops I'll turn over the bottom of the garden, and we can plant around three, when the sun goes to the other side of the house. There's no time to waste. I only wish Papa could be here, because it's hard work trying to dig this soil."

Suzanne read the list.

"You forgot mustard and vinegar and dried vegetables, maman. They have dried vegetables at Lasalle's. I'll get as many as I can."

"Buy whatever you think."

"And dried milk too?"

"I can't stand dried milk."

"We shall need it, though."

"Very well, buy whatever you think will be enough."

Suzanne walked jauntily down the street and up toward the vineyard at the corner of the rue des Saules. She was thinking of the local saying that the wine of the Clos de Montmartre had, in its day, made folk "leap like goats." Wryly she wished she could take something that would make her feel like leaping like a goat. Her blisters had burst and her feet were sore, but food had to be bought and that was that.

As she continued up the hill, Suzanne noticed that a young boy from the quarter was following her. At the corner of the street she paused, turning to ask him what he wanted. The lad blushed furiously as he replied, "I could carry your shopping for you, mademoiselle."

"Why would you do that? I'm not rich enough to pay you."

"You could afford a coffee and a brioche, couldn't you?"

"You're hungry, is that it?"

"Very hungry, mademoiselle."

Suzanne looked at the torn clothes, the cheap jacket begrimed with the dirt of many weeks.

"How old are you?"

"I'm fourteen, nearly, mademoiselle."

"What's your name?"

"Armand Lognon."

"I'm Suzanne Castel."

"I know. I know all about you."

Suzanne reexamined the lad. He looked strong, though his face was pale and his hands and feet filthy. Who was he? And how did he know her name? She paused before entering the oil shop.

"How did you know my name?"

"I've seen your picture outside the Bal Tabarin."

"Have you seen the show there?"

"Of course not. How could I afford that place?"

Suzanne bit her lip and looked over the road to the crémerie under the beech trees.

"Let's go to Mère Gil for coffee and cakes. You could manage something to eat, couldn't you, Armand?"

Armand ran ahead, rushing frantically into the courtyard and plumping down on a wooden bench near a woman serving breakfast cups of café crème to local traders. Mère Gil turned to greet them.

"Bonjour, Suzanne, what can I get you?"

"Two big coffees, some brioches, and a ham sandwich for my assistant."

Mère Gil smiled, cocking an eye toward Armand's cheeky face.

"He looks as if he could eat a horse, that one."

Over coffee Armand explained that he lived in the porch of the church of St. Pierre. He had been living in his parents' home in Lille, but when the Germans arrived they had been shot. So he had hitched a lift to Paris, believing the French capital to be the safest place. Suzanne's eyes widened at the tragic story so casually told.

"But why don't you live in one of the municipal homes? They have refugee children from all over France."

"I like my freedom. I'll never be caged, *never*."

"So you prefer to starve, living in the churchyard and sleeping on graves?"

"Sometimes I starve. Sometimes women take me in."

Suzanne blushed at his implication. Then she burst into peals of laughter.

"You're a card, Armand! Well, I think I might have a proposition for you."

"Go on, I'm listening." Armand continued to wolf down the food as Suzanne explained.

"You must go to this address and ask my mother if she could use you to turn over the garden. Say I promised you lunch and dinner today and tomorrow in return for your help in the garden."

Armand shook hands with her, his face alight with pleasure. "Thank you, Suzanne, I knew you'd be kind. Oh, by the way, I stole the photograph of you from the Bal Tabarin showcase. You'd better tell them to get a new one."

With that he loaded the rest of the brioche into his pocket, solemnly emptied the sugar lumps from the bowl into his handkerchief, and ran off in the direction of the rue Gabrielle.

Suzanne paid the bill and went to the oil shop. She ordered five gallons of the best olive to be delivered, and was shocked to be told that she could get only three. The owner was already serving only regular customers, and stocks had dwindled so alarmingly that rationing had been introduced.

Suzanne paused outside the Lapin Agile, trying to see through faded pink walls and green-painted shutters to the mustard-colored interior. Poverty-stricken impressionist painters had once flirted and drunk themselves to death in that small bar in the days of the belle époque. It was one of Suzanne's favorite places in Montmartre, the spot where she found it easy to imagine that she too belonged to a bygone age. The sun was hot and she felt content despite the distant threatening sounds of the German advance.

In the fish market of Barbes-Rochechouart a vendor offered her a thick slice of tuna. Suzanne looked at the inert blue body and shivered. The stall holder winked, provoked by her innocence and the lush breasts that contrasted so oddly with her slim body. Suzanne passed on to the seafood stall, looking back at the cheeky vendor in his plaid cap, red shirt, and clean white apron. She wondered if he was the man local women gossiped about— Pépé l'Amour, they called him, because he had never been known to let down a lonely lady. She bought shrimps, coquilles, rascasse, and girelle, then tomatoes and celery from a street stall near the place Blanche. On the way back up the hill she stopped in her favorite charcuterie for rosettes from Lyon and a thick black sausage preserved in brine.

As she walked she stopped here and there to order wine as her mother had instructed and tomato purée by the box, tins of tongue, beef, spiced pork, and a twenty-pound cheese bound in muslin. Mission completed, she sat for a few minutes in the cemetery of Montmartre, watching an old man tidying the graves of Degas and Stendhal. Around Suzanne, huge stone tombs with gates and grills formed avenues in the community of the dead. Each tomb was close to its neighbor, and she thought how odd it was that those who had sought privacy in life should have their last resting place in this claustrophobic concrete causeway. Bees buzzed in weeds suffocating the pathways, a priest hurried by, and often loud explosions brought bedlam a little nearer the gates of the peaceful city. Suzanne made her way home through poplar-lined squares and lime-tree avenues until she reached la maison Fleuri. Every now and then neighbors called a greeting and children leaped up to kiss her. Suzanne smiled merrily and kissed them back. Even the black smoke that filled the sky on the horizon could do nothing to dampen the happiness she felt at being in the place where she knew she belonged.

Armand had eaten the leftovers of the cassoulet and drunk a carafe of red wine, and was asleep on the sofa. Nathalie was in the kitchen making omelettes for lunch, having washed and scrubbed her visitor's clothes and hung them on the line. The flowers were gone from the lower end of the garden, and she was well pleased with her new assistant.

"He knows what he's doing, that boy."

"And he can eat, from the look of things!"

"All boys of that age eat a lot, Zizi. They need the food or they get stunted. Let's turn on the radio, shall we?"

They ate in silence as the familiar chimes of Big Ben heralded the latest news from the front. "It has been reported that the French government has left the capital for Tours and the French general headquarters has withdrawn to Briare on the orders of General Weygand. The German army is establishing bridgeheads on the lower Seine at Elbeuf, les Andelys, and Louviers, and German troops are crossing the Marne at Château-Thierry. Reims has fallen to the enemy. It has just been announced that Mussolini has entered the war. . . ."

Nathalie turned pale. "Mon dieu! Italy has stabbed us in the back!"

The newsreader's voice droned on. "The latest news is that at eleven hundred hours today Paris was declared an open city by agreement with the president of the war council. General Herring will command the Paris army and General Dentz will assume the function of governor, remaining behind until the Germans enter the city. This is the end of the news. The next bulletin will be at six P.M. Greenwich Mean Time."

Nathalie began to cry. "They have abandoned Paris! Can you believe it, Zizi, we have been abandoned without a fight!"

Suzanne hugged her mother and tried to comfort her.

"Please don't cry, maman, we'll manage. We're healthy and we have a home, so we'll get by."

"We'll need money when the Germans come. Only the rich will be able to buy things."

"We'll find money, maman. I'm sure Papa intends to send us something."

"If he intends to send us money, why hasn't he sent it already?"

"He will, and if he's dead we'll get a war pension."

Silence. Nathalie stared into space, facing the thought that her husband could be dead. If Jacques had been killed she would have little interest in life. She managed to be brave only by thinking of him and the happy days they would have together when he came home.

Armand woke with a start and sat up, rubbing his eyes and asking why Nathalie was crying. Suzanne told him the news.

"Maman is upset because Paris has been declared an open city. Soon everyone will be advised to leave, to run away because the Germans are coming. The government has given Paris to the Germans without a fight!"

Armand hugged the blanket to his chin and swore defiantly.

"I'm not going to run. I shall stay here, and to hell with the Germans!"

"So will I."

Suzanne was firm and decisive. There was nothing to be gained by leaving the city for destinations unknown. Nathalie interrupted their conversation.

"How can you make such a decision? What are you saying, Zizi?"

"I know what's best for us, maman. We must stay here and look after the house. We don't have enough money to go away from Paris, and I'm *never* going to live in a refugee camp."

"I suppose you're right."

"She's right," Armand said. "I should know. When the Germans killed my family, I left Lille and came to Paris, and look what happened to me! I live in the churchyard and sleep on gravestones or in the chapel when Father Valery forgets to lock the door. But soon I'll be able to better myself."

"How?"

Both women spoke together, and Armand sat back, his face full of hope.

"When the Germans arrive there'll be no food. I'll find food and sell it for a big profit, and I'll find everything folk want and sell it. It's in times like these that a man can make his fortune. I remember Papa telling me how it was done."

Nathalie wiped her eyes and took the dishes to the kitchen. Suzanne turned to Armand and asked him gently, "If traders have no food to sell, how do you think you're going to find any? You have no car, no clothes, and no way of earning enough to buy those things."

Armand blushed furiously, hesitating to tell Suzanne his secret.

"I just met a woman in the rue Pigalle. She runs a hotel and she told me I can work there."

"What will you do?"

"Who cares what she wants me to do! I'm too poor to ask questions. Will you get my clothes, Suzanne?"

For a brief moment Armand thought of his parents, shot by the Germans as a punishment for sheltering English soldiers. He too would have been dead if an English flying officer had not revealed himself and shot the Gestapo visitors. He had not told Suzanne that the woman who ran the hotel in the rue Pigalle was also connected with helping Jews escape from Paris. In this dangerous work Armand intended to help in every way.

Suzanne returned with the newly ironed clothes and handed them back to her guest. Armand waddled to the bathroom in his blanket, returning with a big smile on his face.

"I feel like a new man. That lunch was marvelous, and my clothes feel like new. I won't forget your kindness to me, Suzanne."

They drank coffee and discussed plans for surviving if the Germans took the city. Still they said *if*, not *when,* because they could not countenance confirming that the occupation was inevitable. Outside the sun was shining, and they could feel the advent of summer despite all the tensions and uncertainties of the day. All afternoon they worked, planting the newly bought seeds and bedding plants. As they worked they sang, and Armand told the two women about his former home in Lille. In the evening there was a disagreement when Armand insisted on sleeping outside.

"If I stay inside I'll grow soft. Then when I have to sleep in the churchyard I'll catch cold and die."

"At least take a blanket."

"No thank you, Madame Castel. I must keep myself hard and tough. I'm going to need all I've learned since I came to Paris."

Armand disappeared, and the two women watched as he wrapped the torn coat around his shoulders and instantly fell asleep on the garden bench. They spoke in whispers, afraid lest they wake him. Mostly they talked of Armand and his future once he left the protection of la maison Fleuri. Later they made hot chocolate sprinkled with nutmeg and took it to the sitting room. Suzanne sipped the comforting liquid and asked her mother about things that had been troubling her.

"What shall we do if the mail doesn't start again?"

"It's only two days since it stopped, be patient."

"And what about newspapers? There are none left except the Communist one. We'll never know what's happening."

"We'll get by without papers. We have the radio."

They had been surprised that evening to see some of their neighbors packing their cars with precious belongings in readiness for an early flight to safety. They discussed the matter sadly, uncertain how Paris would feel when the crowds and the traffic jams had gone.

"If all the shopkeepers go, how shall we eat, maman?"

"We'll eat what we grow. Why have we been working like dogs all afternoon?"

"You can't drink cabbage for breakfast!"

"We'll have to learn to live without coffee and tea once our stores run out."

"How empty Paris will be, and how quiet. I can't imagine what it's going to be like. I shall think I'm far away, living in a deserted village in Provence."

The two women kissed each other good night and went to bed. Each one lay awake, running over the situation, trying to make plans for every contingency and succeeding only in succumbing to fear. Outside on the terrace Armand slept and dreamed of better days when he would ride in a big white car. A sudden shower drenched him but he slept on, inured to the damp and the chill emptiness of life.


For two days Suzanne and her mother combed the shops for food. They stored what they purchased in the pantry and, when that room was full, in blanket chests and armoires on the upstairs landing of the house. Armand worked with them until nightfall; then he vanished, to Nathalie's chagrin. She had taken a liking to the lad and had decided to offer him her spare bedroom. By way of explanation she had told Suzanne, "If the Germans come they'll billet their damned soldiers on us, and I'd rather have Armand any day." But as quickly as he had arrived, he was gone. Suzanne looked out on the pink rooftops of Paris and wondered which new woman's house he had invaded.

On the thirteenth of June they heard that the French 7th Army and the Paris army had abandoned advanced positions and had moved around the capital on the east and west along a line marked by the Rambouillet Forest, the Chevreuse Valley, and the Corbeil Seine. Newspapers ceased printing. Communications broke down completely, and the city changed overnight from busy metropolis to deserted, lost community. Those who had once grumbled about the traffic stood mutely by the roadside, looking askance at the emptiness. Posters on every wall mocked the people's trust in the government, the men who had so easily abandoned them: PARIS WILL BE DEFENDED TO THE LAST STONE. In a moment of fury Suzanne tore one of the posters down and trampled it. Then she ran inside the house, distracted by the stillness of the city.

"Listen, maman."

Nathalie looked up, frowning. "I can't hear anything."

"That's because there's nothing to hear. Paris has never been so silent."

As if to contradict her, M. Roger's cockerel crowed and in the garden of the house next to the Marchands old M. Corbeil began to play the "Valse de Mille Feuilles" on his elderly fiddle. Nathalie went to the terrace and looked out, shocked by the change that had come to pass in so short a time. Instead of the bustle she normally saw far below, there was a profound silence. There were no children playing in the square, no gendarmes directing traffic. People had left by the thousands during the previous forty-eight hours. Only a solitary bicyclist rode along the boulevard. Nathalie turned to Suzanne.

"Has everyone gone, Zizi?"

"We're here, and the Marchands and Monsieur Laval and the Rogers and Monsieur Corbeil."

"The Rogers are like us, they can't afford to leave Paris."

"Most of the people of Montmartre have stayed, maman."

"And the shops, are they still open?"

"Most are. The shopkeepers don't want to leave the village."

"And down in Paris?"

"Who knows what is happening there? Perhaps we ought to go to see if the Chambords are still at home. I want to ask if they've heard from David."

"Don't tell me *he's* stayed!" Nathalie's eyes widened and she started in amazement. She had been sure Charles Chambord would be one of the first to run.

"Madame Chambord told me she would never leave, but Monsieur is a fearful coward."

"We'll telephone them, Zizi. That will save going all the way to the sixteenth."

"There are no telephones, maman."

"We'll drop them a line then."

"There isn't any post, and I think it would be foolish to visit them. Monsieur Roger says the Germans will arrive tomorrow, and I don't want to see them."

"Dear God, how things have changed. Will Paris ever be the same again?"


That night Marie-Claude Chambord tried on all she had bought in the previous two days. She was thrilled with her lavish new wardrobe: a piqué evening dress from a shop near the opera; two well-cut suits; a shoulder bag to hold her gas mask and other unsightly objects. A wasp-waisted velvet suit from Chanel and a Balenciaga after-six creation in violet completed the main items of the ensemble. Marie-Claude twirled and whirled and then ran again to look rapturously at the new shoes and boots, furs and elegant tissue-wrapped packages of silk stockings. She sprayed the room with perfume from a cut-glass holder, throwing her head back and letting a thousand invisible droplets fall on her face, her closed eyelids, her naked body. When the dinner gong rang she pouted, reluctant to leave the luxurious paradise of her bedroom. Looking in the mirror at her face, she liked what she saw. At thirteen she had suffered from puppy fat. At seventeen she had blossomed in all the right places and slimmed in those where she had previously been overweight. Her hair was long and red, plaited and intricately beribboned to keep it out of her eyes, which were blue, the strong violet blue that goes with translucent skin and a tendency to delicate constitution. Marie-Claude ran a tape measure around her waist, smiling because it was not a centimeter more than she expected. Then she threw on a dress and tripped down the marble stairway to the dining room. To her relief, the table was full, as always, and she asked herself why there was so much talk of food shortages. Probably Papa had contacts in city business so they would never be without, like other people. She tried to avoid listening as Papa slurped his first course, smacking his lips and expressing the opinion that lobster bisque was the world's finest soup. There was no fresh fish to be had, so Cook had made a rice dish and a silver salver of entrecôte aux échalotes. They drank Chambolle-Musigny with the meat, and Chambord requested another bottle with the Roquefort. He loved Burgundy because it made him feel content, replete and rich. Marie-Claude toyed with chocolate profiteroles, eyeing her father's purple complexion and the moustache he had decided to grow to conceal the false teeth with which he had just been fitted.

"Where is Madame?"

"She's in bed, she has a migraine."

"She drinks too much, Papa, you must do something about her."

"Hold your tongue, child!"

"I'm sorry, Papa, but it's true."

Chambord thought of the row there had been when Carrie discovered she could not go to the country to buy food as she had planned. She had cursed him to hell and back for his false pride, and he had felt compelled to go out to buy every scrap of food he could find in the city to make up for his previous disinterest in the family welfare. It was true they had little food in reserve and he had had difficulty in obtaining meat at any price. Starvation would be unpleasant, Chambord conceded, but surely it would not come to that? For a moment he considered following his wife's advice and having the gardener plant the rose beds with potatoes. Then he shook his head in distaste. It would not do. There was something definitely déclassé about growing food. He was confident that there would always be men who could obtain food in return for money. There was nothing money could not buy, except perhaps good health. Chambord took out a cigar and clipped the end with a solid-gold cutter. Then he retired to his study to look over the latest financial reports from his bank.

Left alone, Marie-Claude finished her coffee and retired to bed. She opened her windows and surveyed the garden, thinking how hot it was, how sultry and altogether too quiet for her liking. Where had everyone gone? What fools they had been to abandon their homes for the unknown. Marie-Claude was full of admiration for her father, who had insisted on remaining in Paris. She had no idea that the gold bars buried in his garden had been the motivating force for such uncharacteristic fortitude. She thought only of his courage and the lamentable laxness of her stepmother. Once when she had searched Carrie's bedroom, she had found a bottle of port, half a bottle of gin, and a box of the most expensive chocolates. Marie-Claude had reported the finding at once to her father, who was opposed to women drinking spirits and perversely mean about buying satin-tied boxes of chocolates.

Marie-Claude despised her stepmother's background. Carrie was an American of English stock, born in a Georgian house in New England. To Marie-Claude's critical eyes, she appeared to have inherited the worst of both races—a steely will and fierce refusal to be intimidated that came from centuries of English colonial rule, and an inability to admit that *anything* was impossible, which came surely from the pioneers who had founded American society. Marie-Claude thought with distaste of Carrie's love of the countryside, of her refusal to change the informality of her ways. She remembered Carrie's barefoot walks on the beaches of Normandy during summer vacations on the coast, and the endless times her father had protested that he expected a woman of dignity as his wife, not a peasant with no shoes. Then, with furious annoyance, Marie-Claude recalled Carrie's comment on the day she had returned home from school having invited friends to tea. Marie-Claude had demanded the solid-gold tea set, an expensive silk box of marrons glacés, and her stepmother's appearance "properly dressed." Carrie had roared with irreverent laughter at her snobbish ways, cutting her to the quick with a cutting reply: "I dress how *I* want to dress, Marie-Claude, and I don't take orders from you or from any of your goddamned friends." Marie-Claude vowed to have her own back someday for all the times Madame had snubbed her, for all the occasions when Carrie had mocked her pretensions, her insistence on socially correct behavior, and her terror of Jews and Negroes.

In her bedroom, the curtains fluttered as the wind rose to a howl. Wrapping herself in a robe, she ran to close the windows, shaking her head in annoyance at the unpredictability of the weather. One minute it was hot and sultry, the next chill and stormy. As the sky lit with the red, gold, and smoky gray of distant explosions, Marie-Claude settled in bed with a society magazine. She had invited some school friends to a party tomorrow. She hoped most sincerely that the sun would shine.

Suzanne and her mother had talked it over and decided that if the Germans were coming the following day, they must enjoy one last night in Paris. After dinner they wrapped themselves warmly against the wind and stepped outside, looking up and smiling at a starry sky. Now and then the whole Butte lit red and white with blinding flashes, and the skyline glowed orange from the light of burning buildings on the periphery of the city. But the two women had decided to let nothing upset them and that was how it was going to be.

"Where shall we go first, maman?"

"To l'Escargot for a drink, and then to les Halles."

"Shall we walk or try to find a taxi?"

"We'll walk, because we shall need a taxi coming back. I don't intend to return home before dawn."

They found the bar almost deserted, though it filled within the hour. Although the floors were covered with sawdust, the walls were decked with priceless paintings left long ago by painters without a sou to pay their wine bills. Peeling olive paint covered the exterior, which had no nameplate or sign except for a grimy gold-leafed plaster snail hanging on a rusty hook and swinging scratchily in the breeze. The owner, Ottoline, was half English and as haughty as could be. Nathalie always came to l'Escargot when she was depressed, because the sound of Ottoline's deep bass voice and the flow of seaman's language contrasting with the hauteur of her manner was balm to the troubled heart. Once, late at night, Nathalie had been in the bar with her husband when Ottoline had been attacked by a Russian seaman intent on taking her night's profit. Ottoline had put the fellow in the hospital with one blow from a sledgehammer she kept under the counter. "My forty-pounder," she called it, and clients had been known to make irreverent plays on her meaning. Tonight Ottoline was draped in the tricolor and waxing poetic as she set the words of the "Marseillaise" to the tune of the German national anthem. The amended words made Suzanne and her mother laugh till tears rolled down their cheeks, and Nathalie kept repeating, "Pray God those German salauds don't speak French!" The bar filled with locals seeking solace in company, and Suzanne watched men playing snooker at a table in the far corner and a local butcher endowing a lottery for a side of Charolais beef. All the tickets vanished before Ottoline could buy some for herself, and she was vociferous in her displeasure. A traveling salesman with news of atrocities in the Ardennes was shouted down by the customers in favor of a lady of uncertain age and obvious experience who told the story of Mme. Bibi's brothel in Ville d'Avray, which had taps that could run with champagne. For days, ever since the news of the German advance, Mme. Bibi and her girls had been experimenting with running tasteless, noxious substances from the taps in order to annihilate every German who imposed his body on them. A cheer greeted her ingenuity, and Ottoline was heard to praise her to the hilt.

Suzanne and her mother arrived at les Halles at eleven thirty. Feeling their way through dark, silent streets, they paused to listen to the chimes of church bells ringing for midnight mass. *Chalandeaux* were walking in groups toward the market, and in distant windows Suzanne could see lovers kissing. She followed her mother around the stalls, peering through the candelight at tomatoes, melons, and peppers fresh from the Midi. They bought parsley, basil, sage, and a string of dried red pimentos. Suzanne chattered excitedly, and Nathalie felt unaccountably happy. Perhaps, she thought, I am happy because the fear of occupation is over, the uncertainty is gone—the Germans *are* coming to Paris tomorrow.

They walked arm in arm to a café on one side of the cobbled square, where they ordered onion soup, goulash, and a helping of tarte tatin. They talked as they had never talked before, exchanging confidences, explaining secret fears and feelings, calmly facing the certain knowledge that they were going to have to live under German rule. From this moment their only aim would be to survive, to keep a happy home and a quiet soul. Fortes from the market appeared, their muscles rippling under cotton vests and rubber aprons. Everyone talked loudly, and men at the next tables invited Nathalie Castel to bring her daughter to share their wine. The men talked of their families, and ordered bottle after bottle of the best until faint streaks of golden dawn began to light the sky. Suzanne looked at the clock, surprised to see it was three thirty. The café was still packed to the doors with market workers, stall holders, porters, policemen, and folk from the quarter reluctant to be alone on such a historic night. At four they all sang the "Marseillaise." Then some went home to bed, and Mme. Castel shed a tear because she could not help thinking of her husband and wondering if he was alive. Having calmed herself, she ordered another helping of tarte and a couple of cafés crèmes. As Suzanne rolled the caramelized apples around in her mouth, she knew that she would taste nothing as luxurious for many a long month. This, she decided, was where she would come when the war was over, where she would bring David, because it was a place that belonged to the happy days of Paris, the days before the enemy came to take what was not theirs to own. She finished the tarte, drained her coffee, and walked slowly past the still crowded bar to the door. The owner waved good-bye, a chorus of male voices saluted the women; then they were out in the street, shivering in the chill air of morning. Nathalie hugged Suzanne sentimentally.

"We had a good night, didn't we, Zizi."

"A perfect night, maman. I'm so glad we didn't stay at home worrying."

"We must be brave when the Germans come, and it won't be easy."

"We'll get by, maman, we have each other."

In the distance church bells chimed the Angelus, and as the two women walked up the rue du Louvre a flock of pigeons flew by, gray wings flapping against a yellow morning sky. A red-clad prostitute appeared from an alleyway, pausing briefly to lean against the crumbling plaster of an old building to take off her shoes. She walked slowly, wearily, upstairs to bed.

Suzanne held her mother's hand tightly, touched by her courage and generosity. It had been a night to remember and treasure, whatever the day might bring. They turned left into the rue des Petits-Champs, right into the rue de Richelieu, disconcerted to

find there were no taxis at the rank. Nathalie's feet were as uncomfortable as those of the belle-de-nuit they had just seen, and
Suzanne's blisters had turned a dull, ominous purple. They were
walking slowly toward the boulevard Haussman, where it became
the boulevard Montmartre, when a strange metallic crunching
sound echoed on the cobblestones, startling them. Suzanne
looked around, saw nothing, and proceeded with her mother
across the road. Then the sound came again, only louder than
before and with a fearful strength that seemed to disturb the
very ground under their feet.

"What's that, maman?"

"I don't know. It sounds as if the Métro's running on the
pavement."

They had passed from the main road to the narrow rue Pele-
tier when the sound came again, almost deafening them. The
pavements seemed to stir, and this time, as they turned, they saw
a massive gray steel German tank rolling along the boulevard
toward the Etoile. Suzanne leaped into a doorway, dragging
Nathalie behind her.

"Say a prayer, maman, the Germans have arrived."

Nathalie crossed herself, closing her eyes and mouthing the
words of the rosary. Trying desperately to be brave, she bit her
lip and brushed tears from her eyes. Who would have thought it
would cut the heart so cruelly to see the stony faces of the enemy
in the spring-filled boulevards of Paris? Nathalie thought of the
apple blossoms on the hill, the smell of cherry trees and chestnuts
roasting on braziers in the evening chill. Would Paris ever recover from the indignity of having been *given* to the enemy? The
two women crouched low, peeping out at a line of tanks with
75-mm guns that menaced all opposition. The leading tank
commander wore a peaked cap, carried black binoculars, and was
handsome in a leathery way. Out of the turrets of the tanks that
followed, young, blond officers, their green uniforms meticulously
pressed, stared in arrogant appraisal and triumph. Some smiled
despite themselves as they looked in wonder at the ancient city
they had taken so easily. Some openly threatened the very air
they were breathing. When the last tank had passed, Suzanne
rose and gingerly stepped out into the street.

"They've gone, maman. What shall we do now?"

"We'll go home, what else?"

"What if the Germans are in all the streets?"

"We'll find a way, Zizi. This is our city, not theirs."

A sudden burst of gunfire made them run for cover. Then there was silence but for the distant scraping of tank treads on cobblestones. Near the cirque Medrano they again heard the ominous rumbling of approaching steel and, no longer ignorant of its meaning, fled to a bar, where they stood staring wide-eyed over the frilly net curtains at the window. The proprietor, who was determined to ignore the German arrival, handed them two coffees and returned to checking his lottery tickets.

This time a longer line of tanks appeared, and Suzanne counted twenty-two. And instead of the empty streets of early dawn, there were silent Parisians standing on the pavements, their faces downcast, their clothes betraying funereal thoughts that obliterated the sun from the horizons of their minds. A child dashed out of a side street, its mother in hot pursuit, grasping it in terror. The Panzer commander looked down and then passed implacably on, followed by his corps of bright young robots atop inviolable barriers of iron. The mighty German army passed on to the boulevard de Clichy and Suzanne thought furiously: They will continue to the boulevard des Batignolles and then to the avenue Wagram. Then they will all assemble at the Arc de Triomphe so they can gloat at their triumph. God, how I *hate* Germans!

People stood talking in small groups as the two women made their way home to the precious peace of the heights of Montmartre. In the garden of a house in the rue des Martyrs a woman was hanging out wash and singing happily as if unaware of the momentous happenings below. Somehow that brief glimpse of normality comforted Nathalie, and she held her daughter's hand, squeezing it reassuringly because she knew Suzanne was speechless with rage. Suzanne wanted only to be home, to rush to her room so she could sob away all the shock and the fear and resentment she felt toward those who had come to steal her city. Vivienne Marchand's fuchsia hedge seemed alive with earwigs, and a cloud of ladybirds appeared near the clematis that grew over their communal wall. Suzanne shuddered, unable to retrieve the happy mood of the early-dawn hours. There was a deathly silence all around. No tourists milled in the place du Tertre, buy-

ing phony van Goghs from traders. Old men who usually smoked
and played boule under the chestnut trees in the square had gone
home to hunch over their radios, waiting to be told their fate.
Children had been sent home from school and were sitting inside
their houses wondering why their mothers were crying. And
below, Suzanne sat in the garden breathing in the scented air
and trying to erase from her mind that first glimpse of the
enemy.

Someday, she told herself, when the war is over, I shall laugh
at this moment and drink a glass of champagne in celebration of
the fact that we survived. But now the nightmare was ahead,
waiting to be lived, and there would be no escape. A scarlet butterfly settled on a frond of mauve wisteria. Suzanne thought how
fragile the butterfly was, how perfect and easily despoiled—like
Paris. Unable to bear the thought of the ignominious passivity
of the French authorities, she ran to her room and closed the
curtains on the stillness.


In stark contrast to the silence of Montmartre, the area around
the sixteenth arrondissement was strident with noise. Tanks had
appeared from every arm of the star of roads that converged on
the Etoile, until traffic all over the area came to a halt. Parisians
were watching from their upper windows, and many ventured
out into the streets to witness in shocked silence the arrival of
the conquerors as German soldiers in steel-basin helmets goose-
stepped up the Champs-Elysées. Regiments holding banners embossed with the German eagle aped Roman legions of long ago as
they brandished their standards on iron arms. And all the while
there was the ominous beat of massed drums that brought to
mind the moment before execution by guillotine in the days of
revolution.

Marie-Claude woke to the sound of a military band playing
below her window. She rose, put on a wrap, and ran to look
out at a passing German group of trumpeters. The men's faces
were intent because they had been ordered to herald the new day
with a show of strength and spectacle that would make the inhabitants of Paris understand the might of the Fatherland.
Marie-Claude ran to her wardrobe and slipped on a new dress.

She left the house and walked to the avenue Foch and then slowly, in awe, in the direction of the Arc de Triomphe. She had never seen so many soldiers as the massed might of the Wehrmacht, the steel mountains of the Panzer divisions, the stiff-backed men of the infantry, and black-clad officers of the elite Waffen SS who stood before dejected Parisians dressed in mourning.

Marie-Claude's heart began to thunder, and she knew suddenly that she was going to faint because the tumult the scene evoked was too much to bear. She stepped inside a building and collapsed at the feet of a black-clad officer of the Allgemeinen SS. The officer called for men to carry the unconscious girl into the porch of a house he had just requisitioned in the avenue Foch. For a moment he looked down at her slender body with its translucent skin, at the gold chain around her neck and the expensive leather shoes on her feet. Then he slapped her brutally, forcing her to consciousness.

Marie-Claude blinked and recoiled, aware of a man leaning over her as she struggled to focus her eyes. The man was tall and fair, with a narrow face and a pointed nose. His eyes were pale and penetrating, and something about him made her feel more frightened than she had ever felt before. As she struggled to her feet, the man asked her name. She replied haughtily, defiantly.

"I am Marie-Claude Chambord."

"Your address?"

Marie-Claude hesitated, but the cold blue eyes compelled, so she answered.

"Place Victor Hugo, number one hundred and eighteen."

The officer smiled as he consulted a leather-bound notebook, and Marie-Claude thought ruefully that he was even more frightening when he seemed pleased than when he was giving orders.

"You are the daughter of Charles Edouard Chambord, president of the Banque de Lyon?"

Marie-Claude hesitated, her eyes roaming over the officer's uniform with its silver epaulets and stark line. How did he know the name and occupation of every resident in the quarter? Who had given him the information? For the first time Marie-Claude realized that some of her neighbors must have contributed to the list.

"I am Charles Chambord's daughter, though I fail to see of what interest that can be to you."

The thin lips broke into a smile.

"I am Oberst-Gruppenfuhrer Heydritch, Reinhard Heydritch."

Marie-Claude was determined not to show the fear that was making her body tremble. Heydritch took her arm and led to her his car.

"Now I shall take you home, Mademoiselle Chambord."

Marie-Claude recoiled in alarm.

"I can walk, thank you, sir."

Sensing her chagrin, Heydritch continued.

"But I insist. I cannot permit you to return home alone in such a weak condition."

Marie-Claude looked into his eyes and sensed in him an insatiable desire and a cruelty that mesmerized her. She allowed herself to be led to the black open car and driven back to the place Victor Hugo. As she rode she wondered if her father would have a stroke when he saw her. And whatever would the neighbors say? Perhaps M. de Justine, who had fought the Germans in the First World War, would fire his pistol and kill the Oberst-Gruppenfuhrer on sight. Marie-Claude shuddered as she thought of all the complications the brief journey would cause. Tears came to her eyes, and she wiped them away with an impatient flick of the hand. What abysmal luck! The Germans had only just arrived in Paris and she was riding home in broad daylight with a member of the SS. She began to pray that no one would see her.

Outside number 118 the Oberst-Gruppenfuhrer's driver stepped down and opened the door so Marie-Claude could step out. She turned to the man at her side and formally held out her hand.

"Thank you for bringing me home, sir."

"You are most welcome, Mademoiselle Chambord."

Heydritch clicked his heels and threw a curious glance up at the impressive house where his companion lived. Then he returned to the car as Marie-Claude rushed inside without a backward glance. She was aghast to find her father waiting in the hall. Chambord screamed in fury at his daughter. "Are you mad! What do you think you are doing?"

"Papa, I—"

"Did you *have* to go out to welcome the Germans to our city?

And, worse, did you have to come home with one as if you'd been out on a date to the opera?"

"I fainted, papa, and that officer, Oberst-Gruppenfuhrer Heydritch, insisted on bringing me home. I tried to stop him, I—"

"I don't wish to hear about your escapades. It will take years for me to live this down with the neighbors. Thank God Madame is still asleep, or I should never have heard the last of your stupidity."

Marie-Claude fled to her room, locked the door, and threw herself on the bed, sobbing as if her heart would break. Chambord had never admonished her so severely before. It was obvious he was ashamed, that he felt she had let him down. After a while she wiped her eyes, blew her nose, and sat up against the pink lace pillows. The encounter with Heydritch had severely frightened her, and she decided never to go out again, at least not until every enemy soldier had left Paris. She tried to analyze the features on the Oberst-Gruppenfuhrer's face, realizing that what remained most in her mind was the evil in his eyes, the sensuous demand inherent in his manner. She sat abruptly on the edge of the bed and then ran to the bathroom, stripping off her clothes, and then leaping under the shower. Cursing Germans for their lack of breeding, their ambition, and their hateful presence, she vowed to avoid them at all costs in the future. She would simply not go out. That was the solution. Decision made, Marie-Claude felt much happier.

The German assembly at the Arc de Triomphe was finally complete. They were all there, the soldiers who had crushed French opposition. Men of the elite Panzer Lehr and the Ghost Squad of the 7th Panzer Divisions mixed with tank crews standing to attention. Overhead the Luftwaffe roared by, adding decibels to the crescendo of military music from the massed bands. Frenchmen in the crowd narrowed their eyes and squinted up to the sky at a black cloud of Heinkels, Dorniers, and ME 109s. Total French bomber strength was not more than one hundred and seventy-five planes, and the British were known to have even less. Old soldiers sighed at the thought that the Germans had almost ten times their air power and enough spare planes to deafen the inhabitants of Paris with this alarming migration of steel. General von Keist, commander of the Panzer divisions, General von Kluge of the 4th Army, and General von List of the 12th made speeches, their voices shrilling in the listeners' ears. Then the band played the German national anthem and the Etoile echoed to the sound of soldiers saluting the Fuhrer and roaring "Heil Hitler!" An epidemic of clearing the nose and spitting broke out in the French crowd, and a young man, overcome with patriotism, ran to put a knife in a German soldier's neck. He was hit in the face with a rifle butt and trampled to death by his countrymen in the undulating crowd. Finally the music reached its climax with the bellow of bugles, drums, and trumpets. The citizens of Paris began to disperse, shaking their heads and trying not to look as beaten as they felt.

Within the hour the streets filled with men pasting up propaganda posters showing a German soldier holding a young French child. Under the picture there was a message that turned the knife in every Parisian heart: ABANDONED PEOPLE, HAVE FAITH IN THE GERMAN SOLDIER. As soon as the posters appeared, gentlemen of a certain age used them as makeshift pissoirs, housewives threw rubbish and excrement at them, and a priest was seen pulling one down from the wall of his church and tearing it into strips. Loudspeaker vans scurried like beetles in the cobbled byways of Paris, and warnings were incessantly screeched, stunning the people into silent disbelief. From this day everything was to be forbidden: wine, lights, the Métro, traveling outside Paris, cinemas, hoarding food, and throwing bricks at enemy personnel.

Suzanne and her mother looked out from the dormer windows of their home, over the uneven rooftops of Montmartre. They had spent one last wondrous night on the town before that agonizing, exhausting moment when the enemy arrived. The parlor clock struck nine. It was time to go to bed. Perhaps things would seem better in the morning.

That night there were no lights in the city, and no church bells rang. The church bells of Paris would never sound again until the city was free.

# CHAPTER TWO

## Summer to Winter, 1940

On the seventeenth of June, three days after the Germans goose-stepped up the Champs-Elysées, the new prime minister of France, Marshal Pétain, addressed the people on the radio.

Frenchmen: In response to an appeal by the president of the Republic, I am taking over as of today the leadership of the French government. Confident as I am of the loyalty of our fine army now fighting with heroism worthy of its ancient traditions in the field against an enemy superior in numbers and arms; knowing as I do that by its magnificent resistance it has done its duty by our cities—and trusting as I do in the support of the old soldiers that I am proud to have had under my command—I now offer my services unreservedly to France to assuage its distress. At this sorrowful hour, my thoughts go to the hapless refugees streaming down the road of France in utmost destitution. I feel for their unhappy plight. It is with an aching heart that I say to you that the fighting *must* stop. Last night I contacted our opponents and on honorable terms they were prepared to find a way, as between soldiers, to put an end to hostilities.

May all the people of France rally round the government whose leadership I am assuming in this hour of tribulation, sinking their private griefs and putting their trust in the destiny of their country.

Parisians listened to the broadcast in their homes, in cafés, markets, and shops all over the city. And as the tremulous voice of the aged soldier explained that France had capitulated, that they would be asking for an armistice, many people wept openly. On the same day as this broadcast, a little-known French general of fifty stepped on English soil after boarding a British rescue plane. He too spoke to the French people: "France has lost a battle. But France has not lost the war!" Few Frenchmen heard the broadcast of Charles de Gaulle, but many of those who did became the first Gaullistes. They were from many walks of life, young and old, rich and poor, from every political party. Their only unifying factor was that they were patriots and first-day résistants. Among these were the Castels and the Marchands. But neither family knew the other's feelings, because confidences were kept within the home. No longer could such matters be openly discussed, for fear of action by collaborators, who had already made themselves known. At Ottoline's, behind the new blackout curtains, there were some who dared ask where M. Laval of the rue Gabrielle obtained the gas for his car. Few people in Paris had gas, because the German authorities had commandeered most of the pumps and requisitioned the remaining cars, trucks, and vans to bring back refugees who had fled.

In the first few days of occupation, it seemed to the inhabitants of the rue Gabrielle as if nothing very different was going to happen. Only the loudspeaker vans and crude propaganda posters informing them of new ordinances intruded on the eye. The Germans were busy pursuing folk who had fled Paris, and cutting off the remains of the French army in retreat. Night and day they engaged with pockets of resistance southwest toward the Loire and southeast toward Dijon. The 14th Corps cut off the retreat of troops withdrawing to Bordeaux. The 16th Panzer Corps attacked defending armies in the east, toward the Langres plateau and the Swiss frontier. The French general headquarters was withdrawn from Bordeaux to Vichy, and the 7th Army fell back to the Loire. By the eighteenth, news had come that the Germans had taken Rennes and liquidated the Brittany redoubt. No one knew if the rumors were correct, but many wept openly in the streets. Old people showed their fear of the occupying force openly to each other.

The poor manifested tragic resignation; the rich hoped to cushion the worst with money. Whores enjoyed the prospect of becoming wealthy. Children fell victim to confusion and anxiety because their parents' fear had destroyed precious security. Newspapers were still nonexistent. The postal system was still paralyzed. Cinemas and nightclubs closed down, to be reopened only when fighting ceased throughout France. The familiar ring of the telephone and the knock that came in the early morning with the postman's round became luxuries to be dreamed of and hoped for with longing normally reserved for a succulent steak or a fat goose from Bresse. Those with radios capable of picking up the BBC told their families what they had heard, but no one communicated information outside the home. People were unsure whether former friends and neighbors were still loyal, as it had soon become apparent that in war friends can also be enemies, that the desire to survive is stronger than anything, even tradition and the preservation of reputation.

Suzanne and her mother remained close to their home, conserving what remained of their cash, because the Bal Tabarin had closed with all the other nightclubs and theaters. Montmartre had seen little of the Germans. They could not run their loudspeaker vans up the steps of the quarter, and motorcycle patrols found the iron railings, cul-de-sacs, and strangely differing levels of the streets impossible to pass. So residents and shop owners who had stayed were free from most of the hectoring noises of the city center. The main cross borne by those who lived on the hill was tourists, off-duty German soldiers who clicked cameras and begged souvenirs at every cobbled corner. Many of the men were rich and greedy, swooping on antique shops, emptying stock and forming queues at perfumeries, where they bought everything in sight. In cafés German soldiers demanded huge meals and second helpings. They were polite and willing to pay for whatever they consumed. It was said that there was never a moment from dusk to dawn when they were not hungry, and after a month Parisians despairingly christened them "Colorado beetles." The Germans were under strict orders to behave with restraint and good breeding, to show themselves as prime examples of the master race. For their part, most Parisians tried to make the best of the calamity. It was not unusual for the Castels to show the way to the place du Tertre to a ruddy-faced German corporal. M. Roger's family served meals to the occupying soldiers in the café on the corner, and even André Marchand had been seen giving a light to a Wehrmacht officer when they met on the steps of the cathedral.

Most ordinary people of the quarter had decided that it was best to relax and play a waiting game until the Germans decided to go home. Former soldiers followed Pétain's lead, sure the old man had not misled them. Hotheads who took to blowing up German staff cars were viewed with disfavor, because the common opinion was that peace must be preserved at all costs. This attitude continued until the armistice was signed. Then it was noted with concern that the Fuhrer, Adolf Hitler, had insisted that this be signed in the same railway carriage as that in which the Germans had surrendered in 1918. He had also toured Paris, posing for photographs near well-known landmarks and standing in uniform, his black leather boots firmly planted, on the steel of the Eiffel tower.

Foreboding came when the terms of the armistice were announced. From now on France would be divided into two separate countries. Paris would be in the occupied zone, and passes to the free zone would be given only under exceptional circumstances. The northern provinces of France would be linked to make a new Flanders, Brittany would be granted autonomy, and Burgundy was to be incorporated into Germany.

Nathalie sat impassive as a sphinx, listening to announcements on the radio. Since the Germans had arrived, she had felt such anger in her heart she thought it might burst with the effort of self-control. And every day things got worse instead of better. She thought sadly of the chaos that was eroding the heart of Paris. The Métro had not run for weeks, so people could not get about. Folk who wanted to work could not do so because theaters had not been reopened and banks and offices were working with skeleton staffs. As if all that was not enough, her money was fast dwindling and still she had no news of her husband. Yesterday a decree had been issued forbidding the people of Paris to own firearms and ammunition of any kind. Nathalie thought of her neighbor, M. Corbeil, who had a selection of guns collected over the past twenty-five years. Would Corbeil hand them over to the authorities? She felt sure he would not. Nathalie scowled furiously at the thought that radios, too, had been banned. Those possessing them had been ordered to hand them in to the municipality. Without the radio they would have no idea what was happening. Nathalie decided to consult her daughter about that particular ordinance. Suzanne was in the attic, occupying her restless mind by sorting through trunks deposited there during the previous forty years by various members of the Castel family. She heard her mother call and ran downstairs.

"Zizi, what shall we do about the order to deposit our radio at the mairie?"

"I've decided what's best. You only have to agree, maman."

"Tell me what you think."

Suzanne sat next to her mother on the sofa, stroking Nathalie's hands to calm her unease.

"I'll go and deposit that little set Papa bought for my tenth birthday. Then we can keep the set that gets the BBC."

"They said failure to comply with the order would be punishable with death. That means a firing squad, you know."

"But, maman, they don't have time to search every house in Paris."

Nathalie considered their position. The threat of death intimidated her, yet she could not bear to think of losing their only link with legitimate news.

"Where could we hide the set? There's going to be an inspection by the billeting officer next week, and we're likely to get some frisé staying here in the house."

Suzanne considered the possibility, stunned to think of having a German living in her home. If anything happened to him, another would come in his place, and perhaps she and her mother would be shot.

While Suzanne was considering a dozen murderous alternatives, Nathalie went to the kitchen to make coffee. She cut slices of Suzanne's favorite pear flan to cheer them, and muttered in disbelief that they were going to have to accept a billeted German.

Suzanne abandoned her daydreams. It was wrong to think of murder—at least, that was what she had always believed. Or did war make everyone a potential killer? Was action against the enemy the only way of remaining sane and alive?

"We must keep our radio, maman. I'll hide it in a very obvious place. No one will look for it there."

Nathalie stared, wondering if her daughter's logic had been disturbed by the shock of occupation. When Suzanne explained what she meant, Nathalie sighed with relief.

"We could put the radio in that old doll's house papa turned into a liquor cabinet."

They tried out Suzanne's idea, and the small radio fit perfectly into the inner section of the cumbersome toy Castel had transformed into a decanter holder, bottle rack, and bitters rail.

Suzanne returned to the attic, and Nathalie tried to read, but she could not follow the story, so she turned on the radio and listened to the news that billeting inspections would begin at eight the following Monday morning. Refugees were flooding back to the city from all over France. Soon there would be food shortages and trouble with the antiquated sewage system.

Nathalie had little money left, and she wondered uncertainly if the Germans would expect her to feed an overweight soldier by herself. She shuddered, her mind rebelling against thoughts of a blubber-bodied yokel from Bavaria slopping soup at her table and sleeping in her spare room. For weeks she had been praying that her husband would return, but there had been no news and she had come to accept the possibility that he was a prisoner in Germany. At that moment, when she was least expecting it, Jacques walked into la maison Fleuri and kissed her. It was a rainy July morning, dark and overcast, but Nathalie thought it the most beautiful day of her life.

"Jacques! Oh, my dear, I am *so* happy you're home. You can't possibly know how much I've missed you."

Jacques held his wife tightly, stroking her hair and kissing her gently to calm a flood of tears.

"You know, Nathalie, thinking of you and of coming home is all that has made me want to stay alive these past few months."

Suzanne entered the room and rushed to kiss her father.

"Papa, why didn't you write? We were thinking you had died in the fighting or that you'd been taken prisoner in Germany. How long can you stay?"

"Only for twenty-four hours, chérie. Now let me look at you. You're prettier than ever, and I'm so proud of you." Jacques settled in his armchair. "Nathalie, have you anything to eat? I don't seem to have had a good meal for months."

Nathalie came to life with a start. First she bounded to the cellar to bring up the one bottle she had left out in case her husband returned, a wine from the area of the Loire where Jacques had spent his childhood. While she clattered pans in the kitchen, Suzanne sat near her father, trying not to look at the scars on his arm as she brought him up-to-date with their news.

"The Germans came to Paris last month and we saw their tanks as we were leaving les Halles. They played such loud military music when they met at the Etoile, we could even hear it up here in Montmartre."

"Have they bothered you in any way?"

"Not yet, but I think we're going to have a German billeted here. I was thinking of throwing him over the wall with a judo throw, but I don't suppose that would be much use!"

Jacques laughed at his daughter's innocence. Then he fell silent, wondering how long it would be before youthful rebellion turned to war-hardened numbness.

"Have you heard anything from your fiancé?"

"Not for a month, papa."

"Not since he was injured?"

Suzanne leaped up, her face ashen, her eyes hurt and confused. Suddenly the war seemed uncomfortably close to home.

"Where was he injured, papa?"

"I heard from one of the officers who was transferred to my unit that David's been fighting with the army in the Alsace region."

"No, where on his body?"

Jacques smiled, pulling his daughter back on the sofa and smoothing her alarm.

"He injured his leg, Zizi, and it was bad, I understand. They've invalided him out of the army, so he won't be in Picardy with the others."

"And where is David now?"

Jacques hesitated, uncertain whether it was wise to tell his daughter all he knew. Then, seeing Suzanne's stricken face, he revealed his secret.

"David has become a résistant. He has formed a group and intends to carry on his own fight against the Germans."

Suzanne was shocked and angry.

"That means I shall never see him again, never! Oh, papa, I could have hoped for better news. I'm always reading about men getting killed when they fight as guerrillas against the Germans. There won't be a single one of them left by the end of the war."

Suzanne sobbed until it seemed nothing would comfort her. She had been hoping David would come unexpectedly to stay at the house and that he would change his mind and love her before disappearing again. She had dreamed of him every night for weeks, praying he would get away from his unit to visit her. Now Suzanne had a strange feeling that she would never see her fiancé again. She would be left forever alone with nothing but memories of what might have been, and David, the most remarkable of men, would die. Remembering what her father had said, Suzanne asked anxiously, "Will David walk again?"

"He'll walk—not as well as the next man, but you know how he is, he won't give in. What he wants he gets, and what he wants most at this moment is to fight Germans."

"I had hoped he wanted to marry me, papa."

"He wants to marry you when he's fought the Germans, chérie. David is longing for a home and a happy married life with children. What hope would there be of that while France is occupied?"

Suzanne cheered when she saw the dinner her mother had prepared: crudités with sugary vinaigrette sauce, smoked eel, and jugged hare with frothy puréed potatoes. Before dessert was served, Jacques had fallen asleep at the table, his face lit by the orange glow of the fire. Suzanne and her mother exchanged pitying glances. The man they both adored had changed beyond recall. His body was skeleton thin, and the calm look of times past had become the hunted look that war inspires. Suzanne whispered to Nathalie, "I forgot to ask where Papa had been fighting."

"Did he say what time he must leave tomorrow?"

"At four, maman."

"So soon? I wish he could stay forever."

When the dinner dishes had been washed, Jacques woke to the smell of coffee. He rummaged in his kit bag and brought out a length of red velvet ribbon for Suzanne's hair. For his wife he had bought a blue-and-white porcelain box of Breton fudge. But when the two women asked him about the north of France, Jacques shook his head wearily, and it was obvious he wanted to forget everything he had seen.

"There were German soldiers sunning themselves on the beaches in Brittany, and a cemetery full of our dead overlooking the sea. You can't imagine how seriously the Germans care for their bodies. Sometimes I wondered if they thought of anything else. I wonder if we shall ever see them leave Paris."

Suzanne went to bed, leaving her parents alone in the living room. As she dozed she heard her mother laughing, the tinkling silver laugh she remembered from past times, which she had not heard for so long. At ten her parents retired, and Suzanne could hear their muffled voices across the landing. She plumped her pillows contentedly and settled to sleep, grateful that for one joyous day her father was home.

In the morning M. Roger's cockerel crowed as if to remind Jacques that he was in Montmartre. He lay cradling his wife in his arms, and trying not to think of what was going to happen after he left Paris. The Germans were surely going to occupy the city for months. Food would become scarcer, and women would be at the mercy of the men billeted in their homes. Knowing that he was powerless to help his wife and daughter, Jacques struggled to remember the lessons of war, that it was best to enjoy every moment for what it was and not to think about tomorrow. He sniffed the familiar smells of morning as they drifted upstairs, and felt suddenly ravenous. Suzanne had gone down early to set a celebration table. She had cooked blood sausage, smoked ham, and new-laid eggs from Vivienne Marchand's hens. There was mint in a vase on the table, because the bright green leaves gave off Jacques' favorite smell. When her father appeared in his pajamas and dressing gown, Suzanne ran to kiss him.

"Do you know where you're going today, papa?"

"They didn't say."

Jacques walked to the kitchen door and looked out into the garden. Suzanne persisted.

"If there's to be an armistice, papa, and our army isn't fighting anymore, how can they consider posting you away from Paris?"

"It's not the French army who are posting me, Zizi. It's the Germans."

Suzanne's face turned pale, and she began to beat the eggs furiously.

"What were you told, papa?"

"My regiment has been ordered to the Gare de Lyon at four this afternoon. They said we shall be working on a new road. When the road is finished we shall come home to Paris."

"Where is the road, papa?"

Jacques considered the question. The Gare de Lyon served Fontainebleau and the East. Was it possible he was being sent to Germany? He shrugged, unwilling to burden his daughter with mere suspicion.

"It could be anywhere. I only know that men are needed."

"By the Germans, papa!"

Suzanne served breakfast in silence. Outside a thrush was trilling on the cherry tree, and in the distance there was once again the faint rumble of traffic. Nathalie came downstairs, and as they ate she chattered and made jokes till her husband's face shone with relief. Suzanne decided to say nothing more about her father's imminent departure. For days the Germans had been sending single and unattached men to Germany to act as forced labor on bombed roads, bridges, and communications centers. Civil servants had been immune from this decree because many of them were needed to keep order among the endless files and red tape bred by new ordinances.

Suzanne swallowed eggs, sausage, and ham without tasting a mouthful. No sooner had life returned to normal than hope was dashed all over again. *Why* did her father have to leave Paris? At last she could stand it no longer, and she burst out with furious questions.

"I think you're being sent to Germany, papa. The Germans need men, and everyone knows they've been sending men to their cities. They must surely have given you some indication of where you're going?"

Jacques raised his hand to silence her.

"While I'm home, Zizi, I want Maman to be happy. We are all aware of what might be. We also know that when the war is over I shall come home from wherever I am, because *this* is where I wish to be."

Suzanne ran to the garden, reluctant to let her father see the bitter tears coursing down her cheeks.

From his attic window M. Laval looked down on her. He had noted the arrival of his neighbor and anticipated Jacques' departure. With Castel gone, there would be two bedrooms free for the use of military personnel. The women could share one of the double beds and a German could go in each of the other rooms. Laval was preparing a list of information on his area for the officer commanding the eighteenth arrondissement. He paused uncertainly when he came to André Marchand's name. Marchand was half blind, so he would be useless on a German labor gang. For the moment Laval decided to let him stay in Paris. But if Marchand continued to talk of resistance and Charles de Gaulle, he would make sure the authorities knew of the radio set the young couple had kept back. M. Laval tried on the new suit he had just bought, a fine suit of charcoal wool that fit him to perfection. Money was important, he thought. Now that he was being paid by the Gestapo, he would soon own a dozen suits, and as the rigors of occupation worsened he would start buying up property belonging to his neighbors as they fell victim to poverty and hunger. He would be a man of power and substance by the end of the war.

Laval adjusted his binoculars and watched Suzanne crying. His eyes narrowed and he sucked in his breath as he examined the fullness of her body under the flimsy cotton wrap. Someday, perhaps, Suzanne Castel would need him. With a little discipline she could be taught to please, and if her need were sufficient she could be made to obey him. He raised the glasses and made a note of the fact that Suzanne had been severely distressed. Then he frowned. Perhaps it was unwise to recommend billeting two Germans in the Castel house. Women alone were tempting to soldiers deprived of entertainment, and men together gave each other confidence to do things a man alone might not attempt. Laval crossed out his previous accommodation assessment and put "one vacant bed" by the Castel house. Then he brushed his hair and went down to breakfast, satisfied that he was doing an excellent job.

Jacques left the house at three and made his way across the city. He had left his army pay book with his wife so she could claim money during his absence. He had helped hide the cash brought back home with him, his savings from the previous six months. His mind was calm because everything was in order with those he loved; all he had to do now was stay alive. Jacques noticed the posters on every wall, and flinched as loudspeaker vans screeched their orders. He passed German soldiers on every corner, and wagons full of Jews being transported out of Paris. It was difficult to remain calm when there were enemy soldiers in every French office, bank, shop, and station, when the air was strident with the sound of alien command. Jacques neared the Gare de Lyon and saw that hundreds of Frenchmen were waiting to be checked through the barriers. His own regiment was there with what looked like half the 1st and 7th French command. Jacques showed his orders and passed through the barrier. But, unlike colleagues who rushed to secure spaces on the train, he lingered awhile. He had an overwhelming desire to see the buffet of the station just once more, because it was one of the greatest remaining examples of belle époque Paris, and the first place he had been brought after his arrival in the city at the age of ten. He had been a country lad, thrilled and stunned by the spectacle and mystery of Paris. The station buffet had been a revelation he had never forgotten, Aladdin's cave in the midst of a busy metropolis.

Jacques slipped past fellow travelers to a flight of stairs near the main waiting room. Then, holding his breath, he opened the buffet doors, his eyes lingering joyfully on pearly chandeliers and pretty painted ladies swinging in merry abandon on the ceiling. On every wall naïve depictions of the provinces of France sprang to his attention, confusing the eye and thrilling the heart. Gradually the atmosphere of warmth and luxurious gaiety lulled his war-blunted senses, and for a moment Jacques felt as he had felt long ago, awed and deeply proud of his city. He stepped inside, closing the door, conscious that he was alone in the vast arched room but for a waiter and one young German officer.

Walking to the windows, Jacques held out his hand to touch the lush red velvet drapes, pushing them aside so he could pinch the web-fine splendor of the Auvergne lace festoons that came between curtain and glass. The German officer rose, paid his bill, and passed close by where Jacques was absorbing the scene. The two men smiled, and the officer inclined his head.

"Once, when I was still at school in Lindau, I saw a photograph of this room in one of my father's books. Now I can see it as it really is. I cannot believe my luck at being in Paris."

"Have you just arrived?"

"I came on the noon train from Baden-Baden. I shall be working in the office of the Propagandastaffel, because I speak French and the seriousness of my back injury prevents my returning to the front."

Jacques thought how handsome and forthright the young German was, how thrilled to be in the city of his dreams. He nodded politely and passed on, giving one last, lingering look at the ornate interior before disappearing to the train.

The young officer walked through the crowded station concourse and disappeared into the sunlight. He was happy to be in Paris, overjoyed by his country's victory, and conscious of his responsibilities in preparing the people of Paris for military government. Paris was a great responsibility, to be treasured and enhanced by the efficiency and application for which Germany was famous. He walked along the embankment, looking down on the bridges of the Seine, at barges passing on unruly wind-whipped water. A young boy was sitting on a crate, fishing with a piece of string; a woman on an iron bench at the water's edge was reading a letter, first smiling, then dabbing tears from her eyes as the words recalled happier times. To be in Paris was a bonus, and the young officer was eager to acquit himself well. As he continued toward his destination in the Champs-Elysées, he saw notices saying NO TIRES, NO GAS, NO SPARE PARTS, NO MEAT, NO POTATOES, REGULARS ONLY. He frowned sympathetically. Obviously Paris in the fall was a lady in distress. He was cheered by the fact that Germany's might would soon redress the wrongs, that Paris would soon sparkle again.

Suzanne sat on the steps of the rue Foyatier looking through to the place Willette, where German soldiers were playing football with small boys from the quarter. She wanted to be alone because she was disturbed by her father's departure. After lunch Nathalie had gone to bed to sob at the agony of parting. Having made an effort to be as attractive and gay as in times past for the precious few hours of her husband's stay, she felt depleted, empty, and without hope. Suzanne thought fiercely that her father was going away to be worked like a dog in a strange country and an alien town where he had no friends. She thought of the ribbon her father had brought home and, touching it, was comforted by the memory. As Suzanne watched one of the German soldiers approaching, tears of anguish and frustration, anger and confusion touched her cheeks. Change was alien to her nature, and the change from freedom to occupation, security to uncertainty, was too much to bear. The mind needed diversion, the body needed to work—but there was no work to be had. She was wiping her eyes and about to return home when the German offered her a cigarette. Suzanne refused politely, explaining that she did not smoke. The soldier pushed the cigarette into her hand, lit it, and then waited for her to smoke, and Suzanne realized that he did not speak French. She shook her head, handing him back the cigarette and miming that she did not smoke. Then she turned and ran back up the steps, aghast when the soldier ran after her. She turned and roared in fury, "Go away! I don't want to talk with you!" The soldier waited nearby, picking his teeth and trying to assess his chance with her. Angry and frightened, Suzanne stood her ground, and after a while the soldier tired of the game and walked away. As soon as his back was turned, Suzanne ran up the stairs, into the rue Gabrielle, over the garden wall, and into la maison Fleuri. Nathalie was making a chamomile tisane in the kitchen.

"A German soldier offered me a cigarette and then followed me up the stairs."

"You should have told him to go away."

"I did, but he didn't understand French. Most of them don't speak anything but German. I think they must be the ugliest, most horrible race in the world!"

"Janine Joel's back."

Suzanne smothered her mother with kisses.

"Where is she?"

"She's at home unloading her belongings and trying to find some money to buy food. The Germans brought the last of the refugees back today, and Janine was one of them. She's been stuck without gas in a farm in the Chevreuse valley, and you know how Janine hates the country!"

Suzanne laughed out loud, overjoyed to know that her best friend was once again in Paris. For as long as she could remember they had been like sisters, at school, at the ballet academy, in the theater. There were those who thought them alike because both had long black hair that fell to the waist and a small-stepping dancer's walk. But Janine's eyes were blue, Suzanne's gold-green. Janine was shorter by half a head than her friend, and had always been more flirtatious, even when young. Since the resemblance was there, however, the girls enjoyed accentuating it by wearing the same butterfly hair slides, the same canvas mules, and by calling each other belle-soeur. Often Suzanne wished Janine could be her real sister, but having her as a special friend seemed almost good enough. When the theaters reopened, Suzanne knew, they would retrieve the threads of lost acquaintance and work together as they had so often in the past.

Suzanne's mood changed, and she helped her mother make dinner, relieved when Nathalie began to talk of plans for the autumn. In those first days and weeks of the occupation they prefaced many of their remarks with the phrase "when the Germans leave Paris." But as time passed they had to admit that the occupation was a long one and that it might never end. They no longer allowed themselves to think of the day when the torment would be over, and they lived only for the present.

With the midsummer heat wave, the officers of the Devisen-schutzkommand arrived in Paris with orders to open all safes and exchange French bank notes for German. They had authority to take over all financial institutions and to issue orders that money "must not lie idle." With the currency protectors came more propaganda workers, and soon the city was inundated with people. The authorities intimated that further accommodations would have to be found, and once again Suzanne and her mother discussed the imminent arrival of the billeting officer. In the early days of the occupation he had visited la maison Fleuri, but the situation then had not been so urgent. The billeting officer had made a note of the spare room but had declined to use it as it was too small and in an inconvenient location. Now Suzanne fidgeted in her chair.

"He'll make us take in a German, won't he, maman?"

"I think he will."

"I'll never speak to him!"

"Of course you will, Zizi. We can't live in a house with a man and never speak to him. We must be polite and kind and hope to God he has good manners."

"There are no Germans with good manners, maman."

Nathalie Castel sighed. Since Jacques's departure Suzanne had been impossible—quarrelsome, contrary, given to sulking and pouting and behaving in an uncharacteristic fashion. She had even put David's photograph facedown on her dressing table, unwilling to look at him and long for him if she could not see him again. Nathalie looked at the long brown legs, the slim fingers tapping the table, the watchful cat eyes that could settle on nothing for more than a few seconds. Suzanne needed to be married, with children to occupy her days, but what hope was there of that? Nathalie started as the doorbell rang.

"He's here. Do stop scowling, Zizi, or he'll put us both in the big bedroom and send two of those wretched Germans to plague us."

Suzanne went to answer the door. She was surprised to see Laval with the billeting officer. Laval sidled inside, smiling unctuously and shaking her hand with a wet-palmed grip.

"I came to translate, mademoiselle."

Suzanne glowered as the tax collector's eyes roamed over her body, and she thought grimly that if Laval were not a collaborator and so a power to be reckoned with, she would kick him out into the garden and crack his skull with a spade. Putting on a mask of politeness, she indicated the stairs.

"You know the way, Monsieur Laval, you can show the officer our room."

"Thank you, mademoiselle."

Laval cracked his knuckles, first one hand and then the other, and Suzanne rushed away to the kitchen to put water on for coffee. She and her mother giggled irreverently at Laval's fawning manner and the sweat that trickled down his face like a waterfall whenever he met a pretty woman. Once, Suzanne recalled, at a street party in the summer of '38, before war disrupted their lives, Janine had flirted outrageously with Laval just to see what he would do. The tax collector had followed her around like a zombie, his wild eyes starting from his corpse-pale face. Janine had let him kiss her and had reported that his breath smelled of Roquefort, his sweat of Camembert. Gales of laughter had echoed in the Castel house that evening, and everyone had agreed it was a perfect description.

Laval appeared in the doorway, startling the two women to silence.

"The billeting officer is satisfied, madame. A German officer will arrive before five, if that is convenient."

"Are you sure he'll be an officer?"

"I have no say in the matter, madame."

"But you know who he is, don't you, Monsieur Laval?"

"I think he will be an officer. You can be sure I shall do my best."

Suzanne smiled, dazzling the billeting officer with her charm. He expressed his hopes for a satisfactory arrangement, via M. Laval, and left having clicked his heels like a robot. When the visitors had gone, Suzanne and her mother went upstairs to prepare the bed.

"I wonder how old he'll be, maman."

"God knows. I just hope he's clean."

"Do we have to have our meals with him?"

"Of course we do. This isn't a hotel, you know, we only have one dining room. I shall be given an allowance to cover his breakfast and dinner, and I shall do my best to keep him quiet."

Suzanne glowered defiantly.

"If he eats as much as all the other Germans in Paris, no allowance will cover the costs. We won't give him wine with his meals, will we, maman?"

Nathalie exploded, utterly exhausted by her daughter's questions.

"Will you *please* stop complaining, Zizi! We must do our best for the German and pray he doesn't expect anything else from us other than meals!"

Suzanne was in the garden when the clock chimed five. She had been praying the new arrival would be kind and not one of those arrogant warlike Germans women in the area dreaded meeting. Some officers billeted with families took over the house, ordering the father and mother about as if they were servants and using daughters and widows as if they were prostitutes provided for the purpose. At ten past five there was a knock at the door. Suzanne ran to open it, and greeted the new arrival with an uncertain smile.

The man before her was not at all what she had expected. He was old—over sixty, she imagined—and his hair was silver white. His pale face had a sagging jawline, and he looked as worried and upset as she.

Over dinner Herr Schulberg explained that he was a bank administrator brought in from Germany to give expert advice to the men of the Devisenschutzkommand. At eight, when Nathalie handed their new companion a brandy, Schulberg talked wistfully about his family.

"I have a wife and five children back home in Germany. Here is a photograph of us taken at Bad Kreuznach at our summer house. During the year we live in Koblenz, where the bank is situated."

Nathalie was surprised to see five smiling children from eight to twenty-eight and a plump wife outside an alpine house of elaborate construction. Suzanne softened despite herself, because she was thinking of her father and wondering if he too was showing photographs of his family to a stranger and hoping for a moment of peace. She poured their guest another brandy, listening eagerly as Schulberg talked.

"I did not wish to come to Paris, but I had no choice. Such a great city needs administrators, and many of your own have gone away to Vichy."

Suzanne nodded sadly. Most of the doctors had fled Paris, some leaving seriously ill patients in the hands of unqualified orderlies. Jews lucky enough to have sufficient cash and somewhere to go had also gone, and so had antifascists who feared German reprisals. Civil servants had been loath to abandon their homes in Paris, but the majority had been obliged to follow the government to Bordeaux and then to Vichy. Suzanne thought of the Chambords, resolving again to visit them when next she was in the area. For a moment she smothered a smile at the thought of Monsieur's chagrin when his bank was taken over. Schulberg continued, determined to cheer the two women.

"Now that we have the Métro running again, we shall soon

arrange that it stops at more stations so it will not be so difficult to get about. Also, bicycles are being imported from the Ruhr, and I shall try to bring you one of the best. I would like to say that during my stay in this house I shall do my best to be pleasant company, and I hope most sincerely that my presence will not be too great an imposition upon you."

They sat near the fire, at peace and resigned to the necessity of preserving an amicable arrangement. At ten Suzanne went to bed, followed within minutes by her mother. Schulberg waited until the women were out of the bathroom; then he walked slowly upstairs. On the landing, he fingered some dried poppy pods in a brass vase with corn picked from a field in Vincennes. As he buttoned his pajama jacket he looked at faded photographs on the bedside table—one of Suzanne when young, in ballet tutu and satin-tied shoes; another of Jacques and Nathalie sitting with laps full of apples under the tree at the end of the garden. Schulberg wiped his eyes and longed for his family, overcome by homesickness and the memory of happier days. This was a nice house, a comfortable home, and the women were charming and kind. He wondered if Jacques Castel was enjoying such pleasant surroundings far away in Germany. After saying his prayers, Schulberg fell sound asleep.

In the weeks that followed Schulberg's arrival, Suzanne and her mother had reason to be glad that he was kindhearted and friendly. Autumn winds were cold, and food had become very scarce. German regulations permitted a total intake of only twelve hundred calories per day, and the allowance was the same regardless of position, so shop assistants ate the same as road workers, pregnant women the same as children. Friendship originally shown German soldiers began to evaporate, and attacks on enemy personnel increased day by day. In the warm, heavy days of summer the food allowance had been enough, but now, with the advent of autumn, everyone longed for beef casserole and mountains of pommes purées. Fuel also had been rationed, and with an icy winter ahead the family could keep the heating at only fifty degrees. Suzanne and her mother took to wearing shawls and scarves inside the house; then, as the temperature fell, they put on caps and coats. Their faces were pinched with cold, though every window had been sealed. Nathalie complained of burst veins in her nose and Suzanne of chilblains everywhere, on toes, fingers, and even around her wrists. Schulberg suffered the hardships without complaint until one rainy day in November when he arrived home with a tree in tow. He had lassoed a rope around its branches, looped the rope around his shoulders, and dragged the trunk downhill from the square near the vineyard. He looked apologetically at Nathalie and explained, "It was in the road. I didn't cut it down, of course."

Suzanne and her mother helped Schulberg haul the tree down the side path and into the garden. Both were amazed by his courage and the strength of his elderly limbs. All afternoon they sawed, one at each end, with Suzanne carrying the heavy logs inside to be dried in the cellar. It was strictly forbidden to cut down trees from the boulevards and squares of Paris, a special ordinance having been issued to that effect. But Nathalie was not complaining. In war, she had long since learned, there were no rules. Schulberg agreed, and soon it was his pleasure to listen to BBC broadcasts every evening, because he was dying to know what was really happening in Europe. After each transmission he hid the radio securely in the cocktail cabinet in case any Gestapo thugs came to call.

In the days of his youth, Schulberg had been a soldier, and he had great respect for the military mind. His patriotism was beyond question, and only on the vexed subject of the Gestapo was his loyalty divided. He had heard stories about how men for the Gestapo and Allgemeinen SS were selected, and rumors about their true reason for being. He knew that many of the men recruited for those branches of the service took pleasure in torturing and taking the lives of innocent people as well as dissidents. Schulberg had already decided that if he had to choose between the Castels and a Gestapo officer come to search the house, he would kill the Gestapo officer, steal a car, and then drive back to Germany, where he belonged. Sometimes, as the situation between the German and French population worsened, Schulberg had nightmares about the Gestapo. Everyone knew about the house in the avenue Foch from which anguished screams came at all hours of the day and night, but Schulberg thought about it more than most. Whenever her lodger cried out in his sleep,

Nathalie rose and made hot chocolate. Then she would hurry with the tray to his bedroom, and they would sit together until the small hours, reminiscing about the days of their youth, when automobiles were new, women were pretty, and gentlemen knew how to behave.

At the end of November the situation became even more tense when twenty Germans were killed after saboteurs blew up the truck in which they were traveling. The officer commanding the occupation force racked his brain for a way to bring the citizens of Paris to heel. He had been trying to avoid open confrontation, because his job was difficult enough without forcing soldiers under his command into actions that would give rise to open hostility. But in the light of the new defiance he passed ordinances that made it a capital offense to go on strike, to deface buildings, not to salute a German officer on the street, and not to inform the authorities of acts of civil disobedience.

Parisians listened stoically, shaking their heads sadly and trying not to think how ugly life had become since the promises of the early days of occupation. Still they were strong, and still long-suffering, working on in the belief that the Germans would vanish as quickly as they had arrived. Farmers from Compiègne, Soissons, and Châlons sent vegetables to relatives in the city, and black marketeers looked after those who could afford their exorbitant prices. With a shrug and a smile, the people of Paris tried to stay calm. They were sure they could do nothing to evict the Germans without help from the Allies. So what was the point of talking of rebellion? There were a few who spoke openly of revolt, but they were soon silenced by the majority, who clung determinedly to the last vestiges of hope that they would remain secure so long as they behaved.

In December the last of the nightclubs reopened, because the German high command considered them a necessary part of the "vie Parisienne." German leaders came to the city to rest, and a visit to Paris was an accepted reward for distinguished service and special valor.

Suzanne was ecstatic when she heard she would soon be working again. She rushed down the hill with her friend Janine, bursting into the Bal Tabarin, greeting the doorkeeper with a kiss and her friends with hugs of affection. The interior of the hall was fusty with a fine layer of dust and the damp feel of a building unused for too long. The wine-colored plush seats and brass-topped tables that glowed in the candlelight of evening seemed tawdry in the harsh white light of day. Twelve dancers were grouped around the piano, some tying their ballet shoes, others adjusting tights and headbands in preparation for half an hour at the barre to unwind muscles long knotted with neglect. The pianist was smoking an acrid-smelling cheroot, the choreographer moaning that they would catch their death of cold in the draft from the unmended windows. Suzanne walked through the tables to where Janine stood talking with the owner. She wondered why her friend looked so glum and why M. Hibbert was wringing his hands and apologizing profusely. When Suzanne sat at Janine's side, the pianist struck a chord and the dancers ran to the barre. As one, they pliéd, one arm on the barre, one balancing them as they began the exercise. Suzanne looked questioningly at her friend.

"What's wrong, Janine?"

"Monsieur Hibbert has just told me he can't continue to employ three acts. Also, he has to choose six of the twelve dancers. It's money, you see, Zizi—he just can't pay all of us."

Suzanne looked to the stage, where the dancers in their black leotards and gaudy striped leg warmers were lifting tired legs to the rousing chords from the piano. The dancers' faces were pale from lack of food and fear at the thought of losing the job they had waited so long to retrieve. Suzanne felt sorry for them and for herself, because she accepted that not everyone was going to return to regular work. Janine filed her nails, and M. Hibbert apologized again.

"It's not my fault, you understand. No one has money except the Germans, and I cannot be sure they will patronize me. As for local trade, well, in past times the rich folk came, but now they stay at home, scared of going out and being questioned about their relatives or their money."

Suzanne watched the dancers' lean bodies. They were smiling now, their cares forgotten as they lifted their legs in strenuous développés. Despite their physical weakness, the girls held their position for the required count, lowering their legs and raising their arms as they turned gracefully away. Suzanne had an idea as she watched.

"If each of the four acts takes less money, you could keep all of us on. And you could ask the dancers if they wanted to work for less salary, too. What do you think, Monsieur Hibbert?"

The vexing question of money was put to the vote. Four dancers refused absolutely to take a cut, six agreed, and two were unable to decide. Hibbert resolved the situation by sacking the four and apportioning the salaries of the remaining eight.

Suzanne and Janine sat together watching the choreographer calling his orders and eight pairs of arms and legs moving in unison. Nearby the wardrobe mistress was sewing ruffles of old tarlatan and net cut from last season's costumes. She looked over to the girls and grumbled.

"There's not a yard of material to be bought anywhere in the city. When I've used the net this way for a few weeks, I shall have to remodel it and use it another way. Then it will tear in holes."

"And we'll have to play Gruyère cheeses."

Mme. Inez laughed at Janine's joke, and Suzanne rose to go backstage to reacquaint herself with the cramped dressing rooms she loved. Behind her Madame was explaining, "I've made the cache-sexes out of some red, white, and blue material I've been hoarding for months. That way, at least we can be patriotic."

Suzanne thought of Janine's lament about her lack of money. *When I came back to Paris I spent everything I had left on food. The rest I had lost to the farmer in Chevreuse when I was bored. It rained every day, and when he offered me a game I agreed. I really* must *stop playing poker, but I was sure he would take me instead of the money I owed. . . .* Suzanne smiled despite her apprehension. Somehow Janine always got by, owing money, fleeing creditors, involving herself with unsuitable men who drained her energy and, before disappearing, took most of what she had.

Suzanne turned on the lights surrounding the mirror in her dressing room. Tucked in the side of the makeup compartment she found a letter from David. It was dated ten months previously and she read it hungrily.

Darling Zizi,
I'm by a stream trying to catch a fish. He's a very fat wily fish because when he was young he took a hook and then

got away. The fish lives under a stone bridge built in
Roman times and occasionally he comes out to take a look
at me. Then he goes right back to the grid where he knows
he'll be safe. The guys here have been trying to catch him
for days, and we've each put one thousand francs on a bet
as to the outcome of the contest. The total sum goes to the
guy who catches the fish. If I win I'm going to buy you a
lace shawl I saw in a shop yesterday. Zizi, I reckon I'll have
to cheat. I'm sure that fish would prefer my hand to a steel
hook. I'll bend over the bank so he can't see me and run
my fingers over his stomach. Wish me luck!

Love, David

P.S. I caught the fish. He was like you, a bit giddy when
touched with passion. Dammit! What a fool I am. When I
looked at him he trembled so much I just had to throw
him back. Never mind, I love you and I'll buy you the lace
shawl just the same.

Suzanne sat at the dressing table, squeezing the note into a
ball. *He was like you, a bit giddy when touched with passion. . . .*
She shivered and threw the note into the refuse box, staring after
it with anguished eyes. What was the point of having a fiancé
if you never saw him, of surging with passion when you slept
alone? Suzanne walked to the door and then ran back to pick
up the crumpled letter, which she straightened meticulously on
the dressing table. Lovingly she kissed it and pushed it into her
purse before returning to her friends in the hall. As she passed
the band room and the costume cellar she sniffed the special
smell of the backstage area—greasepaint and glue, musty satin,
sweat and faded perfume. How good it was to be back where
she belonged.

During the lunch break M. Hibbert informed them that they
would all be required to visit the office of the Propagandastaffel
in the Champs-Elysées in order to obtain work permits. A loud
buzz of protest greeted his statement.

"We don't want to see those German marionettes!"

"If you don't apply you will not have permits, and without
permits you cannot work. But I am not forcing you, mes petites.
Do as you think fit."

The dancers unwound towels from their damp hair and disappeared to the dressing rooms to shower. Suzanne sang a song with the rehearsal pianist, and Janine thought of all she had heard about the business acumen of Leutnant Weber of the Propagandastaffel. Weber liked to make deals. First he had bought a truckload of wine, then a whole harvest of potatoes from a farmer near Lyon. He had sold both at a vast profit in Paris through collaborating intermediaries. Now Janine had heard that Weber was trying to buy city-center businesses, though his efforts had been thwarted by lawyers and civil servants who conveniently "lost" necessary deeds. It sounded as if Weber had money, and Janine had a desperate need of cash. She was three months' behind on her rent, and two months' pregnant by an artist in Pigalle. She decided to wear her best dress when she went to the office where work permits were issued. Perhaps Weber could suggest a way out of her dilemma, and perhaps there would be some way she could be of use to him.

Suzanne's face was soft as she sang a sad love song, and Janine smiled as she watched. She reflected that no one had ever made love to Suzanne, so it was ironic that she sang convincingly of passion. For a moment she envied her friend's innocence and the freshness of Suzanne's vision. Then she returned to mulling over the possibilities of the notorious Leutnant Weber. War made strange bedfellows, and there was nothing to be gained by being too particular. Patriotism was all very well, but it could not be eaten when hungry.

That night Suzanne and her mother were taken by Schulberg to the opening of a new bar cabaret. The situation between the occupying army and the people of Paris had deteriorated so seriously that fraternization was no longer openly seen. But the people of the rue Gabrielle and the area of Montmartre frequented by the Castels were used to Schulberg. They remembered the cheese and chocolate he often gave to hungry children, and the overcoat he had given André Marchand after his bout of pneumonia. So Suzanne and her mother were able to continue treating their lodger as a friend, knowing that no censure would come their way from their neighbors.

They sat at a marble-topped table in the crowded hall, laughing and joking and applauding a new comedian whose rubber features and deadpan humor struck a chord in every Parisian heart. Schulberg, despite enormous efforts at self-control, laughed loudest at jokes about his countrymen. He was unable to resist shedding tears of mirth at ridiculous impersonations of goose-stepping, head-shaven fanatics from the elite corps and steely-eyed eunuchs from the Gestapo interrogation squad. The curfew that night was eleven, so at ten thirty, after drinking a last glass of wine and eating a bowl of bean soup, they made their way back home. Schulberg was telling the two women an involved German joke and trying not to laugh before the tag line when they reached the corner of the rue des Trois-Frères and a shot rang out. With an anguished cry, he fell to the ground, and Nathalie dragged her daughter into a doorway. But Suzanne pulled away and ran back to the spot where Schulberg lay dying. In the place where his right eye had been there was a gaping black hole spouting blood like a fountain. Suzanne noticed that Schulberg seemed to be trying to reach into his pocket, so she bent forward and took out his wallet. For a brief moment his hand pushed against hers; then he breathed a long, shuddering sigh and was gone. Suzanne turned away and was sick. Then she crouched near the body as rain began to fall, watching as water mixed with blood trickled into the gutter. A moment ago they had all been laughing. Now her head felt like the inside of a volcano, and Herr Schulberg was dead. Shock made her shiver, and it was some moments before she could return to where her mother was sitting on her haunches, rocking slowly back and forth. Nathalie's eyes were dazed, though she spoke clearly of practicalities.

"They'll send another one to us after this, and God knows what he'll be like. I must change the sheets and make some bread, they love eating, these Germans. . . ."

Suzanne urged her mother down the street.

"The curfew begins in five minutes, maman. Try to hurry."

Suzanne took Schulberg's wallet and looked again at the wound. Then she ran home with her mother, settling Nathalie in a chair before going to visit M. Laval. She was reluctant to speak to the tax collector, but she could think of no one else to tell of the calamity.

Laval's mouth watered as Suzanne stepped inside. Then, noting the waxy color of Suzanne's skin and the unnaturally fast rise and fall of her chest, he poured her a brandy and asked what was wrong.

"Herr Schulberg has been shot. We were coming home from the new cabaret in—"

"There will be reprisals, mark my word."

"Monsieur Laval, Herr Schulberg is *dead!* Maman and I had to leave him in the street because we didn't know what to do."

"I shall inform the authorities, of course."

"Will another German come to stay with us?"

"That's for the billeting officer to decide, my dear."

Suzanne sipped her brandy, conscious that she felt suddenly too hot and too tightly clad. Her head ached, and a pulse began to pound in her ears as she struggled to retain control. But her efforts were in vain, and as she sucked in the chill air of Laval's living room, she felt the glass slip from her fingers.

Laval leaped up, wincing when Suzanne's head banged against his brass fire screen. He ran to where she lay unconscious on the floor, and loosened her collar and untied the tight sash around her waist. He went to the kitchen and got a glass of water, trying frantically to remember what should be done in such an emergency. Lifting Suzanne into his arms, he tried to make her drink, and all the while patted her cheeks, speaking sharply to ease his own fear.

"Mademoiselle, please rouse yourself! Can you hear me? Don't worry, you are not to worry, I shall take care of everything."

Suzanne's eyes stayed tightly shut, and, looking down, Laval saw that her body was exposed where he had unfastened the blouse. Placing her gently on the floor, he opened the buttons and touched the firm breasts, tracing his finger around the pink-tipped nipples that took his breath away. Then, trembling violently, he refastened the blouse and started to slap Suzanne's cheeks more urgently. At last she opened her eyes and sat up sharply, terrified that she had been unconscious in Laval's presence. He held out the glass of water, which she drank gratefully. Then he accompanied her home.

Nathalie stared at Suzanne's ashen face and the cut on the back of her head.

"What happened, Zizi?"

"I fainted. I'm sorry, maman."

"I looked after her, madame, you have nothing to fear."

Nathalie looked hard at Laval, who excused himself hastily, leaving them alone. Suzanne sat on the sofa, resting her head on a cushion and watching as her mother fussed about the room.

"It's cold, maman, and I'm hungry. I could eat a whole turkey or a full filet of beef. Shall we ever have enough to eat again?"

"Don't worry, we'll get by. We always have, and the occupation can't go on forever."

Late that night, when Suzanne was asleep, Nathalie went to the bedroom Schulberg had used and changed the sheets. She took a cardboard box from the cellar, collected all his belongings, and put them neatly inside. She searched the wallet for an address and found one on a letter from Frau Schulberg. Then, taking all but two thousand francs from the money fold, Madame placed the wallet in the box with the rest of her former lodger's belongings. At 2:00 A.M. she took the box downstairs and put it ready for collection by the door. She wrote a note to Frau Schulberg, enclosing the cash taken from the wallet, and then went to bed. If she left money with the belongings, it was likely that some quick-fingered German clerk would forget to send it where it belonged. Nathalie made a note to ask Suzanne how best the money should be mailed to Koblenz.

In the darkness she lay shivering and thinking of the blood that had congealed in an ugly mass around Schulberg's missing eye. Who could have killed him? Was it one of the locals who disapproved of his friendship with the Castels? Or was it a German who had seen Schulberg laughing so merrily at parodies of his own race? Nathalie thought how Schulberg had done his best for them, returning each day with a parcel of fat, a liter of oil, a side of lamb, or a new pan or shovel tucked under his coat. He had enjoyed a joke, a smoke, and a tale of times past, and she knew it would be impossible to find another stranger more suited to sharing their life. Nathalie shivered with apprehension, knowing that the next visitor to the house could be as vicious as Schulberg had been kind. She shook her head despairingly. In war nothing was certain. Friends became enemies and enemies friends, but who *had* killed Schulberg?

In the small hours her mind turned to thoughts of her husband, and she wondered where Jacques was and why he had not written. Then she thought of Suzanne and how happy she had been to be back at rehearsals for the new show. Nathalie smiled proudly as she remembered how pretty her daughter had looked in her curly wool coat, gas mask and rehearsal music hidden in David's canvas fishing satchel. Then she thought of their depleted food supply and how difficult it would be to replace items already used. Food shops had bare shelves, and all the luxury items in Paris had been purchased by Germans.

At four Nathalie fell fitfully asleep, waking at six as the clock chimed. Normally they were wakened by the insistent cockadoodling of the rooster belonging to M. Roger, but the day previously Roger had necked the bird to provide a supper for his eldest daughter's twenty-first birthday. Nathalie remembered grumbling about the noisy bird. Now she and Suzanne would long for the familiarity of its call. Nathalie looked at the calendar and realized with a shock that it would soon be Christmas. Schulberg had once arrived home with two boxes of "secret" stores, which he hid in the cellar to be used over the festive period. She decided to go and check what they contained as soon as she had had her breakfast.

That morning Suzanne and Janine went together to the offices of the Propagandastaffel. They walked uncertainly up the steps of the gray building in the Champs-Elysées, surprised to find themselves standing in line with unknown club artists and celebrated theater performers. Suzanne peered at those in front of her—a cancan dancer from the Moulin Rouge next to Edwige Feuilleure, who was about to open at the Colisée. Suzy Solidor from the Casino de Paris with two nudes from the Folies Bèrgeres. At the top of the line Jacques Pils from the Etoile stood waiting, and as Suzanne gazed at the faces of favorite stars, Maurice Chevalier emerged from the interview room. She was surprised to think that the Germans had made no distinction between chorus girls and established stars. They, who were so conscious of position, rank, and breeding, made everyone queue, great or small. Smothering a smile, Suzanne wondered if Marie-Claude had grown accus-

tomed to going without food or if Chambord's money continued
to buy plenty in the midst of emptiness. Had the mighty fallen,
or were they still living in the spotless mausoleum as if nothing
untoward had happened? In the months since her birthday
Suzanne had often met Carrie in the city center, away from the
house and the disapproving glances of Chambord and his daughter. They had enjoyed visits to city cafés and talked endlessly
of David over cups of bitter coffee. Once they had managed to
buy a sack of potatoes in the market of les Halles and carried
it all the way back to Montmartre. Nathalie and Carrie had also
become friends, and both looked forward to meeting. But still
Suzanne avoided visiting David's mother at home, and it seemed
to her that Carrie was relieved that Chambord and his daughter
were never mentioned. Suzanne's mind turned again to wondering about David. Was he well or ill, or even dead? How long
would it be before she heard one way or the other? She was no
longer certain that she would ever see him again.

When her turn came, Suzanne walked through to a dark office
lined with books on mahogany shelves. One small window provided the only light, making it difficult to see the antiquated
furniture with which the room was furnished. At the desk there
was a German officer with a beak-shaped nose and gin-pink
cheeks. Suzanne recognized him at once as Leutnant Weber.
Everyone talked about Leutnant Weber, though not all were
impressed by his conniving ways. Weber motioned curtly for her
to sit, and proceeded with his inquiry, writing down Suzanne's
answers on a form that had black-stamped sections for miscellane-
ous information.

"Name?"

"Suzanne Castel."

"Address?"

"La maison Fleuri, rue Gabrielle, Paris Eighteen."

"Occupation?"

"Singer."

"Place of work?"

"The Bal Tabarin."

"Father's name?"

"Jacques Hervé Castel."

"Mother's name?"

"Nathalie Hélène Castel."

"Paternal grandmother's name?"

"Marie-Gabrielle Savoie Castel."

"Maternal grandmother's name?"

"Eloise Lemercier."

Suzanne wondered what relevance her grandmothers' names had in obtaining a work permit. Then she shuddered. Perhaps this was part of the Aryan policy so important to the Germans. Perhaps Jews would not be permitted to perform. Recent legislation prevented Jews from holding public appointments, attending university, broadcasting on the radio, riding a bicycle, and even shopping except in permitted hours. A Jew could work only in the fields or the factory, and all had to wear a yellow cloth star stitched to their clothing. Suzanne looked at Weber's dark eyes, his short, curly gray hair and ugly protruding nose, and thought wryly that he looked very like the composite face that stared out from posters issued by the Allgemeinen SS describing Jewish features in detail so Parisians could "weed them out."

Weber frowned under her scrutiny. The girl was insolent and unmannerly. He had already decided to refuse her a permit. He looked back to the form and resumed his questions.

"Recently you were involved in the shooting of Gunther Schulberg, civilian adviser to the commander of the Devisenschutzkommandos."

"No, I was not!" Suzanne looked defiantly over the desk.

"I have here a report—"

"My mother and I were returning home with Herr Schulberg when he was shot. We were *not* involved in his death, and you have no right to imply that we were."

As Suzanne spoke, the door opened and a young officer entered. He stood in the corner listening to the interchange, and Suzanne noticed that Weber seemed suddenly ill at ease. Peering through the dim light, she saw a tall blond man of slim build whose twinkling blue eyes seemed to follow her every move. As Weber continued to take notes, Suzanne looked more closely at the officer in the corner of the room, puzzled by her own reactions as he moved closer. She felt curiously breathless, conscious of her shabby shoes, her unkempt hair, and the blush she could feel spreading over her cheeks as their eyes met for a brief moment.

When he put down his pen, Weber addressed her like a headmaster speaking to a naughty child.

"You will not argue with me, Mademoiselle Castel. You were ordered here to answer questions without attempting to be evasive."

For a moment Suzanne was silent. Then she roared at Weber like a virago.

"And you will take care of your language, Leutnant Weber. To say that I was *involved* in the shooting of Herr Schulberg is to imply that I conspired with those who killed him. You should have said, 'You and your mother were there when Herr Schulberg was killed,' in which case I should have had no need to argue. If you cannot make yourself understood in our language you should not chastise me for misunderstanding the clumsiness of your words."

Trembling with annoyance, Suzanne forgot about the young man in the corner. Weber was going to turn down her application, so what was the point of being polite!

The telephone rang, startling her, and she was amused to see Weber leaping to attention, raising his arm, and shouting, "Heil Hitler!" What a robot he was, what a fatuous puppet! Derision puckered her brow, and she was tempted to laugh out loud. After putting down the phone, Weber motioned to the young officer in the corner.

"Assist me please, von Heinkel. I must leave at once for headquarters. This artist wishes a work permit. Here are her notes. Assign someone to complete the information, will you?"

Suzanne looked into a suntanned face and direct eyes. When the young officer smiled she felt elated and instantly at ease. They did not speak until Weber had left the room. Then the officer sat behind Weber's desk and offered Suzanne a cigarette from an old-fashioned gold-and-ebony case. She looked at his strong hands, at the softness and thickness of his blond hair, which was combed back and cut in a less exaggerated crop than other German soldiers wore. The officer had an elegance of manner that impressed her, and Suzanne felt a great curiosity about him. When he spoke his voice was deep and resonant, his French flawless and as stylish as the rest of his appearance. Suzanne stared unashamedly, forgetting to answer when he told her his name.

"I am Hans von Heinkel, military adviser to the director of the Propagandastaffel."

Suzanne thought how strong he looked and how handsome. Then she weighed his words and wondered why he was not at the front with the Wehrmacht or on the seas with the blue-clad members of the Kriegsmarine. Hans von Heinkel's bearing was ramrod straight, and she felt sure he was a soldier, not one of the clerks whose only purpose was to destroy French morale. He had said he was a military adviser. Was it necessary for propaganda writers to have advice before writing radio broadcasts full of lies? Probably it was. Suzanne tried hard to dislike the officer, but his eyes sent shivers down her spine as they twinkled with conspiratorial humor. Suzanne thought how devastating his presence was, how impressive and fascinating. Hans van Heinkel was worth ten of almost every other man she had ever met. She stifled the urge to reach out and touch him, the longing to be held close to his chest.

Hans watched her closely, wondering why Suzanne did not answer, why her eyes were so full of longing. He smiled at the violet-sprigged dress, touched by the filigree butterflies in her hair. He was drawn again to the enigmatic gaze in the wide golden eyes. The girl's face was fine, with pointed patrician features and skin like peach down, velvety and soft. Tendril curls at her temples made her look like a cocotte, and yet there was an innocence in her manner that made him feel protective and warm.

Suzanne roused herself from his gaze with a start.

"I was daydreaming, you must excuse me."

"I was telling you that I am Hans von Heinkel, military adviser to the director of the Propagandastaffel. Usually I work upstairs assessing reports from the front."

"But today you'll stay and give me a work permit?"

"Why not? Reading reports is a very boring occupation."

"Where do you come from?"

"My father's estate is on Konstanz, near Lindau. Do you know anything about Germany?"

Suzanne shook her head and watched the long fingers gripping the pen, the grave, handsome face hesitating over the form. What kind of a place was Lindau? Was it town or country elegant or bourgeois? As though reading her thoughts, Hans spoke.

"Paris has been something of a shock to me because it is not at all like the mountains and castles of Swabing and Bavaria. When first I arrived from Baden-Baden I was lost every day in your city."

"Do you live in a castle?"

"Only a very small one."

Hans looked again at the form, noting the black cross in the corner that signified that the applicaion was to be turned down. After a moment's deliberation he took another form from the drawer, wrote in her name and details, and then asked a few questions to complete the required information. Weber's marked form was torn to pieces and safely deposited in his jacket pocket.

"What is the date of the opening of your show, Mademoiselle Castel?"

"December twenty-eighth."

"And the name of the show?"

"It's called *Monocle* and it will be at the Bal Tabarin."

"So I see. Are the bookings satisfactory?"

"Monsieur Hibbert seems satisfied."

Hans stamped the form, signed his name over the stamp, and handed Suzanne a card on which he had filled in her name, address, and age.

"Have you brought photographs?"

Suzanne handed him six small photographs, watching as Hans stuck two on her permit. Then he stamped the photographs and signed them, leaning over the desk and handing the new permit to her.

"Here is your work permit, see you don't lose it."

"I'm very grateful."

"Please come to see me should you need any further assistance. My office is room number eight, upstairs at the end of the corridor."

At the door Suzanne paused, turning to face Hans, who was standing close behind.

"Thank you again. I'm lucky I didn't have to suffer Leutnant Weber any longer."

Hans looked down at the uplifted face and the small, slim hand streched out toward him. There was a moment of breathless stillness, and Suzanne imagined she could hear two hearts beating. Then Hans kissed her hand, clicked his heels, and, returning to the desk, pressed a buzzer to summon a clerk to take over.

Suzanne walked dazedly down the stairs and out into the Champs-Elysées. French policemen were strolling in pairs up the boulevard, their capes blowing in the wind, their tin helmets shining in watery winter sun. She longed fiercely for a café crème and a wedge of chocolate cake, but nearby cafés were offering only ersatz beer and acorn coffee that made the drinker thirsty for hours. Suzanne turned into the rue du Colisée, staring apprehensively at whores in black leather jackets and black spiky boots. They were sitting at window tables in every café, applying scarlet lipstick to icing-white skin and swiveling predatory eyes at German officers alighting from low black cars. The officers, come to inspect the afternoon's talent, looked merry and free from care, their fleshy faces intent and flushed with anticipation. The girls looked well fed, unlike her friends and neighbors in Montmartre. She shrugged. To do what they were required to do made them eligible, in Suzanne's view, for all the food they could consume. She wondered if they felt the same way about all their clients. And did they ever fall in love? She hurried on, wondering if the hard-eyed ladies of the rue du Colisée wore black leather and spiked-heel boots with American Sammies and British Tommies or if, like actresses, they assumed new personalities depending on available trade.

In the street where the offices of the Ministry of the Interior were situated Suzanne saw German clerks with steel spectacles and thin document cases hurrying back after the first sitting of lunch. An old woman approached, muttering unintelligibly about murder and loss of grace, and Suzanne noticed that she was eating putty newly pressed into windows along the way. Near the Théâtre des Mathurins there were queues for seats, and outside the butchers' shops queues for sausages. Sausages hanging from steel hooks in the butchers' windows were a strange color, dirty gray with purple flecks of offal or lights. Suzanne thought wryly that they would soon be eating rats, like Parisians in the Commune, and even each other if the shortages continued. She paused at a bookstall, disappointed to find that even in the city center only old newspapers and dog-eared, secondhand books for exchange were available. In prewar days she and her mother had read two or three books a week and spent all their spare money on sheet music and popular novels. Now even cash would not secure a new book, and the only truthful newspapers were Swiss and Spanish pamphlets smuggled in on pain of death from the free zone.

As Suzanne passed Au Printemps, a young girl in a black beret rushed out of a side street toward her. The girl's face was deathly pale, and she was clutching a brown paper parcel. Drawing level with Suzanne, the girl thrust the parcel into her hands and whispered urgently, "Take this to number six rue des Rosiers, do you understand?" Then she ran on, her face a mask of fear. Suzanne threw the parcel into her canvas bag and continued on her way, her heart pounding like a gong. A black car screeched around the corner, grinding to a halt nearby, and leather-coated men dashed out, grabbing the girl and hurling her into the back of the car before driving away at high speed. A church clock chimed three, and Suzanne thought Paris had never been so gloomy. It was inconceivable that the city of lovers had become the city of threat and violence. It began to rain, and a swirling mist made the buildings seem mysterious and obscure.

Suzanne paused on the steps of an empty house to rest and calm her nerves. As she looked out on the empty street, she was thinking of the well-fed faces of the Gestapo officers she had just seen and the dark hats that masked the look in their soulless eyes. She tried to obliterate the gaze of mute appeal from the girl whose name she did not know, but fear was contagious, and agony, too.

The rue des Rosiers was in the Marais. Since the thirteenth century Jews had lived on the rue des Rosiers, earning their living as moneylenders, antique dealers, and shopkeepers. The Jewish area was a place to be avoided, a place where sinister disappearances were a daily occurrence.

The sky turned prematurely dark, and Suzanne wondered if there was going to be a storm. First she made excuses for not going near the Marais; then she cursed her lack of courage and thought that if only she could find a taxi it would be easy to deliver the package. To walk to the Marais would take an hour. Suzanne shrugged resignedly, knowing that taxis had almost gone from the city streets. The girl had trusted her; she *must* deliver the parcel as she had been asked.

Thankful for the semidarkness, Suzanne turned into the avenue de l'Opéra and along the rue de Rivoli. German tourists were being hustled out of the gardens of the Tuileries, and more were roistering noisily along as she reached the Hôtel de Ville. Suzanne hurried past without looking at the overweight bodies and flushed faces full of pleasure at being in Paris. She had been to the Marais only once and was unsure which street led to the address she had been given. Every step nearer the Jewish quarter frightened her, every car passing seemed to threaten, but she walked resolutely on and at last neared the corner of the rue des Rosiers. Crossing the road, she saw headlights and heard the screech of sirens. A squad of black cars crunched to a halt outside one of the houses, and Suzanne leaped into a doorway, cursing the sentimental stupidity that had brought her to the most dangerous district in the city. She watched, peering through yellow foggy light as men, women, and children from three houses nearby were forced into the waiting cars. When they had gone the street was as silent as a tomb. Nothing stirred, and Suzanne thought it easy to imagine that the houses were occupied only by corpses. She remained rooted to the spot, her eyes searching surrounding porches and alleyways for signs of continuing surveillance. Was anyone left in house number six? Would it not be best to go home, abandoning the parcel in the doorway of the house in which she was hiding?

It seemed like hours before Suzanne was able to make a decision. Then, slowly, cautiously, she made her way down the street to the door of house number six and rang the bell. The bell clanged loudly, shattering the silence all around, but no one answered her call, no face appeared at the window, and when Suzanne felt for a letter box, there was none. Finally she decided to go home, but as she turned to leave she felt herself grasped from behind. Sweat broke out all over her body as iron arms kept her from moving.

"What are you doing here, mademoiselle?"

Suzanne almost laughed with relief. Surely that was the voice of Armand Lognon? Wrenching herself free, she turned to face him.

"Armand! Thank goodness it's you. I thought the Gestapo had come back."

He smiled an enigmatic smile and kissed her cheeks, and Suzanne noticed that he had changed greatly since their last meeting. When Armand struck a match to light his cigar, she examined him carefully. The suit was expensive wool, the overcoat camel's hair. Armand's hair was plastered with pomade and wedged under a fine felt hat. Suzanne thought admiringly that he had certainly come up in the world.

Armand led her to the back room of a nearby house and, looking around, she saw an elaborately furnished sitting room full of red Venetian glass and dark green velvet sofas. On the table there were grapes of pistachio porcelain and death masks in yellowed plaster of Zola and Proust.

"Is this your home, Armand?"

"One of them. I have others."

"You became rich, just as you said you would."

"I have a talent for arranging things, like my father."

Suzanne stared in disbelief at the yellow badge on Armand's lapel. Instead of the obligatory word JUIF, Armand's sported a mocking BRETON. His effrontery made her want to weep and cheer at the same time.

Armand poured two brandies and took the parcel from Suzanne. For a moment he looked sadly at the brown paper wrapping. Then he put it unopened on the chiffonier. Overcome with curiosity, Suzanne questioned him.

"What's in the parcel?"

Armand hesitated as though uncertain whether to trust her.

"Sticks of dynamite."

Suzanne felt herself turn pale. What if she had slipped, or warmed the dynamite by resting the parcel against her chest? What if she had been stopped by a passing German patrol and asked to open the box? She explained in a shaky voice what had happened.

"I got the parcel from a girl who was being chased by the Gestapo. She managed to give it to me before she was caught."

Armand sighed, and Suzanne thought him the oldest fourteen-year-old she had ever seen.

"What's going on, Armand? Can't you tell me what you're doing?"

"It's best you don't know. Some things are better not discussed."

They lapsed into silence. Then Armand began to speak, and Suzanne saw that his eyes were full of tears.

"The girl who gave you the package was my cousin, Rebecca. I stayed with her and her parents when I first arrived in Paris, and we met again by accident a few months ago. She agreed to work with me and knew all the risks involved. The trouble is you never think it will happen to you. I suppose it's the only way to stay sane. Rebecca was sure they wouldn't suspect her because she worked inside Gestapo headquarters as a secretary and had already been cleared as a subversive."

Suzanne looked at her hands, furious that they were shaking like leaves in an autumn breeze.

Armand continued sadly. "I'll take you home, Suzanne. You shouldn't have come to the Jewish quarter, you know."

"You don't have to take me home."

"I will, though, and someday I shall find a way to repay what you've done for me today."

For a moment they sat in silence, reviewing the events of the afternoon. Then Suzanne began to question the wisdom of Armand's choice of hiding place.

"Why are you in the Jewish quarter? Wouldn't it be better to have rooms elsewhere, in the suburbs perhaps?"

"I'm Jewish, so it's my right to be here."

Suzanne looked at the yellow star on his lapel, and Armand explained.

"I don't exist officially in Paris, so the Germans don't know I'm Jewish. I wear this star so they'll think I'm a Breton radical."

"But you live here?"

"No, I only keep this room because the house has been unoccupied for years and the Germans have already checked it."

"And your other rooms, where are they?"

"I keep moving, Suzanne. It's the only way to stay alive."

Armand locked the door as they left the house and walked with Suzanne back to the rue de Rivoli. They chatted happily up the endless length of the rue du Faubourg Montmartre, taking note of the small scenes that were so typical of Paris and so warming to the heart. In the courtyard of Chartier, waiters in black horseshoe waistcoats and white-sheet aprons were throwing dice and calling excitedly. Inside the Paname Bar a fat woman was sitting on a thin stool and regaling the barman with reminiscences of her early life as an artists' model in Montparnasse. And at the corner of the rue de La Fayette a German officer had been run over by a motorcyclist. No one helped him except a girl of seven who was calling shrilly for her mother.

As they walked Armand told Suzanne how he smuggled food, gas, tires, and vegetables into the city and Jews out of Paris to wherever he could contrive. Shocked by the admission, Suzanne wondered how he managed to stay alive.

"I don't know how you sleep at night, Armand."

"Usually I don't, but then I never needed much sleep."

"Will the Germans soon leave Paris?"

"I think they'll stay for years, and so shall I. I intend to stay until all of them are gone, and then to get married and have ten children. I love Paris, it's my city now. I can't go back to Lille, and someday I'll fight for my home, if I'm still alive."

"Take care. Even when you're asleep, take care!"

They laughed and then adjourned for a drink in the bar of Chez Moune. Armand stared at the lesbian bartender, clucking his tongue and shaking his head because she was beautiful and he thought her inclinations a great waste.

They parted in the rue des Abbesses, and Suzanne made her way up the steps, looking back on the city and remembering how splendid it had looked in peacetime. Before the occupation the twinkling lights of Paris had made a fairy-tale backdrop for the ancient lamps and pink rooftops of Montmartre. Now there was only darkness. Two lovers were kissing under a blue-masked lamp. Suzanne hurried on toward the heights of Montmartre. As she walked she thought of Armand and all she had learned from him about the "zouzous," of whom he was an honored member. Armand's words echoed in her mind. *We keep our hair long to show our derision for the frisés. We play American jazz because they hate it and we are free while they are regimented like tin soldiers. . . .* Suddenly Suzanne stopped and stood looking askance at her own reflection in a shop window, shocked to remember that she had forgotten all about Janine. After the interview in the offices of the Propagandastaffel she had walked out of the building and through the streets of the eighth district like a sleepwalker. Suzanne shook her head in amazement. Why had she, usually such a well-ordered person, done such an absentminded thing? Then she smiled, because she knew she had been thinking of Hans von Heinkel. She took out the new work permit and tried to see his signature, but it was dark and she was afraid the rain would make the ink run. She went on, conscious that something strange had happened during her meeting with him, something prophetic and disturbing, to be analyzed at leisure.

Nathalie was at the gate, looking for her daughter and anxiously pacing the garden. When Suzanne approached, her mother rushed up the street to greet her.

"Zizi! Where on earth have you been? You're soaked to the skin. Janine called to find out what happened, and she's been sitting here with me all through the afternoon until half an hour ago. Are you aware of the time? It's almost six. You really mustn't do this again."

"I'm sorry, maman, I wandered into the Marais and got lost."

Suzanne went inside, relieved when her mother hurried to make dinner. She had decided to tell Nathalie nothing of her meeting with Armand Lognon.

"Any news from the billeting officer, maman?"

"A new soldier is arriving tomorrow."

"I thought we might have escaped for a while."

"Did you get your work permit?"

"Of course."

"There's no 'of course' about it. Janine didn't get hers. She has to go back to see Leutnant Weber in the morning, something about quotas, she said. She thinks it will be all right."

Suzanne blinked in puzzlement, grateful that she had so easily acquired her own permit. As she ate a bowl of leek and potato soup and the last piece of ham from their store, she longed for creamy syllabub or an omelette surprise, and her mouth watered as she thought of the hot chocolate she and her mother had enjoyed late at night. There was no chocolate powder left, and only one more sack of coffee beans. Soon they would have to grind acorns or drink only herb tisanes. Everyone in Paris was longing for cream, for rich pungent sauces and fruit soaked in brandy. Suzanne pushed radishes to the edge of her plate, vowing never to eat them again once the bad days were over.

After dinner, Nathalie took out her sewing box and began to darn the heels of some lisle stockings.

"I tried to buy new stockings today, Zizi, but I couldn't find any."

"I'll contact Armand and he'll tell us where to buy them."

"He has a room in the rue Pigalle. I often see him going out all dressed up like a gangster. Goodness knows what the lad is doing these days."

Still Suzanne mentioned nothing of her meeting with Armand. He had said it was best to tell no one about such matters, and she believed he was right.

Nathalie turned on the radio, snapping it off again as sounds

of a German yodeler filled the room. Then she put down her
sewing and told Suzanne the latest news from the authorities.

"This afternoon, while Janine was here, they made an an-
nouncement on the radio saying there'll be no more chocolate
for sale."

Suzanne listened, wondering what was going to disappear next
from the shops when already there was almost nothing. Nathalie
continued imperturbably.

"They announced that pâtisseries must stay shut three days a
week from the New Year, isn't that ridiculous! If I had yeast I
should bake my own. And from the first of February there'll
be wine sales only on certain days of the week. What else? Oh,
yes, fancy bread and rolls have been banned as of today."

Suzanne's mind rebelled against the German love of ordinances. Since the beginning of the occupation it seemed as if they
had become less French and more German, at least in their way
of life. The more orders appeared, the more Suzanne longed to
preserve the very Frenchness the enemy sought to eradicate. Before
the war she had not valued her nationality; indeed, she had never
thought to assert it. Now she and all her friends were absolutely
femmes françaises, and endless German commands only succeeded in provoking the traditional French reaction, that rules
were made to be ignored at every opportunity. Suzanne smiled
with pride at the courage of the résistants, and her mind dwelled
for a moment on David. Then she turned to the window and adjusted the tape her mother had stuck around the frame to keep
out the icy winds of winter.

"I think I'll go to bed, maman."

"I put blankets top and bottom for you, they're warmer than
the sheets. It's the best I can do, Zizi. The hot-water bottles are
full of holes, and we haven't any wood or coal left in the cellar.
From now on we shall have to learn to keep moving."

They kissed and said good night, closing their bedroom doors
and locking them with new steel bolts that had cost a great deal
of money. Nathalie had felt it necessary to purchase the bolts when
she realized that another German was about to be sent to live
with them.

Suzanne looked briefly at her picture of David. Then she put
it away in one of her drawers, between sachets of lavender and her

only silk petticoat. There was no point in longing for the moon. It was more than likely that David was dead. She had heard nothing from him for months. In the bitter chill she turned out the light, her body aching for food, warmth, and the excitement of his touch. After a while she remembered Hans von Heinkel, and leaped up to look at the work permit he had issued. As she read the signature, *Hans von Heinkel,* clear and bold with a curl over the V like a heart, she smiled and her heart began to thunder. She touched the card gently with her finger and turned out the light again. Would she ever see the German again? She thought not. There was no reason to go to the Propagandastaffel. There was nothing to be gained by seeking him out, however attractive he was.

For a few minutes Suzanne listened uneasily to the sound of planes droning overhead, and prayed they would not bomb Montmartre. Unable to settle down, she reran her conversation with Hans. He had said "my father's estate" without a trace of vanity, even with a nuance of mockery. There was an air of wealth and breeding about him that had impressed and pleased her, and his confidence had been that of a man used to command. So why was he working in the office? Suzanne thought of the blue eyes that had smiled, the hands still nut-brown from summer sun, the presence that had touched and awed her, the scent of his body that had made her think thoughts she knew she should not be thinking. How easy it had been to talk with him. It was as if Hans were a Frenchman, not her enemy; as if the meeting had been meant to be.

As the wind brought sleet, Suzanne fell asleep, impatient for the morning, when she was due to begin rehearsals for the new show. During the night she dreamed of walking through a summer cornfield with Hans and eating strawberries and cream from dishes piled high with fruit.

In a small, uncomfortable room on the floor above a bakery in the rue Mercier, Hans lay staring at the ceiling. He was digesting the information contained in a dossier he had copied on Suzanne Castel, nightclub chanteuse and daughter of a well-known theatrical family. He was also debating whether to defy the curfew and walk up to Montmartre to look at la maison Fleur. Then he shook his head. Suzanne was French and, although charming and very beautiful, was not to be considered as a personal friend. Fraternization was to be kept to a polite formality. That was the rule, and Hans thought it a fair one. Discipline was important during occupation because familiarity between the two sides blurred the lines of necessary demarcation. Before long the two melded into unity and the master could no longer control the servant. Suzanne's defiance of the despicable Leutnant Weber came back into his mind, and he smiled. The heart-shaped face had paled, the pointed chin had jutted obstinately like a prizefighter's. The thin hands had fluttered, clasping and unclasping as though gaining courage from contact. Hans thought of Suzanne's figure and the roundness of her breasts. Then he snapped off the light and tried to sleep. How did she sing? he pondered. Did she have that deep, scratchy vibrato so typical of the French race? Would it be wrong to go to the opening of her show? He need not stay to speak with her after the finale.

As dawn etched the night sky with the fleecy pink curlicues of approaching day, Hans put on his uniform and walked to the rue Royatier. He was climbing the steps when, over the garden wall of the Castel house, he saw Suzanne scolding a kitten trapped up a tree. She was calling to the cat in comic exasperation.

"Idiot! Why do you always put yourself in a place from which you cannot escape? You know it's dangerous, you've done it before. You *must* learn to stay in the garden where you're safe."

Hans turned and walked quickly back down the steps. *Why do you always put yourself in a place from which you cannot escape? You know it's dangerous. . . . You must learn to stay where you're safe. . . .* He paused in a café for coffee and aquavit, conscious of the disapproving silence that greeted his arrival. Making an effort to consider his position, he thought of the glow in Suzanne's cheeks, the smile in her voice, and forgot all the rules and regulations of what he *should* do. He took a taxi to the office, thinking as he passed through silent streets of Suzanne in her rose-flowered nightdress with Wellington boots on her feet and scarlet ribbons in her hair. She is French and therefore verboten. He repeated this many times in the turmoil of his mind. She is French and therefore verboten. But Suzanne's face kept flickering before his eyes like a siren, ever beckoning, and on arrival at the office Hans sent his orderly out to buy tickets for the opening night of the Bal Tabarin show. He felt as if he had fallen in love, hot, sick, and deliriously happy. The obsession and constant thinking of Suzanne was just how his father had described passion. But surely that could not be? He barely knew the girl, and the Heinkel men were traditionally slow to develop passion.

Hans took out his copy of Suzanne's work permit, the copy he had appropriated for his own file, and smiled at the direct, almost mocking gaze of her amber eyes. He tried not to think of the softness of her body and the veiled mystery that showed in her expression, mesmerizing him. Her face had an old-fashioned look, like that of a girl in a Renoir painting. Yet Suzanne had strength and a forceful determination that made it possible for him to believe her capable of anything.

At lunchtime Hans found his appetite gone, his mind lost in clouds of titillating imagining. During the afternoon he buckled down to work, determined to be master of himself. But it was impossible, and he found himself reading the same report a dozen times, still ignorant of the meaning. At five he went home, telling himself he was a major in the Wehrmacht, decorated three times for bravery. He had a damaged spine where he had been blown up by a land mine, and he had learned to walk again despite impossible odds. He had always been renowned for his iron will and ability to control the most difficult situation. Was it possible he was now unable to control the longing of his own mind? Hans shook his head defiantly. It was inconceivable that he could be in love with Suzanne Castel. It was not possible they had anything in common. Suzanne was French, he was German, and their two countries were at war. In every thought they would oppose each other. Every tradition by which they had been reared would cause clashes of will and temperament. He could give no loyalty to an enemy, because his life had been given without condition to the Fatherland. So what was the point of punishing himself by longing for a dream?

In the lonely room that was his temporary home, Hans marked off another day on the calendar. One more week and the show at the Bal Tabarin would open. He would send Suzanne flowers, without a card of course, so she would not know about his interest in her. Hans sighed and opened a tin of smoked pork, wishing he were one of the lucky officers who had been billeted with French women who knew how to cook. The thought gave him a brilliant idea, and he spent a restless night waiting to see the billeting lists for the eighteenth district. Was it possible he could bring off such a coup? Hans ate a hearty breakfast, delighted to be able to do something constructive about his perverse desire for closeness to Suzanne Castel.

Hans was unaware that a new man had just arrived in the Castel house, a soldier different in every way from his friendly predecessor, Herr Schulberg. Private Altdorfer was a short, arrogant young man given to thieving and not averse to violence with those older or weaker than himself. He slung his bag on the bed, plumped the springs, and called for coffee to be brought. When Nathalie appeared with a tray, he spoke in a loud voice as though on the parade ground.

"I shall be happy in this house. It's a fine room, though the bed is smaller than I normally require."

Altdorfer openly reviewed Nathalie's body. She was lonely, of that he felt sure—married women were always pining, always thinking of absent husbands and longing for excitement. He poured coffee and put five spoons of precious sugar in the cup. Nathalie winced and went to the door, uneasy at being alone with their new guest while Suzanne was out at rehearsal. Altdorfer called for her to stay. Nathalie looked around, frowning at the puce face and hands, the corpulent body that seemed as broad as it was long.

"Where's your daughter?"

"Suzanne has gone to rehearsal at the Bal Tabarin."

"Does she dance in the nude?"

"No, monsieur, she sings French songs."

Nathalie began to tremble as Altdorfer unbuttoned his jacket. Then he drained his cup and produced a bottle of rum.

"Sit down, don't be scared. I'm a man, not a three-headed monster."

Nathalie sat gingerly down on the edge of the chair, refusing the private's offer of a swig from the rum bottle.

"How old's your daughter?"

"Nineteen, monsieur. Suzanne will be twenty in June."

"Is she engaged?"

"Yes, monsieur, she is."

Altdorfer watched Nathalie closely, pleased by the nervous twitching of her limbs. She was not bad-looking for her age, and her eyes were a beautiful blue. He continued to question her.

"Where's the fiancé then?"

"We don't know, monsieur, he was injured and—"

"When did she last see him?"

"Almost one year ago."

"And you, when did you last see your husband?"

"Monsieur Castel was here in July."

"That's a long time to be without a man."

Nathalie was shocked. She had thought Altdorfer interested only in Suzanne. Now he was grinning slyly, and she turned faint at his implication. Nathalie hurried to the door, appalled to feel the private's breath close behind her. Altdorfer put his hands on her shoulders and swung her around, pushing her back till she was squashed against his stomach and the door. Then clutching her buttocks, he kissed her full on the mouth. Nathalie slapped his face resoundingly. Altdorfer slapped her back, cutting her lip so blood spurted down her blouse. Excited by his strength, he tore the blouse from her shoulders, exposing the slip, which he pulled down with savage impatience.

"Get your clothes off!"

"I'll do no such thing!"

Nathalie ran for the door. Altdorfer locked it and pocketed the key. Then he lifted her in his arms and threw her down on the bed. Nathalie watched helplessly as he tore off her skirt and stockings. She looked up at the skylight window, cursing that there was no escape from the room and nothing with which she could stun the German. Panting like a rabid dog and making lewd jokes at her expense, Altdorfer took off his clothes, pushing Nathalie to the wall side of the bed and grabbing her in his arms.

"I won't hurt you if you behave, and I won't need to touch your daughter if you're good to me. I'm a man who likes women, madame, and either you or your precious Suzanne will have to take care of me."

As he clawed at her body, Nathalie began to cry. Then she felt so angry that she fought desperately to prevent his taking her.

Altdorfer laughed gleefully, delighted that the woman had so much spirit. He pulled her hair from its bun, running his fingers through the silvery length and then holding her down by wrapping the hair around his wrists. Nathalie cried out, but it was futile to struggle, and soon Altdorfer's triumphant laughter echoed in the silent house.

At three Suzanne arrived home and found Altdorfer eating a piece of cake in the kitchen. When Nathalie appeared, Suzanne saw with horror that her mother's arms were covered with bruises, her lip was cut, her neck discolored with bites and thumb marks. Rushing to her mother's side, she cradled Nathalie's head against her chest. Altdorfer lay on the sofa, flicking crumbs from his chest and belching.

"Make some coffee and stop looking sour. I can't stand surly women."

Suzanne marched grimly to the kitchen and filled the kettle. Nathalie retired to her bedroom without a word. Altdorfer looked through to where Suzanne was grinding coffee, and admired her legs. Then, sauntering to her side, he leaned against the door, watching her every move.

"Your mother and I have an arrangement."

Suzanne did not reply. She was debating whether to scald Altdorfer with boiling water or cut off his mauling hands with the carving knife. Annoyed by her silence, he pulled her toward him, pinning Suzanne against the kitchen wall.

"While your mother behaves you can sleep in peace, but the day she says no to me I come to *your* room."

Suzanne remained impassive, and Altdorfer let her go, watching as she put the coffeepot on the tray with two cups and oatmeal biscuits. Her silence so provoked the German that he lunged at her, tearing her blouse as Suzanne leaned forward to lift the tray. Suzanne snarled like a tiger and flicked his face with the carving knife, opening a jagged cut from cheek to chin. Altdorfer screamed in shock and agony, clasping his head and rushing to the hall as the doorbell rang.

When Suzanne answered the door, still holding the carving knife, she was shocked to see Hans von Heinkel on the doorstep with the billeting officer previously seen with M. Laval. Hans paled when he saw the knife, the torn blouse, and Altdorfer howling like a stuck pig in the hall. Nathalie appeared, her face blotchy with tears, her injuries making the situation all too clear. Hans hauled Altdorfer upstairs, handing him a towel to staunch the blood, and packed the private's belongings into his bag, which he handed to the billeting officer. His mind was erupting with fury, and he wondered desperately if he could keep himself from killing the ignorant guttersnipe. As a major, Hans's accommodation had precedence over a mere private's, even if he had arrived much later in the city. So why had Altdorfer been sent to plague a house of unprotected women? Hans thought furiously that money had changed hands; someone had taken a bribe to put the lecherous private where he wanted to be.

Nathalie retired to her room, leaving Suzanne alone and afraid. As she sat on the edge of the sofa, Suzanne wondered what was going to happen to her. It was an offense to attack a German soldier, just as it had recently become an offense to fail to salute one in the street. Both offenses were punishable by firing squad. Suzanne looked up and saw Hans holding out a bunch of Christmas roses.

"I beg you to forgive the disgraceful behavior of Unteroffizier Altdorfer. What can I do to make you feel better? I bought you the roses in the place du Tertre. The old woman who sold them to me has probably bought a large house with what she charged!"

Suzanne smiled, and for a moment they stood awkwardly facing each other. Then she took the flowers and stepped shyly forward into Hans's arms. He stood stiffly, unable to free his mind from self-imposed restriction. Suzanne began to sob like a child.

"Altdorfer hurt Maman while I was at rehearsal and then he tried to . . ."

Hans put his arms around her and closed his eyes, overwhelmed with pity and love. Suzanne's hair smelled of flowers, and her body was soft against his. After a while he spoke, calming her terror and making her feel that there was someone to look after her, someone who really cared whether she lived or died.

"I am hoping I can be the newly billeted officer in this house. One thing is certain, and that is that Altdorfer will not return. Please don't cry, Mademoiselle Castel. I promise I shall be a very good companion, even if I am German. Tomorrow I shall bring chocolate for you and your mother, and it will be best if I arrange for my own doctor to come and examine Madame. One must be sure everything is in order, you understand. Please try to be calm. Is that chicken stew I smell on the stove? I haven't eaten any real home cooking for so very long."

Suzanne smiled up at him. He was hungry and she must look after him. Laughing and crying at the same time, she showed Hans to the room he hoped to occupy. Then she went to the kitchen and made dinner. As she stirred a wooden spoon around the old iron pan, she said a prayer that Hans's stay would be confirmed and that her mother would soon manage to assimilate the agonies of the day.

Hans reappeared looking happy and relaxed. He stood at her side in the kitchen, making a salad from freshly picked winter cabbage, walnuts, and savory from the herb border. As he poured vinegar and oil on the grated leaves he hummed an old French song, and Suzanne had to control the urge to bury herself in the strength of his tall, slim body. Outside it began to snow. Suzanne looked sadly through the window at white flakes settling on the garden. Hans followed her gaze, conscious that the house was very cold, with frost patterns like silver lace on the inside of all the windows. He thought of the black marketeers who sold wood and coal at thirty times the normal price, and the men who stole furniture to be cut into pieces for burning. He resolved to buy whatever he could and bring it back to the house to ease the women's suffering.

"Don't worry, Mademoiselle Castel, I shall find coal or at least something to burn, and I will bring it home tomorrow."

Suzanne smiled happily. How good it was to feel safe, how pleasant to be with Hans.

Nathalie came to join them for dinner, watching as Suzanne and Hans carried in the tureen of stew. She thought how handsome the German was, how fine and honest. Then she looked at her daughter and frowned at Suzanne's radiant, flushed face. It was months since Zizi had looked so happy. Nathalie ate only a small salad with a glass of wine and a wedge of bread. As she ate she stole glances at Suzanne, trying not to think of the complications that could arise from the presence in her house of Hans von Heinkel. Suzanne chatted happily, and Hans savored his chicken stew, teasing her now and then about the size of her appetite.

The fire glowed, and the streets of Montmartre turned white as Christmas came.

Alone in his house, Laval was fuming at the audacity of the German who had arranged his own billet in the Castel house. Who did von Heinkel think he was, with his aristocratic pedigree and his autocratic ways? Laval wondered what Suzanne thought of the German, and jealousy corroded his reason. He would watch Hans von Heinkel every hour of the day and be rid of him as soon as it was possible. Laval could not settle down for thinking of the newcomer. One wrong move from the German and he would call the Gestapo, nipping his desire for Suzanne Castel in the bud.

Suzanne and Hans were looking through an old album of photographs, laughing merrily at some and smiling wistfully at others. Unaware of the danger nearby, they looked forward to a very pleasant association.

# CHAPTER THREE

*Christmas, 1940*

Marie-Claude was miserable. Christmas Day lunch had been a disgusting piece of shin beef made palatable with a bottle of Bordeaux from her father's cellar. There had been watery onion soup, leftovers from the previous meal, and a bowl of rice pudding made with powdered milk. As usual, Cook had put in too little sugar and too much nutmeg to compensate for the lack of taste. For months the family had been obliged to serve itself with meals, because all the male servants in the house had been arrested or expatriated and sent to Germany.

Marie-Claude sat on a damask chair looking at her best silk dress and trying not to cry as she remembered the afternoon Suzanne had called with Christmas presents for the family. Suzanne had looked deep into her eyes, a knowing look, one that delved into the soul, and Marie-Claude had known that Suzanne realized just how frightened and confused she felt about almost everything. For Carrie, Suzanne had brought lavender sachets, for Monsieur a cigar. Marie-Claude had received a small box of chocolates bought from Armand Lognon. She had grabbed the gift from Suzanne's hands, forced a polite "Thank you" from her lips, and rushed upstairs to her bedroom to eat every chocolate in the box. Her mouth watered as she thought of the luscious centers of the chocolates, the nougat and marzipan, montelimar and her favorite lemon cream. When she had re-

turned to the drawing room, Suzanne had teased her: "I hope
you've saved some of your chocolates for tomorrow, Marie-Claude,
they don't grow on trees, you know." Marie-Claude was still
furious and ashamed of her greediness, and every time she thought
of the incident she shuddered.

Looking over to where her father was sitting in his favorite
chair, his hands gripping the walnut arms, his eyes blearily looking at nothing, Marie-Claude wondered what was happening to
him. Was Papa going mad like Great-grandfather Chambord from
Normandy? Was he drunk again? Marie-Claude's eyes turned to
look out on the garden, where Carrie was busy in the makeshift
conservatory she had insisted the gardener construct before he
too disappeared. Bernard, the gardener, had been a Jew, and
Marie-Claude was certain Carrie had given him money to flee
Paris. She stared spitefully out as Carrie watered a profusion of
herbs, clucking over tiny lettuce and radishes that were springing
to life under her care. To combat the weather Carrie had improvised a makeshift cover for each plant from an old Chanel
waterproof.

Marie-Claude thought sadly that in the beginning her father
had been the undisputed head of the household, full of promises
that money would prevail. Carrie had been a secret drinker, without purpose in life except to hide the dissatisfaction she felt with
herself and everyone around her. Now the positions had reversed.
Since the takeover of his bank, Monsieur had drunk himself
into forgetfulness, emptying the cellar of all the best wines. When
he was not drinking, he was complaining that none of his suits
fit, that his head ached, that his shoes pinched, and that life was
nothing without work. Carrie, on the other hand, had ceased
drinking altogether because, as she said, "Someone's going to
have to feed us." She had quickly become the leader of the household, and when the servants disappeared it was Carrie who fought
to keep the old woman who cooked for them. She had succeeded
in this and in everything else, and had learned to grow vegetables
in terra-cotta pots around the terrace. She kept away from
Chambord's precious rose beds, and treated with cutting derision
his continuing obsession with winning prizes. Carrie went out
regularly to comb the shops for food. She had established con-
nections with a black marketeer who kept them in toiletries and

kitchen necessities, and for weeks had been trying to find an honest food-coupon forger, one who would not betray them to the authorities after taking their money.

For her part, Marie-Claude had not been out of the house in six months, except to wander in the garden, staring uneasily at weeds that appeared from nowhere, overrunning everything except Carrie's precious terra-cotta pots. Carrie had developed the habit of humoring her stepdaughter as one humors a sick child, pitying Marie-Claude because she was spoiled, frightened, and unable to think of anything or anyone but herself. They rarely spoke. Indeed, the only sounds in the house were those of Carrie and Cook discussing sparse food supplies, Carrie singing in her bath, and Chambord grumbling as he bemoaned his fate.

Marie-Claude went outside to the garden, wishing desperately that she had something to read. A frosty night had left silver patches on the brown soil, and spider webs glistened in pale December sunlight as they clung to weeds growing near the dividing wall. She looked up at a stone-pink sky and knew that snow was on its way. Black-branched trees reminded her of the desolation all around, and a thin white cat appeared, mewing pitifully for milk. Marie-Claude shooed it away and rushed inside, knocking over one of Carrie's plant pots in her haste. For a moment she looked down in exasperation. Then she kneeled and put the soil back in the pot, pressing and firming the plant so Carrie would not know it had ever been disturbed. Marie-Claude replaced the Chanel mac over the pot, shaking her head disapprovingly at such waste. Then she hurried to her bathroom to scrub her fingernails clean.

Once inside her room, she felt at peace. She locked the door and tripped to the Gramophone, placing the needle carefully on a record of Charles Trenet. She drew the curtains, leaving only a small gap so she would know night from day. Outside, a noisy crow squawked on the garden wall. There was a shot, and the crow fell into the lily pond of the next house, where someone took it gleefully for the stew pot. Marie-Claude threw a bag of rose salts in the bath, though she knew well that their supplies were running low. Then, revolving around and around, she examined her naked body in the mirror. She had lost weight, like everyone in Paris, but it suited her. She noticed that her hair was growing darker, less orange, and this also pleased her. Her eyes seemed even larger in the small freckled face, and her hands even slimmer, Marie-Claude touched her breasts, annoyed that they too had almost disappeared. She stepped into the bath and lay resting her head on a pink waterproof pillow. As she stretched out her arms, she was content because she was alone. Often, of late, Marie-Claude had fantasized about living alone in the house, looked after by a host of servants, never going out, and being visited only by two handsome lovers. Her dreams always included two lovers because she believed that if a woman was attached to one man all her life he inevitably took advantage. It was best to love no one, simply to permit men to pleasure the body before leaving the object of passion happily alone. She wondered idly what love felt like. She was neither avidly curious nor disinterested in the subject, and had never felt the desire to flirt or be kissed by young men who gazed at her when she attended parties. The thought of a man soiling the spotless cleanliness of her body was distasteful and frightening. When she married, Marie-Claude thought, she would try to fulfill her conjugal duties but after love would rush to her bedroom to erase all evidence of her husband's lust. She lifted her legs and scrubbed them with a loofah. Suddenly the light flickered and went out. She sat up, looking around in surprise. Surely a power cut had not been authorized on Christmas Day? Stepping hastily from the bath, she wrapped herself in a pink towel and ran to open the curtains. The new hours of daylight, two hours different from the normal hours, made life totally confusing. When one expected it to be light it was dark, and when it was dark one hoped for it to be light. Marie-Claude disapproved violently of German meddling in French time, intended to make the French work longer for the good of the Fatherland. Outside it was already dusk, and the sky was streaked with violet. Fearing a sudden storm, Marie-Claude closed the curtains and lit a scented candle. How beautiful it was to be home and mercifully alone.

She was experimenting with her hair in an exaggerated chignon when the doorbell pealed insistently. Putting on a swansdown wrap, she jumped into bed. Whoever it was had no manners to call unannounced on Christmas Day! She would not see them, as a sign of her disapproval. She would simply stay in bed! Marie-

Claude stiffened, pulling the bedclothes up around her chin, as the sound of heavy boots echoed on the stairs. Her father's voice came to her, pleading like a whining child with an unseen German officer.

"But, officer, General Gruber himself agreed that there would be no billeting in my house."

Marie-Claude leaped out of bed and ran to the bathroom, locking the door so she could hear no more of the horrifying interruption of normality. After a while she emerged and crept to the bedroom door, in time to hear her father screeching, "What do you mean, my wife and I are to be taken away for questioning? What have I done? I demand to know what I am supposed to have done!"

A quiet, rasping voice replied, "You will return to your home in a few days, Monsieur Chambord. The officers will stay here only when they visit Paris, which is not often. There is no other accommodation of a suitable type for them, so your home *must* be used. There will be no further argument."

"Can I pack a case?"

"That will not be necessary."

Marie-Claude ran to the side of the bed and, throwing herself on her knees, began to pray: "Please, God, make the Germans go away, make them fall down dead." The sound of voices continued in the hallway, but she could not decipher what was being said. She thought with a start that if there were Germans in the house she had best hurry and get dressed. The light returned, and she snuffed out the candle. Then she stood in front of the wardrobe, looking dazedly at racks of clothing. What should she wear? She had best look as prim as possible, in case they tried to take advantage. As she reached out to take a dress, there was a knock at the door. Marie-Claude stared wildly round the room, desperately wanting to escape.

"Oberst-Gruppenfuhrer Heydritch will see you in the drawing room, Mademoiselle Chambord."

Panic rose in her throat like a tidal wave, and she gripped the wardrobe door, unable to answer, unable to summon the strength to work out what to do. The orderly's flat voice repeated the statement. Marie-Claude dropped to the floor and began to pick fluff fallen from her wrap onto the velvet carpet. Absentmindedly she rolled the fluff into a ball as the sound of the soldier's boots echoed down the stairs. Minutes later the sound was replaced by a softer, firmer tread. Marie-Claude ran to the door, staring at the lock and praying it would hold. It was made of heavy brass, the most expensive that could be bought—surely it would not let her down? Ignoring thoughts of the Oberst-Gruppenfuhrer, she sat at her dressing table, brushing her hair. It was necessary to keep calm. She must *not* let him see how frightened she was. Women of breeding did not panic. A stern voice broke into her thoughts.

"Mademoiselle Chambord, open the door!"

Marie-Claude brushed her hair faster and faster. Still she was too shocked to speak. Looking outside to the garden, she saw it was snowing, only the black-branched trees and a red-breasted robin relieving the silent white emptiness that muffled and deadened everything. Unaccountably her mind wandered to the plants that Carrie was growing, and she thought that she must water them if her stepmother did not return in a few days. She was puzzling this odd thought when a loud explosion blew the lock from the door and Oberst-Gruppenfuhrer Heydritch entered, smiling his strange smile and greeting her politely as though nothing untoward had happened. Marie-Claude turned on the pink fur stool, looking furiously at the door and then at her visitor. Without greeting him, she ignored the outstretched hand and returned to brushing her hair.

"You will join me and my friends for coffee, mademoiselle."

Marie-Claude stared at the revolver Heydritch was snapping back in its black leather holster. Seeing shock and panic in her eyes, he paused to enjoy them. The girl was slimmer, tauter, and more neurotic than at their previous meeting, but still she had the style that had first attracted him, the untouchable quality that challenged.

Marie-Claude's voice quavered with fear. "What have you done to Papa?"

"Your father has gone to the offices of the Geheime Staatspolizei for questioning."

"And Madame, what have you done to her?"

"Madame has accompanied her husband."

Marie-Claude leaped up and paced the room, the luxurious

down wrap wafting around her legs. When she could stand the tension no longer, she turned venomously on Heydritch.

"Why have you done this? Whatever did Papa do to disobey the German ordinances—nothing!"

"I am aware of that."

"Then why has he been arrested?"

Heydritch drew the curtains back and looked out on the garden. Marie-Claude winced as he explained his visit.

"I am here on a three-day leave from Germany and I have in mind to enjoy myself. I have brought with me my friends Gruppenfuhrer Hammerstein and Sturmbannfuhrer Rika. We are all in need of relaxation. As you can imagine, life at the front is not amusing."

Marie-Claude's heart began to thunder, her limbs to tremble uncontrollably, and she sat down on the bed, fumbling to fasten her shoes.

"You could have stayed in a hotel. The Crillon is where Reichsmarschall Goering stays. I know because Papa saw him there when he was lunching the other day."

"You are quite right, but you do not live at the Crillon, do you, mademoiselle?"

Marie-Claude walked dazedly to the dressing table and began again to brush her hair.

"There are women all over Paris who know how to please men like you. I am a virgin, you cannot intend to—"

"I intend to use you as my hostess, Mademoiselle Chambord, and I thought you would find it easier if your father was not here. That is why he and Madame were taken away. At such a time it is best for a woman's mind to be free from the concerns of convention."

Marie-Claude brightened momentarily, hoping she had mistaken Heydritch's original intention. She watched warily as he walked to the door, still smiling the mocking smile.

"Please put on one of your beautiful dresses and join me for coffee. I have brought you chocolates from Switzerland and a fine goose from the Ardennes."

She waited for him to leave before putting on the dress. She could not fasten the buttons because her hands were shaking, and even the thought of Swiss chocolate made her sick.

When she could delay no longer, Marie-Claude walked down-stairs to the drawing room. Heydritch rose and introduced her to the men at his side.

"Mademoiselle Chambord, meet Gruppenfuhrer Hammerstein. Otto, this is Marie-Claude."

The Gruppenfuhrer had the pale, saturnine face of a cadaver and eyes like black, bottomless holes. He made a joke as Marie-Claude was introduced to the other member of the party, a young officer commanding an extermination squad. Rika was tall and handsome, with wistful gray eyes and thick, sensuous lips. He held Marie-Claude's hand for a long time, and she wrinkled her nose at the stale smell of his body. When the three had been introduced, they continued their game of cards, ignoring her, and Marie-Claude wondered if Heydritch had posted guards out-side the house. If he had not, there would be nothing to prevent her from walking out and running away. As the men chatted she went to the window and looked out, distressed to see armed sentries near the door and at various points along the street. Obviously the Oberst-Gruppenfuhrer was more important than she had imagined. For a moment she thought of her father, and tears fell down her cheeks, so she had to fumble for a handkerchief and excuse herself. In the doorway of the breakfast room she stood looking out to the terrace and taking comfort from Carrie's plants. She would be like the plants, braving the harsh elements of winter. She would defy the Germans and escape at the first op-portunity. She was a Chambord, whose aristocratic ancestors had defied the guillotine. She too would defy insurmountable odds. As Marie-Claude tried to rally herself, she heard Heydritch's voice behind her.

"Tonight we are going to Maxim's."

"And afterward?"

"Afterward we shall drink champagne and enjoy ourselves."

Marie-Claude looked into his eyes and saw only challenge and merciless appraisal. Haughtily she walked past him and returned to her bedroom, trying desperately to assess what to do, how best to make Heydritch think she was safely in his custody. She thought of the house and every unexpected escape that might be used. She thought of transport, friends who might help, the possibility that the staff of Maxim's, who knew her well, would come to her aid.

But how to alert them to her position without involving them, to their own peril? She lay on the bed, staring at the ceiling, crying now and then and throwing herself on the mercy of God.

At seven they left the house and drove down the Champs-Elysées. This was the first time Marie-Claude had been out in the months since occupation, and her first night out for almost a year. She was shocked by the changed face of Paris and disturbed by the blackness of the night. Ornate lampposts that usually cast a mellow light on the pavements were shrouded in black oilcloth, redundant and forgotten. Night workers scurried by en route to city offices as civil servants returned home, their faces gray with hunger. Most were wrapped from head to toe in shabby shawls, scarves, and voluminous coats, worn indoors as well as outside. Some of the coats were patched with three or four different materials, from old clothes of winters past. She looked down at her own dress, at the star-shaped paillettes glittering silver against expensive blue chiffon frills. Then she listened as her escorts talked, content for the moment to ignore her presence. She considered leaping from the car, but it was going too quickly and it never paused. She began to think of later in the evening, asking herself why Reinhard Heydritch had really come to Paris. Suddenly she found courage and the confidence to know that if she tried hard, she could get away from her captors.

The maître d' of Maxim's frowned on sight of Marie-Claude. Mademoiselle and her father had been frequent visitors since the days of her childhood. Where was Monsieur, and what was the girl doing with three officers of the SS? He handed out menus, bowing deferentially to the Germans and smiling encouragingly at Marie-Claude. The maître d' tried to think what to do, whom to speak with, whether he could help in any way. Marie-Claude's face was ashen, her body twitching with fear. Heydritch ordered for her as if she were not present: aspic Saint-Jacques à l'estragon, sole Albert; Sancerre to commence with, a magnum of Château Margaux to liven the later part of the evening. The maître d' gave the order to the kitchen and passed on to another table. The sommelier withdrew, his face pinched and tense. Marie-Claude started as Heydritch questioned her.

"Tell me, why do you hate your stepmother?"

She looked around desperately, wishing there were someone to help. The owner and manager of the establishment had been banished and a new administrator brought from Berlin. Many of the waiters were young boys, because able-bodied men had been sent away to Germany. Heydritch's hand tightened on her arm, discouraging the urge to run away. At last Marie-Claude answered.

"I don't hate my stepmother. On the other hand, I don't love her. She's strict with me, that's all."

"And you would prefer more freedom?"

"No, I would not. I simply don't understand Madame because she's American and I am French."

"Shall I have her shot? Would that amuse you? You could come with me to watch her die."

Shocked, Marie-Claude dropped a bread roll on the floor. But she replied with all the derision she could muster.

"I find your conversation offensive, Oberst-Gruppenfuhrer. I am not at all interested in having my stepmother murdered. I am quite capable of dealing with her myself."

The three men smiled, and Heydritch turned to them approvingly.

"I told you she was superior. How I admire arrogant women. Only fools are subservient."

Marie-Claude noted that Gruppenfuhrer Hammerstein never spoke directly to her. He ordered food, surveyed the scene, and nodded agreement now and then, but rarely joined in the conversation. But all the while his black eyes returned to their surveillance, roving over her body and hungering for what they saw. Sturmbannfuhrer Rika was quite different. He danced with every woman in the room, even between courses, and disappeared mysteriously for an hour, returning as though nothing had happened.

As the sommelier poured more glasses of champagne, he eavesdropped on the conversation. Heydritch was watching Marie-Claude closely, uncertain of her mood.

"Tell me what you are thinking."

"I'm thinking about Papa."

"He will be safe, because you will keep him safe."

"What do you mean?"

"Let me explain. If you were to run away or to appeal for help from your old friend Maître Duval, I imagine your father would have a very serious accident."

The sommelier disappeared to report what he had heard to Maître Duval.

Marie-Claude watched fellow diners enjoying dinner as they sat lazily on the rose velvet banquettes. For a moment she remembered her first visit to Maxim's, at the age of six, and the wonderful stories her father had told of its past. As the room filled she was surprised to see one of their best friends arriving with Reichsmarshall Hermann Goering. The Reichsmarshall was dressed in a light blue silk uniform covered with medals from shoulder to waist. His gestures were theatrical, and he kept expressing profound admiration for the ambiance. Marie-Claude remembered a comedian she had once seen appearing with a circus. He had parodied a German kaiser of long ago and looked exactly like the Reichsmarschall. She glanced apprehensively toward Heydritch, shocked when she realized he was still watching her.

"What will you have for dessert, Marie-Claude?"

Sick with apprehension, she could barely think of food, but, wanting to prolong the meal for as long as possible, she replied, "I would like peaches in grenadine."

"Peaches in grenadine for Mademoiselle, and some Roquefort for me and my friends."

The band was playing a lilting German waltz as the waiter served coffee. Heydritch held out his hand and took Marie-Claude to the floor. She thought how well he danced, how compelling his looks were and how women in the room seemed to look enviously in her direction. Smiling sadly at her situation, Marie-Claude thought that if Heydritch had come alone she would probably have capitulated, because she would do almost anything to keep her father alive. But now what to do—how to persuade him to let her go? She swirled prettily at Heydritch's side, looking searchingly into his eyes.

"What would I have to do to make you let me go, Oberst-Gruppenfuhrer?"

Heydritch tried to look as though he were considering the question. He was enjoying the game and increasingly excited by Marie-Claude's coldness. When he spoke, her heart sank.

"You would have to win the war for me tonight, and not a moment later."

Marie-Claude persisted, hoping against logic that she could tempt him with money.

"What could I offer you that would change your mind? Money? My father would pay anything if you would let me go. Tell me how much it would cost for you to help me."

"You could not buy my cooperation, my dear. I made up my mind to visit you that morning when we first met. You were so confident and haughty and a little impolite. I found your manner an irresistible challenge, and it has been my sorrow that I have been so long away from Paris."

Marie-Claude saw her chance and, tossing her hair defiantly, looked Heydritch in the eye.

"I see no challenge in your bringing two friends to assist you in your endeavors. A Frenchman would laugh that you need three men to overpower one young girl."

"Touché, my dear, but you mistake my intentions. I need no one to assist me in handling you. Rika and Hammerstein are here to assist me in enjoying you to the very fullest extent. A Frenchman might frown and call my desires bizarre, but I am not concerned with that. I am insensitive to alien opinion. Now shall we rejoin the others?"

They drove home at midnight through streets as deserted as a ghost town. Marie-Claude lingered on the steps, listening to the chimes of the church clock in the rue Mesnil. She had grown suddenly calm and thoughtful. Now that the moment had arrived, she knew precisely what she must try to do.

Heydritch pushed her inside and closed the door. Marie-Claude watched as he locked the door and handed the key to Rika. Then he turned to her and ordered her to bed.

"You had best retire—you look tired, and that will never do."

She glanced uncertainly at the three men, flinching when they laughed at Heydritch's bravado. When she was halfway up the stairs he called out, "In thirty minutes I shall bring you some champagne. Be sure you are not asleep."

Marie-Claude nodded haughtily and disappeared along the landing. Once inside her room, she looked at the shattered lock and shook her head. Then she took a wad of notes out of the dresser drawer and urged herself on; there was no time to be lost. If she was to escape from the Germans, she would have to keep her wits and her strength. She went to the bathroom and locked the door behind her. She climbed onto the window ledge and pushed the trapdoor in the ceiling. A few months before the occupation it had been necessary to have alterations made in the attic cistern; Marie-Claude had been fascinated to learn that all the roof spaces of neighboring houses connected. At her first attempt to reach the attic she fell headlong into the bathtub, severely bruising her ankle and arm. Clenching her fists, she prayed the men below had not heard the noise. To muffle sound, she ran the water into the bathtub. Then she removed scent bottles and boxes of soap from the window shelf, balanced a stool on the wide ledge overlooking the garden, and heaved herself up. With one muscle-straining pull, she was in the attic. She replaced the trapdoor and stepped carefully over trunks and discarded furniture into the roof space of the adjoining house. Then, slowly, cautiously, she passed from house to house until she reached the attic of the property on the corner. A mouse ran over her foot, scuttling into the wainscoting, and Marie-Claude smothered a scream, her eyes filling with tears. She told herself determinedly that all she had to do now was to get through the trapdoor, down into the bathroom, and then away into the street, unseen by Heydritch's guards. Lifting the wooden trapdoor, she looked into darkness. Afraid of making a noise, she took off her shoes and left them in the attic. Then, gripping the edges of the opening, she lowered herself into the bathroom, allowing her body to drop the last few feet. Landing safely, she stepped out of the tub and crept to the door, thankful that the houses of the place Victor Hugo were all built to the same design. The handle creaked as she turned it, and Marie-Claude felt her throat turn dry when she saw a man asleep in bed not more than a meter from where she was standing. Holding her breath, she tiptoed past him to the landing, then slowly, warily down the stairs, cursing every creak and pausing on the landing to peer over the banister into an empty hall. The front door was locked, and there was no sign of the key. For a moment she wondered what to do. Then she made her way to the servants' quarters, where the housemaid was asleep and snoring loudly. Marie-Claude tiptoed by, passing through the unlocked staff door to the steps that led up to the street. For a moment she crouched behind the railing, her ears straining for any sound that might betray the presence of guards. But there was only a profound silence. For some time she remained tense and still, hearing only the sound of distant aircraft droning over the suburbs of Paris. Realizing that she had forgotten her shoes, she swore. It was snowing, and without shoes she would catch her death of cold. But anything was better than remaining with Heydritch and his friends.

At last she ran to the avenue Marceau, wincing as her feet cut on chips of stone and peaks of frozen snow. As she dodged into the shadows to avoid a German patrol, her mind balked at the danger. Then she controlled herself and continued on, taking deep breaths and remembering the horror she had left behind. Her teeth chattered and her feet began to bleed, staining the snow red. But nothing mattered except putting distance between herself and the place Victor Hugo. At the Rond Point, when she was almost exhausted, Marie-Claude noticed a bicycle leaning against the wall of the Palais de Glace. She looked around, then seized it and pedaled away furiously.

Almost at once she realized that she was out after curfew and that she had nowhere to go. Papa's friends would not take her in once they knew he had been arrested, and her own best friend's family had just fled to England. That meant she would have to beg help from the Castels. Marie-Claude frowned. She thought of all the times she had patronized them, all the insults she had hurled Suzanne's way and the disparaging comments she had made to David about his fiancée. She had been right, of course— Suzanne Castel was not a suitable match for David. But now what she needed was a place to hide, and the Castels' house would be as safe as anywhere.

Marie-Claude rode on the sidewalk, close to the wall, praying no one would see her. When she reached the boulevard de Clichy she saw the lights of another German patrol car. She abandoned the bicycle and dived into the basement of a nearby house, covering herself with snow from head to foot. She knew she would not be able to carry the bicycle up the steps that intersected many of the streets of Montmartre; she would have to abandon it.

Soaked to the skin, she went on, panting with effort and fear.

In the rue des Martyrs a drunk appeared, weaving to and fro in the street and calling insults at the wind. Marie-Claude stood against the wall to let him pass, but when he drew abreast of her the man stopped and grabbed her, kissing her full on the mouth and cooing drunkenly, "Liebchen, mein Liebchen . . ." She tore herself away and ran at full speed in the direction of the rue Gabrielle. Outside the Rogers' café, at the corner of the street, she tripped over a black dog asleep on a warm grating. The dog growled, and Marie-Claude knew that hunger had made it dangerous. She walked calmly by, breaking into a desperate run only when she realized the dog was growling close behind. At the gate of the Marchand house the dog pounced, sinking its teeth into Marie-Claude's thigh. She screamed, dragging herself forward to the Castel entrance. Terrified, she cried out, appealing for help and shelter. Startled by the noise, the dog ran away. Then Nathalie's head appeared at an upstairs window.

"What's going on, who's there?"

"It's Marie-Claude, madame, please help me."

"Whatever are you doing out at this hour?"

Marie-Claude sat down in the snow, unable to speak, unwilling to roar explanations to the darkness. A moment later Nathalie helped her inside the house.

"Where are your shoes, child, and what are you doing out at this time of night? You're soaking wet! Have you been swimming?"

Marie-Claude sobbed as if her heart would break.

"A big dog bit me, a black dog. Oh, how ridiculous it will be to die of a dog bite!"

"I'll get some hot water and clean it for you. Don't worry, child, there's no danger of dying."

Nathalie helped her visitor into a chair and rushed to find a bowl and a bottle of surgical spirits. Marie-Claude's face had shocked her, and she tried frantically to work out why the girl was so changed. Her pallor was chalky white, and she looked suddenly old, weak, and empty.

As Nathalie dressed the wound, Marie-Claude told her about the Germans. Nathalie handed her a mug of coffee, precious new coffee given them by Hans before he had left for two weeks' leave in Germany. Nathalie thought of the wood Hans had chopped, the side of beef he had bought, the tins of tea and sack of coffee presented as gifts on his last evening in the house. It would be best to mention nothing about Hans to Marie-Claude.

At three Nathalie helped her unexpected guest onto the sofa and told her to sleep. Then she piled logs on the fire and went to bed, perplexed by Marie-Claude's strange tale. If it was true, what would happen to Charles Chambord and his wife? And if it was a lie, whatever had Marie-Claude been doing out in evening dress without shoes and soaking wet on Christmas night? Nathalie lay in bed weighing the story, deciding at last that it was true. But what was to be done with Marie-Claude? Hans was due back on the twenty-eighth for the opening of Suzanne's show. Marie-Claude would certainly have to be out of the house by then in case she misunderstood their friendship with the German. If the SS officers who had invaded the Chambord house were planning to stay for three days, as they had told Marie-Claude, would they leave once they realized she had escaped? Had they been telling the truth about the length of their stay? And what if Chambord was dead? Nathalie wrestled with the possibilities until the small hours.

Marie-Claude woke to the smell of coffee. Suzanne was setting the breakfast table with a daisy-sprigged cloth and eggcups. Marie-Claude wondered how they managed to buy fresh eggs when she had had nothing but powdered ones for months. She lay back remembering the happenings of the previous evening and resenting the expensive odor of the brew Nathalie brought to the table. How could the Castels, who were poor and without a man, find coffee of such excellent quality? She sat up, rubbing her eyes and examining her feet, which were bound with torn cotton strips. Nathalie called her to the table.

"While you were asleep I took out the splinters."

"Thank you, madame."

"Breakfast is ready. Put on the wrap and join us."

Marie-Claude felt close to tears. Why could she think nothing but vicious thoughts about the Castels? Why had she never been able to accept them as friends? Was there something wrong with her that she always wanted to find fault with people? She looked uncertainly at Suzanne, who was busy grinding pepper into her soft-boiled egg. Marie-Claude rose and put on the wrap.

"Your coffee smells wonderful. Where did you buy it?"

Suzanne and her mother exchanged cautionary glances. Then Suzanne replied with a nonchalant smile, "A friend of Papa's gave it to us for Christmas. He's an importer and he was visiting Paris from the free zone. We're lucky. Most of the neighbors have had nothing but ground chick-peas and acorns for weeks."

"I thought you must have contacts in the black market."

Nathalie's mouth closed like a rat trap.

"We don't have money to buy food, let alone deal with those wretches. Now eat your egg before it goes cold."

Nathalie wondered why she had never been able to take to Marie-Claude. The girl was only just seventeen, so there was time for her to mature and grow tolerant. But something in the arch gaze and petulant manner made her wary of giving trust, and without trust there could never be affection.

Marie-Claude ate greedily, pouring herself two cups of coffee and spreading margarine thickly on her bread. When she had drained the second cup, she looked through the window into the garden with its neat rows of cabbages covered with snow. Suddenly she remembered Carrie and her father's plaintive pleading with the German officer. Should she return home or should she remain in hiding? She felt unequal to making the decision, so she turned to Nathalie.

"Tell me what to do, Madame Castel. I don't know whether to go home or to stay here."

"Only you can decide."

"I think I should telephone the house and see if anyone replies. If they don't, I could go home, couldn't I?"

Nathalie considered this for a moment. The Germans would certainly have left telephone numbers with their adjutants in case of emergency. They would not leave the telephone unanswered and risk ignoring an urgent command from headquarters. She nodded her agreement.

"It seems the best thing to do, and you should telephone your neighbors to check if they've seen the Germans leave."

"I will, madame. May I do it now?"

"We don't have a phone, but you can use the one in the café on the corner."

Marie-Claude looked at the silver-blue dress on a hanger near the door, and, as if reading her thoughts, Nathalie handed her a faded skirt, a pair of old plimsolls, white socks, and a shirt belonging to Suzanne.

"You can use these when you go out, and you'd best go home in them, too. You can't prance around Paris in your evening things. I'll wrap the dress in newspaper so you can take it home with you."

"Thank you, madame, you've been most kind."

Marie-Claude limped to the bathroom, where she washed with a new bar of soap and dried herself on a clean towel that had been put out for her. Borrowing a comb, she parted her hair and plaited it neatly, retying the ribbons. Scrubbed and clean, she looked like a schoolgirl, but as she looked at her reflection she felt suddenly old and uncertain where once she had been sure. She was terrified of going to the café on the corner in case she saw the dog again, and she was too proud to tell the Castels that she had never made a phone call from a public place. She put on the socks and slid her bandaged feet into the plimsolls, looking uncertainly at her reflection again. The pink blouse and skirt suited her and went with the gray jacket she had brought.

Marie-Claude walked out to the landing and looked through a gap in the half-closed door of the spare room. On the bed there was a German uniform, on wall hooks an expensive black cashmere overcoat and a silk scarf embossed with a crest and initials. A photograph of a castle took pride of place on the dressing table. Curious, Marie-Claude crept to the door and pushed it open, staring at the photograph and another of a handsome young man sitting outside a hunting lodge built in the same style as the castle. She was about to rejoin the Castels when she noticed a comic card in Suzanne's handwriting pinned with a gilt tack to the side of the bed. She walked into the room and examined it, shocked by its merry message. *Merry Christmas, Hans, and welcome to la maison Fleuri. This is our castle, and we hope to make it very pleasant for you. Suzanne.*

Marie-Claude returned to the living room, turning over in her mind what she had seen. On the dressing table there had been a letter with a military postage stamp, addressed to Hans von Heinkel. The German must be a billeted officer in the house. He was also rich and handsome, titled and an aristocrat, if her assessment was correct. Marie-Claude felt unaccountably annoyed. It was bad enough to have to face having Suzanne as a sister-in-law, but to find out that she had been sending affectionate messages to a German was too much! She would tell Papa as soon as he arrived home.

She walked haughtily into the café, avoiding Suzanne's curious glance. Once inside the café, Marie-Claude hesitated. She was uncertain what to do, and embarrassed by the open curiosity of men standing at the crowded bar. Suzanne led the way, calling for jetons and then huddling in the corner while Marie-Claude telephoned the first number on her list. She was greatly relieved when there was no reply. To be sure, she rang the number again. Still no answer. The house was empty. She had won—Heydritch had gone away! She smiled delightedly.

"The Germans have gone, Suzanne, there's no answer."

"Try the neighbors and see what they say."

Marie-Claude dialed the second number. A woman answered.

"This is Marie-Claude Chambord. Can you tell me if there are still guards outside the door of my house, Madame Archard?"

"No, dear, they left this morning."

"And the officers, did you see them leave?"

"If you can wait a moment, I'll ask Monsieur."

Marie-Claude's feet began to bleed, and she felt unaccountably nervous. Then Mme. Archard returned to the line.

"The officers also left, Marie-Claude, Monsieur saw them about nine. Is everything all right? I hear your father was arrested."

"Don't worry, madame, and thank you for your help."

Marie-Claude made one further call, receiving similar information and relaying it to Suzanne. Guards and officers of the SS had left in the early morning, the house was empty. They walked back to la maison Fleuri as fast as Marie-Claude's sore feet would allow. Within minutes she was gone, hobbling painfully down the steps of the rue Foyatier. Nathalie Castel had insisted that she avoid returning home by the route she had taken the previous evening, and Marie-Claude was happy to comply.

Alone, and relieved that she had gone, the Castels discussed her.

"Why did you send Marie-Claude by the steps, maman?"

"There's a German patrol car in the place du Cavalaire. I didn't want to alarm her, but I thought it best she avoid any questions."

"I'm late for rehearsal, I must go."

"I wonder what will have happened to the Chambords. Do you reckon they were shot? She didn't seem to have thought of it, did she?"

"Marie-Claude only thinks of herself, maman."

Suzanne collected her music and left the house, taking the same route as Marie-Claude. Minutes later she was in Pigalle, walking past the fish shop where oursins were sold. The fishmonger was placing the spiky black sea urchins in red baskets, which he rested on the snow. As Suzanne passed he waved a cheery good morning, raising his boater and showing all his teeth. A girl stepped out of the house where Armand had his rooms. She was wearing expensive leather boots the color of fine tobacco, and cursing each time they touched the snow. Suzanne wondered if she was a dancer, a barmaid, or a poule from Mme. Francine's establishment. A cyclist came around a corner, wobbling precariously on icy furrows. When he collided with an angry housewife, knocking her to the ground, the lady roared her disapproval and waved a yellow umbrella, threatening to brain him.

Suzanne arrived at the Bal Tabarin and was greeted by a jubilant Janine. They kissed, and Suzanne began to ask questions.

"What's happened, why are you so happy? Did you see Leutnant Weber?"

"I did, and all my troubles are over."

"What did he say?"

"He didn't say much, but he gave me money to cover all my debts."

"And what does he want in return?"

"Zizi, must you always be so curious!"

"And must you always be so secretive!"

Suzanne had an unpleasant premonition that Janine was no longer as scrupulous in her dealing with men as in times past. Once she had fallen in love lightheartedly with every penniless artist she met. Now she was completely preoccupied by money, and Suzanne knew she would do anything to get it. Unabashed by her censure, Janine explained.

"Weber wants to take me out and he asked me help him buy some properties."

"How can you buy properties? You can't even pay your rent!"

"I have to sign papers and pretend I'm the owner. It will really be Weber buying them."

"That's collaborating!"

"My dear Suzanne, you let Hans von Heinkel buy you firewood and meat and anything else you can get out of him. That is collaborating, too!"

When Marie-Claude arrived home, a howling wind was blowing powdery snow in mounds around the black iron railings Not a soul had ventured out except the solitary white cat, which mewed pitifully and grew thinner by the hour. The only colors to be seen were the emerald mold of an iron statue of Apollo and the welcoming rose of a silk-shaded lamp in a neighbor's window. Marie-Claude took out her keys and walked quickly to the door. First she looked nervously right and left, breathing a sigh of relief that the adjacent street was also deserted. How cold it was. How she was longing for some warm soup or a café crème. She closed the door and bolted it, surprised by the homey smell of cooking coming from the basement. Obviously Cook had arrived early. Marie-Claude was happy as she passed down the steps to the kitchen. The room was empty, but on the table there were pans of peeled potatoes and some thick pea soup. She opened the oven, licking her lips at the sight of a goose sizzling on one of the shelves. At least the Germans had had the good manners to leave behind what they had brought! She boiled water and made chocolate from the last of the powder Carrie had hoarded. Then she returned to the hall, balancing the cup and an apple found on the kitchen shelf.

When she entered her bedroom, Marie-Claude smiled. Its visceral pinkness comforted her, and she was greatly in need of something to assuage her shredded nerves. She sat at the dressing table and unwound the bandages, wrapping a towel around her feet when bright drops of blood fell on the rose silk carpet. She drew a bath, using the last of her scented salts and a precious vial of carnation oil. Then, relaxing in the water, she listened to the familiar sounds of home: clocks ticking, boards creaking, birds singing a lonely song in the garden. As the clock struck twelve, Marie-Claude wrapped herself in a towel and ran through to the bedroom. She drew the curtains wide apart and looked happily down on the garden. How good it was to be back, how lucky she had been.

She was sitting at the dressing table, brushing her hair, when she saw the reflection of a black uniform in the mirror and heard the deep voice she had prayed never to hear again.

"I thought if I waited you might return."

Marie-Claude's hands turned to ice, her chest hurt dreadfully, and she was ashamed to feel tears of panic pouring down her face. She watched in mounting agitation as Heydritch unbuttoned his jacket and took off his shoes. Then she burst out furiously, "I telephoned this house and there was no reply. Why did you not answer the phone? Are you not supposed to keep in contact with your headquarters?"

Heydritch was delighted by her spirit.

"Hammerstein and Rika went into the city early this morning. I remained here in case we were called. I can only imagine you called when I was running my bath so I did not hear the bell. By the way, I was greatly impressed by your escape last night. How sad that you have cut your feet so badly for nothing."

Marie-Claude dashed to the door. Heydritch hit her across the chin. She fell in a heap at his feet, struggling desperately to rise, conscious of his hands on her shoulders.

"The game is up, Marie-Claude. The time has come for you to be a woman."

Heydritch threw her back on the bed, smiling down with the hungry, cruel look she had come to know so well. Marie-Claude felt blood in her mouth as her tongue flicked from side to side, exploring a jagged cut. She reached for a handkerchief and wiped her mouth nervously, cautiously, wondering if it would amuse Heydritch to kill her. When he removed his shirt, she saw that he had a long silver scar down the chest from shoulder to heart. She tried to rise, but the blow to her head had made her giddy and she fell back, wondering if her jaw was broken. When Heydritch stood naked at her side, Marie-Claude closed her eyes tightly, unable to look at him. He pushed her unceremoniously away so he could strip off the bedcovers. Then he removed the towel she was clutching and hauled her to his side, kissing her mouth and biting her lip. She jerked her head back in fear and loathing.

"Don't hurt me."

"Be quiet!"

"I want to go to the bathroom."

"I took the precaution of removing the lock, so there would be no point in your trying the same trick again."

Heydritch began to explore her body with urgent, unyielding hands. Marie-Claude writhed away from him, crying out when he slapped her viciously on one cheek and then the other, stunning her so she barely felt him part her thighs. But in a moment of unbelievable torment she heard herself screaming and saw her hands clawing the air in agony. Heydritch taunted her as he pushed inside her.

"Now you can tell me how it feels to be a woman."

Marie-Claude screamed hysterically, but nothing stopped the oscillating, thrusting body that had impaled her. She prayed to faint, to die, to go blind so she could not see the triumph in his eyes.

At last Heydritch lay still at her side. Marie-Claude tried to rise, to rush to the bathroom to cleanse herself of the odious evidence of his lust. But when she turned away from Heydritch, he grasped her by the hair, pulling her back to his side.

"You will not move until I tell you."

"I feel dirty!"

"You cannot be dirty, my dear, you have just bathed, and I had a bath at nine this morning."

"I feel dirty because I'm with you. You're everything I loathe and despise, a degenerate like all the rest of your race."

"And you, my dear Marie-Claude, are like a wild horse. You will be perfect when I have broken you."

Marie-Claude clawed at his face, trying to scratch out his eyes. Heydritch caught her hand in his and squeezed, breaking every nail, so that she cried out in desperation. When he released the hand he was smiling, and Marie-Claude, seeing his desire, began to plead.

"Please let me wash."

"You can wash later. It is now time for your lesson."

"What do you mean?"

Heydritch inclined his head to where Rika and Hammerstein were framed in the dim light of the doorway.

Marie-Claude began to shriek, knowing there was to be no escape, no hope of reprieve. The two men approached, looking down on her in a detached way as Heydritch told her what they intended to do. With a sudden burst of strength, Marie-Claude leaped up and ran through the door, reaching the landing before a blow to the head knocked her senseless. Heydritch dragged her back to bed and threw her down on the pillows, surprised by her continued resistance.

When she came to, Marie-Claude saw Rika putting his clothes neatly on the chair, pressing his trousers here and there between thumb and finger with all the care of a midinette. Hammerstein was wrapping a buckled belt around his fist, his face twitching in anticipation. She winced when he addressed her for the first and last time.

"You are a fighter, mademoiselle, I will concede that. But you are going to need more than determination to deal with us."

Heydritch watched as his victim blinked her eyes, unwilling to force herself too quickly to consciousness. Marie-Claude listened in terror as he discussed her with his fellow conspirators.

"We shall soon know what she is really like under that chill exterior. Will she be as hot as a volcano, or as cold as Siberia? Who knows? Would you fancy a bet, Rika? Come, gentlemen, let us teach this haughty child how we enjoy ourselves."

No one heard Marie-Claude's screams, or if they did, none came to her assistance. Across the square an old road sweeper was brewing tea and a baker's boy scurried home with a bag of gray rolls.

At the Gare de Lyon, Jacques Castel was stepping down from the train. In his suitcase he had some smoked pork given him by the farmer for whom he had been working. Krantz was a gentleman and generous to a fault. He had insisted on giving the pork to Jacques "for the family" so they would know that not all Germans were executioners.

Jacques ordered coffee in the buffet, grimacing at its bitter taste. Looking around, he saw a young German officer drinking coffee and warming himself with a measure of cognac. Jacques looked longingly at the cognac, and the officer, noting his glance, was kind enough to order another. Jacques smiled, touching his forehead in acknowledgment as the German slid the glass along the counter. Jacques drank the cognac, savoring every mouthful, and the German came and sat at his side.

"I must go to this address. Can you tell me how to get there?" Jacques sketched a small map and handed it to the German. "It's not more than five minutes' walk from the station."

"Thank you, I am obliged. This is my first visit to Paris."

After a few words with the German, Jacques went on his way, knowing he had little chance of finding a taxi. Trudging stoically along, he noticed shops with empty shelves, old men with charcoal braziers selling roasted chestnuts and half-bad baked potatoes. There were lines of hungry people waiting to buy the man's maggoty potatoes, and Jacques wrinkled his nose in distaste. Near the Folies Bergères a woman appeared in a doorway, calling out hopefully as he passed by.

"Monsieur, have you a cigarette or perhaps a few potatoes?"

"I have nothing to spare, madame."

"Nothing? I'm so hungry. I would invite you in, I'm alone. . . ."

"I'm sorry, I'm going home."

The woman bit her lip and looked close to tears. Jacques walked on, wondering if all the women of Paris were willing to sell themselves for so little. Had things deteriorated so swiftly since his last visit? Were Suzanne and her mother eating enough? Jacques thought of his daughter and of all the joy she had brought him over the years. He remembered the day she had first met her fiancé, when she was a precociously tall thirteen-year-old and David a poised twenty-one. The images came as clearly to his mind as if it had been six weeks and not six years since that first meeting had occurred. Jacques and his family had been picnicking in the sun in the orchard near the Montmartre vineyard. David had appeared with one of Suzanne's girl friends. It had been a beautiful September day, full of the smell of ripe fruit and fading flowers. Suzanne had been dressed in green and pink, and David had teased her that she looked like an apple. Jacques remembered his daughter blushing furiously and then punching David a blow to the guts that winded him. Jacques laughed out loud at the memory. It had hardly been the most likely start to a romance! After the picnic he had wached his daughter lead David by the hand to the far section of the orchard, where they picked as many apples as her apron would hold. When they returned to the family group, Suzanne was in love and David struggling with his conscience because he was longing to kiss the girl at his side. Wistfully Jacques remembered every detail of that lazy summer afternoon: the smells of earth and grass, the terrine they had eaten, full of garlic, brandy, and chicken liver, the scent of the apricots his wife had stoned for him. Those had been the happy days, the days of peace and contentment.

Jacques reached the boulevard de Clichy and crossed the road, his head bowed against a sudden blinding snow shower. At the corner of the rue des Martyrs he collided with a German officer, knocking the man off balance and dropping his suitcase. Jacques apologized profusely. Then he picked up the suitcase and began the steep climb to the rue Gabrielle. He had gone only a dozen paces when a staccato shout startled him.

"You! Stop at once!"

He turned and looked into the eyes of the German he had just encountered. Shielding his face from the snow, Jacques replied, "Can I help you, sir?"

"Your name?"

"Jacques Castel."

"Address?"

"La maison Fleuri, rue Gabrielle."

"Show me your identity card."

Jacques produced the card and handed it to the officer.

"Are you aware that it is an offense not to salute a German officer?"

Jacques gaped in amazement at the very thought of such lunacy.

"I've been out of Paris since June, working in your country and helping your war effort. I can't be expected to know about orders issued in Paris."

"Next time remember, or you will be shot."

The officer waited until his prisoner saluted. Jacques

cursed the arm that raised itself and the fingers that touched his brow. The German nodded, satisfied that he understood. Then he stepped into a car and was driven swiftly away. Jacques mopped his forehead and ran all the way home, trembling with reaction at the narrowness of his escape. When he reached the gate he saw Suzanne dragging a heavy branch down the path.

"I'm home, Zizi."

"Oh, Papa, I'm so pleased to see you."

They embraced, hugging each other so tightly they could barely breath. Then Nathalie appeared at the kitchen window, her eyes full of tears, and she ran to her husband and buried herself in his arms. As snow fell the three stood hugging each other, their bodies unmoving and silent. They were too happy to express the joy and relief they felt at being together again, so they said nothing.


From his attic window, Laval looked down. He was relieved to see Jacques Castel home. It was a matter of concern to him that Suzanne was left so often alone with the German. Hans's presence and the quality of his bearing had impressed and intimidated the tax collector. An indefinable air of superiority coupled with the uniform was unusual and potent, he imagined, in the eyes of a young woman. Ever since Hans had arrived in the rue Gabrielle, Laval had tried to watch night and day for suspicious signs of a liaison between the two young people. For a moment he turned and saw Vivienne Marchand coming up the street, wheeling her eldest in a pram and panting with cold. Madame was heavily pregnant, and anemic from lack of food. Laval shook his head disapprovingly. It was time André Marchand learned self-control. What was the point of bringing children into the world when there was no food for those already there? Vivienne ran to greet Jacques, throwing out her arms. They collided prematurely because her stomach was so large. The group broke apart, laughing delightedly, and Laval was annoyed to see them all disppearing into the kitchen of la maison Fleuri. He wondered where André was and why he was so often absent from Paris. Was he no longer an attentiste? Had the myopic fool become an active résistant? Laval decided to give Marchand's name to the

Gestapo. That was the best way to keep him out of trouble, to make him realize that he was not free to do as he pleased, impregnating his wife and talking of de Gaulle and other matters that did not concern him.


In the elegant sixteenth arrondissement, in the house in the place Victor Hugo, three officers of the SS were putting on their overcoats, adjusting curved brimmed hats, and marching out to waiting transport. In the basement of the house, the old woman had just arrived to cook lunch. She was surprised to find pans full of vegetables and soup on the stove and a goose cooked to a turn in the oven. Later, when the doorbell rang, Cook hurried to answer, and found Chambord and his wife on the step. They had been forced to hand over their keys to the officers and were unable to enter their own house. Both were pale, tense, and surprised that Oberst-Gruppenfuhrer Heydritch had kept his word. Carrie hurried outside to the garden to inspect her plants. Chambord went to the liquor cabinet and poured himself a large brandy. Cook expressed her relief at his safe return.

"Is my daughter in her room, madame?"

"No, sir, I called Mademoiselle when I arrived at one but she was out. She's been cooking, though, and we have a lovely goose for lunch."

Chambord stared in amazement. What did the old fool mean, Marie-Claude had been cooking? Marie-Claude could not make coffee, let alone complicated meals in the oven. He replied loftily, "My daughter has never cooked in her life, madame, you must be mistaken."

"Come and see for yourself, sir."

"But she never goes out!"

Cook shrugged and disappeared to the basement. Chambord went to the bottom of the stairs and called loudly, "Marie-Claude! Marie-Claude! I'm home."

Impatient and puzzled, he returned to the drawing room and poured another brandy. Perhaps Marie-Claude had gone to stay with friends in order to avoid a confrontation with the officers? That must be what had happened, she had always had such a terror of being alone with men. Chambord sat in his favorite chair, realizing suddenly how exhausted he was. After a while, he closed his eyes and allowed his thoughts to drift. How wonderful it was to be home, how soothing the silence and the snow that made every street in the quarter seem so clean and unsullied. As he dropped off to sleep, Chambord snored gently.

Upstairs in the pink bedroom, Marie-Claude was staring fixedly at the ceiling and trying to make sense of life. Her body was covered with bruises, and blood had congealed on her thighs and on the sheets. She wanted to get up, but she felt so strange that she could only lie still, struggling to survive. They had gone, the men who had hurt her. Had they gone? Her eyes stared wildly round the room as echoes of their laughter returned to terrify. Then she heard a voice calling her name—the voice of her father. Was it her father? Or was it one of the men mimicking his throaty voice? Marie-Claude opened her mouth to answer, but no sound came because her lips were swollen and she was too disoriented to speak. She shook her head, fumbling to wipe tears from her eyes. How long the nightmare had lasted. The Germans' garden of delight had been her purgatory, the hell threatened by priests in the Catholic Church for sins imagined or committed. She moved her legs warily, drawing them up in fetal comfort, and flinched when a cloud passed over the winter sun, casting a shadow on the door. Heydritch had returned! Had he returned? She tried to sit up, to fend off the mouths and hands and the thrusting obscenities that had driven away her reason. Her eyes opened wide as dreadful pictures danced across her mind. They had threatened to put out her eyes, to cut off her nipples if she did not obey implicitly their commands, and she had known instinctively that that was what they really wanted to do. Now they were back—she could hear them moving in the drawing room and on the terrace. As fear turned her mind and pain drove her wild, Marie-Claude opened her mouth and screamed, a hideous, startling howl that echoed like the cry of the dying in the peaceful stillness of the house. Again and again she cried out, roaring appeals for help, her mouth frothing as she abused the black phantoms of her mind.

Chambord leaped to his feet and rushed upstairs, his heart pounding so hard he could barely move his legs. He pushed open the door of his daughter's room and stood helplessly at her bedside, stupefied in horror at what he saw. Carrie followed him up the stairs, rushing into the room and forcing herself not to scream at the gory disorder. Marie-Claude was writhing on the bed, raving unintelligibly, her naked body and bloody thighs thrashing on sheets sticky with the seminal remains of the men who had defiled her. The room had been wrecked in a bizarre orgy of destruction. Lace curtains hung in tatters over broken windows of jagged glass. The carpet was covered with mud, and booted feet had kicked and broken the dainty damask chairs. The chandelier hung askew; the dressing table mirror was cracked in two. Marie-Claude's beautiful new clothes had been torn to shreds, and the bathtub was full of the smoldering remains of gasoline-soaked furs, shoes, and silk underwear. The sin of pride had been punished with destruction.

Chambord began to sob, self-control vanishing as he tried to absorb the desecration. Carrie pushed him from the room, wincing at the broken lock. Marie-Claude was suddenly silent. Carrie looked down at her, then at the squalid remains of what had so recently been Marie-Claude's haven from the troubles of the world. She wondered where to begin, how best to do what had to be done. Then she took the phone and quickly dialed the doctor's number.

"This is Caroline Chambord. Can you come at once, Dr. Picron? There's been a terrible disaster."

"But, madame, I'm so busy. As you know, there are only a few doctors left in the city.

"Marie-Claude's seriously injured."

"So are many of my patients, madame, you know how it is at Christmastime. . . ."

"Get here at once or I'll come right over and drag you away from your goddamned fire!"

Seething with annoyance at Picron's lack of concern, Carrie slammed down the phone. Then she covered Marie-Claude with a woolen wrap and struggled to lift the small body. She ran the bath in the spare-room bathroom, sliding Marie-Claude into the water, where she lay like a log, her eyes staring emptily. Carrie washed her, changed her clothes, and put her into a clean bed, whispering reassurances she hoped the girl could hear. Until the doctor arrived, Carrie sat on the edge of the bed stroking Marie-

Claude's hands and gently brushing her hair. Depression engulfed her as she saw the helplessness of her charge, and she prayed the doctor would hurry.

After examining the patient, Picron emerged shaking his head despairingly. How did one tell a woman that her stepdaughter might never recover? He struggled to find the words to say what had to be said.

"Marie-Claude has been injured in her mind and her body. She cannot or will not tell me what happened, but I imagine that there were two or three men. They were very cruel, Madame Chambord, very cruel indeed. All Germans seem to enjoy inflicting pain. That is something we have come to accept, is it not?"

Carrie wiped tears from her eyes. Marie-Claude was impossible, a troublemaker and telltale, a girl she had always despised. She thought of the times she had wished her stepdaughter dead, all the times Marie-Claude had gone to her father to tell tales, and all the quarrels that had resulted from her troublemaking. Carrie sighed despondently. In the very beginning she and Charles Chambord had been happy. Then, gradually, as Marie-Claude grew older, she had influenced her father against his wife by pointing out with derision that his friends found Carrie odd, alien, a strange wife for one of the richest bankers in Paris. It had not been long before Chambord had paid heed to what his daughter said, and that had been the beginning of the end of Carrie's marriage. She wondered in perplexity what had made Marie-Claude despise her, and could find no valid reason. In his way, Chambord had been responsible for making his daughter spoiled and spiteful. From the beginning he had stifled Marie-Claude with affection, refusing to allow her to be disciplined, pouring money into her schooling as if she were another of his valuable investments. Despite her dislike for her stepdaughter, Carrie resolved determinedly to do her best to help retrieve what remained of Marie-Claude's sanity. No one deserved to suffer as she had suffered and would continue to suffer for the rest of her life. Carrie watched Dr. Picron packing his medical bag and making ready to leave.

"Marie-Claude will have to go to the hospital."

"Are her injuries that bad?"

"Her mind appears to be deranged, madame, and we cannot tell what she might do."

"Give her a chance, Dr. Picron. She's resilient, like all young people. I'll stay with her every minute of the day, and my husband will engage a night nurse so Marie-Claude won't be alone."

"In a clinic for the mentally sick she would have expert attention, madame."

"No! Marie-Claude wouldn't like an asylum."

"Very well, but if she has not improved substantially by next week, I shall insist."

Carrie showed the doctor out and then went in search of her husband. Chambord was in the cellar, counting the remains of his collection of port.

"Charles, Marie-Claude's very sick. I'm going to need your help looking after her. We'll have to take turns because Picron doesn't want her to be left alone. He wanted to put her in the clinic, but I said we'd take on a night nurse instead."

Chambord showed her a dusty case of port. "My father gave me these for my twenty-first birthday. He bought a hundred cases from a domaine once owned by the Empress Josephine. He had taste, I'll tell you. *He* wouldn't have made the mistakes I have." Drunk and unwilling to face reality, Chambord glowered meaningfully at his wife.

Carrie persisted. "Please listen, Charles. Your daughter is very ill. Picron wants her to go to the asylum!"

Chambord continued counting bottles, dusting them, ignoring his wife completely.

"How cold it is, Carrie, and I'm hungry. Isn't lunch ready yet? I'm so tired and so sick of all this."

Carrie turned her back on him and rushed upstairs, disgusted by her husband's weakness. As she ate lunch she began to think longingly of the hot, heady summers of New England. Wistfully she recalled how in her youth she had been popular, always surrounded by loyal family and friends, danced attendance on by young men in brand-new cars who wanted to take her dancing. She had been confident of the future, certain of her own abilities, an eternal optimist to whom nothing seemed daunting. But since marrying Charles Chambord, Carrie admitted to herself, she had felt like an outcast, patronized by his friends, despised by his daughter, and eventually denigrated constantly by him for not being French and, worse, for not being willing to try to appear more French. Carrie shrugged her shoulders defiantly. It was time to leave France, time to abandon the fiasco of a loveless, hopeless marriage. But first she must look after Marie-Claude, at least until her mind cleared.

While Carrie was eating a small wizened pear for dessert, Marie-Claude began to scream. Carrie rushed upstairs to the bedroom and held her tightly until she fell asleep again. For hours she remained in the room, returning after dinner to tell her stepdaughter stories about the parties they would throw when the war was over, the food she would eat when she had recovered, the fun she would have when she went to finishing school in Switzerland. Marie-Claude stared at the ceiling, trying valiantly to understand what was being said. But the phantoms of her mind were playing tricks and frightening her with clear, cold visions of the men who had devoured her innocence and disfigured her mind. That night she began to scream hysterically, and it took Carrie an hour to calm her. The following morning Marie-Claude was catatonic, her arms held rigidly at her sides, her eyes staring wildly at the door. Carrie resigned herself to the prospect of a long wait for sanity to return.

Two days later Chambord got drunk and fell down the cellar steps, breaking his leg. And as the old year gave way to the new and snow blanketed the city in white, it took every ounce of Carrie's strength of mind not to give in, not to run away and forget her responsibilities. Then, as she was lighting the candles on the dinner table that would herald the New Year, Marie-Claude appeared in the dining room, her hair disarranged, her nightdress slipping from her shoulders.

"What day is it today, Carrie?"

"Tonight's New Year's Eve, and tomorrow all the bad things from last year get left behind."

"Men came to the house, Carrie, they . . ."

Tears began to fall, and Marie-Claude sobbed desolately, despairingly. Carrie held her like a sick child, silencing her husband's questions with a glance.

"Why don't you join us for dinner, Marie-Claude? We thought of asking you, but I said you'd be too tired."

Marie-Claude sat down close to Carrie, her back rigid, her face empty of expression. Hungrily she ate a bowl of soup and drank a glass of wine. Then, without warning, she rose and walked from the room. Chambord watched his daughter with fearful eyes. At the door Marie-Claude turned, struggling to voice her thoughts.

"Did you know that Suzanne is in love with a German? I saw a note she wrote him in his bedroom."

Chambord cursed and Carrie held her breath as Marie-Claude began to laugh hysterically.

"Imagine being in love with a German! I could *never* love one, never, never, never. . . . Oh, God! Please let me die, let me die, let me die quickly."

Marie-Claude ran upstairs, sobbing incoherently, and Carrie decided to let her be. Only time would heal the damaged mind.

At midnight, as the clocks chimed twelve, Carrie thought of the bells that used to peal all over Paris to herald the New Year. She roused her husband, and they took glasses and their last bottle of vintage champagne to Marie-Claude's bedroom. As he turned on the light, Chambord dropped the tray in horror and disbelief at what he saw. Marie-Claude was swinging like a rag doll from the chandelier hook in the ceiling, a woven silk scarf around her neck, her legs revolving slowly, so her body cast grotesque shadows on the wall. The violet eyes were wide open, staring in disbelief at the cruel blow fate had dealt. The once pale, elegant face was puce and puckered, and they knew at once that she was dead.

Carrie began to cry. Then, as she sat despairingly at the side of the bed, she saw a pad of sheets covered with Marie-Claude's childish handwriting. Flicking through the pages, Carrie flinched at the tragic tale. Their names and ranks, their strange tastes and the agony each had caused were all clearly described. It was as if Marie-Claude had been given one precious moment of lucidity before plunging inescapably into the vortex of self-destruction. Carrie showed the sheets to Chambord. Then she folded them and hid them away, engraving the names Marie-Claude had written forever on her mind in case the murderers were tempted to return.

That night, when the body had been removed and her husband was asleep, Carrie went to the bureau in her bedroom and took out her gun. In the days of her youth she had enjoyed shooting and had won prizes at county fairs. Satisfied that the gun was in good condition she returned it to its hiding place and retired to bed. Someday, surely, the men would return, determined to re-capture the ecstasy they had found. Before she went to sleep, Carrie repeated their names: Heydritch, Rika, Hammerstein. Marie-Claude had written of their promise to come back and of her determination to thwart them. Outside, an icy wind froze the snow. Carrie thought it was like living in a tomb.

# CHAPTER FOUR

## *New Year, 1941*

On New Year's Day Jacques was due to return to Germany. In the early morning hours he had lain in bed going over every happy hour spent with the family, every laugh they had had, every mouthful of food Nathalie had cooked for him. He stroked his wife's hair lovingly, wondering why she had sobbed so desperately when they made love. Crying was not her style—whatever could have happened to so distress her? Jacques shrugged sadly. War was hateful and disturbing. Probably when the Germans had gone from Paris Nathalie would return to her former high spirits and be well again. As he dressed, he looked out the window. On the steps, the old priest from St. Pierre was on his way to morning mass. Father Valery was talking animatedly with a disreputable-looking fellow who saluted a German officer with ridiculously exaggerated respect. Then, when the officer had passed, the unkempt fellow turned and made a rude sign at the German's back that indicated that his father had not been married to his mother. Jacques laughed delightedly, wondering what business the priest could possibly have with such a wanton. He was surprised to see the two men pause as they reached the middle level of the steps, and Father Valery hand the man money before going on his way with a trusting handshake. Jacques was suddenly afraid that the old man was placing himself in jeopardy. Valery had always been a maverick, taking on anyone and everyone, even the Vatican when he disagreed with its edicts. Now, surely, he was an active résistant. Jacques looked at the clock, hoping fervently that Laval was still asleep.

In the kitchen, Suzanne was making breakfast. Hans was reading a Swiss newspaper confiscated from a vendor and calling to Suzanne to hurry with the eggs. Jacques thought what a handsome pair they were. Then he checked his thoughts and tried to force himself to remember that Hans was part of the occupying army—but it was impossible to think of the handsome young man as anything but a friend. The family liked Hans and trusted him implicitly; indeed, Nathalie had gone so far as to say that she would be utterly lost without him. Jacques shook his head in confusion. War was the great divider, an inefficient means of resolving conflict that decimated the population and ended in desecration. He thought for a moment of David, wishing he had told Suzanne of the wanted posters he had seen all over the East: DAVID CHAMBORD, ENEMY OF THE FATHERLAND, WANTED BY THE GESTAPO. But what was the point of letting her know that David's life was worth substantial money to the quisling who could find and report him? Jacques prayed fervently that his daughter's fiancé would never be tempted to come back to Paris. The new commander of the interrogation unit was said to be a man who enjoyed his work. Standartenfuhrer Gunther's reputation was known in Germany and in every occupied country where his actions had led to countless deaths. Jacques shuddered, and Suzanne teased him about his daydreaming.

"What's wrong, papa? You look as if you've seen a ghost."

"I was thinking of Standartenfuhrer Gunther of the SS, who's just taken charge of activities in the avenue Foch."

Hans looked up from his paper, surprised.

"I thought Tristan Slagel was in charge of interrogations."

Hans ate his eggs and buttered his toast as though unaware that they were discussing matters that had connection with his own life. Jacques smiled indulgently, knowing instinctively that Hans was as horrified as he by the happenings in the house of horror. He explained what he had heard.

"On the train there was a compartment reserved for Gunther. The blinds were drawn and no one was allowed to go near except his personal guard. Apparently he likes working with Slagel, that's why he's been transferred to Paris. I found out all about him from one of the guards on the train. The poor fellow wasn't at all happy with the responsibility of trying to keep Gunther alive, and I didn't blame him—I think he should have been destroyed at birth."

Hans looked quickly toward Suzanne, aware that she had a dread of the men who operated from the house in the avenue Foch. Anxious not to upset her further, he changed the subject.

"At what time will your train leave, sir?"

Jacques smiled at the adroit reversal.

"I'm to report by three to the Gare de Lyon."

"I shall be at the office for some time today, so I shall not be here to wish you bon voyage."

Suzanne looked surprised.

"It's New Year's Day, why are you going to the office?"

"I have to collect a present for you which I forgot to bring the other day."

Nathalie appeared from her bedroom. Though she greeted them cheerily, Suzanne noticed that her mother was pale and listless. She debated what could be bothering her. Was it that Maman had found it difficult, or even impossible, to accept her husband's affection, feeling herself soiled by Altdorfer's greedy advances? Or had she told Jacques and suffered because of his reaction? Suzanne looked across the table to her father, who was arguing cheerfully with Hans. He looked so happy that she felt sure he knew nothing of what had happened. She wondered if her mother had caught a chill, and she put more wood on the fire, anxious to relieve Nathalie's melancholy.

At twelve thirty Jacques left the house. Hans walked with him as far as the boulevard and then made his way to the office in the Champs-Elysées. Jacques sauntered along, pausing to buy a second-hand newspaper at a stand near the Villemin Hospital. At the corner of the rue de Nancy, Jacques had a beer at the counter of a shabby bar. A young lad approached, offering cigarettes and promising coal at a dozen times its real market value. Jacques told him sharply to go away. He thought angrily of the Germans occupying the city and what they had done to the lives of ordinary people. Enemy soldiers had bought up all the lace, liqueurs, jewelry, perfume, and luxury clothing. They had commandeered all supplies of fuel, so only the occupying force had warm offices and homes. Fresh food and vegetables and fish from the Channel ports went straight to German-controlled restaurants and hotels where high-ranking officers lived. And Germans controlled the black market, which operated in everything from gold coins to goat cheese. Jacques hurried from the bar as a bread-coupon forger arrived to distribute his work among the clientele. Would Paris ever be as she had been? Jacques wondered. Would she ever rise like a phoenix from the ashes of war and be a great lady as in times past? He walked on, disturbed by scenes of poverty and deprivation all around.

Suzanne ran down the steps of the rue Foyatier and in the direction she knew her father would have taken. Unwittingly he had left behind his wallet, containing his train pass and identity card, and she hurried to overtake him. The pristine snow of previous days had turned to slush, and each time a van or truck passed she had to leap against the wall to avoid getting soaked. Reaching the boulevard de Magenta, Suzanne passed the Ville-min Hospital and far ahead, near the place St.-Laurent, she saw her father stepping out of a bar, adjusting his shoulder sack, and changing the heavy suitcase from one hand to the other. She called to him, but Jacques did not hear because the wind was howling and the sound of German sirens deafened his ears.

In the place de la Bastille three German squad cars ground to a halt. Jacques paused on the pavement near a woman and a young lad with long hair, obviously one of the city's rebellious zouzous. Jacques smiled at the lad's courage, wondering where he had stolen the jacket he was wearing and the leather shoes that looked a size too large. A German officer called to the boy to follow him; another turned to Jacques, ordering him to follow the boy. The two stood against the wall, and Jacques saw, as he looked around, a poster advertising a new production of *Macbeth* at the Théâtre Montparnasse. He shrugged, waiting for the Germans to return to explain what they wanted. As he blew on his hands in the icy winter wind, a gray steel truck appeared, full of men from the local jail. The men were herded out and lined up with Jacques and the boy against the bright-colored poster on the wall. Looking down, Jacques was shocked to see the zouzou crying.

"What's wrong with you! Fancy crying in front of the Germans."

"They're going to shoot us."

"Nonsense, we haven't done anything wrong."

"Haven't you heard what they do? Where've you been all these weeks?"

"I've been working on a farm near the Rhine."

The boy spat on the ground and wiped his nose on his sleeve.

"I curse every one of them, but who's going to take care of Maman when I'm dead?"

Suzanne reached the place de la Bastille, halting sharply at the corner of the square. Twenty men were standing in line against a blue-and-purple play poster, and Suzanne started when she saw that her father was one of them. She recoiled in horror as another gray truck appeared, carrying tin-helmeted German soldiers and a machine gun. Suddenly she knew what was going to happen. For weeks the Germans had been collecting hostages from local jails—men who had been arrested for being out after curfew, unwise black marketeers, and the occasional drunk who broke windows in the city center. When executions were due these men were rounded up and put in crowded squares so everyone could see what happened to those who did not obey German ordinances. If the men in jail were not enough, folk were taken from the streets to augment the number.

Suzanne walked forward numbly toward the spot where the German officer was roaring orders. The machine gun was placed on the cobblestones, equidistant from each end of the line of men. Some of them were twitching nervously, and all were doing their best to look defiant. Suzanne made a sudden dash toward her father, but a soldier pushed her back and she heard Jacques calling for her to go home. She could not obey, and stood paralyzed with fear and horror. Jacques whispered to the boy at his side. The boy smiled and nudged the man next to him, till the whole line was grinning broadly. Suzanne wondered what her father could have said to so cheer the men. Conscious that she was going to see her father die, she turned away to wipe tears from her eyes. She must be brave. She must not let her father down. As she wiped her eyes she heard her father's voice singing the "Marseillaise." Soon the men at Jacques' side and everyone in the square were singing joyfully, defiantly:

> "Allons enfants de la patrie,
> Le jour de gloire est arrivé . . ."

Suzanne listened as the German officer ordered his men to be
ready. She heard the tumult of voices that drowned the metallic
clicking as the gun was maneuvered into place, and watched in
stunned resignation as the German raised his arm, lowering
it with a bark of command. Bullets spat back and forth, back
and forth, their clattering sound deafening the onlookers. The
men against the wall threw up their arms in mute appeal and
fell in the muddy snow. For a moment the song faltered, the
sound diminishing as the victims' voices were lost. Then a
challenging crescendo filled the square, and Suzanne was touched
to see the Germans hurrying to remove themselves from the
uproar.

> "Aux armes, citoyens!
> Formons nos bataillons.
> Marchons! Marchons! . . ."

Louder and louder the people sang until the enemy was gone,
their faces grim as the anthem reached its climax. When the
Germans were out of sight there was a sudden deathly silence, the
funereal still of a cemetery. No one moved, because none
wanted to be the first to look at the bloody bodies against the
wall. The sky darkened to thunder gray, subduing the light; a dog
barked, breaking the moment of trancelike immobility; and
gradually people began to go home.

Suzanne walked reluctantly to the wall and looked down at her
father's body. His face was unmarked; his right hand still clutched
that of the zouzou at his side. Only a red patch soaking his overcoat betrayed the hopelessness of her vigil. As Suzanne bent to
touch her father's cheek, she was shocked to see a solitary tear
fall on her hand. Jacques was dead. The zouzou was dead. Only
an old man groaning at the end of the line was still miraculously
alive. Men came to carry the injured man away to a nearby
house, out of reach of any loitering German patrols.

Suzanne looked up at the poster and then down at her father,
her body trembling with anger and shock. It was not so very long
ago that her thoughts had centered on singing in the theater and
getting married to David. She had planned only to have fun and
a pleasant life in the chestnut-lined boulevards of Paris. Now

she thought of nothing but survival, of outliving and outlasting those who had come uninvited to ruin French lives. And most of all she longed for Paris to be as she had been before the occupation, unsullied and everlasting, a grande dame unconquered by the rabble.

Suzanne was wondering what to do with her father's body, when a man came and told her that the corpses would be removed before the Germans could return and placed in a communal grave in the churchyard of St. Michel. She walked slowly, unsteadily home, her mind fumbling over how to break the news to her mother. The streets of Paris were unnaturally silent, as often they were after a reprisal. Parisians in nearby bars and cafés were thinking of rebellion and wondering if they dared confide in those with whom they were drinking. The complacency and resignation prevalent in the early days of occupation had eroded, and now people questioned everything, even their own fear and desire for self-preservation. For the first time the people were trying to assess how and when they could do something to help themselves, how they could force the Germans from Paris.

At the corner of the rue de Cligancourt, Suzanne bumped into Armand Lognon. He saw immediately that something was desperately wrong.

"Has something happened, Suzanne? What's wrong with you?" He took her by the arm, pulling her to a halt, and shook her gently till she looked up at him. "What's wrong, Suzanne?"

"Papa has just been shot by the Germans."

Armand put his arms around her and tried to contain her trembling.

"Where did it happen?"

"In the place de la Bastille. The Germans have a fine sense of humor."

"You saw everything, I suppose?"

"The men who were going to be executed sang the 'Marseillaise' and the crowd joined in. I wanted to sing but my throat had gone so dry I could hardly swallow. Then the machine gunner mowed them down. . . ."

They walked past a wall poster edged in black, with blood-red letters giving a list of names of men executed in a reprisal the previous week. Suzanne thought numbly that soon her father would be just another name on a reprisal notice. It was even colder than before, and walking up the icy streets of Montmartre was dangerous and difficult. Armand pushed Suzanne into a bar and ordered sweet tea and a bowl of soup. She ate as he urged and listened as he spoke.

"Wait until your mother has eaten, then tell her the news. Women faint when they get a shock on an empty stomach. You'll *have* to be strong, Suzanne. Your mother hasn't looked well for weeks. I don't know how this is going to affect her."

Suzanne continued on toward la maison Fleuri. Children of the quarter waved a greeting, but she saw nothing of her surroundings. Laval was in his bedroom window; M. Corbeil was in the back garden, clearing rotting cabbage from the slushy ground of his vegetable patch. Suzanne passed by like a sleepwalker.

When she entered the house, Suzanne smelled the tempting aroma of fresh fruit. She was surprised to see new books on the table, and her mother looking radiantly happy and relaxed for the first time since Altdorfer's departure. Nathalie took Suzanne's jacket, babbling excitedly as she hung it in the cupboard.

"Hans brought us books. He said you'd been complaining that we had nothing to read—and he brought these, too."

Nathalie touched an orange lovingly. Suzanne sat on the sofa, staring at the luxurious gifts as her mother continued to explain.

"Hans had to go back to his office for a meeting, so he won't be back till eight. I'm making fruit flan and a chicken stew for his dinner, you know how he loves chicken."

Nathalie twirled around the table, holding a bowl of ripe apricots and smelling their elusive scent. Suzanne tried to think where Hans had bought the fruit and how much it had cost.

Suddenly her mother was on guard, aware for the first time that Suzanne was shivering with fear. She sat at Suzanne's side and stroked her hands lovingly.

"What is it, Zizi, what's wrong?"

Suzanne struggled to remember what Armand had said. She should let her mother know about the calamity after dinner. She must not let Nathalie see how upset she was. She shook her head sadly, knowing she could never tell lies or keep anything from her mother, however bad. Nathalie spoke sharply, startling Suzanne into action.

"Zizi! Tell me at once what is wrong, what's the matter with you?"

Suzanne poured them each a brandy. Then she sat at the table and slid one glass over to her mother.

"There's been a very dreadful happening, maman. I don't know how to tell you."

"Your father's been hurt, hasn't he? He's had an accident— which hospital is he in?"

"Papa has been killed in a reprisal shooting."

For a moment the two women were motionless. Then Nathalie whispered softly, "It's not possible. Jacques was on his way to the station, on his way to Germany to work for *them!*"

"I saw it, maman. I'm so sorry."

Nathalie stared blindly at her daughter. Then she drank the brandy and walked mechanically to the kitchen to make dinner. It was not possible that Jacques was dead. Only a few hours ago they had been in bed together and he had asked what was wrong, why she had been so sad during his visit. Men for reprisal shootings were taken from the Feldgendarmerie except when there were not enough to make up the required number. But Zizi had said she had seen her father die. Nathalie peeled potatoes and put them in a colander. She was about to light the gas when she felt a painful constriction in her chest. For a moment she struggled to breathe normally, but the pain grew worse, spreading from breast to neck and rib to arm. She called desperately to Suzanne and slid down the wall, clutching her chest and gasping.

"I can't breathe, Zizi. Run for Dr. Remouille and tell him to hurry, the pain is dreadful."

Suzanne sprinted to the corner of the street, where she hammered on the doctor's door. There was no reply, so she knocked even harder and pressed her face anxiously against the window of the empty surgery. An old woman passing by called out, "Remouille went with all the rest of his kind when the Germans came. He won't be back, you mark my words."

Suzanne looked frantically at the door, desperate to know what to do. Panic-stricken, she called back to the old woman, "Where can I find a doctor? My mother's been taken ill."

The old woman shrugged.

"In the city, perhaps. You'll have to run down to Paris and ask in one of their fancy clinics."

Suzanne ran home, relieved to find that her mother had dragged herself from the kitchen and was sitting on the sofa, propped up on faded cushions. Her pallor had improved, and she made a brave attempt to smile. Suzanne plumped down at her side.

"Dr. Remouille isn't there, maman. He left Paris when the Germans came."

"I feel a bit better now, so don't trouble yourself. When I can I'll go upstairs to bed. There's chicken stew in the pan and potatoes peeled in the colander. Make the fruit pies for Hans, I promised him pies in return for the gifts he brought us."

Suzanne helped her mother upstairs, lifting her gently onto the bed and punching the cushions so Nathalie could sit upright, in a position in which she could breathe. Then Suzanne went downstairs and, telling herself she must do everything her mother had asked, made apple and apricot pies. She boiled the potatoes and added peas and parsley to the stew. She did not cry because her mind and body were numb, deadened by the disasters of the day. As she cooked she was thinking of her father as he lay dead on the cobblestones of the place de la Bastille. She was in a curious state of mind, beyond normality but within the confines of hysteria. Sounds meant nothing to her, and Allied aircraft bombing the suburbs no longer terrified. Even the luscious fruit and elegant books she had longed for held no pleasure, because she was unable to feel anything but grief. Now and then she went upstairs to check her mother's condition, taking a cup of beef bouillon, which Nathalie could not resist, or a solitary flower from the garden. Then, alone in the kitchen, her mind returned again to the tragic scene of the afternoon, and Suzanne wondered if she would ever forget the horror she had witnessed. Would her mind keep returning to the blood and the brains that had frothed in the gutter? Would she forever hear the rattle and clatter of the gun and the voices singing defiantly? For an hour she sat in semi-darkness, trying to calm herself. But she felt only a suffocating panic, a longing to run away from men in uniforms who would remind her of the end of family unity.

At eight thirty Hans appeared, smiling widely. One look at

Suzanne told him something was dreadfully wrong, one touch of her icy hands that she was ill or at least dazed. He threw his overcoat on the chair and ran to her.

"Suzanne, tell me, what is the matter?"

Suzanne looked at the Wehrmacht uniform and saw in her mind's eye the execution squad with its cumbersome machine gun raking along the wall. Hans felt his blood run cold as she stared through him, and for a moment he was unable to bear the condemnation and anguish in her eyes.

"Can you tell me what is wrong, Suzanne?"

"Papa was killed today by your colleagues."

Hans held his breath, shocked and unable to accept what she had said.

"What are you saying? Your father was going back to Germany."

Suzanne turned on him, her eyes blazing feverishly.

"Papa was shot by a German reprisal squad in the place de la Bastille at one thirty this afternoon."

"On his way to the station?"

"I was there, I saw everything."

"How could this happen?"

Suzanne served dinner and sat facing Hans across the table.

"How could it happen? What does it matter how it happened? Papa's dead, and all you can do is ask questions. I don't want to hear your questions. You're my enemy, *his* enemy, and the enemy of all my friends!"

"Suzanne!"

"Don't touch me and don't try to say you're sorry. All I want from you is that you bring Papa back to this house alive and well, but even a German can't perform miracles."

Hans pushed his plate away. For a moment his eyes dwelled on the books and the fruit he had bought from men with access to the impossible. He had expected Suzanne to be as happy as her mother had been with the gifts. But in a few hours everything had changed. Jacques Castel was dead and his own relationship with Suzanne irreparably damaged. Suzanne looked at him, her eyes full of contempt.

"I'll take maman something to eat. She collapsed with shock when she heard the news."

"I'm sorry, I'm deeply, truly sorry, Suzanne."

"You should be glad. Today twenty Frenchmen died. That's twenty less for you to impress with your stupid, lying broadcasts!"

Suzanne ran from the room, her eyes full of tears, her body shaking uncontrollably.

Hans took his overcoat from the chair and walked resignedly from the house. It was over. There was nothing he could ever do to make Suzanne forgive him. Nothing. He could not bring back the father she adored, and he could never eradicate from her memory the uniforms of the men who had executed Jacques Castel. In an icy wind Hans walked down the hill, wondering where to go. Local bars no longer welcomed enemy personnel, and clubs for German officers of rank bored him. The clubs were full of bloated men boasting about German power, and loitering around the entrances there were women with painted faces hoping to be invited in for a meal. Hans walked on, shivering with apprehension, shock, and bitterness. Perhaps his old room was still vacant. There at least he could be alone. He approached the bakery, relieved to see a light in the window, and after a word with the owner walked upstairs, remembering the lonely nights he had spent in the room, the tasteless food he had eaten from cans. Since arriving at la maison Fleuri he had felt at home, at peace with the world and happy despite all the tribulations of occupation. For the first time he had understood the futility of war, because the Castels were his friends. Loyalty to Germany had, of necessity, been divided and shared with them, whatever his preconceived notions of correct behavior had originally been. Once he had tried to decide what he would do if it came to a choice between Suzanne and his own military integrity, and had been disturbed to find himself unable to face the truth of his feelings for her.

As night came there was the usual hollow silence of the blackout. Hans lay fully clothed on the bed, thinking of Jacques Castel. Jacques had been a fine man, a warm, sympathetic listener and someone he had felt he could trust implicitly. What right had anyone to murder him? What right had the reprisal squads to shoot indiscriminately? That was not war, but cold-blooded murder. The German commander of Gross Paris had warned the French that he would take an eye for an eye, a Frenchman for every injured or killed German soldier. Hans frowned. In the

Bible it said that one should turn the other cheek, that to meet hostility with hostility and death with murder was to propagate the very situation one sought to avoid. He struggled to find an answer, and knew in his heart that Germany was in the wrong. Paris was the capital of France, a beautiful city beloved by its inhabitants since time immemorial. What right had the German high command to inflict its forces on the French, bleeding them dry of their lifeblood? Troops had commandeered forty thousand French locomotives, then three hundred thousand freight cars, well over half the total in all of France. These had been sent back to Germany to be melted down for munitions. Then they had stripped French farms of half a million horses and mules, destroying agriculture and ruining output. In the first year of occupation the authorities would send a million tons of food back to Germany to be fed to the starving, leaving nothing for the French. And as if that were not enough, they had made the conquered nation pay the billeting costs and an indemnity of four hundred thousand French francs. Was it any wonder that Parisians sabotaged and rebelled? The only wonder was that they had not devastated every rail line and communications center in the city.

Unable to sleep, Hans walked to his office and read the dossier on Suzanne. Once again, as he studied her photograph, the direct gaze charmed and he longed for her. Then he shook his head despairingly. Love was an illness he was never going to overcome. He sat at his desk thinking of the opening of the show at the Bal Tabarin and his joy when Suzanne had performed her spot. How beautiful she had looked in the black dress, a solitary red rose at her breast. Her innocence had exploited feelings of gallantry long dormant in every man's heart. After the show he had waited to take her home, and together they had walked through the darkest, narrowest streets of the quarter, because Suzanne was concerned for his safety and at pains to avoid a repetition of the Schulberg calamity. But now what did she really feel? Had her denunciation been merely hurt at her father's death? Was she already regretting what she had said? Or was the friendship over, nipped in the bud before it could blossom into fragrance and beauty? Hans sat alone in the empty building wrestling with his thoughts until dawn. Then, as the sky lightened, he began to long for coffee and walked to a café around the corner from the office. He nodded to col-

leagues who frequented the place, conscious that he felt no em-
pathy with them and they did their best to ignore him. Hans's
family was a military institution in Germany, and there were many
who disapproved of his decision to depart from tradition by entering a new profession as an architect. Destruction, not construction, was the mood of the moment, and annihilation of tradition
the policy. The Fuhrer's strategy had been proved effective in
Poland, Norway, and Holland. Fellow officers turned their backs
on Hans, impatient with his romantic view of the occupied city,
and after a while he returned alone to his office. It was icy cold,
but the sun was shining brightly, melting the snow and revealing
the tips of evergreen hedges in the small gardens of the eighth
district. Soon spring would come and the streets would be full of
people out for a walk, a talk, and a saunter along the boulevard.
Hans thought of the Castels' garden with its neat flower borders
and vegetable patch. There was work to be done in the garden, and
he had promised to organize it. He thought lovingly of Suzanne
digging up potatoes and boiling them with mint for dinner. Then
he shook his head, rebuking himself for yearning for what might
have been.

At seven Suzanne woke and looked at the windows of her room.
They were clear of ice because Hans had brought enough wood
and fuel to keep the stove burning overnight, at least for a few
weeks. She was tired and listless because she had not slept well.
Remorse had pounded at her mind until the small hours, and she
had wished she had known where Hans had gone so she could
follow him and apologize for her harsh words. He, of all the
Germans in Paris, was different. He understood the longing in
every Parisian heart, the desire to be free, to walk unmolested
down city streets breathing in the smell of chestnuts roasting on
autumn evenings and the heady scent of lilac in the spring. Suzanne rose, her heart heavy, her shoulders bowed because her
father's death still shocked her. How stupid she had been to quar-
rel with Hans, how hasty and ill-advised! She thought how
bleak the house seemed without the caring presence who provided
food, warmth, and the elusive glow of admiration that encouraged her to be brave.

On the way downstairs, Suzanne paused outside her mother's room and called softly, "Did you sleep well, maman?"

There was no reply, and knowing how fitfully her mother usually slept, Suzanne decided to let her be. She would make eggs in creamy cheese sauce for breakfast, a special treat made possible because Hans had brought cream and a large chunk of Trappistenkase back from Germany. Suzanne looked sadly at his empty chair, missing the cheery good morning and the light that came into his eyes whenever they were close. She opened the garden door, relieved to see the sun. In the long days of winter everything seemed much worse than it was, and the occupation appeared to be never-ending. When summer came, she knew, she would feel more hopeful, and with luck the Germans might go home.

As she cooked eggs and made coffee, Suzanne thought what she must do. She would go to Hans's office and apologize for her outburst of the previous evening. She would tell him about the pies she had made, and grovel if necessary so he would believe her penitence. She picked parsley from a pot on the windowsill and put it in a glass to decorate her mother's tray. Then, having polished the silver sauce boat on her sleeve, she dropped a wool warmer over the coffeepot and carried the tray upstairs. The room was in darkness, so Suzanne deposited the tray on the dressing table and pulled open the curtains. As she turned to greet her mother, she stared aghast at the waxy face on the pillow, the wide-open eyes and the arm outstretched at an odd angle on the counterpane. Approaching the bed in disbelief, Suzanne called frantically, "Maman! Maman!"

In her heart she knew her mother was dead, but she struggled to remember what should be done to check the inevitable. Stumbling out of the room, she ran to find a mirror to slide under her mother's nose for signs of the mist that would indicate there was still breath in the body. She was distracted when the mirror was clear. Nathalie was dead. She was now alone in the world. Alone, alone, alone—the word echoed in her head like a death knell. Why *did* David not write? Where *was* he? For a moment she wished she had never met him, so she would be saved the constant aggravation of wondering if he was still alive.

Suzanne went downstairs and ate her breakfast, moving mechanically like a puppet, her mind cranking and jangling with confusion. If it became known that Nathalie was dead, Hans would not be permitted to remain in the house. But if her mother never again appeared, there would be questions. Was there anyone she could trust besides Vivienne and Hans? Suzanne thought fearfully of Laval, shuddering as she imagined him reporting every move to his masters in the Gestapo. She must at all costs stop *him* from coming to the house. Absentmindedly she spilled coffee on the cloth, staring helplessly at the spreading stain. Was it possible to concoct a lie of such dimensions? Was it possible to pretend Nathalie was still alive? Suzanne's mind turned again to thoughts of her father and the events of the afternoon when she had seen him die. Then she wondered if she could ask Janine to come and stay. She rejected the idea because Janine was having an affair with Leutnant Weber, who would want to call at all hours of the day and night and who would surely know of Hans's presence. She had never previously considered the possibility of being unable to confide in Janine. Now she often caught herself guarding her words and carrying on superficial conversations with her best friend because she was afraid to talk of things that really troubled her. Was war responsible for her change in attitude? Suzanne thought it was. War changed everything, upending ideas long ingrained in the mind and disappointing when loyalties weakened.

When she had washed the dishes, Suzanne put on her coat and walked briskly from the house. She paused to have a word with Mme. Roger at the corner café and then half ran, half walked to the boulevard, where she caught a bus to the Arc de Triomphe. When she neared Hans's office she began to run because she was frantic to see him. On the stairs of the Propagandastaffel she collided with Leutnant Weber. Weber frowned, remembering Suzanne's face from their previous encounter. What was the Castel girl doing in the office? He paused to question her.

"Where are you going, mademoiselle?"

Suzanne wondered how to convince Weber that she was in the office on legitimate business. Then she had an inspired thought.

"Janine Joel asked me to call here to leave a message for a friend."

Weber looked pleasantly surprised.

"And what is the message and the name of her friend?"

"He's called Herr Zimmer."

Weber beamed, and Suzanne was relieved that Janine had confided her pet name for him.

"What is the message you wish to give to Herr Zimmer?"

"Janine said she'll meet him at the Bal Tabarin after the show this evening."

"I hear you are working with Janine?"

Suzanne thought it best to affect respect. "Yes, sir, I am."

Weber eyed her with suspicion.

"May I ask who signed your work permit?"

Alarm bells sounded in Suzanne's head, and she lied desperately.

"I don't know who he was but he took over from you when you had to go out. I'm very grateful to you, Leutnant Weber, for telling the clerk what to do."

Weber passed her on the stairs and left the building, puzzled by the strange statement. He decided to check the signature on her work permit when he returned and so find out which clerk had dared defy him.

Suzanne rushed upstairs to the next floor, pausing at each door until she reached office number eight. When she knocked, she was relieved to hear Hans calling for her to enter. His face lit with pleasure when she stood shyly in the doorway.

"Suzanne! Thank you for coming. I've been trying to work, but I couldn't stop thinking about you."

"I need your help, Hans."

"And I need your company."

"Can you come home at once?"

Hans looked into the stricken face and knew that Suzanne was close to tears.

"Is Madame ill again?"

"Maman died last night. When I took her breakfast, she was already cold."

Hans gripped her body, his mind struggling to make sense of this second tragedy. Then he went to his desk and told Suzanne what he thought it best to do.

"Go home, I will follow as soon as I can. I shall ask my doctor to sign your mother's death certificate, that way no one will know what has happened. We must say nothing of her death to the neighbors, not even to Vivienne, because if the news comes out I shall have to leave, and I do not wish you to be alone."

"What about Laval?"

"The collaborator?"

"He's always asking questions, and when he does he expects a reply."

"Tell him Madame is ill with heart trouble and cannot be disturbed."

"What if he tries to search the house?"

"There's no reason for that."

Suzanne remembered her encounter with Weber.

"May I use the telephone?"

Hans nodded, and Suzanne dialed Janine's number. He watched her, admiring the narrow wrists and tapered fingers that gripped the telephone so earnestly. Everything Suzanne did she seemed to do with great intensity, and this both excited Hans and made him love her.

"Hello, this is Zizi."

"Hello, Zizi. Are you well? You sound a bit upset."

"I'm fine, thank you, but I need you to confirm a lie I just told your friend Weber."

"Of course. I love lying to the wretch."

Janine laughed merrily, and Suzanne smiled despite herself.

"And what message am I supposed to have given him?"

"I said you'd meet him tonight after the show."

"Damn! I was hoping to see Gérard."

"Weber seemed very pleased with the news."

"He would, the dirty little bastard."

When Suzanne put down the phone she explained to Hans what was happening.

"Weber asked me what I was doing in the office. I said I had a message from Janine, because I didn't want to say I had come to see you."

"And Janine will confirm the lie?"

"Yes. Weber also asked who signed my work permit."

"Really? What did you tell him?"

"I said a clerk signed it, a man who took over when he went out. If he checks he'll think I thought you were a clerk."

"If he checks he'll find your dossier missing."

"Is that serious?"

"Hardly. I stole it and put it in my filing cabinet."

"Shall I take it home with me and hide it?"

"Probably it would be best."

Suzanne left the office and returned home. She felt less tense despite everything that had happened, and content that Hans would soon be home. She queued for over an hour outside a butcher's shop in the Madeleine, then for twenty minutes at the grocer's on the hill. As she stood in line she listened to a new sound that had come to Paris, the clip-clop of womens' wooden shoes. No one had enough money to buy black market leather and there were no bargains in the shops, so women had improvised hinged soles. For a moment Suzanne thought of Marie-Claude, who had bought twenty pairs of shoes as soon as she knew about the occupation. Was it possible Marie-Claude might sell her a pair? She decided to call on the Chambords next time she was in the sixteenth district. The shirtmaker was hanging shallots on hooks on the door of his shop. The piano tuner was painting potato prices on his window, the seamstress offering rain-sodden cabbage at exorbitant cost. Suddenly everyone was selling food, even the antique dealers. Suzanne thought of M. Rosenberg, who had bought the brushes and clock from her mother. Would he still be in his house, or had he fled Paris with the rest? The shop had been locked for weeks and there was no sign of the antique dealer around Montmartre. Of late people had been vanishing mysteriously in the night, as if the inquisition had returned in a modern guise that was called the Gestapo.

Suzanne climbed the hill, waving to friends in the square and pausing to talk with some schoolchildren. In the rue la Vieuville she stopped to stare at a poster of David Chambord. ENNEMI DE LA RÉPUBLIQUE was written under the photograph, which was a good likeness of her fiancé. Suzanne read through his "crimes," almost cheering as she skimmed the list: sabotage, currency irregularities, attacks on German personnel, arson, and aiding undesirables to escape from France. Fiercely proud, she tore down the poster and folding it neatly put it in her shoulder bag.

Near the café on the corner Mme. Roger's youngest was playing boule with a gray pebble, and Monsieur was showing the gap in the waistband of his trousers where his paunch had previously been to a friend from the rue des Saules. Suzanne smiled, touched by the resilience of her neighbors and the unchanging atmosphere of the street. When she reached Laval's gate there was a screaming of tires. Suzanne looked around, aghast to see a low black car stopping outside the Marchands' house. Two men in leather coats entered the property; another remained at the wheel of the car, his face hidden by the familiar fedora. Suzanne ran inside her home, rushing upstairs to the spare-room window to watch as André was led away. Vivienne stood at the door, a tiny, pathetic waif just delivered of her second child. She was holding her older child by the shoulder and trying not to cry. Suzanne turned away and buried her face in her hands. Things were deteriorating rapidly. Promises made at the time of the armistice had not been kept, and now the Germans were killing at will. She wondered if André was going to be shot and if there was any hope of his escaping before arriving at the dreaded interrogation center.

Some time later Hans returned, and Suzanne ran to meet him.

"The Gestapo have arrested André Marchand."

"I know. I saw them driving him down the rue Lepic, but they were unable to hold André."

"What do you mean?"

Suzanne stepped back, looking delightedly into Hans's face as he explained.

"When the Gestapo car reached the rue Lepic a man blocked its way with a wheelbarrow full of straw. Then others came from the market and began to hack at the windows with sledgehammers. André ran away in the confusion."

"How do you know about all this?"

"I was walking home via the Parc Monceau and saw it all. I should be angry but, being acquainted with André, I was praying for his safety. Pour me a brandy, will you, Suzanne?"

Hans's face had lost its usual glossy tan, and Suzanne realized that he was severely shaken by something he had not yet revealed.

"What happened after André got away?"

Hans paused as though reluctant to remember.

"The people who were in the rue Lepic dragged the Gestapo officers from the car and killed them. I saw a midinette put her scissors in their mouths, and the fishmonger cutting their throats so casually you would have thought he was slicing cod. Then the bodies were trampled into the snow."

"What about the car, won't someone find it when they search?"

"Men came and took the car apart. In ten minutes it was all gone. Then the bodies were hung on meat hooks from the lampposts. I never saw such gruesome faces, Suzanne. It made me pray that if I am ever lucky enough to father children they will never experience war."

For an hour they sat calming each other until the atmosphere in the house brightened to normality. Hans's doctor arrived at one and left ten minutes later, having made the necessary examination of the body. Suzanne served lunch, and Hans told her what he planned.

"Madame will be buried outside Paris. Dr. Meyer will tell us where at a later date. I'm sorry you won't be able to be there, Suzanne, but it's too risky for everyone concerned."

Suzanne felt suddenly profoundly moved by the thought of her mother being buried without the benefit of a blessing. Hopelessly confused, she felt unable to go on talking normally, acting as though nothing had happened, and she began to cry not just for the loss of her mother but for the loss of her own certainty about David. Hans made coffee and held her to his chest. Then the doorbell rang and Vivienne arrived, her eyes red with tears.

"You know the Gestapo came and took my André away?"

"Tell her what you saw, Hans."

Hans poured coffee and cut slices of apricot pie, handing them to the two women and giving his handkerchief to Vivienne so she could wipe her eyes. He wondered whether it was wise to tell what he had seen, because to divulge his presence in the rue Lepic was to admit that he had done nothing to help his countrymen. One look at Vivienne's desperate face changed his mind.

"Your husband escaped, madame, and the officers of the Gestapo were killed by the crowd."

"Are you telling the truth?"

"Of course. Why should I lie?"

"To comfort me, perhaps."

"I saw their throats cut and heard their screams, madame. Your husband ran away in the direction of the cemetery of Montmartre."

"I wonder where André has gone."

"He will have gone to join the résistants. There are more of them every day."

Waking from a moment of reverie, Suzanne brought David's poster from her purse and showed it proudly to her friends.

"Look what I took from a wall."

Hans looked down on a strong, determined face, a firm jaw, dark curly hair, and eyes as clear and mocking as Suzanne's. He was surprised by the resemblance.

"So this is David. I believe I have seen the poster before—we have one in the office, and there are others like it in every German squad room."

Vivienne touched the photograph admiringly.

"David was always a fighter. I pray God he'll come back safely when the war is over."

When Vivienne had gone, Suzanne turned to watch Hans, who was sitting in her father's armchair examining the poster of his rival. She had always been honest about David, calling him "my fiancé," but it had been obvious that she thought him dead, and Hans wondered if the confirmation that David was alive would change things. A thousand questions flooded his mind as he looked toward Suzanne. It was said that everything was fair in love and war. Would it be fair to steal her from her absent fiancé? He was sure now that he loved Suzanne, in war or peace-time, and despite every obstacle. Suzanne sat at his feet looking into the fire, and in the warm coral glow Hans stroked her hair, watchful of the wistful expression that flickered on her face.

"Are there pictures in the fire?"

"Only pictures of the past and memories of the good times."

"And what of the future, Suzanne? Have you dreams of the future, are there good times for you and me?"

He felt her sigh and longed to touch her. The smell of soap and rose oil that clung to her body excited him, and he was glad that it was dark so Suzanne could not see the struggle he was fighting. Sensing the tension in him, Suzanne spoke.

"Are you unhappy, Hans?"

"Of course not, I am very content. Do you realize this is the first time we've really been alone?"

Suzanne looked him over with an indefinable, questioning gaze, and Hans asked himself what she was really thinking. How difficult it was to know her, how enigmatic the expression on her face. He sighed. Would there be time to delve into her mind?

Would there be time to know her as he longed to know her, deeply, lastingly, like a husband?

Suzanne was feeling confused as she sat in the firelight glow. She felt traitorous to David and afraid that the body upstairs would be aware of the treachery. Perhaps when her mother had gone from the house things would be different. Perhaps not. How did one resolve such a conflict of loyalty? Could a woman love and want two men, both with equal longing? Was it possible she had never loved David, that all she had felt for him was juvenile infatuation? Suzanne thought of the happy times they had spent together, the promises they had made, the home they planned and that she still wanted fiercely, defiantly. Then she looked up at Hans, beckoning him so he sat at her side, resting her head on his lap so she felt safe and secure. At this moment what she wanted was Hans. To long for David was to want the impossible, because he would never live until the end of the war.

Hans whispered to her, "I have some leave coming. While I'm free, will you show me Paris?"

"How? We can't be seen together, can we?"

"We could go sightseeing after the curfew, if we were very careful. I won't wear my uniform, so we should be safe. Only the neighbors in Montmartre know I'm a German officer. In the city center they will take me for a fine Frenchman."

"Would you like to see Paris in the dark?"

"I would like to see it with you."

Later men came to take away the body. When Suzanne had wept until she could weep no more, she made a pot of chocolate and sat with Hans in the stillness of the night, holding hands and dreaming.

"What will you do when the war is over, Hans?"

"I shall return to Germany to manage my father's estates."

"Have you any brothers and sisters?"

"I have two, both younger than I, and one sister, who is the youngest member of the family. Marguerite is beautiful. Papa has already had four offers of marriage for her, and she is only fifteen."

Suzanne looked at the handsome face, noting every curve and line, every flicker of a smile, every passing frown. Her heart thumped with excitement at being near him, yet she felt inexplicably dead inside. She wondered fearfully if her father's death had destroyed something precious deep within. Was she now just a hollow shell, able to talk and smile but unable to think of anything but incipient death and calamity?

Sensing her momentary depression, Hans said he was ready for bed. They turned out the lights and walked upstairs together, parting on the landing and closing the doors of their rooms. Hans lay awake thinking of Suzanne, his body on fire though he knew that this was no time to pursue love. Suzanne was still numb with shock at the double tragedy that had hurtled into her life so unexpectedly. It was best to wait until she had settled to the idea of being alone. In her bedroom, Suzanne lay thinking that she would move Hans into the main bedroom the next morning. There was no point in his using the cramped spare room when a better one was available. She smiled as she remembered childhood years when she had rushed to her parents' room in the early hours of each new day to snuggle in between their warm bodies. She wondered if Hans was asleep, and tossed restlessly from side to side, unable to settle. At midnight she crept from her room into his and for a moment stood looking down on him as he lay sleeping. Then, in the moonlight, she kissed his cheek, savoring the country smell that lingered on his skin and closing her eyes as waves of longing flooded her soul. Gently she pulled the bedclothes up to cover his neck, returning to her room vibrant with longing. Wearily, she smiled. Only a few hours ago she had thought herself an empty shell. Now she was warm and hungry for love. Controlling desire, Suzanne lay barely moving because she wanted to preserve the brief moment of intimate contact with the man she adored.

In the bedroom across the landing, Hans opened his eyes and sat up against the pillows. He was exultant. Suzanne had kissed him. Suzanne had come secretly to his room in the darkness to plant an innocent token of regard on his cheek. He had feigned sleep, but his body had felt the intoxicating triumph that comes from being loved. He wondered what Suzanne would think of his home in Lindau, the stables full of fine horses, the stone castle on the banks of the lake. For a moment he ached with homesickness. Then he thought again of the girl in the next room, and closed his eyes in ecstasy. Tomorrow he would accompany

Suzanne to the Bal Tabarin. Then they would go adventuring, curfew or no. They would walk together in the silent streets of Paris, hidden by the darkness and protected by the night. And someday he would show her how much he adored her. Hans tried to sleep, but at dawn he was still making plans. Tomorrow and the next day they would be together, and with luck he would never let Suzanne go. All he now wanted was to survive the war and live forever protecting and adoring her.

At seven the smell of coffee roused Hans, and he leaped up happy in the knowledge that this was the beginning of a new and exciting period in his life, when the sun would shine amid the hazy grayness of war. Outside, the snow had melted and the rooftops were bathed in watery sunlight. Hans had never felt so content.


Laval also was eating breakfast and digesting the contents of a letter of instruction he had just received from the Gestapo command. He smiled slyly, pleased that they had taken note of his report.

# PART II

# CHAPTER FIVE

*May, 1941*

Suzanne rose at five. She was excited because today was the first of May, the traditional day of lovers. Every Frenchman left in Paris would present the lady in his life with a token in the form of a sprig or bunch of muguet de bois. Rich dilettantes with a desire to impress would give pretentious bouquets suffocated in cellophane, young lovers would exchange simple tributes, and she had a surprise stolen from the Parc Monceau for Hans.

She ground coffee and put it in the pot. Then she went to the garden and inspected the pear blossoms, the beanrows, and the herbs that were flourishing around the edges of the beds. Hans had done well with the garden in such a short time, considering the hostile winter and the unusually dry spring. Out of the corner of her eye Suzanne saw Laval, still in his nightcap, staring at her from the attic window of his home. For a moment she shivered with apprehension. She had kept Laval's curiosity satisfied by telling him her mother was confined to bed with heart trouble, and Hans's doctor had called every week to foster the lie. Then three days ago, when Laval had insisted on calling at the house to see Madame, Suzanne had been forced to tell him that her mother had gone away to stay with her sister in Versailles. Laval had almost choked with rage and suspicion.

Suzanne held a sprig of lavender under her nose, considering the lies she had poured out to calm him, the compromise she had been forced to make to satisfy Laval's concern. From the beginning of the previous week Vivienne Marchand had come after work, around nine o'clock, to sleep in the house, chaperoning Suzanne's nights alone with Hans. Vivienne's mother-in-law had moved into her house many months previously to look after the children while she worked, so they were satisfied no one would suffer from the nightly absence. Suzanne thought the whole business ridiculous. If she and Hans were going to have an affair they could do so at any hour of the day, not just at night, when Vivienne appeared to sleep in la maison Fleuri. She had thought herself in no need of a chaperone, whatever Laval might believe, but as spring came and the scent of blossoms filled the air, Suzanne knew that her feelings for Hans had reached the point of decision. She wanted him, right or wrong, but she could still not equate her feelings for Hans with her love for David. Was it possible to love two men? Or did she love neither? Was she just impatient for love? Or was Hans the symbol of her rebellion against the war and Germany and David, who had vanished when she needed him most?

Suzanne shook her head in confusion, deciding not to think of such a vexing problem on such a beautiful day. She drank a cup of coffee and remembered the exciting times she and Hans had enjoyed in the months since January, her eyes misting sentimentally as she relived their adventures. At least once a week they had ventured into the city to marvel at buildings Hans had only dreamed of during his days as a student. They had held hands in the Palais Royale, kissed in the place des Vosges, and wandered under the elegant arches of the rue de Rivoli in pitch-darkness brightened only by the moon. Once they had almost been caught by a German patrol, and on a dark February evening they had been clambering over the garden wall at two in the morning when they spotted Laval pacing restlessly back and forth on his back porch. The tax collector had developed insomnia, and Suzanne wondered what was keeping him awake. Was his conscience beginning to prick, or was something else the cause of his deteriorating stability? She dismissed thoughts of the collaborator with an impatient shrug. Now that spring was warming the city with sunshine, she had decided to show Hans some of the sights of Paris during the daytime. He had suitable clothing bought from black marketeers and chosen with the intention of giving him a Gallic air. His French was flawless, so there seemed no valid reason why they should not enjoy themselves once they were out of Montmartre. Suzanne thought of the places she wanted to show Hans, the Bois with old men playing boule under the willow trees, the bird market on the quai de la Mégisserie, and the flower sellers of the Ile de la Cité. She would take him to the Parc des Buttes Chaumont and to the dark cloisters of Notre Dame. As she made breakfast, Suzanne's mind raced excitedly with plans for the summer. She was taking bread rolls from the oven when Vivienne appeared.

"I slept like a Vincennes drunk, and my hair looks like it."

"It's getting very long. Why don't you plait it and tie it on top of your head?"

Suzanne put coffee, rolls, and a pot of red plum jam before her companion, and Vivienne cast a curious glance at her young friend.

"Why are you up so early, are you still sleeping badly?"

Suzanne shrugged, and Vivienne noticed an air of controlled excitement about her. She sighed despairingly. She had already known for months that Hans was besotted with Suzanne. Now she was forced to admit that it was possible Suzanne felt the same way. Where would it end? Vivienne accepted a bunch of mint and some spring onions from the garden and went home to make breakfast for her children. She was concerned about Suzanne because she knew that any liaison between the two young people could be perilous. Vivienne saw Laval at his window and frowned, furious at his constant vigilance. Laval claimed to be a patriot and in the name of France denounced his neighbors. Hans, on the other hand, was supposed to be their enemy. Vivienne thought wryly how she cherished the German's friendship and longed to see Laval dead. War was total confusion, demolishing ideas long ingrained in the mind and making nonsense of conventional loyalty. As she prepared to go to the factory Vivienne let her mind dwell on the flush in Suzanne's cheeks, the tension in her body, the brightness of her eyes. The girl was in love. For a moment Vivienne was shocked. Suzanne was in love with a German! As she chattered to her children, Vivienne conceded that Hans was easy to adore. She tried not to think of Suzanne's predicament. Everything would be resolved in the end. There was nothing to do but pray for her.

When the clocks chimed seven, Hans sat up in bed. Today was the first of May and he had some surprises for Suzanne. He leaped up and looked out the window, smiling because the sun was shining and there was a smell of magnolia in the air. As he looked around the now familiar room he was happy. From below came the scents of morning—new-baked rolls, coffee, and rare smoked bacon Suzanne had begged from a susceptible farmer in les Halles. In the living room he kissed Suzanne and settled at the table, eyeing her expectant face and loving her so much he could barely keep from throwing his arms about her and drowning her mouth with kisses. Suzanne handed him a blue glass vase in which she had placed three sprigs of lily of the valley and a curl of maidenhair fern. As she kissed his cheek she whispered, "I stole it from the Parc Monceau because I wanted to be sure I could give you a token. Papa used to buy Maman a bucketful, but this is the best I can do."

Hans left his breakfast untouched and took her to the garden shed. Blinking in the darkness, Suzanne watched as he waved his hands like a magician.

"Voilà! Pour toi, mademoiselle."

Hans turned a switch and the shed was lit with light from a solitary ceiling bulb. Suzanne looked up and saw that he had fixed a shelf around each of the walls, painted it green, and placed on its surface dozens of tiny pots, some blue, some white, some pink, each one containing a lily of the valley plant. Her face lit with surprise, and as Hans turned out the light she threw herself at him, whispering the phrase she had never dared say or even think before.

"I love you, Hans. . . . You must think me brazen to say it, but I love you."

Hans held her close, afraid to break the perfection of the moment. Then he bent his head and kissed her, not the loving gentle kiss of a brother but the thrusting, urgent, demanding kiss of a lover. The kiss took her breath away and Suzanne closed her eyes, allowing herself to drift to a secret place that felt like paradise. When she stepped back, she looked questioningly up at Hans. Then she thought of Laval and knew she must hurry

back to the house. Hans put the pots on a tray and carried them
back to the living room.

"My bacon has gone cold."

"Those little pots of muguet are worth the inconvenience of
cold bacon. Thank you for a lovely surprise, Hans."

They ate in silence. Then Hans asked what she was thinking.
Suzanne bit her lip and remained silent, too excited and apprehensive to speak. They drank more coffee, their eyes full of longing, uncertainty, and tacit agreement. And as the sun rose high
in the sky and the house was lit with a warm golden glow, Hans
thought it time to say what he had been wanting to say for
months.

"You know I want you."

"I know."

"How do you feel about me?"

She hesitated, unable to explain all the thoughts that were
crowding her mind. Hans pressed her for a reply.

"Since the first time we met in the office I've been wanting to
care for you, Suzanne, to give you everything I have, and to be
with you always. At first it seemed an impossible dream, but
now I don't know. You said you love me, but do you *really*
understand all that means?"

She kneeled at his side, stroking his face and putting a finger
over his lips to silence the questions. Her eyes told him all he
wanted to know and after a moment's hesitation Hans took her
in his arms and carried her upstairs. In the bedroom where once
her parents had slept, Suzanne looked at the faded Spanish bed-
spread, the rose flowered mirror frames, the lanterns Nathalie
had bought from a gypsy peddler in the Midi. Hans took off her
robe and led her gently to bed, lifting her nightdress and throwing it to the floor. Suzanne shivered violently because she had
never been naked with a man before. She had waited so long
for love, dreaming the foolish dreams young girls enjoy until
the images became insufficient and unsatisfying. She lay in bed
watching Hans undress, remembering the days before the occupation when longing had plagued her nights and she had feared
dying before she felt the tantalizing intrusion of a man's body.
In those days she had imagined this moment would happen
with David, that he would teach her about love and make her

truly *his* woman. For a moment Suzanne felt bitter pangs of regret. Then Hans was at her side, holding her close to his chest. Suzanne forgot everything as she listened to the drumming beat of his heart mingling with the fluttering of her own. She longed to please him, though she had no idea what to do to make him content, and all the while Hans was whispering reassuring, loving words that made her writhe with longing. At last he held her gently against the pillows and edged closer and closer until theirs were no longer separate bodies. Suzanne cried out, her mind rushing along dazzling corridors of delight. She closed her eyes, enjoying the tingling spasms of passion until a flutter of ecstasy heralded the sunburst of release and she heard herself calling out as Hans's body exploded in her own. For a while they lay still, half drowsy, half drunk on the heady wine of fulfillment. Eventually Suzanne sat up on her elbow, kissing her lover's cheek and tracing her finger along his upper lip.

"I didn't expect love to feel like that."

"Was it better or worse than you imagined?"

"A million times better, and a thousand times different. I love you, Hans."

"How do you love me?"

"I love you as I love bluebells in the spring."

Suzanne burrowed her head on his chest, sniffing the freshness that had first made her want him.

"Have you decided what we're going to do today? We could go to the park or to the Ile de la Cité. Hans, say something, don't fall asleep."

"It's been so long since I made love, I am out of practice."

"We'll practice often."

"Wicked child, and I thought you were so innocent!"

Suzanne closed her eyes, pretending the war did not exist. Despite her endeavors she kept remembering how the nightly broadcasts smashed hopes of an early end to the gangrenous spread of hostility. Germans were clashing with the British in the desert of Africa. Germans were conquering the Allies at Nofilia, El Agheila, Mersa Brega, and Benghazi. Would it never end, this march of steel on the world's soft belly? Once she had prayed for the conflict to be over, whatever the outcome. Now, after love, Suzanne did not know what she wanted. When the war was over Hans would return to his castle in the mountains, and whatever he might say, there would be no future for her in Germany. She listened as he talked, content for the moment to let fate have its course. Hans was teasing her gently and telling her of his plans for the two-day leave.

"I've decided what to do today. We will leave the house and meet in the bar next to that building in the rue Fontaine where the concierge has fish eyes and is always knitting socks."

"Where shall we go?"

"I want to see the Café des Deux Magots."

"And La Coupole?"

"There too, but I can't resist the Deux Magots because I read that waiters take a vow never to smile at the customers."

"Then where?"

Hans thought awhile, stroking Suzanne's shoulders and sniffing the smell of roses that always reminded him of her. He wondered what she would most enjoy, what to do to make the day indelible. At all costs he must keep his special secret. Waiting for her approval, he continued.

"Then we shall go to the flower market and then to say our prayers at La Sainte Chapelle."

Suzanne thought of the building, one of her favorites in the city, a stained-glass pavilion of splendor supported by pillars etched with gold. How well Hans had remembered her reminiscences of the winter months. She kissed him passionately, burning with longing for his body and touched by his consideration.

"Tell me, what else will we do?"

"Then, my beautiful Suzanne, I intend to surprise you."

Suzanne bit his ear, and Hans took her into his arms, tempting her with his need and teaching her that there are a hundred ways to soar on silver clouds. When the clocks had chimed nine, half past, and ten, Hans rushed to the bathroom, pretending he was escaping a villainous eastern houri. Suzanne lay back in bed, staring at the ceiling and wondering why love made her feel so alive, so warm and full and complete. She gazed sentimentally around the room at photographs on Hans's dresser, his tortoise-shell brushes, and the silk muffler bought in the rue de la Paix. What was it about him that so charmed her? She decided it was everything. The complex being that was Hans von Heinkel was a joy in every way. The contrasts within him, the forthright statements and diplomatic lies, the jokes, the seriousness, the exciting body that had waited so long. Suzanne slid cautiously to the edge of the bed and stood in front of the mirror, staring at her reflection and wondering why she looked the same as she had an hour ago. Was it possible that everything inside her had changed and nothing outwardly? She touched her cheek and smiled, thrilled by the lyrical memory of new love.

Hans went downstairs, calling that he would make them a drink before leaving. Suzanne went to the bathroom and stood under the antiquated shower, reluctantly washing away the traces of first love. As she toweled herself dry she looked again in the mirror. There were pressure marks on her chest and arms, and a blush around the nipples where Hans had tasted her. A shudder of longing thrilled as she paused to savor the events of the early morning. Then she brushed her hair and tied it with yellow ribbon. She had decided to wear a new dress, one that her mother had made too small the previous year and that now fit perfectly. Suzanne examined bands of forget-me-nots on the pattern, remembering the day when she and Nathalie had bought the material at a street market in the rue Mouffetard. It was only a year ago, and yet it seemed like ten. As she recalled the happy times she and her mother had spent before the war, Suzanne wiped a tear from her cheek. She must *not* think of unhappy things today. Today was the first of May. Today was the day she and Hans had become lovers. She wiped her eyes in the mirror and then, satisfied that she looked her best, tripped downstairs to the kitchen.

Hans looked up admiringly. "You're becoming more beautiful every day."

Suzanne blushed with pleasure and looked at the fine gray silk shirt he was wearing.

"Is that new?"

"I brought it from Germany for a special occasion."

"It's beautiful."

"I didn't know if you'd like the color, you always say you hate gray."

"You'll be the handsomest man in Paris."

Hans left the house at eleven. Suzanne followed at a quarter past.

From his window, Laval cursed grimly. What had those two been doing? And why had the German grown pots of muguet de bois? Was it to satisfy Suzanne's whim or was it a lover's tribute on the first of May? Laval looked down at Suzanne's radiant face and knew in his heart that she was changing rapidly. Was it possible the German had already taken what *he* craved? Surely the blossoming of Suzanne Castel had not happened without reason? Laval hesitated to call the Gestapo about Hans. If he was not careful, he knew, he would sound like a jealous old fool. Already he had been censured for the troubles that had ensued after André Marchand's arrest. He had been told he should have known of the hostility of the people of Montmartre and the plans of those in the rue Lepic. There would have to be a sound reason for calling the authorities about Hans von Heinkel, a valid, factual reason, not a trumped-up excuse for causing trouble. Laval paced the attic in agony because he was jealous and frustrated. Suzanne had become his obsession and he could do nothing but try to work out ways of making her aware that her life depended on his whim. Sometimes of late Laval spent hours staring into space, thinking of Suzanne, and he had begun to have strange lapses of memory when whole days disappeared from his consciousness. He looked wearily to the wardrobe that held a dozen fine suits bought with Gestapo payment. What was the point of having fine clothes when there was no one to impress? Laval wondered if he could follow Suzanne to see if she met up with Hans once they were out of Montmartre. In a city full of bicycles, he and his fellow collaborators had the only gasoline apart from that issued to German officers and staff vehicles. Laval shook his head sadly. There was no way he could follow Suzanne, no way at all. For weeks he had not dared use his car because he was too frightened to proclaim his position. Once he had been proud of his cooperation with the authorities, but now he was terrified. Only a few days previously someone had stuck a penknife in his thigh when he was drinking coffee at the crowded bar of a local café. Laval had limped home, unable to find anyone to blame for his dilemma but himself. In the past few weeks his coal bunker had been raided, and fuel bought at high cost from illegal dealers had vanished as soon as it was delivered. He could not sleep at night and was hard pressed to stay awake during the day. Laval hoped self-righteously that the Germans realized

how much he was suffering. He wondered if he should consult
a doctor about his lapses of memory, deciding it was best to tell
no one about his problem lest the Gestapo find out and abandon
him. As he looked out the window, he saw Father Valery walking
down the steps. Laval's eyes narrowed as he watched the priest
greeting a girl in a black beret. The black beret had come to
signify resistance—how dare the old fool be so open about his
allegiances? Laval decided to follow the priest, because he had
begun to suspect that mass was not all Valery was giving his
parishioners. He hurried from the house and down the steps,
catching up with the priest as he reached the place St.-Pierre.
Father Valery paused suddenly as if to catch his breath, and
Laval bumped into him in his eagerness not to be left behind.
He apologized with ill grace.

"Excuse me, father, I hadn't seen you."

"You're in a hurry, Monsieur Laval. Allow me to let you pass."

Father Valery stepped aside, but Laval stood his ground, disconcerted by the twinkle in the old man's eyes. He sniffed con-
descendingly at the priest.

"They tell me you're growing mushrooms in St. Pierre?"

"I am indeed, Monsieur Laval, and soon we'll have mushrooms
growing in all the church crypts of Montmartre. I have the knack,
you know, the way of making things flourish. And you, how are
you? I don't recall seeing you at confession since the Germans
arrived."

Laval cleared his throat nervously, eyeing the old man and
wondering warily if Valery was deliberately goading him.

"I'm too busy to come to church, father."

Father Valery nodded wisely.

"Indeed you are, Monsieur Laval. I see you up there at your
window at all hours of the day and night. What *do* you find to
do? By the way, your eyes are very red. I think you should visit
the optician. At your age eyestrain can be dangerous."

Laval nodded curtly, seething inwardly at the old man's comments. He hated Father Valery, who, despite being a priest, was
known to be able to drink every man in the area under the
table and was rumored to have once had more than a paternal
interest in his housekeeper, Mme. Bettine. Laval stamped away
down the steps, and Father Valery smiled. The collaborator was

beginning to feel the strain of betrayal, as Judas Iscariot had felt it. Soon Laval's mind would deteriorate until his usefulness to the Gestapo was diminished. Then they would discard him and he would be left friendless, with nothing but the wrath of his neighbors for company. Father Valery hoped to have the strength to forgive the tax collector his sins. He reached the chapel and called to his young assistant, Father Chanson, "Any news from Archbishop Salliège?"

"Nothing yet, father, but I'm sure he'll find a way to let us know if the children arrived safely in England."

"I just met Laval."

"I saw him yesterday and he asked me if I knew the names of my parents and my grandparents and their parents and grandparents. Can you imagine such a question?"

Father Valery laughed out loud.

"He obviously suspects that you're the only Jewish Catholic in Montmartre."

They put baskets of mushrooms on the bench and took up empty ones, which they filled with the pick of their crop. Father Chanson paused in the sun to look out over the pink rooftops of Montmartre, and Valery asked about the new children they would help escape.

"Have you heard how many there'll be this week?"

"Lognon said thirty or thirty-five, father."

Valery started, his mind racing. Such a number seemed impossible. For weeks the number of Jewish children to be evacuated from Paris had been increasing. Now another thirty or thirty-five were to be taken through enemy lines. Father Valery looked in mock appeal to heaven.

"God will help us, preferably with a large bus and a squad of German soldiers to pass us through the roadblocks."

In the peaceful stillness of the chapel yard the two priests plotted, knowing the children's escape was going to be a difficult and perhaps fatal exercise. But Armand Lognon, the escape-route organizer, would provide them with everything they needed—he always had, and would continue to do so until someone denounced him.

With a dozen baskets of mushrooms, the two set off for the nearby market. There they handed over what they had grown to local housewives, touched when the women cried at the sight of the free food they had desperately needed. That afternoon both men were to be seen giving the presbytery a thorough spring cleaning. Mme. Bettine, Father Valery's housekeeper, had broken her ankle and was supervising their actions from the chaise longue. Neighbors smiled in amusement as they passed up the steps. Father Valery grumbled that cleaning was not his métier, and the priest's laughter could be heard through the windows, relieving the tensions of the day.

Suzanne and Hans were kneeling, looking up in awe at the windows of La Sainte Chapelle. Carmine, cobalt, and green cast a dappled light on their faces, and the sense of holiness was profound. Both felt as they prayed that this was a moment of sanctification of their new relationship, and they held hands, unwilling to be parted even for a moment. From the aisle near the altar a visitation of nuns appeared, their pale faces alight with reverence. Choirboys in scarlet and white were preparing hymnbooks for evensong, and one young chorister was practicing an anthem in a clear child's voice. Hans led Suzanne from side chapel to altar, where, as a shaft of sunlight touched his hair, she kissed him. Hans allowed himself to pretend that they had just been married. The thought made him so deliriously happy he threw his arms around Suzanne, to the surprise of other visitors. From the church they went to the quayside where flower sellers with wooden carts were offering bunches of gyposophila, pots of muguet, and early carnations to passersby. Hans stopped at a cart with scarlet-painted wheels and bought pink, red, and yellow daisies, feathery-leafed love-in-the-mist, and an orange potted begonia. They continued at a leisurely pace to the quai de la Mégisserie, where they watched dog washers, poodle clippers, and old men selling birds in fragile cages to children in need of something to boss. In a café near the Louvre they drank pastis and joined in an argument about the best substitute for butter. A local woman favored castor oil, another liquid paraffin, the two provoking gales of laughter from irreverent men in the bar. Suzanne laughed merrily and Hans watched the scene contentedly, relieved that he was accepted without question.

In late afternoon, when the sun had shaded the buildings mellow rose, Hans led Suzanne around the corner to the Ritz Hotel. Once, in the coldest day of the winter, Suzanne had told him how she dreamed of luxury: "I would just like to go and register at the Ritz. I would pretend I was a foreign princess so no one would dare ask me to sign the bill." In great secrecy Hans had reserved a suite so she could indulge her favorite fantasy, to be wealthy and a lady, warm and well fed in the womb of the famous hotel. Even in wartime it was rumored that inside the gilded porticos of the Ritz Hotel want was left behind, to be forgotten in the luxury that still reigned supreme. True, there was no longer filet mignon in the restaurant, and the chefs had gone to war, but the elderly waiters had learned to improvise from what was available, and their service was impeccable. Hans looked at Suzanne's enraptured face as they registered and knew that his secret was a success. The concierge beamed at them, and a boy was delegated to take them to the bridal suite. Suzanne dissolved into peals of laughter, delighted at the realization of her dream. At four they bathed and changed, at five champagne arrived, at eight they left for a new restaurant Hans had heard about, only to find it already closed. They returned to the hotel grill room and enjoyed lamb chops. Suzanne was thrilled by the ornate dining room and impressed by the elegant linen cloth, the heavily embossed silver. The meal was delicious, the wine superb, and her glowing face made Hans feel omnipotent. He kissed her often, to the amazement of staid diners in the room.

Later in the evening they went to a club recommended by the waiter, where they giggled at nudes in red boots, black tights, and silver skullcaps, provoking the audience with a saucy chaloupé. Their nipples pointing, the rows of girls exposed their buttocks, thrusting out their hips to clients in ringside seats and encouraging those who looked rich enough to touch. Suzanne's attention wandered from the dancers across the smoke-filled room to a man whose fleshy neck and rigid stance betrayed his nationality. Another man sat at his side, a slim, almost feminine figure with ice-blue eyes in a tallow-pale face surrounded by silvery hair. The young man was dressed in black, and Suzanne saw that his boots had square toes and steel-capped heels. She shuddered, and Hans touched her hand.

"What's wrong, Suzanne?"

"I'm sure those two men are SS officers."

"My dear Suzanne, most of the men in the room are German and many will be SS officers. What's the matter, are you unwell?"

"Look at them, Hans, don't you think they're a very frightening pair?

Hans looked across the room as the older man rapped an out-thrust buttock with his cane. The chorus girl winced and ran away. The younger officer ignored his companion and the girls in the line above him. He was looking disinterestedly around the room when his eyes came to rest on Hans. For a moment their eyes met. Then Suzanne tugged at Hans's sleeve and urged him to go home.

"I'm tired, let's go back to the hotel."

"Very well."

"Why is that man so curious about you?"

"I didn't notice that he was curious."

"I wish we hadn't come here!"

"Suzanne, I am not doing anything wrong, and neither are you. But if you're worried, we'll return to the hotel."

A comedian came onstage, choking on the acrid atmosphere and telling jokes first in French, then in German. Suzanne followed Hans toward the door, relieved to be escaping the claustrophobic feeling in the club and the man who had frightened her. Blinded by the spotlight, she stumbled as she reached the velvet curtain that separated auditorium from entrance foyer. A hand gripped her wrist, and she looked up into the eyes of the young German officer she was trying to escape. His piercing gaze mesmerized her, and Suzanne felt certain he knew what she was thinking. She paled, withdrawing her arm from his grip, and making her way again to the foyer. His voice was sibilant and scratchy, as though an impediment restricted his throat, and Suzanne prayed to get away from him.

"Hauptsturmfuhrer Slagel."

"Thank you for helping me, sir."

"Your name, please?"

Suzanne wondered whether to lie. If she gave a false name and was found out, she could be in trouble. Reluctantly she answered, "I am Suzanne Castel."

Slagel was joined by his overweight companion as Suzanne

stepped into the lighted foyer. She looked around frantically for Hans, starting when the older man touched her arm.

"I hear you have already met my assistant. I am Standarten-fuhrer Gunther."

"Suzanne Castel, sir."

Gunther smiled, titillated by the fear in the girl's face. Slagel watched the two, his mouth a thin line, his eyes unblinking like the eyes of a cobra. Suzanne was relieved to see Hans coming from the cloakroom, carrying his overcoat and her wrap. She grasped the wrap and hurried with him to the door, but before they reached the street Gunther's voice held them back.

"Won't you introduce us to your friend, Mademoiselle Castel?"

Suzanne's stricken face touched a chord in Hans's heart, and he turned autocratically to the two men, nodding curtly as Suzanne introduced them.

"Standartenfuhrer Gunther and Hauptsturmfuhrer Slagel, this is Major Hans von Heinkel."

Pale blue eyes assessed Hans's tanned and handsome face, and Suzanne realized that Slagel was insatiably curious about her lover. Gunther also watched with interest, but his was of a pro-fessional nature. He was asking himself why the girl was so terri-fied and why, if she was a résistante and afraid because of their meeting, she was with an officer of the German Wehrmacht and on such familiar terms. He watched as the two made a hasty exit from the club. Tomorrow he would check the files of Major Hans von Heinkel and the record of Mlle. Suzanne Castel.

Suzanne did not stop running until she reached the Ritz Hotel, and Hans chided her for her imaginings.

"Suzanne! Those men are concerned with Frenchmen who break the law. Please try not to worry about things which do not concern you."

Suddenly Suzanne longed to be home in her own bed in la maison Fleuri. If only she could hear the clocks chiming and the cat next door meowing and the rattle of bean sticks in the garden. But she said nothing to Hans, because she was anxious not to ruin the perfection of the day. Looking around the hall of the hotel, she frowned at elderly dowagers in expensive clothes, their wrinkles clogged with makeup. Old men in the bar had purple faces and port-filled paunches, and the elevator attendant was a hunchback of eighty. Suzanne thought that in the luxury of the Ritz Hotel, more than anywhere in Paris, she felt the decay of war. The only Parisians left, or so it seemed, were the old, the infirm, and those with more money than sense. As she stepped out of the elevator, Suzanne thought how regal the place was, how homeless and false. Her fantasies of the winter had been like all fantasies, disappointing in the reality. Home was much nicer in every way than the Ritz Hotel. She would never long for the unknown again.

An hour later Suzanne was happily sipping hot chocolate and laughing at her fears, because love was reassuring and Hans's kisses had been intoxicating. She fell asleep replete and satisfied, but in the darkness she had nightmares of torture, death, and a catafalque of slimy bodies. Awake and alone with her fears, she sat up in bed listening to every creak in the corridor outside and the contented breathing of the man at her side. She decided to say nothing of her terrible dreams. It would be wanton and unpleasant to spoil Hans's leave with the foolish imaginings of a woman in love. But why had Slagel's eyes shone with such malevolence? And why had Gunther so carefully weighed first her and then Hans and then them both as though they were conspirators? Had her own fear shown, making Gunther suspicious? His loyalty to Germany was of a fanatic dimension, and no inquiry was enough if he suspected that someone had faltered in duty to the Fatherland. She prayed he would already have forgotten her, but in her heart she was deeply afraid. At dawn Hans woke and kissed her. Then, sensing that Suzanne was weary from lack of sleep, he held her and told her his plans for the day. The night's black spectres slipped from her mind, and Suzanne ordered a hearty breakfast and relished every mouthful.

Outside it was a perfect day, a day to remember, full of sunshine and songbirds. While Hans showered, Suzanne lay thinking how lonely she would be without him. Suddenly she was uncertain about everything and terrified of the occupying army, where once she had been full of defiance. Was this a natural reaction? she asked herself. Had love made everything more precious? Her mind returned momentarily to the two men who had intimidated her the previous evening. Then, impatiently, she leaped out of bed, determined not to succumb to panic. Unexpectedly she began to think of David, wondering why he had never written and why he had so deliberately vanished from her life. Then she checked herself. What did it matter? She was in love with Hans, she must put David out of her mind. As she sat at the dressing table putting on lipstick and combing her hair, Suzanne thought that being a woman was not easy. Why could she not have been born a man so she could love every woman she fancied and be hailed as a wondrously virile fellow? Why was it different for women? Then she smiled. She was happy as she was and unwilling to change. She put on her dress, shadow-boxed with an imaginary German general for a few seconds in the mirror, and then breathed in the clear fresh air of morning.

They ate lunch in the Parc des Buttes Chaumont on the hill to the east of Montmartre. Swans were swimming on the lake, young children scampering under the magnolias, and a band of army pensioners was practicing an old French tune. As they listened to scratchy fiddles and shabby drums, the lovers applauded, and the old men bowed. Later, the two rested by the lake and Suzanne lay back watching Hans, her eyes full of admiration, her heart full of love. When a boat became free they rowed across the water and took photographs of each other beaming happily outside a reproduction Greek temple. Suzanne squinted in the strong sunlight, laughing outrageously as Hans snapped her screwing up watery eyes. "Is this how you want your children to remember you?" he asked. Airplanes droned overhead as the lovers sat on the steps of the temple, but they heard only the peaceful sounds of the park. Hans kissed her neck, her cheeks, her ears, and Suzanne ran her fingers through the water, tickling a goldfish sunning itself in the balmy calm.

"You know, Suzanne, when I first came to Paris I was very miserable because I could no longer fight at the front. My back injury had made me feel useless, and as it is not in my nature to sit all day behind a desk, I felt ridiculous."

Suzanne listened to the deep voice, shivering with longing as Hans explained his thoughts. What a perfect day it was, unsullied by war and the frightening presence of enemies. She closed her eyes, grateful for the sun and the presence of her lover.

"I wish we could hide here until the war is over. I wish I need never go back to Montmartre."

"Of course you don't, you would miss your home in a day! You've been missing it already, don't think I haven't noticed."

Suzanne blushed at his awareness of her feelings.

"I didn't mean I wanted to leave home because I didn't like it. I meant I wanted to be far from Paris until the occupation is over."

"And when the war is over, what then, Suzanne?"

"I don't know."

"Someday you must think about that. David will be returning to Paris and—"

"He'll return only if he hasn't been killed, and most résistants end their lives in a field with a bullet in their head!" Suzanne burst out wildly, furious at this idyllic moment to be reminded of the man she felt she had betrayed.

Hans held her hand and said gently, "David sounds like a survivor to me. There are some people who can overcome any adversity because they have special luck and a talent for making fate obey them."

For a moment they were silent, each one thinking about Suzanne's absent fiancé. On the bank a wild duck squawked, a little boy cried, and the air was heavy with the scent of orange blossoms. At last Suzanne voiced her thoughts.

"David *is* one of those people. The war will hurt him and damage his body, but he'll do his best to come home. I don't know if he'll succeed—he's chosen the most dangerous way of spending his time, and the most dangerous place, too."

Her voice faltered in admiration and uncertainty, and Hans decided not to press her to make up her mind. Suzanne had only just learned about love, and the war was far from over. There would be many months, even years, for her to make a decision.

They walked home hand in hand, pausing to make a wish under a centuries-old oak before leaving the park for the boulevard. Near the Canal St. Martin they watched night streaking the sky with gray, rose, and gold. Towering above them there was a statue silhouetted against the pink dusk, showing a boy blowing a horn, his legs gripping the sides of a winged horse flying upward to heaven. Suzanne sighed as she looked up at the statue, because she too longed to leap to safety far away from the threatened city. With something of a shock she realized that she was not only afraid of Germans, she was also afraid of the people of

Paris, her own people. She fell into a deep reverie as Hans led the way home, his short leave almost over. Soon she would commence rehearsals for the new show and Hans would spend his days at the office. Only at night and in the hours of early morning would they be completely alone and together. Suzanne held Hans's hand, kissing it and holding it against her breast. She felt a great reluctance to relinquish the perfection of the day, because moments of happiness were rare in the black days of conflict.

On the last day of Hans's leave the lovers went for the afternoon to the Bois de Boulogne. They left the house at eleven, separately, as always, in order not arouse Laval's suspicions. They met, as was their custom, in the Bar Yvette on the rue Fontaine, where they drank watery lemon tea and chatted with the owner. Then they pedaled across the city on the bicycles Herr Schulberg had purchased, kept chained in the cellar of the Bar Yvette. There were chestnut trees in full blossom in the boulevards, and copper beeches glowing in the sun in the squares of the seizième. Suddenly Suzanne remembered David's parents and was conscience-stricken that she had ignored them for so long. She promised herself she would call on the way home, and pointed out their house to Hans as they circled through the place Victor Hugo.

"That's the house of David's stepfather, Charles Chambord."

"It's a fine mansion. He's lucky to be so comfortable in these hard times. When did you last see them?"

"I don't know exactly, it was some months ago. I must call on my way home."

From the place Victor Hugo they pedaled down the avenue Bugeaud, which ended in the place du Paraguay and the bois end of the avenue Foch. Suzanne glanced up the avenue Foch, noting a squad of squat black cars outside number seventy-four, the mansion that housed the Gestapo interrogation section. SS guards in black uniforms were all around the building, and from the first-floor balcony a black iron eagle had been erected, its wings outstretched and demanding like the enfolding wings of death. Suzanne pedaled away furiously, entering the park by the Porte Dauphine and forcing herself not to think of Gunther and Slagel. Once inside the bois, they dismounted and threw themselves on the grass, watching old men rowing their grandsons on the lake

and a woman talking furiously to herself as she walked by, ignoring the beauty all around. Hans picked a bunch of buttercups,
tickling Suzanne's nose with them and questioning her about her
thoughts.

"What are you thinking?"

"I was wondering how to show you all there is to see here, the
waterfalls, the race courses, and the Bagatelle Pavilion."

"We don't have to see it all today. There'll be other leaves when
we can be together."

Suzanne looked deeply into his eyes. Was it true? Would there
be endless days of love and summer? She lay back on the grass,
sniffing scents of pollen, fern, and the pure country fragrance of
honeysuckle. At this moment the war seemed far away, an aber-
ration to be dismissed impatiently. Bees buzzed in the hawthorn
hedge, and there was a great stillness broken only by the plop of
an oar in the water and the shrill squeal of a delighted child.
Suzanne thought how long it had been since they'd seen rain. If
the dry weather continued there would be no fruit on the apple
tree, no strawberries in the garden. An aircraft droned by, and she
edged closer to Hans.

"I heard on the radio that seven hundred men were killed last
night when the English bombers came. Two thousand more were
badly injured."

"Don't think of the war, Suzanne. This is the last day of my
leave and I want it to be perfect. I'm so sick of everything to do
with fighting and hate."

They lay in silence, their hands entwined, whispering about
places they still wanted to visit, shows they wanted to see. As she
lay in Hans's arms Suzanne asked him about his home.

"Tell me about your house in Germany."

Hans lay staring through the poplars at the sun. As light
dappled his body he realized how homesick he was and how far
from his family. It seemed an age since he had been home, living
the life he enjoyed without a care in the world. He thought of his
sister and wished he could have been there to see Marguerite blossom into beauty. He had received a letter from his younger
brother, Helmut, saying that the other brother had enlisted
against his parents' wishes. Hans frowned. Horst was barely seventeen, a wild boy with a strange need for speed and excitement
that would someday be his downfall.

Suzanne touched his hand, hesitantly, uncertainly, waiting for him to speak.

"Why are you so sad, Hans? You seem a thousand miles away."

"Only a few hundred miles, to be precise. I was thinking of my brother Horst, he joined the army last week."

"You had a letter from Germany?"

"From young Helmut."

"Are your parents well?"

"As well as older people can be in such terrible times. Now that you have reminded me of Lindau, I am homesick."

Suzanne was silent, her conscience pricking because Hans looked overwhelmingly sad. She was conscious that her feelings for him had annihilated grief about her own parents' death too quickly for decency, a thought that troubled her often. Suzanne shook her head. Nothing was forever, not parents, or war, or love, or loyalty. It was best to grasp every opportunity greedily, to devour the rich meal of experience and live every day as if it were the last. She snuggled against Hans as he began to speak of the home he adored, the family he missed, and the fear he felt that something might happen to his once perfect world.

"On the banks of Lake Constance there are orchards as far as the eye can see, at least there were. The house is—"

"The castle."

Suzanne corrected him because she enjoyed the fairy-tale visions evoked by this grandiose word. Hans smiled indulgently.

"Very well, the castle of Bodensee was built in the fifteenth century. It is an austere building of gray stone, not at all like the picturesque Neuschwanstein. Inside, though, it is splendid. The hall is twenty meters high, and the staircase is solid rock hewn into steps by master builders of long ago."

"And what is your room like?"

"My room is in the watchtower. It is very large, and from my window I can see to Langenargen and on a fine day even to Switzerland. There are pine trees everywhere, and the air is very fine and healthy. Someday you will see it for yourself, though, so there is no need to speak of it."

As he thought about his home Hans yearned for Germany, and Suzanne sensed his depth of longing and the sadness he tried hard to hide. She rose and Hans followed, wheeling his bicycle and guiding hers as they made their way to the rose gardens and the

Bagatelle Pavilion. Hans continued his story, and Suzanne was happy because as he spoke he began to smile.

"The furniture in the house is a mixture. Some has been made by the local craftsmen, some is very old, from my ancestors. In the hall there is a reindeer chandelier, and on the walls swords and shields used by every Heinkel in the family since the eleventh century. They were a warlike band. I can tell you, I am not at all like them."

They ate lunch in a deserted restaurant on the allée de Longchamp, wrinkling their noses at strange-tasting meat-labeled "kid" on the menu. When they reached the dessert course it began to rain, and soon startling flashes of lightning came with the roar of distant thunder. People enjoying the park ran for cover, and small boys leapfrogging under the trees raised their shirt collars and shook small fists at the sky. And everywhere there was the smell of lindens, damp ferns, and the reassuring pungency of rich brown earth. Hans turned to Suzanne and kissed her. His leave was almost over. Tonight would be the last of the sweet clover days.

"It's time to go home."

"Why so soon? You said we'd spend the whole afternoon here."

"I shall go back first. You want to call at the house of your friends the Chambords, and I have one more surprise for you, which I am impatient to prepare."

"First the Ritz Hotel, now this?"

Suzanne laughed delightedly as Hans paid the bill. Then he led her over damp shingle paths toward the exit.

"Once when you were very tired and worried you told me you wanted to register at the Ritz. So I booked the suite to surprise you."

"Now you're going to surprise me again."

"With something you very often want. On your way home you can try to remember all the other things you've been craving during the winter. Then you can choose which one I have managed to obtain for you."

"Tell me now, you know I can't bear waiting!"

"Certainly not, and stop scowling like a vixen!"

They kissed at the Porte de la Muette. Then Hans cycled away and out of sight. Suzanne pedaled round the corner, wiping rain from her face and leaning her bicycle against the railings of the house in the place Victor Hugo. She rang the bell, smoothing her dress and pushing wisps of wet hair from her face. At first there was no answer; then Suzanne heard a shuffling of feet in the hall. She was shocked to see Charles Chambord answering his own door.

"Monsieur Chambord?"

He looked blank, and Suzanne felt obliged to remind him who she was.

"I'm Suzanne—Suzanne Castel. May I come in?"

Chambord scowled and turned his back on her, grumbling under his breath that visitors were not at all welcome. Suzanne followed him into the hall and closed the door, amazed by the deterioration in the house and its owner. The place smelled musty and damp, and she noticed areas of mold edging from floor to ceiling, staining the paper with green spots. In parts the paper had peeled and was hanging down. Suzanne looked at Chambord in puzzled apprehension.

"Is Madame in?"

"Who knows? I don't know anything anymore. Perhaps she's in the garden. Madame is always in the garden. If she were not, I should have starved months ago."

Suzanne hesitated. Would it be impolite to leave Monsieur and go to the garden to see Carrie? Chambord was obviously sick or drunk. She wondered if his mind was deranged or if he was simply befuddled with drink. Knowing how besotted he was with his daughter, she ventured to ask about Marie-Claude.

"Is your daughter well, Monsieur Chambord?"

Chambord started violently. Then a tear fell down his cheek and he walked away, shaking his head despairingly. Suzanne went to the garden, where she found Carrie in trousers and a cook's white apron. Carrie was at last digging up her husband's rose bushes.

"Hello, Suzanne, how are you? Have you heard from David?"

"He hasn't written to me for many months."

"We had a letter in November postmarked Lyon, but nothing since. Have you seen the 'wanted' poster?"

Suzanne unfolded her copy of the poster from her purse, carefully straightening it and offering it to Carrie.

"I have it with me all the time. I'm so proud of David."

Carrie was surprised to see tears in Suzanne's eyes and a look of sheer misery on her face. Concerned, she took off her gardening gloves and led Suzanne to the kitchen.

"I've no coffee left, but I've been hoarding some lemon tea for a special occasion, and I have some oatmeal cookies, I remember you liked those."

While Carrie made tea Suzanne looked carefully at her, puzzled that David's mother seemed fitter and browner than when they had last met. Carrie had blossomed as her husband had withered, and this was very odd. Suzanne longed to ask why there had been such a deterioration in the house, why Chambord was so changed, and what was going on in their world of privilege. Suzanne looked down as Carrie turned to her, and for the first time she was aware that her new relationship with Hans was embarrassing. She hurried to think of something else, and told Carrie what had been happening since their last meeting.

"Maman died earlier this year."

Carrie's face showed shock and tension.

"She seemed so full of life the last time she came to lunch. What happened?"

"She died of heart failure after Papa was shot in a reprisal raid. The war had made her very tired and depressed, but none of us expected anything really bad to happen."

"Sometimes I'd like to go out there and shoot every German I meet, but what's the point? There are just too many of them. I'm so sorry about what's happened, Suzanne. If there's anything I can do, you know you have only to ask."

Carrie thought of David and Suzanne drank her tea, uncertain whether to ask what had happened to their house. Carrie poured them another cup and explained her own predicament.

"Marie-Claude was . . . Marie-Claude killed herself a few months back."

Suzanne dropped her cup. As it shattered, she struggled to work out what could possibly have provoked such a self-possessed girl to the ultimate desperation. She listened in horror as Carrie continued.

"Marie-Claude was badly injured by three German SS officers who came to stay in the house. When Charles and I returned from Gestapo headquarters she was ill, and for days her brain was deranged. Sometimes she seemed calm, then she'd start yelling so crazily we'd almost decided to let Picron have his way and put her in the clinic. Then on New Year's Day she hanged herself in one of the guest bedrooms. Marie-Claude was everything to Charles, and he's gone to pieces since she died. He drank every bottle of wine in the cellar and all the spirits in the house, then he began on the cleaning fluid. Sometimes he knows folk who call, but mostly he's so drunk he can't tell what he's doing or saying."

"Would it not be best to have Monsieur put in a hospital?"

"I've been thinking of going home, Suzanne. I'll get Charles into the clinic and then I'm going to get out of this city if it kills me."

Suzanne thought of the travel restrictions that prevented even members of the Vichy government from entering and leaving Paris. How could Carrie get away? Was it possible or impossible? She thought of Chambord's purple face, the sickly smell of his rancid breath, and the mold that was fast engulfing the hall. Carrie *must* be helped. Was it possible Armand could smuggle her out? She decided to introduce Carrie to her friend.

"I have a suggestion, madame."

"Call me Carrie."

"Carrie, I know a young man who might help you—at least I think he might."

"When could I meet him?"

"Can you come to my house on Sunday? I don't want to risk bringing him here, it's too near to the offices of the Gestapo."

"I'll come after lunch. How about three o'clock?"

"That would be fine."

Carrie hurried to the storeroom to put some shallots and potatoes in a bag.

"Take these, Suzanne, I have plenty more."

Suzanne kissed the bony cheek and shook Carrie's hand. Then she walked down the hall, pausing outside Chambord's study when she heard him discussing something with his daughter.

"You know, my dear Marie-Claude, you really *must* decide which will please you. La Martine is excellent, and l'Alpine is in no way inferior. One specializes in languages and the other in etiquette and home management. . . ."

Carrie led Suzanne outside, whispering sadly and shrugging her shoulders helplessly.

"Sometimes Charles talks with her for hours. I just can't make him admit Marie-Claude's dead. He can't face reality, and he never will."

Suzanne wanted to run from the house, but she forced a smile as she wheeled her bicycle to the road.

"Goodbye, madame . . . Carrie. I shall look forward to seeing you on Sunday. Don't worry if you're late, it takes ages to get to Montmartre."

"I'll be there by three."

When Suzanne arrived home she smelled an unusual smell. At first she did not recognize it. Then, as she greeted Hans, she realized that it was the smell of roast beef. Her mouth watered like a fountain, and she blinked disbelievingly. Hans had often tried to buy a filet of beef from his black market contacts, but even money had not been sufficient. Suzanne opened the oven door and peered in, squealing with shock and happiness at a whole filet cooking on the top shelf. The outside was already crisp and dark. The inside would be pink and bloody. Suzanne kissed Hans's ear and then his cheek, his mouth, his throat.

"Where did you buy it?"

"I didn't buy it."

"Who gave it to you?"

"No one gave it me."

"Then how did you get it?"

"I stole it from the Hôtel Meurice."

Suzanne stared at his smiling face. The Hôtel Meurice housed German officers of high rank, men who ate like kings, according to popular rumor. Was it true that Hans had risked his reputation for a piece of beef?

"Are you telling the truth?"

Delighted to have surprised her, Hans explained.

"I went to the kitchens of the hotel as the butcher's van was delivering. I had checked the time of the delivery each day for two weeks. Never let me say again that my army training has not come in useful. When the meat was delivered I took the filet and put it in my basket. Then I pedaled away as fast as I could and came here to put it in the oven."

"And no one saw you?"

"Of course not. I made sure to arrive when the chefs were commencing their preparations for dinner. The meat deliveries are usually signed for by an orderly, but he was not there."

"Where was he?"

"I asked him to telephone certain facts to my office, so he was busy checking his records."

"And while he was out you took the filet?"

"My dear Suzanne, why are you so amazed? You've been telling me for months how your mouth waters at the very mention of beef filet. Now stop asking questions and set the table. The potatoes are boiling. We have a fresh tomato salad and a bottle of wine which I dug up from under the apple tree. I remembered to wave to Laval as I was digging, but he seemed not to enjoy the gesture."

They ate with relish, and Suzanne marveled that Hans, who was always so honest, had for her stolen from his own colleagues. A dozen times she leaned across the table to kiss him. Then she told him all she had seen during her visit to the Chambord residence. Hans thought of Charles Chambord and the rumors circulating about the daughter of the house. Marie-Claude had been exploited by the SS officer German soldiers called "the hangman," and Heydritch's nickname had proved ominously apt. He remembered the day when he had met Oberst-Gruppenfuhrer Heydritch on a battlefield near the Norwegian border. Heydritch had been sent to visit the troops to raise morale, but his presence had had a curiously dampening effect on everyone he met. Hans sighed at the thought of the women who had accompanied the Oberst-Gruppenfuhrer, girls with red-gash lips and grim bright eyes. Then he recalled the weals on the back of one of the girls, which she had shown off with great pride after dinner in the officers' mess. He looked over to Suzanne, admiring the silky black hair and the eyes that needed nothing artificial to make them compelling. Suzanne was explaining about Carrie's longing to leave Paris.

"I've asked Madame Chambord to come here on Sunday to meet a friend who might help her get out of the city."

"I had best go out before your friends arrive."

"Why?"

Suzanne looked hurt, and Hans explained what he had thought she would understand.

"I cannot be party to such a plan, Suzanne. Carrie is reliable, I'm sure, but a man who helps others escape from Paris in return for money might give my name to the Gestapo if I were to appear sympathetic to such a meeting. Perhaps it would be safer if you met him outside the house."

"Whatever you say, Hans."

They were silent, aware of an invisible barrier between them, the barrier of divided loyalty. Suzanne swallowed the last of her meat, wishing she were not so often reminded that she and Hans were at the same time lovers and enemies and that they would have to remain so until the war was over.

Later in the evening they sat happily toasting bread on the fire. Vivienne arrived, said hello, and retired exhausted to her room, leaving them free to make plans. Glad to be alone, Hans raked the embers and spread anchovy paste on his toast.

"This is delicious, but it's time to go to bed."

"What shall we do, where shall I sleep?"

"With me, of course. Vivienne never comes to your room, does she?"

"She hasn't, but she could."

Suzanne shrugged uneasily. Then she ran upstairs, unable to refuse Hans anything. But after love, when he was asleep, she stood at the window looking out over the darkness that was Paris. The golden loom of prewar days, the twinkling lights and shadowy majesty of the tower was invisible. No church bells rang. No traffic roared by. No radios playing too late disturbed the ear. Suzanne sighed. How things had changed since the Germans came to Paris. In a year, every value she had known had shifted, and even friends no longer seemed reliable. Her mind turned to Janine, her most valued companion for so long. Janine had been generous at Christmas, giving her a bottle of expensive perfume and a box of marrons glacés. Suzanne knew she was going to get some silk material from belle-soeur for her birthday, and though she was delighted by the prospect of the gift, she felt curiously embarrassed by the knowledge that Janine's German suitors were increasing by the day. The new show would be Janine's last, because she had decided that her vocation for the theater should be postponed while she made as much money as she could from the officers who flocked to her door. Suzanne wondered if her friend knew she was drifting into prostitution. Then she shook her head resignedly. Of course Janine knew, how could she not? It was best not to think of such troublesome things. Perhaps when the war was over Janine would return to her old ways, forgetting this frenzied desire for money. But in her heart Suzanne knew this would not be so. Once Janine left the show, she would never return, and would eventually spend her days waiting for clients in a home bought from her earnings.

Suzanne stood at the side of the bed, looking down at Hans. Should she stay or should she go back to her own room? It was nice to sleep by her lover's side, but too risky now they were home. She was afraid of Laval bursting into the house with his Gestapo colleagues, of Vivienne being called in for questioning about André and confessing what she could so easily discover. Suzanne tiptoed to her own room, sure it was best to continue sleeping there. She and Hans could make love when Vivienne was out of the house, adjusting their days to accommodate the fiery pangs of passion. Her mind resolved, she felt better and slept soundly until morning.

On Sunday, Hans went to the countryside to buy seed potatoes. After giving Carrie coffee on the terrace, Suzanne walked with her to the house in the rue Pigalle. She had already told Armand Carrie's story, and he had agreed to try to find a way to get her out of occupied France. It was a burning hot day, and the two women were relieved when they reached number eighteen, the address Armand had given. Suzanne rang the bell, and a young girl appeared, dressed in black with a frilly white apron.

"We're here to see Armand Lognon."

"What is your name, mademoiselle?"

"I'm Suzanne Castel, and this is Madame Chambord."

"Just a moment, please."

The maid closed the door, and Carrie turned uncertainly to Suzanne.

"I thought you said he was expecting us."

"Armand has to be very careful, I suppose."

The door was opened again, and a hard-faced middle-aged woman stood before them. Carrie stared at her in amazement.

The woman was over six feet tall and weighed at least two hundred pounds. Her eyes were black-ringed, her mouth deep red, her dress a sheath of claret beads that jangled when she walked. With a commanding nod, she ushered them inside.

"I am Madame Francine."

Suzanne and Carrie exchanged glances, then stared at the red talons extended in welcome. Carrie winced at the pressure of Madame's hand.

"Armand told me you were coming to see him, but he has not yet arrived. I can assure you he is always on time for his appointments, but today I don't know what has happened. I hope he isn't in any trouble. Madeleine! Drinks, if you please."

Madame called her order like a sergeant on parade, and as the two women accustomed their eyes to the dim light of the hall they saw that she was inviting them into a private parlor. The room was decorated in Burgundy style, with Biedermeier sofas, beaded lamps, and drawings by Lautrec. Carrie looked closely at the drawings, trying to decide if the ladies of the rue des Moulins were prints or originals. Was it possible they were real? Mme. Francine followed her gaze.

"Those are real, the first studies Lautrec made for his paintings of the women in the bordellos of the rue des Moulins. Everyone envies my art collection."

Suzanne wondered where Madame had found the money to acquire such marvels, and as though reading her mind, Madame spoke.

"I have always invested in art, ever since I was a very young girl. The Lautrecs cost me almost nothing from an old fool in Honfleur who was really trying to sell me a bureau. The Corot I found in the attic of the first house I ever owned. I call it my bonus, because it cost nothing at all."

While Madame was speaking the two women were surprised to hear distant voices raised in the reverent phrases of the nunc dimitis. Mme. Francine went to the window and looked out, frowning impatiently.

"There's a convent behind this house and the nuns are always singing. When they are not singing they are praying or scrubbing the cloisters, and in the evenings they beat themselves with ropes as a penance for their imagined sins. It's too much, I tell you. My gentlemen get so excited watching them, I have to keep two of my girls permanently dressed in habits! It's a hard life, mesdames, a very hard life."

When Madame had departed to the salon, Carrie whispered to Suzanne, "This is a brothel!"

"I'm sorry, Carrie. Armand just told me he lived in a house in the rue Pigalle."

"I don't care what kind of place it is so long as Armand gets me out of Paris, but where *is* he?"

Suzanne walked to the window and looked out over the wall to the cloisters of the Order in the next street. She wondered wryly what the nuns thought of the cavortings in Mme. Francine's establishment and what sins provoked their own demeaning penance. Just then the doorbell rang, and Suzanne was disturbed to hear the sound of guttural German voices. She felt her heart pounding violently as the callers mentioned the boy for whom she and Carrie were waiting.

"Where is Armand Lognon?"

The maid's anxious voice drifted to their ears. "Armand went to Bordeaux two days ago, sir."

"We shall search the premises, step aside."

Madame appeared with two fluffy ostrich-feather wraps.

"Put these on and go to the salon as fast as you can. If those Gestapo pigs ask you for your papers, tell them General-Oberst Stilber is responsible for you."

Carrie sniffed the wrap, wrinkling her nose at a heavy pansy perfume. She and Suzanne sat drinking with the other girls and waiting anxiously for the officers to question them. First the men searched the house and loud protests could be heard from the upstairs rooms, with one or two hastily slammed doors. Finally they came to the salon, where Madame's unoccupied girls were filing their nails, reading magazines, and eating expensive chocolates.

"You! What is your name?"

"Violet, monsieur."

"Show me your papers."

"My papers are in the bedroom, monsieur."

"Get them at once."

"Would you like to accompany me to my room, monsieur?"

Violet giggled, and the Gestapo officer flushed with annoyance as Madame's laughter echoed in the hall. He turned to Carrie and pointed.

"You!"

"Yes, monsieur."

"Your name?"

"Caroline, monsieur."

"Nationality?"

Carrie hesitated, and Suzanne held her breath.

"Italian, monsieur."

The senior officer frowned as he looked Carrie over.

"You're somewhat old for this kind of work, aren't you? Take my advice and get out while you can, madame."

When the Gestapo had gone, Francine retrieved her feather wraps. Suzanne noticed that her hands were quite steady and she had a German Mauser stuck through her sequined belt.

"That was close! Now where in God's name is Armand? That boy is like a son to me, and he worries me more than all my girls put together."

By five they were concerned for Armand's safety. At six Madame invited Suzanne and Carrie to stay for dinner, and they sat with the rest of the girls in the basement, enjoying a bowl of vegetable soup. After the soup there was hare cooked in wine Madame imported from Bordeaux, and apricot flan, rich and satisfying. They had despaired of Armand's arriving when there was a tapping noise at the window and, looking up, they saw him standing outside, his head tied with a bandage, a bloodstain spreading from his ear to his neck. Mme. Francine leaped to the window in alarm.

"What happened, have you been shot?"

"The Gestapo almost caught me in Neuilly."

"And they've been here looking for you. You've been denounced, my dear. Who would have done such a thing? I shall *kill* them when I find out."

Madame was indignant. Violet turned a trifle pale. Armand was shaken, but his manner was polite as he shook hands with Carrie and kissed Suzanne's cheeks.

"I'm sorry I'm so late, Suzanne."

"Sit down. You look awful."

"I had to walk home because they also shot my bicycle from under me. Those big houses around Neuilly are full of collaborators, you can't trust yourself an inch. I only stopped to post a letter and suddenly *phut!* the air was full of bullets."

Armand drank a cup of soup and then turned to Carrie.

"I understand from Suzanne that you want to leave Paris?"

Carrie nodded, still speechless at the realization of Armand's youth. The boy did not look a day more than sixteen.

Armand spoke softly, as though conversing with himself.

"There's only one chance for you, Madame Chambord, at least from me, because I'm going to have to lie low for a long time until I can be seen again around the city."

"Tell me what you have in mind." Carrie had decided that anything was better than remaining forever in Paris with a deranged husband in a house of bitter memories.

Armand looked her over, assessing her toughness, her courage and ability to stay calm. She certainly looked the part he had in mind. He began to speak, watching Carrie closely as he outlined his plan.

"I need a woman who can pretend she is from a Catholic orphanage."

Carrie waited. She had already ceased to be surprised by him. Armand continued thoughtfully.

"There are thirty Jewish children waiting to leave Paris. I've made arrangements for them to travel by bus to Quimper in Brittany. From there friends will take them to England in fishing boats."

"What then?"

"Then the kids will be on their own."

"Why do you need a woman?"

"The party's supposed to be a group of Catholic children with consumption going to the beaches for a holiday. Father Chanson has agreed to come with us, but I need a woman because girls wouldn't be sent without one. I'm a Jew but I know that much."

"Have you passes for the party?"

"Not exactly."

"What does that mean?"

"We'll drive along roads where there aren't any checks."

"Through fields?"

"We'll have to pass through one roadblock in the suburbs of Paris. We don't need passes to go to the suburbs. Once we're outside the Gross Paris area we'll have to travel on country roads and cart tracks."

Carrie knew it was a foolish scheme, a mad flight to even greater danger on the open sea in a fishing boat. Suzanne remained silent, unwilling to influence her friend in any way. Having poured drinks for her guests, Mme. Francine and her girls withdrew to the salon, and from time to time Suzanne heard the sound of men laughing and the doorbell constantly ringing. Carrie thought awhile and then asked, "Who'll drive the bus?"

"I shall."

"Have you a license?"

"I'm not old enough to have one. I won't be fifteen until tomorrow."

Armand looked despondently at his hands. For weeks he had been trying to find someone to share this perilous escapade, but the last three drivers had been shot within days of returning to Paris. Friends and associates knew this and had declined to take part in further daring escapades until they knew who had been feeding information to the Gestapo. Armand looked appealingly at Carrie.

"I just can't find a driver, madame. So I have to drive, what else can I do?"

"Have you ever driven on uneven ground?"

"No, madame."

"Have you any experience of driving a truck or a bus?"

"None whatever. I'm sorry, madame, there's just no alternative. I can't keep the children here in Paris and I can't take them out by train or by any other method. I've thought about it for weeks, and this is the way it has to be. Someone betrayed my last three drivers and other members of my group. Today, as you know, the Gestapo came for me. There's a leak within my organization and I don't know where it is. That's why no one will drive for me."

Impressed by his honesty, Carrie made her decision.

"I'll drive the bus. I'm not risking my neck with a fifteen-year-old kid at the wheel."

Armand shook her hand delightedly.

"I was hoping you'd offer, madame."

"Now you can stay home and hide from the Gestapo."

"That won't be possible. I speak German, so I'll have to deal with any sentries or roadblocks we encounter."

"I thought you said we'd be driving on lanes and country tracks."

"I did, but you can never be sure you won't meet Germans, even in the country."

"If Father Chanson can't drive, can he use a gun?"

"Priests don't kill, madame."

"But can he shoot?"

"I didn't ask him."

"Give me his address, will you? I'd like to meet him before we leave."

Armand scribbled it on a paper. Then, after a last drink, the two women left the house and made their way to the place Pigalle. They were silent, each one mulling over what she had seen during the afternoon. The Sphinx was open, the Eve closed and barred, and outside the Folies Pigalle there was a queue of impatient German soldiers waiting for the evening performance to begin. Cigarette papers littered the square, along with a dead rat or two, and painted wooden swizzle sticks from cheap clubs all around. Suzanne thought how depleted and dirty the place looked; how, like everything else, it had changed.

"I'll leave you here, Carrie."

"Thanks for everything, Suzanne. I know it's a crazy scheme, but I want to get out of Paris and I reckon I'm as well off with Armand as anyone else."

"Did he say when he wants to leave?"

"The fourth of July. It's an appropriate day for an American, isn't it?"

Carrie went downstairs to the Métro, Suzanne climbed the hill to Montmartre, and the two men who had been watching Mme. Francine's house separated, one to follow Suzanne, the other to keep watch on Carrie.

Unaware of the danger, Suzanne paused to look in the window of a toy shop in the rue André and to watch children playing catch in the place des Abbesses. The thought of seeing Hans made her hurry, and she was delighted to find him already home, sitting on the terrace reading a newspaper bought in the suburbs. There was coffee on the stove and wildflowers in vases on the table. Hans kissed her and handed her a cup of coffee.

"Did everything go well?"

"Not really. The Gestapo arrived to search the house while I was there. It was a brothel, Hans. I've never been in one before, you can't imagine how strange everything was."

Hans looked questioningly at Suzanne's radiant face. Then, after considering the implications of her statement, he spoke firmly, making her gasp with fear and apprehension.

"War is not a game, Suzanne. If the Gestapo raided that house, you are now a suspect because you were there. Were you followed home?"

Suzanne stared uncomprehendingly, her throat dry from shock.

"I don't understand. Why would anyone follow me?"

"Armand Lognon is a wanted man. He lives in the house you visited in the rue Pigalle. The Gestapo probably went there to arrest him."

"I think they wanted to arrest him, but he wasn't there."

"So they searched the house and took everyone's name?"

"They searched the house, but they only took the names of two of the girls."

"Not yours?"

"No, I don't think they noticed me."

Hans sighed with relief. Perhaps everything was in order. Suzanne had been lucky that the Gestapo had been interested only in Armand Lognon. He tried to reassure her.

"You may be safe. I don't know, to be truthful. There's no way of telling what those people think."

Suzanne plumped down on the sofa, shocked to the core by the concern in her lover's face. She resolved at once never to go to see Armand again and not even to walk in the rue Pigalle in case someone mistook her intentions. Hans's remarks had taken her appetite away, and she only toyed with the cherries he had bought in the country.

"Where did you go?"

She looked at Hans's suntanned face, trying to concentrate when he replied.

"I went to Menilmontant."

"Edith Piaf was born there."

Suzanne's mind wandered to the men who had searched the house in the rue Pigalle. She had been stupid and she knew it. Hans was right. War was most certainly not a game. Hans continued, determined to take Suzanne's mind from the danger both knew she could be in, the shadow of the Gestapo that had momentarily darkened her day.

"I bought seed potatoes from a gardener in St. Mande, and I was lucky enough to find a German officer leading a pig and six piglets from an apartment building near the Bois de Vincennes."

"He was keeping pigs in an apartment!"

Suzanne's laughter cheered them both, and Hans hugged her to his shoulder and forgot about the Gestapo.

"I think he was trying to keep the pigs in the garden behind his apartment, but his French neighbors kept stealing them for food, so he insisted that I bring one home with me."

"And where is it?"

Hans pointed to the garden, and, looking out, Suzanne saw a curly-tailed pig eating clover on the lawn. Hans had penned the pig so its run included the grass and a stretch of daisy border. Suzanne hugged him gratefully.

"Whatever should I do without you? Tell me how you managed to bring him home."

Hans frowned at the memory of the uneven contest.

"I almost lost him a dozen times when he jumped out of the bicycle basket. So I walked with him under my arm until I was given a lift near the boulevard Magenta."

"Who gave you a lift, a collaborator?"

"No, an SS officer who works in the house in the avenue Foch. I didn't care where he worked. I was so tired of trying to hold on to the pig, I should have been happy to ride with the devil."

Suzanne thought of Tristan Slagel and wanted suddenly to run away from Paris, to hide in peaceful fields watching cows interminably munching, anything to avoid thinking of the house in the avenue Foch. She almost laughed at the reversal of former cravings, for excitement, danger, speed, and exhilaration. Now all she wanted was a quiet life, a home, and enough food to survive.

"Did the officer mention Slagel and did he ask you for your address?"

"He didn't ask for my address, and about Slagel he said only that he was brought up in a series of orphanages, that he has no friends, and that he lives not far from here in the boulevard des Batignolles. Apparently Standartenfuhrer Gunther is a father to him. Slagel follows instructions blindly, never believing Gunther wrong. I had the impression the officer I met did not really approve of either!"

Suzanne paced the room, determined not to think of the pair who had so frightened her. Hans took her in his arms, trying to comfort her.

"Stop worrying about Slagel. If you must, worry about what you did this afternoon, because that was dangerous. From now on you must not see Armand, and your visits to the Chambord house must be terminated. Madame is on her own in this adventure. She is old enough to have weighed all the dangers of her plan and to have accepted the risks in trying to leave Paris."

That evening they made an inventory of the food remaining in the storeroom. Oil, soap, sugar, and potatoes could not be bought in the city, and soon, Hans feared, they would not even be available on the black market except to German generals and Parisian millionaires who could pay anything to have what they wanted. Material also was scarce, and new clothes were becoming hard to find, so city dwellers had started combing the flea markets of the Porte de Cligancourt, Malik, and the rue Mouffetard for ancient taffeta dresses and Victorian lawn underwear to be remodeled for present-day use. Old ladies were said to be keeping themselves in black market food by selling off the contents of their trunks, and some daring women were wearing men's trousers. Suzanne felt sure they would all be wearing trousers by November, when icy winds would defeat redundant ideas of propriety. She jotted items down as Hans called them out: two sacks of rice, one sack of peas, four dozen dried pimentos, one half sack of flour, one liter of oil, one kilo of sugar, one packet of coffee, a few grams of corn flour, seven bottles of wine retrieved from the garden, one small box of soap, one liter of green liquid shampoo, a ball of string, a pile of ancient newspapers. Not much to eat, Suzanne decided. She must make an effort to scour the markets and to pay a visit to her friend Mme. Hazard in the morning.

At nightfall the lovers sat on the terrace, hidden from view by a screen Hans had erected to thwart Laval's surveillance. Suzanne listened as the piglet snored, wondering sadly how much longer it would be before they slaughtered him.

"Who's going to kill him when the time comes?"

"Monsieur Roger will kill him in return for some of the meat. We'll also give Vivienne some, and Monsieur Corbeil. Then we shall all be very happy and very full, at least for a week or two."

That night Suzanne slept at Hans's side, unable to force herself to return to her own room. Her mind went over and over the events of the day, the comic moments with Mme. Francine and her scarlet-suspendered young ladies, her fear when the leather-coated men came to search the house, her admiration for the businesslike way Carrie had questioned Armand Lognon. Would Carrie make it safely to the Breton port and back to America? Suzanne knew it was unlikely, but she accepted that it was in Carrie's nature to try. And the children, what would they do? Thirty Jewish children had been rescued from the Gestapo in France, Germany, and Poland. They were all orphans, all confused and frightened, without homes or future security. They would surely be no match for German tanks and the steel-helmeted sentries blocking every main road.

Unable to sleep, Suzanne wandered downstairs to the kitchen and made a pot of herb tea. As she carried the tray to the lounge, she stood for a moment looking up at her mother's portrait. In the frilly drawers and pink tights she had once worn for her trapeze act, Nathalie had been a beautiful, exuberant creature. Suzanne thought perplexedly that it was still hard to believe that her mother had deteriorated with such suddenness. She wandered around the room looking at familiar posters of past theatrical events, at the pebble collection and cased butterflies her father had put together over twenty years. As she examined the objects, she realized that the room was her parents' room, not her own, and she resolved to buy some paintings for the walls and to fill the shelves with new books once the war was over. The old ones could be relegated to the guest bedrooms and the landing.

Suzanne reconsidered the room, deciding to buy a new carpet as soon as she was able, one in bois-de-rose, her favorite color. The rest she would leave as it was, because it was home and she loved it.

She was polishing the table with a duster when she heard a sound in the hall and, walking to the door, saw a grimy envelope on the tiles. She hurried back to the sitting room, closing the door softly so Hans would not hear. Then she tore open the envelope, half afraid, half ecstatic, because the writing on it was David's.

Dear Zizi,

I'm sorry I haven't written for so long but I was injured and I've been hoping to be able to tell you that I'm just as nimble as before. I realize now that that isn't going to happen because my leg's damaged and I'll always have a limp. I'm not too depressed because I can walk and run and sit and stand, and that's fine by me after the doctors said I'd never walk again. You've probably heard that the Gestapo has a reward out for me. That's another reason why I've stayed out of your life. But right now I just can't wait any longer to have news of you. Write me with all your usual chatter and leave the letter on your doorstep the night after you get this. I've fixed for it to be collected by the friend who's delivering this one. I'll be in Paris soon for a month or so, and it's going to be dangerous for both of us because the Gestapo probably know you're my girl. I'll be thinking about you all the time, Zizi, and resisting the temptation to chase up the hill to see you only because I don't want to involve you with those murderers from the avenue Foch. When the war's over and we're married, with only babies to disturb our sleep, I promise I'll *never* leave you again. For now you'll have to be content because I love you, and though I keep trying to stop thinking about you, I never succeed.

David

Suzanne felt tears in her eyes and a pain she thought must be the agonizing pang of conscience. Did David really suspect nothing of her affair with Hans? Had none of his contacts told him of her outings with the German or her visits to his office? Suzanne decided that David would probably be the last man in Paris to be told anything of the association, because none of his friends could know with certainty that Hans was anything but another German officer billeted in a French home. But David said he might return at any time. What if the two met? How could she avoid a confrontation? Wistfully Suzanne thought of David's impetuous nature, his passion, and the courage that could make him decide to walk into her home, defying the Germans, the Gestapo, and all the banshees of hell if he so chose. She thought firmly that she must not panic. She must not think of such complications.

Tucking the letter into her pocket, she went to the kitchen to wash her cup and saucer. Then she sat at her father's desk and wrote a reply, because she could not countenance letting David think her unresponsive. She decided not to tell him about Hans, because she was still unsure whether David would survive the war. Why burden him with a loss about which he need never know? Why trouble about Hans at all?

Having rationalized the omission, Suzanne went to bed. She was excited and deeply happy because David was alive and he had said he still loved her. At last he had made contact—everything was perfect, absolutely perfect. As she slid under the bedclothes, Hans took her in his arms.

"Where did you go? I missed you."

He was asleep before Suzanne could reply. She snuggled against his chest, savoring the scent of his body and the firmness of his skin. As she lay at his side she thought of the letter from David, and the happiness it had given her made her aware for the first time of the full extent of her own duplicity. Someday she might have to decide between the two, but which one and how? If she loved David, how could she want and adore Hans? And if she loved Hans, how could she need to retain contact with David? As dawn tinted the sky yellow, Suzanne was still trying to work out her feelings. A faint hum of traffic echoed on the hill, an explosion startled passersby, and in a house below la maison Fleuri a new baby gave its first lusty cries. Suzanne closed her eyes, confident that everything would be decided by fate. She fell asleep as the clock struck six, and dreamed of getting married in the old church near the Montmartre vineyard. When she turned to kiss the bridegroom, under the priest's watchful eye, she saw Hans and David standing side by side, imploring her to make a decision. She woke with a violent start as the clock chimed seven. Hans was standing beside the bed with a tray of coffee and rolls.

'This is the rue Gabrielle Ritz Hotel, mademoiselle."

"Thank you, sir."

"Vivienne just left for work, so we are alone."

"Do you have any plans before you desert me for your office?"
Hans got into bed and poured the coffee.

"I might think of something while I eat my rolls."

Their laughter echoed in the garden, and Laval, who was on the terrace of his home, looked up in shock and anger. The sun rose and the bedroom glowed pink as it shone through the curtains. Suzanne forgot her preoccupation of the previous evening as soon as Hans kissed her. In wartime every day must be lived to the full, every moment treasured. She put down her cup and turned toward him, kissing his face and his neck and the smooth skin of his stomach. Hungry and eager for love, she abandoned caution and enjoyed his body. For the moment, David was forgotten.

# CHAPTER SIX

## Autumn, 1941

Carrie was packing her belongings: some clothes, souvenirs of the early days in Paris with David, favorite books, and small pieces of silver. She had two leather suitcases, and that was all she intended to take. The weather was still suffocatingly humid, and every effort made her feel faint because she was hungry and had been for days. The trip to Brittany with the children had been twice delayed, but that morning she had been told to be ready. They would depart on the fourth of September, two days hence.

Carrie looked out at the garden, shaking her head ruefully because she hated the thought of leaving all the vegetables she had worked so hard to grow. The next morning Chambord was due to be taken to the clinic of the Cistercian Sisters near the Bois de Boulogne. Dr. Picron had had no hesitation in certifying the banker, because Chambord had taken a shot at him with a revolver no one knew he had hidden. Carrie sighed as she thought of the bloated, sedated body lying on the bed upstairs. Once Charles had seemed a handsome, debonair Frenchman, as well ordered as her first husband had been chaotic. His lack of courage had not been apparent because courage was needed only in times of adversity. But from the moment the Germans arrived in Paris things had been different, and after Marie-Claude's death purgatory had enveloped the house, tormenting those who had to contend with his drunken aggression and petulant forgetfulness.

Carrie thought of the children she was to accompany to Brittany. In the last few weeks she had come to know the Haussmans well. George was thirteen, a brave boy who had hidden his brothers and sisters out of reach of the men who had dragged his mother to the train that would take her to Buchenwald. Irena was a bluestocking of eleven, and the twins fierce little tomboys of nine. The other children in the party were being housed in a warehouse on the Seine. Armand had engaged an elderly aristocrat to teach them drill and anything else that could be useful on their journey. Sancerre, who had charge of the children, was seventy, a ramrod-straight gentleman who had once been an officer in the Chasseurs à Cheval. He had grown so fond of his charges that he had volunteered to travel to Quimper with the party. Sancerre could still fire a gun; his sight was good and his hearing perfect, even if he had arthritis in the knees. So that was how it would be—one old man, a woman, a priest, a boy of fifteen, and thirty children from five to thirteen, all fleeing for their lives.

Carrie opened the window and took in a breath of warm air. She was so hungry, she decided to dig up the last of the potatoes and carrots so she could make a pan of stew to last the two days before departure.

Later, when Carrie had picked lettuce and radishes for a salad, she took a spade from the garden shed and strode to the potato patch. She had dug up two bucketsful of potatoes, carrots, and spring onions when her spade struck something hard. Bending to investigate, she found a gold bar wrapped in black oilskin. Dazed, she continued digging, piling her find in the wheelbarrow until she had twenty small gold bars, each wrapped in soil-stained tarpaulin. Exhausted with excitement, she carried the bars through to the kitchen, poured herself the last of the brandy, and drank it at a gulp. So that was why Chambord had insisted on staying in Paris, when she had been so sure he would flee the occupying force! Carrie laughed delightedly. Then confusion made her feel like crying. Money had been the only mistress her husband had ever had, and an intoxicating one.

When she felt calm again, Carrie wiped her eyes, lit the stove, and put the vegetables on to cook. Then slowly, painstakingly, she carried the gold to the drawing room and went upstairs to empty her suitcases. She could do without books and clothes. Books could always be bought again, except the old, precious ones, which she would take with her. These she selected and put under her arm, along with some changes of underwear and clean trousers and sweaters. Carrie took the things to be repacked downstairs, placing them beside the gold bars. Carefully she packed the books under and over the oilskin-wrapped bars, with her clothing on top. In the kitchen, the vegetables were simmering. Carrie inhaled the fresh country smell and felt hungrier by the minute. She checked to be sure she could lift the cases, trying one and then the other until she was satisfied they were a manageable weight. Then she went to the kitchen and ladled herself a bowl of soup. Upstairs, newly dosed with the sedative Picron had prescribed, Chambord was snoring loudly. Carrie finished the first plate of stew and ladled out another, surrendering to hunger and leaving the table full for the first time in weeks. She was halfway upstairs to her room when the phone rang. Carrie ran back and answered it, surprised when a young girl spoke her name.

"Madame Caroline Chambord?"

"Yes. Who are you?"

"Your son David told me to tell you 'David Kelly' so you will know I have a message from him."

"Is something wrong with David?"

"No, madame, but in fifteen minutes, perhaps less, the Gestapo will search your house and arrest you. Get out at once."

Carrie heard a click and the line went dead. She stood in the hall looking at the mold that was creeping insidiously up the mildewed walls. David Kelly had been her son's infant name for himself, because he could not pronounce his father's surname, Kellerman, the name he had relinquished to please her. Carrie wondered what to do. The clock struck the half hour. It was six thirty on a peaceful September evening and the Gestapo was coming to arrest her. Fear made Carrie find sudden strength, and she carried one of the suitcases to a neighbor's house, returning for the other before locking the front door and hurrying away. The sun was setting, and there seemed to be an uncanny silence in the square. Carrie wondered who the caller had been and how she knew what the Gestapo were doing. She was explaining what had happened to her old friend Mme. Bontron when she heard the squeal of tires and saw two black cars stopping outside her house. Carrie shuddered as men rang the bell, watching as they tramped down the servants' stairway to break open the lower door. Half an hour later they emerged, one carrying the metal file in which Chambord kept his papers, the other holding a gold statuette from Carrie's dressing room and the jewel case she had packed and then left behind. Carrie thought of Marie-Claude, tricked into returning to the house when she imagined it empty of her enemies. Marie-Claude had found them waiting for her, and the result had been calamity. Carrie debated whether to go back to see if Chambord was still safely asleep in his bed. But after a few moments' consideration she decided it was best, assuming he was still alive, to leave her husband to the offices of Dr. Picron. At eight the following morning Picron would arrive to take Chambord to the clinic. Carrie handed her house keys to Mme. Bontron with instructions to admit the doctor. Then she wondered where she should go, debating whether to remain in the Bontron house and deciding against this because neighbors in the square had seen her enter and any one of them could betray her to the Gestapo. Unwilling to involve her friends in any further risk, Carrie made her decision and, borrowing Madame's bicycle, pedaled around the corner to the luxurious Raphael Hotel. After registering and depositing the first suitcase, she returned to the house and collected the second suitcase. Then, bidding her friend good-bye, she cycled past the majestic house that had been her home and without a backward glance of regret turned into the rue Copernic and across the boulevard to the hotel she had selected as her hideaway.

The hall of the Raphael was supremely elegant, with silk Persian carpets, bois-de-violet bureaux, and equestrienne sculptures by Duchamp-Villon. Rococo mirrors reflected peace and calm as guests sat reading in the library and sipping drinks in the velvet plush bar. The writing room was green-walled and silk-curtained, with boiserie painted faux maplewood and tapestries of uncertain age. Carrie noticed a bull-necked giant of a man reading a paper on the terrace, and another drinking beer in the bar. Was there anywhere in Paris that had not been invaded by the enemy?

Once in her room, she relaxed and ordered a pot of chocolate and a strawberry flan. Then she went to the bathroom and inspected a marble bath on which there was no soap. As she ran the bath, a white-gloved waiter appeared, his gaunt face taking in every inch of Carrie's clothing, the tough ranginess of her body, and the cautious way she answered his questions. The woman was obviously an English spy. Old Dubois was thrilled by her audacity in registering at the Raphael, which was full to the doors with high-ranking German officers. He smiled respectfully as Carrie signed the check, and when he reached the door paused to impart what he considered might be useful information.

"If you need anything, madame, please be so kind as to call me. If I do not come at once, it's because the Germans on this floor are very demanding."

Carrie nodded gratefully. Dubois polished his spectacles meticulously and continued.

"The Boches go to dinner from seven thirty to eleven each night and are always out of the hotel by nine in the morning. Service will be impeccable during the hours of their absence, madame."

"Thank you, you're very kind."

Amused by his comments, Carrie picked up the telephone. There was only one person in Paris who would know how she could contact Armand Lognon.

Mme. Francine answered at the first ring.

"Hallo, ah, madame, how kind of you to call. We have been hoping you would contact us."

"Has the time of departure been fixed yet?"

"Indeed it has. May I ask where you are?"

"I'm at the Raphael, in the avenue Kléber."

There was a pause while Mme. Francine digested this information. Carrie waited interminably; then madame came back on the line.

"We are distraught that you should consider staying so far away from us, so I shall send my sister to collect you in the morning. What is your room number, madame?"

"I'm in two one eight."

"Very well, Ottoline will come at ten. Au revoir, madame."

For an hour Carrie sorted through her belongings. Then she

decided to have a bath and go straight to bed so she would be
fresh in the morning. She was lying back enjoying the scented
water when there was a knock on the door. Carrie fastened her
wrap and opened the door, surprised to see Dubois hastening inside with a woman who bore a striking resemblance to Mme.
Francine.

"Time to leave, Madame Chambord. I am Ottoline, Francine's
half sister. Francine said I would come tomorrow morning for the
benefit of that little louse on the switchboard who reports everything to the Gestapo."

Dubois fastened Carrie's suitcases and carried them to a trolley
outside the door. Carrie hurried into her clothes and followed
Ottoline to the service elevator. A green car was parked in the
alleyway leading from the hotel kitchens. Ottoline hurled the
suitcases in the back as if they weighed nothing and drove away,
having thanked Dubois profusely.

"He's a good man, that one, a first-day résistant, you know,
madame. He's seventy now, but he's still as alert as ever."

Carrie held her breath as Ottoline hooted her horn at the
Mercedes of a Generalfeldmarschall and one or two low black
cars from the avenue Foch. Twice, Ottoline's booming voice
roared disapproval of the Germans' road manners, and Carrie
began to wonder if they would ever reach their destination alive.
But at last they came safely to a halt outside a shabby old house
in the suburb of Bagnolet. Next door there was a bar, closed and
vandalized, and all around there were the shells and the rubble
of homes that once had been. Carrie thought it a most depressing
area. On either side of the road there were terraced cottages with
peeling paint, broken windows, and gardens full of stinging
nettles. There were no children to be seen, no dogs, policemen, or
workers on bicycles, only the threatening flashes of explosions on
the distant skyline and the sound of airplanes droning overhead.
Carrie wondered if the area had been evacuated. Then she saw
Armand watching her from an upstairs window. Ottoline pushed
her inside the house and plonked the suitcases down.

"Good luck on the journey, madame. Tonight you must not
go outside unless Armand says it's all right."

Carrie sat on the dusty sofa, suddenly exhausted by the excitement of the day. She would never return to the city, and Paris

would someday become part of the past, a decade of her life to be forgotten as quickly as possible.

Armand appeared from the upstairs bedroom, rubbing his eyes sleepily. He held out his hand in greeting and shouted so Carrie could hear him above the sound of falling bombs and shattering windows.

"I hear you had a bad day, Carrie."

"Were you asleep just now?"

"I feel cold and my bones are aching. I hope I'm not getting an attack of the grippe. I'm going back to bed in a few minutes so I can get as much rest as possible. If you're hungry, the kitchen cupboards are full of food. I've thought of everything, I can assure you."

Carrie sat in the shabby living room wishing she had brought a book to while away the hours. The night would be long and frightening if she was to remain alone in the lounge throughout the air raid. To comfort herself she thought of her son, proud of David's courage and the fierce independence that made him what he was. She would ask Armand in the morning if he knew David and could deliver a message from her. She dozed awhile, wakened at eleven o'clock by the arrival of Father Chanson. The priest was dressed in a black pullover and trousers, with a heavy overcoat and a fine felt hat. Chanson kept rubbing his hands together as if frozen, and Carrie teased him about this.

"Don't tell me you're cold on a night like this, father?"

"I always feel cold when I'm afraid, madame. Is there anything to eat? I haven't eaten since this morning."

"I can give you canned beef and noodles."

"That would be perfect."

While Chanson was eating, Carrie investigated the sleeping arrangements. There were quilted bags in one of the bedrooms, with pillows and mugs of water. Armand, it was true, had thought of everything. Carrie put out the clothes she would wear in the morning and placed her suitcases inside the bedroom door. Then she went downstairs to make tea for herself and Chanson.

"How long will the journey take, father?"

"About four days if we're lucky. After that we shall all be dead, or you will be on the sea and I will be back in Paris with Armand."

Carrie looked into the dark, luminous eyes, at the slim hands and dark hair that framed a poet's face. Father Chanson was of Italian parentage, but he looked Jewish. Carrie prayed that they would not encounter any Germans who were keen on the Aryan policies of the Fuhrer. At midnight she went to bed. Father Chanson followed a few minutes later. Carrie smiled. For the next few days the priest would be living in close proximity with a woman, on terms of the greatest physical intimacy. She appreciated the courage that had made Chanson volunteer for this dangerous expedition, and was touched by his reserve in her presence. That night her companion talked in his sleep. Carrie wondered who Rosa was, his lover, his mother, or a figment of his imagination. Tossing and turning restlessly, she tried to keep her mind from dwelling on the hellish noise outside, but sleep was impossible and she lay awake thinking until the dawn.

At first light Carrie rose and went down to the kitchen to make hot drinks for herself and Chanson. Then she began to prepare the sausage and eggs that Armand had bought for breakfast. At six Sancerre arrived with the children, who sat silent as the tomb while Carrie gave them their breakfast. She was impressed by their discipline but saddened by their frightened faces. Armand appeared at seven, still yawning, his arms full of bags and paper packages wrapped in string. He gave Carrie the ammunition she had requested, and rifles to Sancerre and George Haussman, with pouches of bullets for their jacket pockets. No one spoke, and in the unnatural silence Carrie thought of the bus. What if it had been blown up in the raid the previous evening? She looked now and then to Armand, but he was calmly eating his eggs and talking to the priest.

When breakfast was over, Armand called Carrie aside and led her to a piece of open ground in the street adjacent to the house.

"Voilà! This is your bus, Carrie. I bet it's much better than you expected."

Carrie looked admiringly at a solid vehicle, its exterior camouflaged in green and brown. The interior had seats of real leather, and as Armand started the engine she realized that the bus was capable of doing whatever she required. She was pleasantly surprised, and she said so.

"Where did you find it?"

"I stole it from the Gare de Lyon."

"From a German consignment?"

"Of course. Usually these buses are used to take guards to and from the prison of Mont Valérien at Suresnes."

"Who did the paint job?"

"I did. I don't trust outsiders with that kind of work, Carrie."

She ruffled his long brown hair, and Armand smiled engagingly, delighted with her praise. Then he squinted up at the sun and led Carrie back to the house.

"It's a fine day for our trip."

"Let's hope we're not the only bus on the road!"

When the children were ready, Carrie took one of her suitcases from the bedroom. Chanson carried the other, joking about its contents because the weight surprised him.

"What do you carry in this, madame, lead bars?"

"No, father, gold ones."

They laughed and then stepped outside into the sunlight of a hot September morning. At the end of the street Carrie saw piles or rubble that had recently been a school, a bar, and a terrace of houses. The ruins were still smoldering as she examined them, and she thought how lucky it was the bus was undamaged. Inside the bus the children were pressing their noses to the window, and George Haussman was cautioning his brothers that if they got lost or stepped away from the vehicle they would be left behind. Armand repeated this warning to the rest of the assembly.

"If we stop at night we shall do so in a field. There must be no talking, no stealing, and no making contact with neighbors. Nothing must betray our presence to the enemy. I want us to be as invisible as we can throughout the journey. And if we meet a German patrol you are to say nothing. I shall personally shoot any child who cries while the soldiers are with us. You will address Madame as Madame Martine and Father Chanson by his own name. Is that understood?"

"Yes, Monsieur Armand," a chorus of anxious voices replied, and Carrie saw that the children were terrified. Frightened children often made mistakes, and one mistake on this perilous journey would be the end of them all. She turned and spoke softly to reassure them.

"We have to treat the trip as a kind of game. We're going to play hide-and-seek with the Germans, and if they stop us we're going to lie our way out of trouble. We've just *got* to be cleverer than they are. And when we get to Quimper I'm going to buy all of you a steak and some potatoes fried in butter."

"And petits pois, madame?"

"And ice cream?"

"And mousse au chocolat?"

The children's faces lit up with pleasure as they called out their favorite foods. Shushing them gently, Carrie edged the bus from the rough ground, turning onto the cobblestone roadway of the boulevard Davout. This Armand had warned would be a dangerous section of the journey, but there was no way they could avoid it. At the place Cardinal Lavigerie Carrie turned left toward the Bois de Vincennes and then southwest through Charenton, Ivry, and Kremlin Bicêtre on the road that would eventually lead to one of the main exit roads from the city. At one corner Carrie saw a German patrol car approaching and, ramming her foot down, she swung the bus into a nearby garage. The patrol car passed by, and the garage owner wiped his forehead and congratulated her.

"The Germans will be going to the avenue de Fontainebleau. I suggest you cross by the avenue Gallieni. There isn't a checkpoint there—at least there wasn't yesterday."

Carrie drove back into the street and slowly past the cemetery of Gentilly. To avoid the Porte d'Italie they would cross rough ground for the first time. Suddenly she saw a roadblock ahead. It must have been erected during the night, and there was no way to avoid it. This was their first unexpected setback. At the checkpoint a young soldier asked where they were going. Armand replied that the children were consumptives being taken for a ride in the country. The soldier blinked uncertainly at Carrie and the children and then back at Armand. It was his first day on a roadblock and he was loath to search a woman, whatever his orders. Then he spotted Father Chanson and grinned with relief. He had been to mass at St. Pierre and knew both fathers well. The sentry called out cheerfully, "Good morning, father."

"Good morning, Gersberger. Do you fancy a ride?"

The young man beamed, relief flooding through him that nothing was amiss.

"I need a change but I shall have to wait until Christmas. When will you be back, father?"

"Late tonight if we haven't been killed by the Allied planes!"

"Bon voyage, father. Let them pass."

As the sentry waved her on, Carrie drove confidently down the avenue Gallieni, turning the bus off the road and catching the wheel as it was jerked from her grasp on the rough, stony ground. Suddenly she heard the sound of children crying and, looking through the rear mirror, saw that three of the youngest members of the party were sobbing as if their hearts would break. They had contained their terror of the German sentry because Armand had told them he would shoot anyone who wept while being questioned. But now fear made its voice known, and soon there was loud nose-blowing and sniffling from every section of the bus. Gradually, as they jolted up and down on the rutted furrows of a cornfield, the children began to feel sick. Within fifteen minutes most of them had turned pale and were holding their stomachs, and soon Carrie had to stop to allow those who could wait no longer to get out. Looking up to the main road that ran above them, she saw German patrol cars and supply trucks passing by. Following her gaze, Father Chanson prayed that no one from the German convoy would look down to the field below. When the children were ready to return to the bus Armand handed each one a candy.

"Take it and it will keep your stomachs from hurting."

Carrie raised an eyebrow, and Armand grinned.

"I got these from a pharmacist. The children will probably sleep until we reach Quimper!"

"Are you sure they're safe for kids?"

"Carrie, you know me—I check *everything*."

They stopped for lunch on the edge of a river. An old man was fishing in the sultry heat of the afternoon. Armand did not know if he was French or German, so they ignored him, keeping a cautious eye on his every move. Tension robbed the children of their appetites, and they fell asleep in small groups under the trees. Carrie drank a bottle of lemonade. Father Chanson peeled a pear. Only Armand felt well enough to tuck in two slices of smoked ham, tomatoes, and an endive salad made him by Mme. Francine. During the early afternoon they dozed for an hour. Then they had a drink and resumed the journey. The sun was still scorching down and in the lanes hungry dogs barked as they passed by en route for Maintenon.

Nearing their first night's destination, the scene was idyllic, dark fir trees as far as the eye could see and here and there a lake, a castle, a fairy-tale spire on the horizon outlined against the gold of the setting sun. All was peaceful emptiness and Renoir-red poppies until Carrie turned off the road to avoid the city of Chartres. Then, seemingly from nowhere, a black car appeared, its roof turned down, exposing two Germans being driven by a taut-faced chauffeur. The men were dressed in the black uniform of the SS, their silver shoulder flashes glinting in the setting sun. There was no room to turn, no field into which Carrie could drive to avoid a confrontation, so she continued boldly on, maneuvering the bus onto a grassy verge to permit the black car to pass. The officers looked up at the children, the woman, and the Catholic Father. Then they nodded graciously and passed on. Armand put the grenade he had been gripping back in his bag, and the children relaxed their watchfulness.

The party was to spend the night at Iliers, a location chosen by Armand's contacts in the area. When they reached the field where they could hide the bus, they found six men shot dead near bales of newly stacked hay. Father Chanson said prayers over the bodies, and the older boys helped Armand bury the farmers. Still the children did not cry, and most barely spoke because they had been trained to be quiet at all times. During the previous six months most of the children had seen parents and grandparents put to death, their homes razed to the ground, their pets destroyed in the inferno. Fear reigned in their minds as they sat huddled together, and they were unwilling and unable to trust anyone. In the darkness, a woman appeared, her eyes red-rimmed from crying. She spoke in a whisper, handing them sandwiches of crispy bacon cut from the pig in her larder. The woman was the wife of one of the dead farmers, and when Armand questioned her she told him everything she knew about German military presence in the area.

"We thought we were safe because we hadn't seen any Germans since last year. There are often English soldiers escaping from Germany, but we always recognize them because they cannot say a word of French except bonjour and bonsoir, which they say in answer to every question. When the English escape from the prison camps they come through Switzerland and then via Bourges and Orléans to St. Malô or Brest. We have often entertained them, so we thought nothing of the two men arriving here and asking for something to eat."

"You're sure they were English?"

"Of course I am. They told us all about their homes in England as we ate dinner. Then the Germans arrived and shot my husband and every man from the nearby farms as a punishment for helping the English."

Armand was shocked, as always, by the savagery of the German reprisal.

"What happened to the Englishmen, madame?"

"They vanished when the Germans drove up the drive. I don't know where they went."

"When was this, madame?"

"Last night about ten."

"Perhaps they're still around?"

The farmer's wife shrugged sadly.

"Who knows? Certainly the Germans are everywhere. There's an infantry unit at Le Mans and field units at Châteaudun and Brou. Would you like some more bacon, Armand? I have plenty to spare."

Armand looked to the children, who were sleeping under the trees, and shook his head. Father Chanson was smoking a pipe of foul-smelling tobacco, and Carrie had gone to the river to wash her clothes. Armand wondered at the meticulous ways of Americans. The farmer's wife wished him good night and left bacon for the morning, having promised to return with new-laid eggs at first light. Armand watched her walk back to the house, a woman made redundant by war. Then as he settled he went back to the beginning of his career as an escape-route organizer and thought of all the people who had died helping him. His aunt and uncle, cousin Rebecca, and both her brothers were all victims of torture in the avenue Foch; three of the drivers and endless farmers, tradesmen, and local guides had all been killed. Often it was his fault, because the Gestapo were determined to obtain information as to the whereabouts of Armand Lognon. For the first time that he could remember, Armand felt lonely and afraid. He watched as Carrie wrapped herself warmly for the night, her arms sheltering the smallest child, Loulou, a tiny, rebellious girl who had survived the destruction of her Polish village. Darkness came and there was nothing but the sound of rats scampering about the undergrowth, planes droning overhead, and, as dawn broke, the quarrelsome cackle of magpies in the rowan trees. Armand stretched his legs and walked to the lower field, where he surveyed the surrounding countryside through binoculars. Now that he had been told the Germans were in Brou and Le Mans, he would have to change the route. He was debating which would be the safest road to take when something moved in the undergrowth to his right. Armand pocketed his binoculars and walked calmly back to the clearing, his mind racing. If there were Germans about, he would soon be shot, and if the watcher was a French quisling, the party would be betrayed to a passing patrol. A twig snapped as he reached the fire. Armand took a grenade from his bag and then, calmly forking bacon into the pan, called to the bushes, "Venez manger. Il y a du jambon et des oeufs."

A mellow voice called back, "Bonjour, monsieur."

Armand smiled with relief, That surely was not a German. He called again, only louder.

"Venez, monsieur, et bienvenue."

"Bonjour."

Carrie strode to the edge of the clearing and shouted, "Get the hell out of there before you scare us all to death!"

A dapper man of about fifty appeared. He was wearing tennis shoes, a filthy beige drill suit, and a bowler. He was followed by a tall, fiery-haired Scotsman who stepped out of the ferns in a kilt and red tam o'shanter. The Scotsman was powerfully built and about thirty, heavy-bearded, with sparkling green eyes. The children stared in disbelief at his kilt and at the red pompom wobbling on his hat. Then they forgot fear and laughed till tears rolled down their cheeks. The two men introduced themselves to Carrie and Armand.

"Major Angus McGregor, ma'am, First Regiment Scots Guards."

"Colonel James Watt-Smythe."

"We've escaped from a wee prison in Poland."

Armand beamed delightedly as they shook his hand, and Carrie tried hard not to laugh at the colonel's bowler hat.

"Where *did* you get those clothes, gentlemen?"

The colonel coughed, and McGregor looked dumbfounded.

"This is ma regimental tartan, ma'am. I've worn it everywhere since the war started, even in Auschwitz. The colonel had a bit of trouble putting his outfit together for the escape, you cannae find clothes in those places. His bowler belonged to the camp commandant, and he stole his shoes from one of the gas-chamber orderlies. We're proud of ourselves, ma'am, because we've escaped and that's every officer's duty."

Armand introduced everyone and explained their journey to Quimper. Carrie fried more bacon for the "Englishmen," as the children called the new arrivals, listening as McGregor's soft Scots burr prized information out of Armand.

"Have you room in your bus for us?"

"There's room, sir, but you would involve us in risk if you were to continue wearing your national dress."

"That's true, old boy. Best we ask the lady of the house for some clothes."

The colonel and McGregor conferred, but the Scotsman was adamant. He would wear his kilt and continue on foot, meeting up with the party at prearranged night stops wherever possible. Watt-Smythe would borrow clothes from the farmer's wife and accompany the party to Quimper.

At eight the following morning the colonel drove the bus away, having left details of their route with McGregor. The Scotsman loaded his bag with bread, bacon, and some apples from the orchard. Then on sturdy legs he tramped down the lane, taking a lift here and there on a hay cart or a motorbike until he reached the outskirts of Montoire. McGregor slept in a barn until he was refreshed, then plodded on, cursing the flies and the thirst and the humidity that made him sweat. Someday, when he was back in his beloved Highlands, he would eat himself sick of mutton pasties, potted hough, and cock-a-leekie cooked all night on the stove. He would enjoy a glass of whisky and fish salmon from the river. His mouth watered and he wondered about his sister Mary, alone in the big house on the Kyle of Lochalsh. As he thought of her his step quickened and he almost ran along. There would be

no Germans in Scotland, and if there were, his sister would have
their measure. McGregor began to sing "Bonnie Mary of Ar-
gylle," and many a Frenchman looked askance as he made his way
toward the sea.


On the evening of the third day Carrie and the children were
hiding under a stone bridge near Savenay. The green bus had
been discovered by a patrol from Nantes, and they had been
forced to run for cover. Two of the party had been injured in the
shooting that followed, and since then they had remained under
the bridge, afraid to move on for fear of revealing themselves to
the Germans. Carrie bandaged Sancerre's wounded arm and the
gash on Loulou's head. She looked up anxiously as Armand returned from a reconnaissance trip, cursing violently and deathly
pale. Carrie took him to one side and questioned him.

"What happened? Are the Germans still there?"

"They just blew up the bus. I could hear them laughing about
it from the road. What in God's name are we going to do now,
Carrie?"

Carrie returned to hugging Loulou, and Armand sat despondently at her feet. The colonel was silent, his mind comput-
ing the risks of continuing on foot with thirty young children,
some injured, some on the verge of a nervous breakdown. It
would be wiser to go on alone, but he could not countenance
leaving the children undefended. He was touched when the
Haussmans brought him bread and cheese, sitting admiringly on
the ground at his feet and urging him to tell Armand what to do.

"Armand's grenades were in the bus, sir."

"I know they were, George."

"All our belongings also, and the ammunition. You are a
soldier, sir, and Armand is not. You *must* tell him what to do."

"We'll get to Quimper, don't worry."

"But how shall we get there?"

"We'll just have to find a way. If you want something badly
enough, George, you get it. That's life."

The Haussmans looked at each other and subsided into silence.
If the English colonel said there was a way, it must be true.

Beyond the bridge it was pouring rain, and there was the roar of distant thunder. Carrie wondered disconsolately if the German patrol was still waiting for them to emerge from their hiding place and how long it would take to get to their destination without transport. The children huddled together, looking questioningly at her, then Armand, and then the Englishman they had come to admire. The colonel knew he would soon have to leave the hiding place to reconnoiter their surroundings, and he was amused by the pounding of his heart. It had been a long time since he was a fighting man, though in his youth he had been in action many times. Since he had reached the age of forty-five he had been desk-bound, directing British intelligence operations in Poland and Silesia. Every German soldier would know his face from the wanted posters, and the reward for killing him would be speedy promotion and a holiday in Paris. He pulled on a dark sweater lent him by Father Chanson and prepared to leave the bridge. Just then the party was startled to hear McGregor's loud voice singing: "Sure by Tummel and Loch Cranoch and Loch arbor I will go, wi' heather tracks and heaven in their wilds. If it's thinkin' in yer inner heart braggots in ma step, you've never smelled the tangle o' the isles. . . ." There was a burst of gunfire, and a loud curse from the Scotsman. Then a couple of grenades exploded nearby, and the listeners were pitifully grateful to hear McGregor's voice calling, "Are you there, Colonel? Call out, will you, I cannae see you. Your bus is burned to a frazzle and I just blew three Jerries to kingdom come."

The children ran behind Carrie to the field, where their bus was a smoldering mass of debris. McGregor was inspecting an intact German patrol car, and one of the older lads was putting on a German steel helmet.

"This one fits me."

"I'll wear one of the others, because I speak German."

George Haussman began to take off his clothes so he could don a German uniform.

"I'll take the other."

Armand dragged a dead German away and began stripping him of his jacket. George watched as Carrie gave the children what remained of the Germans' meal—a small quantity of rabbit stew in a pot over the fire. In the corner of the field the two Englishmen were conferring.

"Well, Colonel, we've come this far, what now? Will we stay with the children or will we go on alone?"

"I intend to stay. You're free to do as you please, McGregor."

"There's room in the car for eight."

The colonel considered how best to divide their resources.

"The priest and Madame will have to go with the youngest children, that's the Haussmans and Loulou. Those who have German uniforms will have to pretend they've taken the others prisoner."

"And that old fellow with the wounded arm?"

"Sancerre will lead the children to the next rendezvous while you and I bring up the rear."

"How far is it to Quimper?"

Watt-Smythe studied his map.

"About a hundred and fifty miles if we stick to the roads, forty miles less as the crow flies."

"It's a long way with little children and a few nonfighting men."

Armand's voice reached them across the field.

"I'm not staying here in case another patrol comes by. Get ready to move on."

Surprised, Carrie looked up. Armand was waking the children who had fallen asleep and telling them to collect their belongings. Obediently she stepped into the patrol car with Father Chanson and the children. They arranged to meet up with the rest of the party at la Roche Bernard the following evening. Then Armand drove away. When the patrol car had disappeared, Sancerre lined up the remaining children, and they began to walk wearily through the fields. At a distance, McGregor and the colonel brought up the rear. It was a cold, moonless night, and Sancerre could hear the chattering of the children's teeth as they trudged along. He was not happy about their chances.

On the outskirts of a village, he saw a bicycle rack leaning against the wall of the community hall. One of the boys whispered longingly, "Do you think it's wrong to steal, Monsieur Sancerre?"

Sancerre remembered that the archbishop of Paris had recently excused food theft if it was to keep one's family alive. He shook his head confidently.

"In this instance I think not. Hurry and take one bicycle each!"

The older boys ran ahead, returning with machines for Sancerre, the two girls, and themselves. Then, cautiously, as quietly as they could, they all pedaled through the village. The church clock struck 1:00 A.M. as Sancerre led his party through the silent main street, confident that no one had seen them. Armand had told him to travel by night as much as possible and to rest by day in order to avoid the frequent German patrols. The God-sent bicycles cheered everyone, and soon the Sancerre party was well on its way to Pontchâteau.

In their turn, the colonel and McGregor also chose bicycles and rode after Sancerre. The Scot was in high spirits because he was now well on his way home, and even the colonel had begun to express the hope that the mission might be successful.

Fifteen kilometers behind, a German night patrol discovered the bodies of their colleagues in the field. A phone call alerted all roadblocks within a fifty-kilometer radius of the field, and the military commander sent extra men to find the escaping English.


Unaware of the drama at his rear, Armand drove into la Roche Bernard and through the ancient village to hide near the estuary in an unused warehouse two hundred meters from the bridge. He had told Sancerre to meet him in the largest empty port building. It was now up to the old man to find them.

While Armand hid the car, Father Chanson went in search of food. He found nothing, because nearby fields had been devastated by bombs. Chanson knew that the children were ravenously hungry, so he walked into the village and knocked on the door of the first house he reached. A frightened woman appeared and asked him what he wanted.

"Madame, have you anything to eat? I'm very hungry, and my bicycle has a flat tire, so I cannot get home."

The woman ran to the kitchen, took bread, cheese, and a basket of field mushrooms from the table, and thrust them into Chanson's hands. Then she slammed the door in his face. Puzzled, the priest started back down the road, his mind turning over the expression on the woman's face. She had been terrified and

ashamed, but why? Chanson was unaware of a German officer
watching him from the bedroom window of the woman's house.
But as he reached the water's edge he became conscious of someone following him. When he paused, the footsteps paused. When
he hurried on, they came after him at the same speed. Chanson
stepped into the shadows, knowing that under no circumstances
must he lead a German back to the children's hideout. His pur-
suer walked toward the alleyway where Chanson was hiding. In
his hand he carried a revolver, and he was elated at the thought
of killing a résistant. When the German's head appeared around
the corner, Chanson hit him with a log from the woodcutter's
pile. The German grunted and fell to the ground, a trickle of
blood from his mouth staining the Father's shoe. Chanson tried
to still the trembling in his limbs, the feeling of agony in his heart
because he knew the man was dead. Then, gathering up the food
he had been given, he ran back to the warehouse, where Armand
was waiting.

"A German followed me, you'll have to help me get rid of the
body."

Armand gulped in surprise as Chanson handed the mushrooms
to Carrie. Carrie pretended she had not heard what the priest
said, but her eyes followed Armand and the dark figure of Chanson as they walked back along the quayside to the alley where the
German lay. A loud splash signaled that they had disposed of the
body. Carrie thought sadly that a priest who had killed would be
a man with a conscience the size of Normandy. It would be wise
to keep a careful watch on Father Chanson.

In the morning they were joined by Sancerre's group and the
two Englishmen. The colonel volunteered to keep watch, and it
was not long before he woke them.

"Armand, there's a convoy of German military vehicles on the
far bank of the estuary."

Armand blinked sleepily.

"How many, Colonel?"

"Five, as far as I can see, approximately fifty men."

For a moment Armand hesitated. Then he handed an address
to the Englishman.

"Take this, Colonel, and go on ahead with Madame and the
children. I'll stay behind to try to delay the Germans. How long
do you reckon they'll take to get to the bridge?"

"About half an hour."

The colonel hesitated, unwilling to sacrifice the young man who had for so long provided the only truly successful escape route from Paris. His thoughts were interrupted by McGregor.

"*You* go on ahead, laddie. If your fishermen friends dinnae see you they'll mistrust the lot of us, and we cannae risk it. I'll stay behind with the Germans."

"And I." Chanson took a rifle and stepped down from the car.

Carrie smothered a tear. Was the priest going to sacrifice his own life to pay for the one he had taken? She watched as George Haussman and Sancerre also stepped down.

"We too will fight in the rear guard."

Armand saluted and drove away. At his side, Carrie held Loulou, and on the back seat Irena Haussman was responsible for her brothers and the youngest children. The rest of the party, led by the colonel, followed on bicycles. Sancerre waved until they disappeared from view. Then he looked across the winding, narrow road on the other side of the estuary. It would be twenty minutes or more before the trucks reached the bridge. Was there time to do what should be done? He explained his thoughts to George, who immediately ran to McGregor.

"Is it true you carry dynamite, sir?"

"Ay, and dangerous stuff it is in this weather, though I've not much of it left."

George looked longingly toward the bridge and then back to McGregor. The Scotsman understood.

"Come on then, wee George, we can only try. Let's hope they're carrying explosives in those lorries."

Father Chanson stood with Sancerre, watching the red pompom on McGregor's hat and the swinging pleats of his kilt as he disappeared toward the water. Chanson paced the warehouse like a caged animal, his mind a mass of agonizing contradiction. Why, he asked himself a thousand times, why had he not placed his trust in the Almighty? He had not placed his trust in the Almighty because he had not enough trust.

Watching him suffer, Sancerre was provoked to comment. "Yesterday you killed a German, father. If you had not he would have discovered the children and they would all be dead or prisoners again. Now you must make peace with yourself. There is no room for self-indulgence on a mission of this kind. Our

thoughts must be of the children, not of ourselves, if you'll forgive me for saying so."

Chanson looked into the aristocratic face, at the gnarled hands
and elegant tie pin at odds with the rest of Sancerre's outfit.

"You're right, of course, and I shall do my best not to allow the
events of last evening make me forget why I came on this trip."

The two men waited until McGregor returned with George
from the bridge. The boy's face was alight with admiration, and
he called out as he neared the warehouse.

"Major McGregor has made a wonderful job, we'll see all those
Germans blown as high as the sky. When I get to England, sir,
you must teach me and my sister Irena how to handle explosives."

McGregor weighed the boy's match-thin arms and the lines of
suffering already etched on his youthful face. Then, concealing
the emotion he felt, he reproved George.

"When you get to England, laddie, you must learn to earn
your living. You'd best forget about bombs and explosives, because you'll be a free man, and that's the most precious thing on
earth."

George remembered his mother's face pressed against the bars
of the carriage in which she was traveling like an animal to
Buchenwald. Her last words had been almost the same as Mc-
Gregor's. *Go to England, George, and try to forget everything
you have seen. It will only make you vengeful, and that will fill
your life with hate and unhappiness. . . .* George edged nearer the
major, because the sight of his huge body gave him courage. Now
and then he looked into McGregor's green eyes and received a
reassuring wink. For the first time in months, George felt happy.

When the convoy was on the bridge, McGregor blew the central
section. Suddenly the air was filled with black smoke, and the
explosion was heard for miles around. From houses in the village
Germans appeared, shouting and calling to comrades in the
water. There were three more explosions as ammunition in some
of the trucks ignited. Fire wagons, fishing boats, and local volun-
teers were brought to the rescue, and in the confusion the Scotsman led his companions across daisy-filled fields to Muzillac.
From there they rented a horse and cart and proceeded as fast as
they could to Ste. Anne. There, the exhausted horse dropped
dead, and they had to hide until sunset.

McGregor was reminiscing about the Highlands when a young

girl crossed the field on a bicycle. The major stared at her long blond hair, the pale face with its sensuous blue eyes, and the intent way she was searching for them. When he called out to ask if she had anything to eat, the girl ignored him, addressing herself to Sancerre as she jumped off the bicycle.

"Monsieur, I came to warn you. I was at home when you passed by about one hour ago. I saw you, and so did the German patrol from Vannes. They are behind me on the road. I don't know if they will think of looking for you in the fields, but they could."

"They'll not find us here."

The girl frowned at McGregor's interruption, and he eyed the tiny waist, the pretty hands, and the scarlet rope-soled espadrilles that covered her feet. She was a bonny lass and clever, he decided, and not a day more than eighteen.

The girl blushed under his scrutiny and then asked, "Can you tell me where you are going?"

McGregor frowned suspiciously. At such a time questions were unwelcome, and what business was it of hers? He mumbled a noncommittal reply.

"We're going wherever we can get."

"I could lead you to Dinard. From there you could get a boat to England. Or if you prefer I can help you to Brest."

"No thanks, lassie."

McGregor turned away, and the girl shouted furiously, "I am not lassie! I am Yvonne Marie-France Beaujean, and I am not a German spy, whatever you think. Two days ago my father was shot by the Germans. That is why I came to help you—I was hoping you would let me come with you to England."

Tears filled her eyes, and Sancerre offered his handkerchief.

"We have to be very careful, mademoiselle. You must forgive the major's manner."

Yvonne turned her back on McGregor, and he chuckled with delight at her fiery temper. Then again she tried to persuade him to trust her.

"I can lead you somewhere the Germans will never find, through underground passages and caves all the way to Hennebont."

McGregor agreed at once, and they picked up their gear and followed her. The caves were dark and craggy, with sharp-pointed

spikes that caught the Scotsman's head and tore Father Chanson's
shoes to shreds. Bats wheeled overhead, and there were the unfamiliar noises of animals who never saw the light of day. For an
hour they walked, pausing now and then to rest because the air
was damp and thin. Then, at a fork in the rocks, Yvonne began
to hurry and McGregor asked her why she was running.

"I have a surprise for you, Major."

"My name's Angus McGregor."

Yvonne pointed, and they saw an old mine wagon ahead on
twin rails leading to a tunnel.

"What's this, lassie?"

"I am not lassie!"

"Tell me, what is it?"

"Once there were miners in this area. They were hoping to find
treasure or gold, I don't know which, but for forty years there
has been no work in the mine."

They stepped onto the wooden trolley and trundled along the
rails for what seemed like hours. Sancerre was relieved for the
respite, because he was exhausted. McGregor was eyeing Yvonne
and wondering if he could persuade her to come with him to
Scotland. Father Chanson was dreaming of Paris and the presbytery in Montmartre where he and Father Valery lived in happy
camaraderie.

When the rails ended they walked again, emerging eventually
from a shaft hidden under dense undergrowth outside Hennebont. It was only a few more miles to their rendezvous at Pont
Scorff. Yvonne rummaged in her pocket and produced a thick wad
of French money.

"It's all I have, Monsieur Angus McGregor. Will you take me
with you to England?"

McGregor stared at the money, then at the girl.

"What about your mother, would you leave her behind?"

"My mother was killed in an air raid in 1940. I am alone in
the world except for my aunt who lives in Quebec. That is why
I followed you. I knew you could not be Germans, because only
an Englishman would appear in public in a woman's dress."

McGregor opened his mouth and closed it again.

"I'm a Scot and that's nae a dress, it's ma clan tartan, ma kilt.
And I'm Angus McGregor, McGregor's ma last name."

The major bit his lip. It was going to take months to turn Yvonne into a good Scots lassie. He pushed the wad of notes back to her.

"Keep your money, you'll need it when you get to England."

A burst of gunfire cut short their conversation. The party dived for cover, but Sancerre had been shot in the chest. Father Chanson ran back to the path, picked the old man up by the shoulders, and dragged him back to the ditch. Then he mouthed the words of extreme unction, because he knew Sancerre was dying.

McGregor threw his last grenade and waited. After the explosion, there was silence. Then, when the smoke had cleared, the birds began to sing again and they heard the welcome sound of foghorns in the bay. Warily McGregor rose and led the way to their rendezvous, pausing to call to Chanson, who had lingered behind with the dying man.

"Hurry, father, we cannae be hangin' about."

Sancerre pushed the priest away.

"Go quickly, father, it's all over with me. Tell the children I pray for their safe arrival in England."

In semidarkness Chanson hastened along the road, straining his eyes as he followed the French girl's satiny blond hair. When he had almost caught up with the party, a shot echoed in the stillness and the priest fell to his knees, a look of profound regret on his face. So, he was never to return to Paris, never to help Father Valery with his work again. Chanson closed his eyes and prayed for the safety of his old friend and all the résistants they had ever known. Another shot hit the priest, and Chanson fell dead in the roadway. Yvonne too was hit, a bullet shattering her calf. She did not cry, though blood poured down her leg onto the shingle path, soaking her socks and the new shoes she had been saving for her trip to freedom.

McGregor ran back to the clearing, mad with rage at the sniper's cowardice. Tempting the gunman to take aim, he stood looking up, his eyes searching the leafy dimness. Suddenly a shaft of moonlight caught the barrel of a rifle. McGregor fired, and a collaborator fell from the gnarled oak tree into the meadow. The Scotsman ran back to the couple on the road and examined Yvonne's wounded leg. He was surprised to find his hands trembling with agitation, his breath shunting through his lungs like a train through a tunnel. The girl would not be able to walk, so McGregor handed his rifle to George and picked her up in his arms, wondering why he felt so light-headed with relief.

"We've not far to go now, so don't cry. God, you're heavy, and I'm as tired as a hound after the hunt."

McGregor hummed a lilting Scottish lullaby, and soon he felt the blond head fall against his throat and heard the deep breathing as Yvonne slept.

George whispered as they reached the outskirts of Pont Scorff, "Will you marry Yvonne when you get to England, sir?"

McGregor considered the question for the first time.

"I'm no a hasty fellow, George, I think I'll wait a week."

George smiled happily. If McGregor's house in Scotland was large enough and if he had a wife to look after him, there might be room for the Haussmans as well. George was already thinking seriously about how to find someone to adopt him and his brothers and sister without splitting up the family. He held the gun lightly, his eyes searching the undergrowth because he was proud the major had trusted him with his life.

As they neared a derelict barn they saw Armand smoking a dried-grass cigarette. His face was ghastly pale, and it was obvious he was severely shaken. McGregor ran toward him calling a question.

"Is something wrong, laddie? What's happened?"

Armand looked curiously at Yvonne, but he said nothing about her presence with the Scotsman.

"Six of the children were killed today when a mine exploded on the road."

"And the colonel?"

"He's inside comforting Carrie."

"Sancerre and the priest are dead too. They were killed by a Frenchman, though they didnae know it, thank the Lord."

Armand thought of the old soldier who had volunteered for one last mission and the priest who had forgotten his vows for long enough to save all their lives.

Tomorrow, with luck, they would reach Quimper. Armand had stolen a truck to make sure the party could all travel together. He sat looking at the fire and wondering if praying was really a help.

Carrie removed the bullet from Yvonne's leg, applied bandages, and gave her painkilling tablets.

The French girl slept at McGregor's side, his tartan shawl around them both, his brawny arms enfolding her. When next she opened her eyes, Armand was brewing coffee and a small girl with flaxen hair was trying to wake Carrie. Yvonne smiled at the child's persistence.

"What's your name?"

"I'm Loulou."

"Where do you come from, Loulou?"

Loulou stared suspiciously at the newcomer.

"I don't know where I come from."

The little girl ran to Carrie and buried her head in her wrap, knowing she must never answer questions from strangers.

When everyone was awake, they ate fried bread and watercress picked from a nearby stream. Then Armand checked the truck and George Haussman scrambled into the front passenger seat with the colonel, who had elected to drive. The rest of the party wedged themselves in the back of the vehicle, eager to set off on the last leg of the journey.

It was dark for 8:00 A.M. as Watt-Smythe edged them onto a country road bordered by foxgloves and meadowsweet. White horses pranced in a nearby field, saved from requisition by an ingenious farmer. Along the banks of the river among the cow parsley, women were piling apples into rosy red mountains to be made into local cider and calvados. It was a peaceful scene, and for a brief moment the colonel imagined himself home in England. For the last twenty-five years he and his wife had lived alone in a rambling country mansion left him by a rich uncle. There had been no children, and adoption societies had shunned their applications because of his work as an intelligence officer. The colonel was deep in thought when, as they rounded the corner near a bridge, a German sentry stepped out and challenged them.

George Haussman replied, "We are traveling to Brest with prisoners."

Dissatisfied, the sentry waved his rifle, ordering them all out of the truck. Watt-Smythe hesitated briefly, then shot the sentry between the eyes.

As he drove on, George Haussman shivered. How cold the Englishman was, how sure in every action. George wished his hands would stop trembling. Then he thought of McGregor and began to dream of Scotland and fishing salmon in the Highlands.

On his left the colonel could see the jagged gray-beige rocks of the Breton shoreline. The sea was pounding mercilessly on the beach, and everywhere there was the sound of gulls screaming. On Armand's instructions he drove down a sharp incline to a fisherman's cottage on the beach. Then, having examined the layout of the house, he called to Armand.

"We'll stay here with the children while you go and get your friends. We won't move until you come to pick us up."

"Very well, Colonel. I shall return as quickly as I can. Their house is not very far from here."

Armand ran to the road and within minutes had hailed a lift from a man with a pony and trap. The colonel went to the door and knocked. There was a moment of silence; then a monocled German colonel appeared. Watt-Smythe hit him with the butt of the rifle, and McGregor dragged his unconscious body inside. A quick reconnaissance of the property revealed that it had been commandeered as a weekend home by the German. They found his companion, a widow from Lorient, in the storeroom, taking a jar of peaches from a shelf. McGregor tied her to a chair and gagged her. Then he went outside and carried Yvonne to the bedroom. Across the highway, squat Breton cottages shone white among the cornfields. And on the headland a lighthouse flashed its warning to ships at sea. McGregor stood for a moment re-membering Michelet's words. *All these rocks that you see are sunken cities. And those whispering sounds which seem to be made by the storm are the Crierien, ghosts of the shipwrecked asking for burial. . . .* He wondered if folk in the houses nearby had seen them arrive, but there was nothing to be seen, only fishing boats on the far distant horizon and a row of blackbirds cawing on the fence.

Inside, Carrie was making soup, and Loulou was wiping sweat from Yvonne's feverish face. McGregor took his place near the bed, praying the French girl would recover.

In the evening the gale rose and the sea pounded the low wall around the garden. On the beach gray thistles stood strong against the onslaught with prickly couch grass that was the only covering on the dunes. The children crept into McGregor's bed, onto the colonel's sofa, and under Carrie's sleeping bag, but no one slept. They were all waiting for the knock on the door that would signify capture or the chance for freedom. Suddenly one of the children remembered.

"Carrie, you said you would buy us steak when we arrived in Quimper."

"I think I'll buy it when we get to England. We'll be happier in England, because we won't have to worry about being seen by the Germans."

"Whatever you say, Carrie."

At 1:00 A.M. Armand arrived with two rugged Breton fishermen. Carrie bundled the children into their clothes, and the colonel led them to the boat. Then he returned and thanked Armand for his help. Armand smiled delightedly.

"I am honored to have met you, Colonel, and you, Major McGregor. Good luck to you both."

As the two men waded out to the boat Armand called, "If you have any spare rooms in your houses in England you can let some of the children stay with you. They are all without homes, as you know."

Carrie admired his persistence. McGregor had already agreed to adopt the four Haussman children. She was to take Loulou, and the colonel and his friends the rest. Carrie smiled as she recalled his words. *If there's any trouble with the authorities I shall turn my house into an orphanage and to hell with bureaucracy. . . .* The children's reaction to the news had been to cry and sob for an hour, releasing all the tensions and uncertainties of the past few months. Then they had approached their new guardians with shy kisses and tiny gifts saved from former homes.

Carrie called over the rail to Armand, "Tell David I'm safe, and don't forget to keep out of Paris for a few weeks."

"I shall be very careful, Carrie, and I shall always think of *everything*."

Carrie blew a kiss, amused by his youthful confidence. Then she looked at the children and wondered what they would make of the colonel's stately home and the seat of the Laird of Kyleakin. The fishermen cast off, and in a howling gale they drew away from the solitary figure on the shore. Some of the little ones cried at the parting; some fell asleep as though nothing untoward had happened. Armand waved until the boat was a speck on the horizon. Then he walked to the station at Quimper and took the night train to Paris.

Satisfied that he had done his best for the children, he dozed, dreaming of Suzanne Castel and the night he had gone to see her show at the Bal Tabarin. At 3:00 A.M. he ate some bread and cheese and drank a flask of coffee given him by the wife of one of the fishermen. Soon he would be back in Paris, hiding in one of his safe houses and being visited by Mme. Francine, who was the nearest thing he had to a mother. Armand thought fondly of her as he dozed. The train was almost deserted, and soon he felt able to sleep for a while. Outside it was raining, and jagged flashes of lightning lit the compartment as Armand snored.

In the early hours of the morning, an SS officer boarded the train and sat facing Armand. The officer's hair was white blond, his eyes ice blue, and something in their strange expression made Armand want to hide. Instead he looked steadfastly out the window, forcing himself not to succumb to panic at the arrogant amusement of the officer nearby. An old woman boarded the train at Chartres, and Armand chatted with her and ate some of her apples. When she stepped down at the next station he fell to thinking of the future, doing his best not to think of the officer's eyes, which never left his face. Armand thought they were the eyes of a snake, unblinking and soulless. Was it possible this was the man he had sought so strenuously to avoid?

When the train drew into the station in Paris, Armand walked down the corridor whistling a cheeky tune. He was relieved that the journey was over. He had made it. The children were safe, and he would soon be out of reach of his Gestapo enemies. He walked down the platform and gave his ticket to the guard, shocked to see the black-leather-gloved hand of the SS officer taking it from the old man. For the first time the officer spoke, and Armand clenched his fists to stop himself trembling at the sound of the hissing voice.

"You are Armand Lognon?"

"No, I'm Jacques Vanion, here are my papers."

"I am Hauptsturmfuhrer Slagel. You will accompany me to the interrogation center in the avenue Foch."

Slagel pocketed Armand's ticket and marched the boy at gunpoint to a waiting car. The ticket collector waited until they were out of sight; then he hastened to a call box and dialed Mme. Francine's number.

In the car, Armand was thinking of David Chambord, who was hiding in a château in Neuilly, in the very midst of a host of collaborators. Standartenfuhrer Gunther wanted David Chambord as much as any other résistant in France. His mind was in a turmoil as he considered Suzanne and her German lover. Suzanne had told Armand nothing of her liaison with the German, but he had sensed that she was infatuated with Hans the first time he saw them together. Would Slagel torture him until he told of the chains of communication through which he had been working these past months? Would he betray the Breton fishermen who risked their lives with every tide? Would he talk of Suzanne, who was the most beautiful woman he had ever met? Armand felt panic washing over him like waves on the shore, and the scent of fear emanating from every pore.

Slagel smiled exultantly. Standartenfuhrer Gunther had been waiting for months to question Armand Lognon. With luck, he would lead them to Rol Tanguy, the Communist resistance leader, and Pierre Lefaucheux, who was determined to mastermind insurrection and the liberation of Paris. And most important of all, they would ensnare David Chambord, whose groups were now operating all over occupied France.

By the time they had reached the corner of the avenue Marceau, Armand had decided what he must do. For a moment he smiled with relief, and Slagel looked askance at his expression. What was making the Jew so happy? Slagel thought grimly that Lognon would not grin for long. Indeed, within a couple of days, once Slagel had extracted every scrap of information, Armand would be sent for execution to Mont Valérien, if he had not already died.

Armand thought of the pharmacist he had visited on the advice of one of his resistance friends, the capsule he had been given "in case the worst ever happens." He had never thought that it would, but now he was glad that he had truly thought of everything. For a brief moment he congratulated himself. Then the car turned into the avenue Foch and sped toward the building with the black iron eagle. Armand rolled the poison capsule around in his hand and thought of the happy days of childhood in Lille and of his mother, who had fought so bravely when the Gestapo arrived. Then he thought of Suzanne, with whom he had fallen hopelessly, ridiculously in love. He took the capsule between thumb and finger, and when Slagel leaned forward to speak with the driver, pushed it into his mouth. For a moment he lost his courage and hesitated, his eyes looking longingly at the chestnut blossoms in the sunlit boulevard. Then he bit hard on the capsule and screamed one agonized lament as the corrosive liquid burned his throat. In seconds Armand was dead.

Slagel screeched for the driver to stop and, leaping out of the car, dragged the body onto the pavement. First he shook Armand's shoulders. Then he roared abuse at the corpse, his face paling, his eyes glinting with fury. It had happened again— he had been cheated of his triumph, and this time by one of the most important résistants he had ever captured. Speechless with rage, Slagel paced back and forth, back and forth, looking in loathing at the contorted body. When he searched the shabby suit he found one Métro ticket to Bagnolet, one half-smoked cigarette, a packet of American chewing gum, and a letter from Armand's mother, dated May, 1940. Slagel cursed the courage and the cunning that had defeated him. Then he felt again in the inner lining of Armand's jacket and took out a photograph, the kind displayed in theaters and nightclubs. Despite his anger, Slagel smiled, his face puckering with triumph as he looked into the alluring face of Suzanne Castel. So, the wide-eyed girl was a résistante and a close friend of the most troublesome Jew in Paris. She was also the fiancée of David Chambord, one of the three leading résistants in Paris and a man Standartenfuhrer Gunther dreamed of capturing. Slagel wondered what connection Hans von Heinkel had with the girl, remembering the night they had met in the nightclub near the Ritz Hotel. Stirrings of intense emotion made Slagel's mind wander, and he had to force himself to hurry back to the office to consult his files.

Forgotten in the roadway, Armand lay staring at the sky. An hour later a passing taxi driver picked up the corpse and delivered it to Mme. Francine in her house in the rue Pigalle. Madame looked down at the stiffening body and tenderly touched Armand's cheek. Tears fell down her cheeks as she whispered, "For you, my dear, the war is over."

# CHAPTER SEVEN

## December, 1941—January, 1942

Suzanne was preparing for the final show at the Bal Tabarin. She and Janine sat side by side at the dressing table, rouging their cheeks and painting their mouths with minute scraps of lipstick from depleted makeup boxes. A new curfew had just been decreed to punish recalcitrant Parisians for their increasing defiance of the occupying force. The unnaturally early hour of the curfew meant that theater and club owners were facing the prospect of a shutdown over the lucrative Christmas period. Janine did not care, and as she powdered her nose she was happy and excited. She had just received the keys to a new apartment in the most fashionable area of the eighth district, one converted floor of what had previously been the Navarin Hotel. Her bank balance was healthy, and for six months she had been buying every scrap of gold she could find from friends, bankrupt jewelers, and other less reputable sources. For Janine things had never been so good. To salve her conscience, Janine had bought Suzanne a fabulous Christmas present. Originally she had intended to give it to Suzanne on Christmas Eve, which they had always spent together, but this year Janine had been invited to a party at the home of the German commander of Gross Paris, and she had no intention of missing such an important occasion. She puckered her mouth and applied a coating of liquid paraffin as a gloss for her lips. In the harsh white light of the makeup mirror she looked exquisitely beautiful, unreal and hard as a diamond. Suzanne watched her, half admiring, half hesitant, still overwhelmed by the sudden change in her friend. She pulled on the old black dress she had been wearing for her solo spot for over a year, clipping the broken zipper and expertly engaging the teeth so the catch slipped smoothly up her back. Janine frowned, aggravated by Suzanne's acceptance of her deteriorating condition.

"If you mend that zipper again, Zizi, I swear I shall scream."

"If I throw it away I'll have nothing to wear."

"Wear this instead."

Janine pulled a shiny white box from under the bench, and Suzanne saw that it came from Schiaparelli. She watched in increasing excitement as Janine went to the wardrobe and took another box from its hiding place.

"You were so impressed by my new outfit last week, I thought I'd get you one like it. I'll be wearing mine later tonight when I go out, so for a few minutes we'll be able to be belles-soeurs just one last time."

"I can't believe this is happening."

"These are my Christmas presents to you, Zizi. I do hope you'll like them. I'll be working over the holiday, so it's best I give them to you now, in case we don't see each other for a while."

Suzanne held her breath as she unloaded an exquisite black dress from its wrappings. Janine watched, touched by the wonder and innocence in her friend's eyes. Suzanne fingered the fine draped wool, the cluster of beads around the neck, the silk lining that revealed its exorbitant price.

"I don't know how to thank you, Janine. This must have cost a fortune."

"Open the other box too, Zizi, and hurry, it's almost time for the overture."

Suzanne opened the box labeled REVILLON, knowing it to be from the best fur designer in Paris. When she saw the voluminous white fox wrap, she threw her arms around Janine, bowling her over.

"Shall I wear it now? Help me out of this old rag, will you?"

Janine pulled down the zipper and dragged the shabby black dress from Suzanne's shoulders, throwing it with a grimace of distaste into the bin.

"Best throw it away in case you relent and decide to try to wear it again."

Suzanne fastened the new dress and gazed at her reflection in stunned admiration.

"How much did it cost? No, don't tell me or I shan't dare wear it."

Janine reckoned on her fingers.

"I'd say that outfit cost me two General-Obersts, one General-leutnant, one Oberst-Gruppenfuhrer, and a few frisés I don't want to remember. Don't look so sad, Zizi, whoring's no worse than dancing, typing, or singing for your living. You just wear out a different part of the body."

Suzanne stroked the soft fur and thought that she was as much of a collaborator as Janine for accepting such a gift. She kissed her friend, determined that Janine should never know how sad she felt at her flippant attitude toward her new profession. Outside the door, the call boy shouted, "Overture and beginners."

Janine ran downstairs, relieved to be leaving the grimy club where she had worked for so long. From the moment she had started earning money from the Germans she had thought herself elevated in the world, and as she looked at M. Hibbert's dancers waiting in the wings, their faces pinched with hunger, their tights full of clumsy darns, their shoes worn down, she knew she had made the right decision. Janine straightened her dress and smoothed her hair. Then she peered through the velvet curtains into the body of the hall and saw M. Orloff, the Russian conductor, waving short, fat arms at what remained of his orchestra: one drummer, a pianist, and an old lady flautist from the conservatory. The audience was restive, and there, alone at his usual table near the wall, was Hans von Heinkel. Janine ran an expert eye over the rest of the assembly, shrugging because there was nothing of interest to her, just the usual café society slumming and locals from Pigalle and Montmartre, who could afford the cover charge, staring into the folds of the curtain as they waited to ogle their favorite girls. Janine looked over a table of SS officers, but her deliberations were cut short as the curtain rose and she heard the tap-tap of the dancers' feet on the catwalk. She followed them onstage, bowing gracefully as she acknowledged the applause of her admirers.

When the time cafe for Suzanne to do her spot, she thought of no one but Hans. Knowing this to be her last show, he had filled the dressing room with flowers—early hyacinths, roses, and narcissus that scented the air with the heady perfume of spring. Suzanne had no idea where Hans had managed to buy such blooms in December, but she was touched by the gesture. When men sent flowers they usually sent boring formal bouquets. Hans had sent a whole hothouse of splendor. As the spotlight pinpointed her face, Suzanne could see nothing of the audience, so she sang just for Hans, and every man watching believed she was singing for him.

When she came offstage, two nudes were bickering over a sequined G-string. Suzanne looked at their lush bodies and thought that they, like Janine, had decided that taking German lovers was preferable to starvation. For some time it had been possible to tell virtuous women from sexual collaborators and honest families from those whose men were working on the black market, because the ones convention condemned were not showing the massive weight loss of the rest of the population. Suzanne looked at her own reflection in the mirror. She had grown thin and she looked older, no longer the inexperienced girl from the rue Gabrielle. She shrugged, knowing that she too was a collaborator, a woman with a German lover. Defiantly she told herself that without Hans she would have starved. From the moment of his arrival he had cared for her, going farther and farther afield to buy food and contacting forbidden members of the black market despite his position. Lately Hans had often returned empty-handed, and Suzanne tried not to think what would happen when all the food was gone. On the way upstairs to the dressing room she met Janine on her way down for the finale. Janine kissed both her cheeks.

"Zizi, I have to change and dash when the show's over. I have a date with a General-Oberst tonight."

"Can't you even stay for one drink so I can show off my new outfit?"

"No, my sweet, I can't, I shall have to miss the party altogether. Anyway, you know how I hate good-byes."

Suzanne repaired her makeup and donned the luxurious white fur wrap. For a moment she stood entranced by its sensuality. Then she ran down to join her colleagues onstage for the finale. Loud applause greeted the colorful spectacle, and some of the girls burst into tears as the curtain fell. Men left their seats in the hall to head for the stage door, and onstage Suzanne exchanged small gifts with the dancers. Hibbert had given them each a bottle of Bordeaux to take home for Christmas, and he had put a trestle table on the empty stage and loaded it with the remaining bottles of champagne from his cellar. The girls eyed each other, all of them wondering how they were going to survive with a 6:00 P.M. curfew, which prevented any theatrical work. To save fuel the cinemas had ceased afternoon showings, so they could not take jobs as ushers, as was their custom when "resting." It might be possible to get work in hotels, bars, or shops, but club performers had no experience to recommend them, and the girls knew life was going to be hard. Hibbert poured them another glass of champagne and proposed a toast.

"To our next show, may it be very soon."

The girls smiled wanly, and Suzanne thought she could feel despair in the air. In the new order of things it was unlikely they would work again for months. Everyone tried to avoid thinking of this, but soon they fell silent, and by midnight they were drifting back to the dressing rooms and preparing to go home.


Outside it was a dark, moonless, frosty evening that nipped the cheeks and made the night walker breathless. Janine cursed that she could not find a taxi. Gas was almost unobtainable, and people with cars had not been able to use them for months. Taxi drivers were busy converting their vehicles into gazogènes, to be run on wood fuel, bringing a new smell to the boulevards. Janine shuddered as she saw dark forms scrambling over piles of refuse. The streets of Paris were alive with rats, which were breeding as never before. She hurried on, trying not to think of the scratchy sounds all around or to see the rodents' glimmering eyes.

The man following Janine kept his eyes on the outline of the white fox wrap. He was grim-faced and tense with excitement. Suzanne Castel looked wealthy despite all the privations of the occupation. The man clenched his fists and fumbled for the knife in his pocket. For days he had been sharpening it, examining it, enjoying it, and he was impatient for the moment when he would use it.

When Janine reached the rue St.-Lazare, an air raid siren

sounded. She ignored its wailing and turned left into the narrow
rue de Mogador. Hearing footsteps behind, she hurried on, looking over her shoulder now and then but seeing nothing in the
inky blackness except the red and black stripes around endless
reprisal posters giving lists of names of Parisians who would
never return to their homes. An icy blast made Janine resolve to
ask one of her more powerful lovers for a car or, better still, a
driver to be at her disposal during the evenings. She hurried on,
wishing it were springtime, full of the scent of magnolia.

The man ran forward, his body straining with effort and
excitement. Suzanne would scream and beg his mercy, but it was
too late, the damage had already been done. He stayed close to
the wall as Janine searched the darkness for the familiar blue-
painted headlights of a taxi. When none came, she resigned
herself to walking all the way to her destination. She was going
to be late. Hell and damnation! Janine thought of the waiting
General-Oberst and cursed. At the corner of the rue Charras a
German patrol car passed by. Desperate not to miss this chance,
the man drew closer to Janine. She paused, puzzled because the
footsteps following her seemed suddenly very near, and turning
she called to the emptiness beyond.

"Who's there? Why are you following me?"

The sound of her voice was lost as the patrol car screeched by.
The man pressed his body against the wall so she could not
see him, and as the car passed he lunged forward, grasping
Janine's black hair and pulling her toward him. His hands tight-
ened around her throat, making her choke and writhe in agony.
When he spoke, she was shocked to the core.

"You should have been more careful, my dear Suzanne."

Janine tried to protest her identity, but the man's hands were
like a vise around her throat. She knew he was going to kill
her, that he had mistaken her for Suzanne, and as he ran the
blade over her chest she tried desperately to fight him off, but
she could not match the manic strength of his limbs. Beyond
reason, the man exulted in his brief moment of domination.
Then he cut her throat, moaning in ecstasy as warm blood gushed
over his body. An upsurge of power released chains long melded
in the man's mind, and he knew that at this moment he could
do everything he had ever wanted to do. He hacked at the body

again and again, plunging the knife into the soft, giving flesh. Then he pushed the corpse away, watching as it slid down the wall, the damaged face pressed against the peeling paintwork of a charcuterie. The man threw back his head and laughed when he read the sign on the door. It was fitting that the pig should die near a pork butcher's establishment. For a moment he looked up at the dark sky. Then he mopped his suit with the fur wrap and walked, with it still in his hands, into the night. Suzanne Castel was dead. Her body had trembled against his own, her hands had gripped his in the final paroxysm of death. He walked on through the inky blackness, clutching the wrap, sniffing its perfume, and grimacing as the blood congealed, sticking the pristine fluffiness into hard brown knots.

When she had finished packing her makeup, her clothes, and the photographs she kept around her dressing-room mirror, Suzanne said good-bye to her friends and left the stage door with Hans. They walked arm in arm through the familiar alleyways of Pigalle, avoiding the main roads and pausing to kiss near a fountain of stone dolphins in an ancient square. The champagne had made Suzanne relax, and she pressed her body close to Hans, caressing him tenderly.

The man felt drained of all energy. His hands hung limply at his sides and he was wondering how he would ever get the blood off his clothing. Ahead, he saw a flash of white moving slowly toward the rue des Martyrs. Her ghost had come to haunt him! He shook his head wearily, cursing his imagination. The dead were dead; only the living could move and breathe and tantalize the senses. He crept nearer the white shape that had so startled him, gazing in disbelief as Suzanne's voice came to him in the silence of the night.

"I'm a little drunk from all that champagne."

"I like you this way."

"Shall we save the wine Monsieur Hibbert gave me for Christmas?"

"I imagine that was what he intended."

"Oh, Hans, I'm so tired, so very tired."

The man stopped in the middle of the road, stunned to disbelief. If Suzanne Castel was alive and well, who was the woman lying dead in the rue Charras? He had touched her hair and felt the butterfly slides, the same slides Suzanne wore when she was appearing in the club. He had recognized the outfit she had worn so proudly on her last night at work, the clothes the German had surely bought her. He stumbled on, forcing his legs to move and holding his aching head, barely able to keep from screaming hysterically at the white-clad figure ahead. His brain felt like a white-hot furnace, his body like a ton of steel. What was to be done? How to be rid of the temptress who was driving him mad?

The morning papers were full of the murder and l'artiste assassinée was the subject of every conversation, not because the people of Montmartre were unused to death but because Janine had been one of them and the killer was an enraged deviate. Hans read the headlines, aghast when he saw Janine's name on the sheet, her photograph on the front page. The killer had cut her throat and slashed her body in a frenzy. Hans read the account in horror: *a blood bath, Jack the Ripper, a madman on the loose in Paris* . . . He walked home, pausing to speak with Vivienne and to raise his hand to Mme. Roger, who called hello from her bedroom window. Nearing la maison Fleuri, he helped M. Corbeil measure his wall in preparation for the building of a new greenhouse, and nodded to Laval, who was on his way to the shops. Laval stared clean through him, hurrying along the street, his head bowed against the wind. How dare the German acknowledge him? They were not friends. How could he think they were? Laval cringed with loathing as he passed out of sight.

Suzanne was happy. That morning the sound of a cockerel had broken her sleep, and she had imagined herself in the balmy days before the occupation. Everyone on the Butte Montmartre was busy buying hens, ducks, guinea fowl, and even catching thrushes so they would have something to eat if things worsened. Women were becoming adept at making pies from cabbage and leftovers, and cheese was the latest luxury. Suzanne ran to greet Hans, pulling him to the table and handing him some tea.

"I have a surprise for you, Hans, we've been given some beautiful cheese made by Monsieur Corbeil's sister who lives in the country. And she brought some salt pork for our storeroom. I hope we'll be able to buy another pig."

"We have meat for Christmas. After that I shall have to think again."

Hans drank his tea and tucked the newspaper under his seat. Suzanne wondered why he was so pale and anxious that she should not see the morning paper.

"Is something wrong, Hans?"

"Eat your breakfast, we'll talk later."

Stung by his tone, Suzanne fell silent, toying with her eggs and wishing she did not care so much what Hans thought and said. A strong word from him made her cry, a rebuke pulverized her stability. She pushed her plate away and poured another cup of tea.

"I had a letter from Carrie today."

"Is she well?"

"She's back in America, and she has a new house near where she used to live when she was young."

"Where's that?"

"Somewhere in Connecticut, not far from New York. Hans, tell me, what's troubling you?"

Hans hesitated, uncertain how to break the news. Then he explained what he had learned.

"Janine is dead. She was murdered last night by a madman. I don't think you should read the paper, Suzanne. The account is very gruesome and upsetting."

Suzanne fled to her room and locked the door. First she sobbed until she could cry no more. Then she sat on her bed and cursed war because it destroyed everything, love, friends, family, and security. She looked up at the white fur jacket and the dress on its padded satin hanger. Janine had been generous to a fault, whatever her profession. Now she was gone. They would never work together again. They would never make plans and tell each other secrets they told no one else. Suzanne thought of their last meeting and Janine's words. *You know how I hate good-byes. . . .* The remembrance made more tears flow, and she paced the room trying to envisage what could have happened. Later, Suzanne

went downstairs and read the account of Janine's death in the
paper. Hans was outside, busy preparing the soil for planting. For
a moment Suzanne watched as he raked compost over the beds.
Then she looked again at the news headline, shivering in horror
as she scanned the lurid details and the picture of the broken
body against the wall. Blood had spattered the pavement, the
shop window, the road, and a nearby notice announcing the
names of men killed in a reprisal. Near the body someone had
scrawled WHORE. Suzanne's distress turned to anger, and she
began to think about Janine's friends and clients. Most had been
German officers considerably older than belle-soeur, men of a
certain elegance and wit, anxious to foster an image of virility
by being seen around the city with a dazzling beauty. Janine had
had no jealous lover in the background, no discarded fanatic who
would have wanted to kill her, and her nights had been nights
of mechanical passion, not moments of white-hot emotion likely
to provoke such an attack. Suzanne went outside to talk with
Hans. Laval, who was in his garden, watched, his ears straining to hear every word. Now and then he twitched with rage at
their obvious familiarity, and as Suzanne disappeared into the
kitchen with her lover, the collaborator returned to his work,
cursing her shamelessness. The sky was pink with the approach
of snow, and Laval had little to eat and no fuel for the fire.
Traders in the area were refusing to sell him supplies, so he had
been forced to buy everything on the black market at exorbitant
prices. Since November, two of Laval's sources of information had
vanished from the city, and he knew that if he did not make
some attempt to impress the Gestapo they would drop him, leaving
him to starve before the spring. He threw pine cones on the sparse
fire in his hearth, watching dazedly as they spat on the carpet.


In a bare white office in the avenue Foch, Hauptsturmfuhrer
Slagel was reading through his files, the same files he had been
combing since the death of Armand Lognon. This he did at
least once a week, and sometimes in the still of the night when
everyone else had gone home. He was determined to find some
clue to the personality of David Chambord, something that would
reveal how to ensnare him. Thus far he had found nothing, and

daily Standartenfuhrer Gunther grew more impatient, more frustrated by his lack of success in arresting the leaders of French resistance. Slagel read through the file on Suzanne Castel, frowning at the mocking eyes and determined mouth. Castel appeared to be a young girl whose only interest was her profession and her fiancé. Slagel wondered idly what her true feelings were for Hans von Heinkel. Laval, Gunther's spy in the area, was obsessed with the girl, so his reports had to be read in the light of this disability. Everyone else who had been questioned about Suzanne—at the Bal Tabarin, in Mme. Francine's establishment, in shops and houses around Montmartre and Pigalle—had said the same thing: that she was interested only in surviving and that she was an innocent disinterested in rebellion. Slagel picked up the morning paper and looked at the headlines, reading the account of Janine's murder and looking closely at the photograph of her body. Then he stood to attention and saluted Standartenfuhrer Gunther, wrinkling his nose in distaste at his superior's new toilet water.

"Anything new, Tristan?"

"Nothing, sir."

"Perhaps we should simply arrest the Castel girl and see if Chambord comes to rescue her, as he did her friend Lassalle."

"I have no grounds for arrest, sir."

"You have the photograph taken from Armand Lognon."

"Yes, sir, but with respect, anyone can steal a photograph."

"I am aware of that."

Gunther walked to the window and frowned at the falling snow. Snow would impede his morning exercise, and he was worried about his weight. He thought of the directive he had just received from Berlin: "All résistants are to be exterminated." It was pointless to arrest one man here and there, because others immediately replaced them. So this morning Gunther had had two hundred and fifty known résistants arrested and shot at Mont Valérien. Now he *must* find their leaders, the three most important men in Paris. Once he had them he would make at least one of them talk, and so achieve what he most wanted—an intimate knowledge of the chains of communication and available manpower plus details of plans being prepared by those who were determined to free France from German rule. An idea suddenly struck Gunther, and he turned to Slagel, watching his assistant's reaction with relish.

"I think we should send for Major von Heinkel. I have a feeling he may be able to help us."

Slagel's face brightened with pleasure, and he ordered a car to be sent to collect Hans from the house in the rue Gabrielle.

Gunther sat by the window, waiting impatiently for Hans to arrive.

"Have you anything for me today, Tristan?"

"There's a woman in three, sir. I shall be questioning her again at eleven."

"How many times has she been interrogated?"

"Four times, sir. This will be the last."

"At what time will she be ready?"

"By midday, sir."

"Very well. I shall speak to Major von Heinkel, then I shall go to my appointment with the masseur. I shall be back by midday."

When Hans arrived at the house in the avenue Foch, he was taken immediately to Gunther's office. As he stood waiting in the corridor he heard the hysterical screams of a woman whose fingernails were being slowly, agonizingly removed. Hans tried to shut out the sounds emanating from the basement interrogation rooms, but they drummed on his brain, making him fearful as to the reason for his own summons to the Standartenfuhrer's presence.

Gunther was drinking coffee from a silver pot when Hans appeared. Hans saluted and stood looking down at the notorious pair. By the side of the desk Slagel was taking notes, his pale face blotchy with excitement, his hands clutching a cheap black pen. Gunther spoke firmly, authoritatively.

"I have today received a directive from the Fuhrer which instructs me to destroy all resistance in France and specifically in Paris. One hour ago two hundred and fifty men were shot at Mont Valérien and tomorrow a further hundred résistants will be executed. I must now make strenuous efforts to find the three leaders of the opposition."

Hans listened in wonder at the casual way Gunther spoke of his duties.

"I have asked you here, Major von Heinkel, because you are in a position to help me obtain invaluable information on one of the three men."

Hans's face was impassive, and Gunther began to feel irritated by the coldness of his attitude. Slagel looked admiringly at the unyielding expression on Hans's face, thinking him the very finest example of Germanic breeding. Gunther's sharp voice cut into Hans's thoughts.

"You are lodged in the home of Suzanne Castel?"

"I am, sir."

"Mademoiselle Castel's fiancé is David Chambord, who heads the resistance in southern France, Lyon, and Aix-en-Provence, and who has recently established a group here in Paris."

"I understand that Mademoiselle Castel's fiancé is David Chambord."

"Does she ever speak of Chambord?"

"I recall her mentioning that she had seen Chambord's face on a wanted poster and that she thought he would never come back alive after the war."

"How very true. Does she ever see Chambord?"

"Not that I am aware, sir. I think she has not seen him for over a year."

"Anything else that might be of interest, Major?"

"Nothing that I can recall, sir."

"I wish you to observe Castel at all times and to call me if Chambord should ever make contact, whether by post, by messenger, or in person."

"I am not a surveillance officer, sir."

"You have eyes, use them."

"I am an army officer, sir. This is a job for the SS or the Gestapo."

"I shall have you seconded to me if you prefer."

Hans eyed the Standartenfuhrer with distaste, and Gunther rose and walked around his visitor. How insolent von Heinkel was, and how reluctant. He returned to his desk and looked arrogantly up at Hans.

"What is your own relationship with Castel?"

"I am billeted in the house, sir. I try not to be an imposition."

"You are a personal friend?"

"I am a loyal officer of the Wehrmacht, sir."

"But you are Mademoiselle Castel's friend?"

"I have only the most casual relationship with the family, sir. I leave the house each morning at nine and arrive in the evening about eight. I barely know Mademoiselle, though she did once offer to show me the sights of Paris."

"I'm sure I don't need to tell you the consequences of any dereliction of duty in this matter, Major. Do you understand what I am saying?"

"Yes, sir."

"You may return home now. If you have anything to report, please contact Hauptsturmfuhrer Slagel, who will inform me of any relevant information."

"Yes, sir."

Hans stood to attention, relieved to be dismissed. As he walked smartly from the building he thought that if he had not agreed to watch Suzanne, someone infinitely more dangerous might have been sent to observe her. When he was well away from the avenue Foch he leaned against the wall of a café and mopped the sweat from his forehead, his mind returning again to the icy eyes of Tristan Slagel, the clipped, mechanical voice of Gunther, and the screams that had punctuated the entire interview. Gunther and Slagel had appeared not to hear the sounds from the interrogation rooms. Was it possible to become so used to human suffering that it had no effect on the nerves? Hans hurried back to Montmartre, relieved that orders of a more serious nature had been avoided.

Slagel watched from the window until he was sure Gunther had left the building. Then he returned to poring over his files. At eleven, when a secretary brought him coffee, Slagel took a break and assessed the contents of another folder hidden in his desk, the information file on Hans von Heinkel. He savored the Heinkel family history, envying it because he had no idea of the identity of his own parents. Poring through the photographs, he took pleasure in those that showed Hans being decorated by the Fuhrer, and he looked in wonder and admiration at the picture of the Heinkel castle on the lake. No wonder the gallant major was so regal, a king or a knight from medieval times in present-day uniform. Greatly impressed, Slagel hid the dossier away and returned to his scrutiny of the information on David Chambord and Suzanne Castel. So intent was he on his work that he heard nothing of the routine sounds of the building: phones ringing, hard snow sliding down the roof, prisoners calling for help, and detainees in the interrogation rooms screaming in agony. He was concentrating fiercely on helping Gunther carry out his orders. Nothing else mattered; nothing must be allowed to interfere.


On Christmas Eve Suzanne was alone in the house. Hans had received an urgent communication from his mother telling him that Horst had been killed in an explosion, his father had had a stroke, and Marguerite, his beloved sister, was dying of malnutrition. Hans had begged compassionate leave, and after apologizing to Suzanne for leaving her had taken the next train to Baden-Baden. Before departing he had bought what food he could find and had given Suzanne an expensive leather satchel to replace David's torn canvas fishing bag, which she had been using for so long.

Alone in the house, Suzanne sat listening in vain for the Christmas carillons that had once disturbed the peace at this time of year. But no bells rang, and the only sounds were those of hungry dogs barking, hens clucking, and occasional explosions set by résistants determined to rid Paris of German personnel. It was late but Suzanne did not feel like sleeping, and as the clock struck twelve she wandered into the garden. The scene before her was dazzling white, like a vast, ethereal lake. She looked over the wall to the steps of the rue Foyatier, the diamond-shaped flagstones pale in the moonlight and dappled with black as the trees shivered in the breeze. There were no late-night toilers up the hill because the new curfew prevented people from going out in the evening. Paris was as silent as a cemetery, its streets emanating fear and bewilderment. Feeling the cold, Suzanne returned to the kitchen and put on a pan of water.

In the living room, the curtains fluttered and a man stepped inside.

Suzanne poured boiling water on the cocoa and stirred it vigorously. Then she added a drop of milk and a lump of sugar and carried her drink on a tray to the sofa. The icy draft made her look up, and as she did so she saw that the door to the terrace was ajar. She sat very still, aware that she had closed it earlier in the evening. She was trying to work out what had happened when Laval stepped out from behind the curtains. In one hand Suzanne saw a white fur wrap caked with dried blood and in the other there was a long, silver filleting knife, its edge brown and dirty. She put down her cup, her mind fumbling to grasp the implications of the wrap, the knife, and the man standing before her trembling with rage and anticipation. Laval had murdered Janine! Suzanne felt suddenly sick and full of panic. What could she do? How to elude him and the knife he had brought to kill her? She backed to the kitchen. Laval followed, trying to explain what had happened.

"I thought Janine was you. The wrap misled me, you see. Who would have thought there would be two like it? I thought she was Suzanne Castel, the girl who gave herself to a German."

Panic and anger made Suzanne shout at the intruder.

"You have no room to talk about loving Germans, Monsieur Laval! You are the only collaborator for the Gestapo in the whole of Montmartre."

Ignoring her, Laval approached, and for the first time Suzanne knew how it felt to face death. She thought of David, who loved her, and of Hans, who would return from Germany and find her mutilated body on the floor. Laval was mumbling in a dazed monotone.

"You should have shown me more respect. All my life I have craved respect . . . I have powerful friends and I can do much harm . . . you've never realized what I can do, you refuse to see me for the man I am . . . ever since the first time we met you've laughed at me and made your friends treat me as a joke . . . I am not a joke! . . . I am a man who will have his way!"

Laval stooped to avoid a string of garlic hanging from the kitchen ceiling, and as his head bowed Suzanne hit him with an iron saucepan from the drainboard. He stumbled, and she darted past him to the living room. Momentarily stunned, Laval reeled in pain. Then he staggered back to the living room and advanced menacingly on Suzanne.

"You have one chance left, my dear Suzanne. If you cooperate I shall forgive you for selling yourself to the German. I have needs . . . I have . . . needs . . . I'm a man and I have a right to dream."

Suzanne held her breath in horror as Laval tore open her blouse, watching as he tugged at the tight tweed trousers she had borrowed from Vivienne's wardrobe. She knew she must get to the kitchen door and to safety through the garden, but how? Laval fumbled with her breasts, and Suzanne recoiled, unable and unwilling to save herself as he desired. As he was gazing in awe at her nakedness, Suzanne grasped a paperweight from the table and crashed it down on his forehead, but Laval's madness had given him superhuman strength and, shaking his head, he came back at her, gripping her throat so she could not speak. Suzanne fought for her life, beating his face with the paperweight and grasping his knife with all the desperation of the doomed. As Laval lunged toward her, Suzanne pushed the knife into his chest.

Only when her attacker screamed in agony and slid slowly to the ground did Suzanne realize what she had done. Then, freeing herself from his weight, she looked disbelievingly at Laval's face. He was dead. Was he *really* dead? Panic rose in her throat, and she edged slowly toward the kitchen door, wiping Laval's blood from her stomach and trying to avoid his staring eyes. Suddenly there was a tap on the door. For a moment Suzanne stood like a statue, frozen into immobility. Then she turned and found David smiling down at her. Sobbing like a child, she flung herself into his arms.

"I've killed Monsieur Laval! He attacked me and I killed him. What am I going to do?"

"Calm down, Zizi, I'll take care of everything."

"Oh, David, I'm so sick of what this war has done to me. I'm a murderer! I'm a murderer just like all the people I keep saying I hate."

Suzanne fell to her knees and stared disbelievingly into space.

Ignoring her, David picked up the knife with which his fiancée had killed Laval and washed it under the kitchen tap before hiding it in his valise. Then, unable to lift the corpse over the garden wall, he called to Suzanne, "Get your clothes on, Zizi, and come help me."

Suzanne hurried to obey, fumbling to fasten her skirt and button her cardigan.

"David, were you on your way to see me?"

"No, I was passing the alleyway at the end of the Marchands' garden when I heard you screaming. I forgot all about the Gestapo and ran to help you. Let's hope they haven't got men following me."

Stumbling to her feet, Suzanne took a jacket from the sofa and ran to the garden to help David lift the body over the wall into the garden of Vivienne's house. Her mind kept going over the fact that David was home and going to help her conceal what she had done.

She was miraculously still alive, and with the man she had loved for so many years.

Moving like an automaton, Suzanne helped maneuver Laval's body to the door of his own house. Then, satisfied that no one would suspect her involvement, they climbed back over the walls of the three neighboring gardens and returned to la maison Fleuri. In the kitchen David kissed her tenderly, surprised by the fire of Suzanne's greeting. Zizi had certainly matured. For a moment he asked himself who had taught her new ways. Then he locked all the doors and drew the curtains, settling to talk on the sofa in the living room. For a moment Suzanne sat like a stone, numb from shock and paralyzed with fear at the explanations to come. She laughed, then she cried in confusion and relief, and David knew it would be hours before she could think clearly. When she spoke, her voice was brittle and stiff.

"I thought I should never see you again, David."

"Why? I wrote as often as I could."

"Résistants are always being shot. I know because we read about them in the newspapers."

"Not all of us get shot, Zizi. I'm still pretty fit, aren't I?"

Suzanne took hold of his hand, examining the strong fingers and flexing the forceful grip that made her feel how it had always made her feel. Wonderingly she looked into David's eyes and touched his cheek.

"How suntanned you are."

"I've been in the Midi since November."

"Where were you?"

"In the mountains of the Alpes Maritime, first in Draguinan, now in Sospel."

"Are you alone there?"

"I have a group of ten men with me, sometimes more. But tell me your news. How's everyone, are you working, and have you been getting enough to eat?"

Suzanne was panic-stricken. There was so much David would

have to be told, and none of it would please him. She asked herself all the while how to say what he would never accept— that she loved Hans and could therefore never marry him. Could she never marry David? Suzanne flinched because she knew her feelings for him had never changed. The fact was she adored both men and was loath to hurt either. Was she spoiled or superficial in her emotions? Was her predicament the foolishness of an immature girl, or had fate played her a cruel trick? There seemed to be no easy solution to the conundrum of her emotions. Suzanne examined David's face, surprised that he seemed more vibrant, more forceful, even handsomer than she remembered. The roguish gray eyes twinkled, and the dark curly hair gave him the air of a gypsy or a pirate from story books. Desire confused resolve, and Suzanne looked down, ashamed to meet his gaze. David waited patiently, puzzled by her restraint and the emotions parading before his experienced eyes. In Suzanne he recognized fear, shyness, longing, love, and duplicity. The Zizi he remembered would have screamed with delight to be so surprised by his reappearance. This Zizi was infinitely more cautious, slimmer, older, more knowing, and to him more fascinating in the curious ambivalence of her manner.

"What are you keeping from me, Zizi?"

Suzanne leaped up and paced the room, unable and unwilling to answer the question. But David caught her and cupped her face in his hands, gazing deep into her eyes, almost mesmerizing her with the power of his presence.

"What's wrong? Were you hoping I wouldn't come home?"

"Of course not, don't be silly."

"Are you happy to see me, or would you rather I went away?"

Suzanne was tongue-tied. David stroked her hair and decided to be patient.

"I have a few days before I must go back to the South. I've been planning to spend them here with you. Is there some reason why I can't stay with you, Zizi? Have you changed your mind about me?"

"A German officer lives here now, he was billeted in the house."

"Where is he?"

"He went to Germany on compassionate leave because his family is in trouble."

"When will he be back?"

"He said on the thirty-first of December."

"I'll be gone by then, so what's the problem?"

Suzanne went to the kitchen and began to beat eggs for an omelette. Her hands were shaking, and David saw tears dripping into the pan as she moistened it with oil. Suzanne forced her voice to normality.

"Are you hungry?"

"I haven't eaten all day. What's the German's name?"

"He's called Hans von Heinkel, and he works in the offices of the Propagandastaffel."

"They're the dregs of the German army, the ones who are unfit for medical reasons and the academics who wouldn't know a rifle from a rump steak."

Suzanne's eyes blazed, and she folded the omelette with such force that she broke it in two.

"Hans is *not* the dregs of the German army. He was a Wehrmacht officer and he won the Iron Cross. He works in the offices of the Propagandastaffel because he had injuries to his spine that made it impossible for him to return to the front."

David walked back to the living room, reluctant to believe his instincts.

"How long has he been here?"

"Hans arrived just before Papa was shot."

"And they let him stay here alone with you?"

"Vivienne comes to sleep here almost every night. Monsieur Laval insisted I have a chaperone."

"Did you need a chaperone, Zizi?"

The scarlet flush that crept into Suzanne's cheeks told David what he needed to know. For a moment he felt the hollow emptiness of loss. Then, as he ate, he assessed this surprising development. Who would have thought Zizi could bring herself to have an affair with a German? David shook his head disbelievingly, though he knew war to be the ultimate leveler. Then he thought of Anya, his own friend of many months, a Russian girl who had been his lover since the summer night when he had rescued her from a firing squad. Anya was a ballet dancer, temperamental, difficult, and so jealous of Suzanne that she had torn up every photograph he possessed on the night they first became lovers.

David finished the omelette, his mind far away from the homey room in which they were sitting. War aroused needs well dormant in the balmy days of peace. At this moment he needed Anya and the animal feelings she aroused. Obviously Suzanne had needed the German because she had been unable to wait and unwilling to hoard precious innocence for a man she believed might never come home. David looked at her with renewed interest. Perhaps Suzanne had been right to grasp love wherever she could, but it was sad that she had wasted herself on a German. He enjoyed a glass of wine from one of the bottles Suzanne had hidden in case he ever returned. Then he took her in his arms and they lay side by side on the sofa. When Suzanne was feeling better, David asked her to tell him everything. She looked at her mother's portrait on the wall and the familiar mementos of times past scattered around the room and knew she must tell the truth. To lie would be to insult David. To tell the truth would be to suffer, but there was nothing else to be done. Suzanne took a deep breath and began.

That night air raids razed part of the suburbs and Red Cross ambulances rushed to the scene, their alarm bells clanging. There was nothing left of certain areas but rubble and dogs howling at the dawn. All over Paris, throughout the blackout of the night, there had been a series of explosions set by resistance officers. Part of the Hôtel Meurice had been blasted, and two senior-ranking Germans had been killed. An SS Oberfuhrer on leave from Dachau had been blown sky high by a booby trap in his car, and men were still busy scraping the remains of his body from the façade of the German interrogation center in the rue des Saussaies. Frenchmen smiled delightedly at the news, trying not to think of the reprisals that would inevitably follow. Once they had condemned the hotheads of the resistance. Now they too listened to the broadcasts of de Gaulle and waited for the day when they would fight for Paris.

Suzanne and David were still talking at 6:00 A.M., when M. Corbeil's new cockerel crowed and a shaft of watery sunlight lit the room. Sleepily, Suzanne went to the kitchen and made tea. She had been truthful because David had wanted to know everything and because she was aware that if she did not tell him about the affair someone else might. David watched the sun rise, his mind mulling over what Suzanne had said. His love and admiration for her remained undimmed. A coward would have pretended spontaneity, a fool would have lied about the liaison, but Suzanne had told the truth and offered to release him from their engagement. He thought how she had cried and how he had longed for her. David was twenty-eight, with a mountain of experience that had made him mature beyond his years. He had already decided that he wanted Suzanne whatever her relationship with the German. If he could need Anya Davidoff, Suzanne could need Hans von Heinkel. War had taught him that women were men's equals in courage, and he was determined that Suzanne should be his partner in everything. His mind turned to Hans. The German had bought food for Suzanne, spending hours every weekend visiting country contacts and supervising work on the garden. Hans von Heinkel was in love with Suzanne, and according to her he was not in the mold of the Teutonic warmongers who governed Paris. David sipped his tea and held Suzanne's hand across the table.

"I'm famished. What's for breakfast?"

"I have some eggs from Vivienne and cheese Hans . . ." Suzanne bit her lip. Did she *have* to keep mentioning her lover? "Hans bought it last Sunday from a farmer in the Chevreuse valley."

"Is he rich?"

"He can buy from black marketeers, so I suppose he must be."

Despite everything, David felt a great curiosity about his rival. He was sure of one thing—he had been lucky to avoid meeting Hans, because an officer of such distinction would have reported his presence to the Gestapo. David shook his head at the thought of succumbing in his fiancée's house while celebrating Christmas, instead of on the battlefield, as he had always anticipated. He decided it was best not to think of Hans. It was Christmas Day. To hell with Germans, to hell with war. It was time for love and a moment of peace on earth. David took his rifle upstairs and leaned it against the wall of Suzanne's bedroom. His ammunition he hid in her lingerie drawer, enjoying the rose smell of the room and the trinkets and souvenirs of happier days that decorated the walls. Avoiding the room where Hans slept, David looked around the house, drawing curtains where they gave onto the steps and locking all the windows. He felt safe and sure Suzanne still loved him, whatever her confusion and the compassion she felt for the German. On his way back to the living room David took a tissue-wrapped gift from his pocket.

"This is for you, Zizi. Knowing your bloodthirsty streak, I thought you'd be amused."

Suzanne unwrapped a gold chain that had swinging from its links the bullet that had recently missed David's head by an inch. She kissed him and put the chain around her neck.

"Now I'm ashamed I have nothing for you."

"You have everything I've ever wanted wanted, Zizi."

David eyed the long hair, the nervously flickering lashes, the look of curiosity and longing in the golden eyes as Suzanne kneeled at his feet. He touched the petal-soft cheek and listened as Suzanne questioned him.

"Why didn't you make love to me before you went away?"

"You know why. I didn't think you were ready for love, and I couldn't risk leaving you in trouble."

"I'm ready now, and I don't care about trouble."

There was a brief silence while David considered the implications of her statement. He had been patient for so long, too patient by far, ignoring the fact that Suzanne had wanted him since she was a young girl. He stroked the long black hair and kissed her forehead.

"Are you *sure*, Zizi?"

"Of course I'm sure."

They lay together on the fur rug in front of the fire, and David smothered her mouth with kisses as he unfastened her clothes. Suzanne felt the light-headed, intoxicating feelings he had always inspired, and knew instinctively that she would never feel this with another man. She could love Hans and worship him. She would always admire and respect him, but only with David would she experience the delicious stupefaction of being truly possessed. As David began to touch her body, she lost herself in the joy of dreams fulfilled. She and David were together again. The world was perfect and untroubled. As David took her, Suzanne's control vanished and she cried out, writhing in passionate abandon as sunbursts of the mind drained her. For a brief moment everything seemed clear, and as she felt the urgency of his need, all sadness faded and she knew what she must do. Only after love, when they were lying side by side, did images of Hans return. Then the agony of betrayal reappeared, only this time *he* was the victim.

David and Suzanne ate lunch in silence. As she thought of the exciting moments they had shared, Suzanne blushed in confusion and disbelief. David was trying to equate the childish girl he had left behind with this woman of many delights. When their eyes met they laughed, and often they held hands and looked searchingly at each other. Sprigs of holly decorated a tiny Christmas cake Suzanne had made from fruit and flour saved meticulously from her rations. David smiled at its diminutive size and at the way Suzanne cut it in half so carefully. She handed him one half and then cut her own in two so she could save Hans the piece she had promised him.

"I told Hans about the cake and promised to save him some. He'd be disappointed if I forgot."

"Has he a sweet tooth?"

"Not really. He likes fish and meat, but I can't buy them very often."

They left the remains of the meal and went upstairs to Suzanne's bedroom. Love seemed even more exciting now that the uncertainties of reacquaintance had passed. Satiated, they slept, intending to rest for an hour. But when they woke it was dark. Suzanne leaped up, shaking the bedside clock in disbelief.

"It's five o'clock!"

"Quit waving your arms and come here. I love you, Zizi, I've loved you since that first day in the orchard, when you kept trying to kiss me."

"I never tried to kiss you."

"You sure as hell did."

Suzanne blushed at the memory of her youthful forwardness, and David held her in his arms and was content.

"I'll never stop loving you, and when the war's over I'm coming right back to Paris to marry you. I'm not going to let Hans stop me, so you'd best resign yourself to the inevitable."

Suzanne looked admiringly at the jutting jaw and the determined hardness in David's eyes. At this moment, she realized that she loved him more than she had ever thought possible. When David spoke again, she felt sad and empty.

"I have to leave the day after tomorrow, so remember what I've just said, Zizi. And now stop staring at the ceiling and come kiss me."

Hours passed in exploration and exciting conspiracy. A new dimension had entered Suzanne's life, and she reflected that she had changed. Where once she had been indecisive, she was now even more confused. There was no doubt in her mind that she loved David, and none that Hans was precious to her. But when David touched her she forgot everything, even Hans. Where was it going to end? Suzanne rose from the bed and looked wistfully down.

"I'll bring us something to eat on a tray."

"That sounds like a pretty good idea."

On the day of David's departure, Suzanne was making breakfast tea in the kitchen when she heard the sound of a key in the front door. She jumped up, her face turning pale as Hans stepped into the room, his arms outstretched to greet her.

"I came back early, Suzanne. I just couldn't stand the thought of you being alone, I . . ."

As he kissed her, Hans saw over her shoulder David eating his breakfast at the table. For a moment he was so angry his head ached, his fists clenched, and his face became a mask of displeasure. Suzanne would not have deliberately contacted Chambord without his knowledge. The resistance leader must therefore have arrived unexpectedly at the house, placing Suzanne in an impossibly risky situation. Had he simply been unable to resist seeing his fiancée again? And what danger had David brought upon them with his untimely arrival? Suzanne fluttered to the table to introduce Hans.

"David, this is my very dear friend Hans von Heinkel. Hans, this is my fiancé, David Chambord."

The two men shook hands. Then David poured himself another cup of tea, wondering warily when Hans would try to leave the house to call the Gestapo.

Hans took off his coat and watched suspiciously as David went to bring another cup from the kitchen. For the first time in his life Hans felt panic-stricken, not from fear of David but from terror at his own unwillingness to do what he had been ordered to do. He decided at last that he would take his lead from the American, because to spoil Suzanne's Christmas with hostility would be against his better nature. He looked into Suzanne's face, watching her uncertainly as David poured him a cup of tea. When David pushed the cup across the table, Hans nodded formally.

"I have been longing for this all the way from Germany."

"How were things at home?"

David asked the question casually, waiting to see if Hans made any move to arrest him. He was shocked by the German's composure and stunned by the realization that Hans appeared to have no desire to do him harm. Hans tried to still the pounding of his heart and the premonitions that haunted him that the Gestapo would soon arrive to disturb their peace. He looked closely at David, thinking how handsome he was and what strength lay hidden in the muscle-packed body. He eyed David's coarse silk jacket and the rucksack packed in the corner of the room. Was David about to leave? Hans struggled to reply to the question.

"Things in Germany were very bad. I promised to bring you cheese, Suzanne, but I could find nothing, not even for my own family, who were starving. The destruction of the cities has been appalling. Some are left with nothing but mountains of rubble, and people are sleeping on the streets. I feel as if I came back from hell."

David was moved to pity Hans. He thought admiringly that Suzanne had been right, Hans was not at all like the other Germans he had met. He watched as Suzanne leaned forward, eager to catch her lover's every word. He was impressed by Hans's military bearing, the quality of his looks, and the breeding inherent in his manner. Five hundred years of history, tradition, and excellence marked the Heinkel family tree. Was it any wonder Suzanne had been fascinated by him? David looked down at his own wound and thought of the limp that had so appalled Suzanne when he reappeared in her house. Then he poured them all another cup of tea and watched as Hans stared thoughtfully out the window. David imagined he knew just what Hans was thinking. Hans was remembering his meeting with Standartenfuhrer Gunther. He knew he should act, that David Chambord must be arrested at once, but the thought of betraying such a courageous man to a murderer like Gunther was repugnant to him. Hans looked at the clock, then at Suzanne, who was awaiting the decision she knew he would have to make. He shrugged wearily, knowing he would never do anything to distress her. It was Christmas and he was home.

During the morning the two men helped Suzanne prepare lunch. In the afternoon they tidied the cellar and storeroom, lifting heavy boxes and rummaging in sacks of potatoes for the supplies Suzanne had requested for dinner. Relaxed in each other's company, they chatted, and Hans ventured a few questions because he was longing to have another opinion about the possible duration of the conflict.

"Have you heard anything of the Allies' plans to liberate France?"

"I've heard nothing. I think they're too busy elsewhere to think of it. In the Midi I'm concerned with staying alive. I have to move every few weeks to keep out of the way of the Gestapo. The longest time I've had in one place in the last year has been six weeks. I get news after you get yours in Paris, but generally folk seem to think that next year will be crucial for Germany."

"What's the gas situation like in the South?"

"I have to steal every liter."

"I too stole gas so I could take my father and Marguerite to the hospital."

"How old's your sister?"

"Marguerite is seventeen, and I think she will die very soon. I had always expected her to have such a happy life. Now I barely recognize her. She cannot walk, and though she tries to read, she has not the strength to hold a book."

David pitied the girl, despite her nationality, and Hans too, because he seemed like a friend. He could not dislike a man who risked his life by conspiring to befriend a wanted résistant, and he could not keep from admiring Hans for his dislike of the Gestapo.

When they had finished tidying the cellar David handed Hans a cigar and they sat on a potato sack, smoking. Hans spoke quietly, aware that each word was treason and shocked that he no longer cared.

"Just before I went to Germany to see my family I was called

into the Gestapo headquarters and instructed to keep watch on
Suzanne."

David's face was intent and angry.

"Why? What has Zizi ever done to upset those bastards?"

"They were not interested in Suzanne, only in you. They
ordered me to check in case you tried to contact your fiancée.
If you did, I was to inform Standartenfuhrer Gunther at once.
For two weeks he has been arresting résistants all over Paris.
Three or four hundred were shot at Mont Valérien only a few days
after I saw him."

"I was told about that."

"Gunther wants the three main leaders of the Paris Resistance
more than anything in the world. He has files on you, Colonel
Rol Tanguy, and Pierre Lefaucheux. He is confident that if he can
capture any one of you he will be able to torture you until he
obtains the information he needs, which is the location of every
resistance group in France and the names of all the leading members."

"What are you going to do?"

"I have met you and done nothing. I shall continue to do nothing, but if you contact Suzanne again, David, I cannot be sure that
Gunther will not find out. I may not be the only person to whom
he has spoken."

"Thanks for telling me what you know, Hans."

"I am telling you to protect Suzanne, and *please,* whatever you
do, don't mention anything to her. She has a terrible fear of
Hauptsturmfuhrer Slagel and his superior."

"I reckon they should both be destroyed."

"I agree, but many have tried and failed."

"Let's hope the next one will make it. Now let's go upstairs, or
Zizi'll be wondering what we're plotting."

Suzanne was relieved to see the two men sitting facing each
other across the table. She poured some wine for them and adjourned to the kitchen to make the evening meal. From time to
time she looked around the door to where they were reading parts
of a newspaper Hans had found on the train. Suzanne laughed
as she heard Hans's voice.

"There's an article here which says a white Russian has made
twenty million francs from his activities in the Paris black

market. Surely that is the fellow from whom I've been buying our meat."

David leaned over to read the article, detaching a page of household hints from Hans's hand.

"Give me the scissors and I'll cut out the fashion stuff for Zizi."

He cut carefully around a picture of the couturier Coco Chanel, her apelike face grinning at a Nazi general's wife. Behind, swanlike models preened, and underneath the picture a captain stated that the famous French designer was creating a new line specially for Frau Hassler. Looking closely at the hausfrau's waistline, David thought that a new shape was exactly what was needed. Hans began to ask about the prices on the black market in the Midi, and like two housewives the men compared notes. David frowned as he recalled the last bag of food he had had delivered to his hideout in Sospel.

"I pay about three hundred francs a kilo for potatoes, and a leg of lamb would cost five thousand if we could find one."

Hans looked outside to the garden.

"I don't buy many vegetables because we have room to grow them. But I spend most of the weekend going to the suburbs and the country to try to buy oil and sugar and flour. In the last weeks it has become almost impossible to find those things."

The two men watched as Suzanne set the table. It was eight o'clock, and David knew he would have to leave as soon as he had eaten. The brief respite was over. In twenty-four hours he would be back in the South, fighting again, hiding again, and killing every German he met. He looked across the table to where Hans was sitting and admired the finely chiseled features, the determined set of the body. Despite his reservations about Suzanne's relationship with the German, David felt at ease because he knew Hans would look after her. Suzanne appeared with a massive curl of sausage and crispy fried potatoes. A salad of winter savory and parsley completed the meal with the last bottle of Romanée St.-Vivant. While Suzanne was cutting the sausage, David bounded upstairs, remembering something he had brought for her amusement. When he returned to the table, Hans proposed a toast.

"My toast is to friendship and to peace."

Moved by the occasion, Suzanne wiped tears from her eyes. At this memorable moment she was acutely aware of the ludicrousness of war. They clinked glasses, and David proposed his own toast. He spoke softly, almost wistfully, Hans thought.

"To the end of the war and whatever the future holds for us. To our happiness."

Hans met his eyes, and they both looked to Suzanne. Then they touched glasses, and David handed Suzanne a printed replica of the menu from the Restaurant Voisin for Christmas Day, 1870, after besieging Prussian troops had cut Paris off from her food supplies.

"Remembering your appetite, Zizi, I thought this would give you a bit of hope. At least you know you're not *that* short of food."

Suzanne read the ornate writing, looked back at David, and then began to laugh.

"Where did they find those things? 'Le civet de kangourou, le chat flanqué aux rats, consommé d'elephant.' "

"They slaughtered all the animals in the Paris Zoo and ate those that weren't poisonous."

They all hooted with laughter, and Hans took the card from Suzanne, his face full of disbelief.

"I have never heard of such things. Bear chops and donkey's head farcie—imagine!"

The two men wiped tears of mirth from their eyes, and Suzanne giggled at Hans's incredulity. They chatted animatedly until they had eaten the Christmas cake that had been saved for this special occasion. Then, as Suzanne cleared the table, David looked at the clock. It was time to leave. He went upstairs for his rifle and re-appeared dressed for the journey. As Hans rose to see him to the door, they shook hands.

"Don't let Zizi go hungry, and see you take care of yourself, Hans."

"I shall, and I wish you bon voyage on your journey to the South, David. I am honored and grateful that we are friends and not enemies."

Suzanne watched sadly as David left the house and climbed clumsily over the walls of neighboring gardens until he reached the end of the street and escaped through the alleyways of Montmartre. She thought how his leg must pain him and how brave he was to act like an acrobat after sustaining such an injury. She stood, full of admiration for his courage, straining her eyes to see through the darkness, but David had disappeared. When Hans called, she blinked back tears.

"Come inside. Whatever will David think if I permit you to catch pneumonia?"

Suzanne closed the door and went back to the living room. Hans was raking the fire embers and whistling happily. Suzanne sat looking at photographs on the coffee table of David in their secret hideway in the orchard, her mother and father in the garden of la maison Fleuri, Janine in the dress she had worn for her first solo spot four years previously. She and David were the only two still alive. Would they survive until the end of the war, or would David's name soon grace a stark white cross in a field of bitter memories? Hans watched closely, aware that Suzanne had been deeply disturbed by her fiancé's visit. When he tried to kiss her, she recoiled, because her body was still with David in the big bed upstairs, her mind still with him on his perilous journey. Hans drew back and sat on the sofa.

"What's wrong, Suzanne?"

"Nothing. I'm just sad David's gone."

"Now you have seen him again, have you made a decision?"

"I don't want to make a decision."

"But, Suzanne, it's time you did. I want to marry you, and I cannot propose while you are still engaged to another man. I love you and want to spend my life with you. I have thought of nothing but our future since I went to Germany."

"Please, Hans, not now."

They sat in silence, far apart on the sofa. Hans was thinking of David and conceding that he would not blame Suzanne if she still loved her fiancé and still wanted to settle with him. But *he* had loved her for so long. Had he been nothing more than a convenient means of affection, a man to buy food, a stopgap until her real love returned? What *was* Suzanne thinking? Unable to control his anxiety, Hans turned to her and spoke.

"Suzanne, forgive me, but while I was away I made many decisions and I want to tell you about them. I have decided to hand over the estate in Lindau to my brother Helmut. He loves the house and will care for my mother when my father and Marguerite are dead. I shall return there just to make sure everything is in order. Then I intend to come back to Paris. This means you won't have to live in Germany. I know you've never been happy with that idea."

Suzanne barely listened as Hans continued.

"Until now I have been very patient, I think you will agree. I knew you loved David, and I am aware that you still fear for his safety. But do you still wish to spend your life with him? If you do, I must go away."

Suzanne sat very still, unable to find adequate words to explain the turmoil in her mind. Hans poured the last of the wine and chided her.

"At least say something, Suzanne."

"How can I? There's nothing but sadness for us both if I make a choice."

"You must have some idea what you want."

"I love you and David, *that* is what I feel and what I seem to want."

"But you gave yourself to me, not to David."

Suzanne hesitated. Then she spoke in a whisper.

"Before the occupation David thought I was too young for love. But when he came back, I slept with him. I wanted to, and I don't regret it."

Hans's face flushed with anger, and he rose and put on his overcoat.

"I love you, Suzanne, I have since the very first moment we met. I think I have shown the truth of my feelings for you in every possible way. But I cannot have a relationship with a woman who is under the impression that she loves two men. I do not believe this is possible. I'm sorry—as far as I am concerned, it is over between us. I shall return tomorrow to pick up my belongings."

Hans left the house in agony because the dream he had cherished for so long had ended.

Suzanne ran after him, but the sound of the front door slamming made her cry, and she returned to the living room and sat vacantly on the sofa, unable to work out where life had gone wrong. Two years ago she had been a successful artiste with a career in the theater and a fiancé who loved her. She had considered herself a lucky person, a winner, a woman who got everything she wanted by charm and luck and determination. Then war had dislocated her life and she had fallen in love with Hans. Loving him had undoubtedly made her silly and indecisive.

Suzanne leaped up and looked in the mirror. She was still Suzanne Castel. She still had her talent and her career and two men who loved her. She was not some stupidly indecisive schoolgirl from a bourgeois home in the eighth arrondissement. She must pull herself together and be how she had always been, tough, strong, and determinedly her own person. If she could not decide which one of the men in her life to love, she would love both of them. She glowered at her reflection and felt better. Love was an illness that changed a person's nature. She had fallen victim to it and become ridiculously confused. From this very moment she vowed to enjoy every day, every caress, every moment of passion, and to hell with anything that stood in her way. When Hans returned, she would love him as he had never been loved, and with luck he would change his mind about leaving. She rushed upstairs and changed the sheets on his bed, putting on his favorite lilac ones, then spraying the room with scent and putting Christmas roses in a vase near the lamp at his side. Then she went downstairs and waited for him to come home.

Hans turned right at the gate and right again down the steps of the rue Foyatier. Suzanne's statement had shocked him, and he had spoken recklessly. He sighed, because he knew that though he was right in principle, he could never be angry with Suzanne for very long. Nothing would be gained by allowing his heart to be broken by a girl too immature to know her own mind, but how could he stop loving her?

Father Valery passed by, panting as he raced up the stairs. Hans nodded a greeting, puzzled when the old man pointed surreptitiously to the shadows farther down. In the darkness Hans strained his eyes. The scratching of a match produced a flame that briefly illuminated a man in a fedora and brown leather coat. Hans continued down the steps, walking smartly past the watcher but doubling back into the place St. Pierre so he could observe the man on the stairway. He was relieved to be wearing his dark overcoat and thankful that the moon was a thin silver crescent. In one of the houses nearby he heard a couple arguing

and a baby hungrily crying. A light switched on incautiously in
the bakery brought a roar of command from a passing gendarme.
Then there was silence. Half an hour later Hans heard footsteps
below on the road and a voice softly calling, "Schultz, where are
you? I'm here to take over."

"Be quiet, the girl might hear you."

A second man joined the watcher, and Hans strained his ears as
they talked. What he heard made his heart pound in disbelief,
and he felt panic rising in his gullet. Once the new man was
alone, Hans moved soundlessly away, returning to la maison
Fleuri via the steps of the rue Drevet and almost colliding with
another surveillance officer leaning against the recessed doorway
of an empty shop in the rue Gabrielle. Hans bade him a polite
good night, and the man started guiltily, betraying the fact that
he too was watching the house. Hans took out his key and let himself into the hall, bolting the door behind him and pausing to
collect his thoughts. Suzanne ran out to meet him, and her words
touched a chord in his heart.

"I'm so glad you're home, Hans. Don't let's fight, there aren't
enough hours left to waste them. We could all be dead, like
Janine and Maman, and think of all the happiness we should
have missed."

"Sit down, Suzanne."

"Is something wrong?"

Her hands clutched his arm, her eyes filling with tears.

"Have they killed David? For God's sake, tell me."

"Suzanne, the Gestapo are watching this house. They have a
man on the steps of the rue Foyatier and another in the doorway
of the shop that used to be Leonardo's."

She heard what Hans said but could not reply because a nightmare montage of images bred on rumor shot into her mind. Tortured faces, emaciated corpses, and girls with their intestines
dripping blood appeared and disappeared, and with them the
death's-head face of Tristan Slagel. Suzanne leaned back on the
sofa, conscious of sweat trickling down her forehead.

"Why? Can you tell me why?"

"I don't know. Either they have been interested in you ever
since you went to the rue Pigalle, which I doubt, because they
would already have arrested you . . .''

"Or?"

"Or Laval has invented something very recently to make the Gestapo suspicious."

"Laval's dead. He attacked me and I killed him with his own knife."

"When was this?"

"On Christmas Eve. He'd killed Janine by mistake because he thought she was me. If you remember, we were wearing the same clothes on the last night of the show. Laval had Janine's fur wrap, and he got into the house when I went into the garden."

"Where is the wrap?"

"In the waste bin."

"Bring it at once, we must burn it."

Flames sprang up the chimney, and Hans's mind raced ahead to what might happen. Obviously the surveillance team had been ordered because the manner of Laval's death had made the Gestapo suspicious. Had they seen David arrive in the house? How long had they been there? Had the watchers seen David leave?

Hans took Suzanne's hand in his own and led her upstairs to bed.

"Forget about making decisions, Suzanne, you have other things to worry about now. I'm afraid this is a most serious development."

"Hold me tight and let's pretend the war is over."

In the darkness, after love, Suzanne sat in bed listening to the wind howling. She shivered as cold drafts came through the window, and watched enviously as Hans slept the settled sleep he always enjoyed when he was fulfilled. Suzanne wondered if she would ever sleep peacefully again. She could not settle because every muscle was straining, waiting, fearing the knock that could come at any moment. Her mind kept wandering back to the precious hours she and David had spent together over Christmas. Had he succeeded in escaping from Montmartre? Or was he already dead, another statistic on Standartenfuhrer Gunther's list of triumphs?

Below on the steps the surveillance officer also shivered. The man he had relieved had gone home, and soon he would be off duty.

He hoped his wife would have something substantial for breakfast. From time to time he looked up at la maison Fleuri, but there was nothing to see. He spat on the ground, furious at the wasted vigil. Not a soul in sight, what a waste of valuable time! He had a mind to go home to the warmth of his bed and make up a report.

In his office in the avenue Foch, Tristan Slagel was waiting for the report of the first surveillance officer. He tapped his fingers impatiently on the desk and often walked to the window, scanning the night sky for signs of dawn. When the report was delivered, in the early hours of the morning, Slagel rushed to his desk and began to read.

# CHAPTER EIGHT

## Autumn, 1942

Slagel walked smartly through the streets of Paris toward his office. As he passed along the boulevard des Batignolles, sullen Frenchmen scowled and women in turbans spat as soon as he was at a safe distance. Slagel's face was impassive. He knew most of the men, women, and children he encountered by sight, and was satisfied that they were all too terrified of him to contemplate harm. In the doorway of a house near the Cinéma de l'Empire an old man sat carving a dove of peace. When he saw the Hauptsturmfuhrer the man ran inside, slamming the door in fear and loathing. Slagel noted that many of the commercial establishments in the avenue Wagram were deserted, including a celebrated restaurant whose door was padlocked, its lace curtains dank and green. In the horlogerie at the corner of the rue Brey a young boy was polishing the brass face of a valuable grandfather clock for which there was now no sale. His mother was offering shallots from her garden to hungry-looking housewives at a stall outside the shop window, and doing a brisk trade.

Slagel paused to light a cigarette from a case which he treasured. The exterior had been made from the facial skin of a young Jewish girl, and each time he used it he remembered the thrill he had felt at the moment when the light faded from her luminous dark eyes.

An out-of-work musician in a first-floor window blew a rude

arpeggio as Slagel walked by. The Hauptsturmfuhrer did not hear him. He was thinking of David Chambord and the frustration and futility of the surveillance Standartenfuhrer Gunther had mounted from the previous December to the end of March. There had been nothing whatsoever to report except that on the very first night of the operation a shadowy figure had been observed vaulting over Suzanne Castel's garden wall to safe obscurity.

The previous day Standartenfuhrer Gunther had decided it was again time to mount a strenuous campaign to round up the main resistance leaders in Paris. A special SS force was combing the catacombs and sewers of the city in search of Colonel Rol Tanguy, and a squad of Gestapo officers were on round-the-clock surveillance of every known contact of Pierre Lefaucheux's. The Castel girl would also be followed everywhere, and men would remain outside her home at night, doubling their watch at weekends and holidays, when it was thought most likely Chambord might try to make contact.

Slagel hurried on, impatient to be in the office, where he felt content and secure. As he walked he remembered his superior's rage and frustration of the past few months, and was desperately anxious that the new initiative be successful. Surely with full-time surveillance over a protracted period they would manage to secure at least one of the wanted résistants.

At the corner of the rue le Sueur an out-of-work diamond cutter lay unconscious from hunger on the pavement. Slagel stood over him, smiling that elusive smile his colleagues had come to recognize as a warning of imminent danger. He leaned forward and took the man's papers from the threadbare jacket. "Jean Goujon, 25 boulevard de Reims." Slagel would arrange for the man to be picked up and questioned. If he was willing in return for money to spy on his neighbors, he would be set free. If not, he would be sent to Mont Valérien and shot. Slagel thought self-righteously that the Fuhrer was right, Paris must at all costs be rid of its Jews, its lunatics, vagrants, and sexual deviates. He bounded up the steps of his office, ignoring secretaries, clerks, and adjutants in the rooms off the hall. This was his kingdom, and it was a fine day for the hunt.

Standartenfuhrer Gunther had risen at seven, exercised vigorously till seven thirty, eaten a hearty breakfast of sausage and egg and three cups of coffee thick with sugar. After breakfast he had walked a mile, around and around the Jardin des Tuileries, near his home, keeping precisely to the same route as on the previous day, avoiding dogs, which terrified him, and returning to change and scent himself in readiness for a most unusual encounter. Gunther studied himself in the mirror and frowned. It was too bad he was putting on weight. He put this down to the intense satisfaction his job gave him and to the fact that he could not resist eating too much each evening in the German officers' club. Paris was an exciting place, the most enervating posting he had ever been given, and in many ways the most fulfilling. Gunther's mouth watered as he thought of Slagel's work in the interrogation rooms, the men who broke miraculously before his eyes and the women sent for his gratification when nothing more could be gleaned from them. Then he thought of the plan he had formed for the capture of David Chambord. He *must* satisfy Berlin by taking at least one of the leading résistants. But it was not easy, and his lack of success had recently brought Gunther the first serious criticism of his entire military career. He frowned as he thought of Rol Tanguy safe in his slimy stronghold in the sewers. Lefaucheux was frequently out of the city and had more safe houses than any other résistant in Paris. Only David Chambord traveled in and out of the city like a modern-day Pimpernel, daring everything. The capture of Chambord had become Gunther's primary objective, and he spent hours each day thinking of ingenious ways to accomplish it.

Today, however, Standartenfuhrer Gunther had decided to allow himself an unusual diversion, and at eleven he walked to his car and ordered the driver to take him to the Théâtre Mogador. Outside the theater he stepped down and dismissed his driver, having pretended he was going to visit friends. Gunther walked the rest of the way to Mme. Francine's house in the rue Pigalle, looking at his watch every few seconds because he was obsessed by punctuality. When she had been to the avenue Foch to be interrogated, Francine had promised the Standartenfuhrer something special, and today he had asked that she keep her promise. Gunther smoothed his gloves and tilted his hat at a rakish angle, pulling in his stomach and tapping the lion's-head knocker six times precisely.

Mme. Francine opened the door and led her visitor down the hall. Gunther was at ease and secure in the knowledge that one of his best informants worked in the house. In the bar he ordered brandy, delighted when Madame herself served him. Gunther had often been heard to lament that the only good woman was a dead one, but, hearing Mme. Francine's robust voice and watching her towering frame, he was filled with admiration. What an operation the woman ran, as neat as any military exercise.

Madame calmly eyed her visitor's sallow face as Gunther raised his glass and finished the brandy.

"I know your taste, sir. You hate women with spirit, that's why you have to use those poor girls when Hauptsturmfuhrer Slagel has done his work on them. Don't worry, I understand and I know how to be discreet. That was why I wanted to invite you here, to enjoy something specially tailored to your needs, something you'll never forget."

"Where is she?"

Gunther was impatient to meet his prize.

Madame whispered conspiratorially, "She's in number eight, on the top floor. I shall personally accompany you."

Madame smiled enchantingly, and Gunther did not see that her eyes were alight with loathing. Since Armand's death, Mme. Francine had continued to entertain influential German visitors, waiting her chance for revenge on the men from the avenue Foch who had hounded him and the quisling who had betrayed his trust. Thus far three SS Obersturmfuhrers had vanished without a trace after visiting the establishment. As the men rarely told their colleagues about such visits, Madame had never been under suspicion. Now the leader of the SS interrogators was in her sitting room. Mme. Francine felt well pleased. Gunther refused a second brandy but accepted a cigar. Madame clipped the end and lit the cigar. Then for a few minutes they watched the girls fussing over their clients, twirling in prettily absurd outfits, stretching their legs and coyly allowing eager companions to investigate their plumage before disappearing for an hour of expensive make-believe. Gunther rose decisively when he had smoked the cigar and Madame led him upstairs, past the blue bedroom doors of the first floor and the silver ones of the expensive suites on the second floor to the attics, where specialized clients came to indulge their fantasies. Gunther's face was shiny with sweat, and Madame wondered if he had a respectable wife far away in the home he never mentioned.

Taking a key from her châtelaine, Madame opened the matte-black door of number eight. Gunther strained his eyes to see, but the interior was in total darkness. As Madame relocked the door he noticed the odor of lilies and a heavy, sweet, sickly smell that reminded him of something he could not quite remember. Then Madame lit four tallow altar candles, revealing her secret. Gunther gasped in shock, his eyes bulging in enraged disbelief. In a black coffin lined with ebony velvet and sprinkled with arum lilies lay Violet, his informant from the house. He rushed from the door to the side of the coffin, peering down in the dim light to see if his eyes were telling the truth, that Violet was dead and not play-acting for his amusement. Madame watched the Stand-artenfuhrer's beringed fingers fumbling to remove some of the lilies that covered the body, and with pride explained her position.

"She died only a few hours ago, sir, and I thought it would amuse you to have the woman of your dreams, a dead one, not just a mutilated wreck without the strength to defend herself. You may do as you wish with her, Violet is *all* yours now."

"How did she die? I demand to know how she died."

Madame looked remorselessly down at the ivory face and the eyes so innocent and blue.

"I poisoned her, sir."

"You will be arrested within the hour."

"I think not, sir."

Gunther swayed as she spoke. He was seeing two of everything, two towering Mme. Francines, two coffins, two bodies prettily rouged and coquettishly beribboned in violet. He ran toward the door, collapsing with a cry at Madame's feet. As he fell, she pushed his arm aside with the thick black heel of her shoe.

"Oh, my dear sir, you're feeling ill. Could it be that you drank something which disagreed with you?"

Francine laughed delightedly as she swept from the room, leaving Gunther unconscious on the floor. Within the hour she had her prisoner removed in Violet's coffin to a safe house outside the city center. Madame had plans for Standartenfuhrer Gunther that would take some time to accomplish.

That night Violet's body was unceremoniously dumped into the Seine. As she watched from the Pont Neuf, Madame spat derisively. The traitress was dead. Violet would betray no more innocents to the butchers of the avenue Foch. On her way home, Madame thought sadly of Armand, who had been the son she had always dreamed of having, the plucky little sparrow she had so admired. She had waited patiently, planning meticulously every detail of her scheme to avenge his death, and was confident that she could bring the plan to fruition. Many had tried to rid Paris of Standartenfuhrer Gunther. There had been five assassination attempts that Madame knew of, and all had failed, resulting in massive retaliation against the civilian population. Madame felt sure it was best to neutralize Gunther's effectiveness and then return him to the avenue Foch in readiness for the most brilliant coup—the murder of the notorious interrogator, made to look like suicide. Pleased by her own ingenuity, Madame thought that all she now needed was a little luck to complement her calculations. She looked up at the starry sky and saluted, her fist clenched. *Nous triompherons, Armand!*

The following afternoon Suzanne and Hans were in the place de la Madeleine, standing outside the cheese shop, debating whether they could afford a wedge of newly arrived Brie. Normally the pungent odor from massed cheeses inside the shop could be smelled from fifty meters away, and in peacetime the rush-latticed shelves had been a work of art. Suzanne looked at the empty spaces and thought of the heart-shaped Coeur de Roblet that used to lie next to the crusty fromage Normand, the wheels of Brie that had graced the top shelves, and the Lisieux, Camembert, Reblochon, and miniature country cheeses wrapped in plain leaves that had been her mother's favorites. The wartime shelves were empty, the jugs of parsley in the window display gone, and she and Hans were trying to decide if they could spend half a week's budget for a taste long absent from their menu. Realizing the foolishness of such extravagance, Suzanne led the way to the other side of the square, where Hans bought some bedding plants. There were queues of people waiting at every stall, and it took them over an hour to secure a solitary green peppercorn and a bony boiling fowl. They walked on to a part of the square where three elderly artists were displaying their work. One of the paintings caught Suzanne's eye, and she examined it wistfully, touched by the happy memories it evoked. The painting showed a field of scarlet poppies blowing in the breeze from an ancient windmill. Hans asked the price.

"I shall buy it for you, Suzanne."

"Thank you, it's beautiful."

"Remember when we had a picnic in a field just like that one, the week after we first were lovers?"

Hans kissed her, and Suzanne's face glowed with pleasure. She was thinking she would carry the painting home and put it in a prominent place to cheer the dark nights of winter. Holding it at arm's length, she was touched by the memory of happier days. Hans paid the artist, and they walked to the café where they had left their bicycles.

"You go on ahead with the painting. I'll take both the bicycles and leave them in the Bar Yvette. Then I will carry all the shopping back home."

"Why can't we go home together?"

"You know why. We don't walk together in Montmartre for fear of upsetting your friends and neighbors. Laval is dead, but we cannot be sure that everyone approves of our relationship."

As Hans cycled away, Suzanne walked thoughtfully up the rue Caumartin, pausing here and there to look in shop windows at sparse goods artistically displayed. Hans was right to be cautious and Suzanne knew it, but the pretense necessary to keep their true relationship secret never failed to irk. Suzanne felt slightly nauseous as she climbed the steep street. She had not eaten any meat for two weeks, and wondered if she had become anemic, like everyone else, or if her strange cravings were the action of the mind relieving tension by dwelling on the most unlikely and unobtainable objects. For a week she had scoured local shops for a pineapple, her mouth watering at the very thought of its sharp-sweet juice. There had been no pineapples in Paris, but Suzanne would have given a month's money to buy one. She crossed the square and proceeded up the rue Pigalle. This was the first time she had been in the street since her meeting with Armand, and she was curious. She passed Fred Payne's bar, which was closed and shuttered, and the Hôtel Trinité Palace, which was full of dancers, black marketeers, and out-of-work artists from nearby clubs. Darned tights flapped in makeshift rows at the hotel windows, and here and there gaudy underwear betrayed its owner's profession.

As she drew near Mme. Francine's establishment, Suzanne was astonished to see that it was empty and deserted. Curiosity overcame her, and she ran across the road and looked in through the windows. The house looked as if it had not been lived in for years. The walls were bare, the furniture gone, and on the door there was a card on which Madame had written CLOSED TILL THE END OF THE WAR. Suzanne laughed out loud at Madame's sense of humor and the large, aggressive handwriting. She passed on, puzzled that Francine had chosen this moment to move. How had Madame obtained passes to leave Paris? And where else would she find business booming? Suzanne paused to rest in the rue des Martyrs, hurrying on when she had her breath back.

On the steps of the rue Drevet a young girl collided with Suzanne. The girl apologized profusely and ran away, leaving Suzanne clutching the note she had pressed into her hands. She wondered who the girl was and why she had been so frightened. Once inside la maison Fleuri, she read the message and frowned uncertainly: "Zizi, Standartenfuhrer Gunther is going to have you followed. Please take care. D." She ran to the kitchen, lit a match, and burned the message to acrid cinders. Then she put water on to boil and walked outside to calm the pounding of her heart. Mme. Crystalle, the opera singer who had bought Laval's house, was practicing her scales in the garden. When she saw Suzanne she called out.

"Hello, my dear. A young girl just came to your house but you weren't in. I asked if she had a message, but she ran away, and I must say she looked frightened to death. Is anything wrong?"

"What was the girl wearing?"

"She had a red skirt and a blue-and-white check blouse."

The girl who had handed Suzanne the message had been dressed in red, white, and blue. Suzanne's face paled, and she wondered if the Gestapo were already watching the house. Had they seen the girl? Or had they been following her around the city?

Mme. Crystalle called out cheerfully, "Did you hear that one of those Boche pigs died today in the bar in the old square?"

"In Ottoline's?"

"That's the place. He choked to death this morning while he was having a coffee. I think she put glass shavings in it, or sawdust. While he was choking everyone sang the 'Marseillaise.' It's done me a world of good."

Suzanne returned to the kitchen to make an herb tisane. Mme. Crystalle was a patriotic Frenchwoman who had been collecting guns of every kind since the coming of the Germans. She had ignored all the ordinances so she would be ready to "defend and fight for Paris." Since arriving in the rue Gabrielle, Madame had been the leading light in the training of the street's own defense corps, the Free Paris Association. The Association was led by M. Corbeil, whose own attic was also like an armorer's store. Between them the militant pair had made sure that every man and woman in the near vicinity was armed and able to use their rifles and revolvers. For hours each week there were training sessions when everyone practiced in case they should be needed to help in the liberation of Paris. In streets all over the city men and women were doing the same. Those who had saved guns and ammunition hid them in attics, garden sheds, and boxes buried in the ground. Those who had nothing better, sharpened bed ends, iron staves, and old bayonets from the First World War, determined to be as dangerous as possible when the moment came. Old women were sewing forbidden tricolor flags from remnants of skirts, curtains, and bedspreads. Children were running errands and carrying messages for résistants unable to move around the city during the daytime. And everywhere there was growing impatience for the call where once there had only been apathy.

Suzanne wished she had some coffee or even a few spoonfuls of tea. But there was nothing left, only dried sage and mint for infusions. Hans had combed Paris for coffee, his efforts frustrated because the only drinkable beverages had been requisitioned for German clubs and the offices of the high command.

Suzanne wondered what Hans would say when he heard about David's message. Then she shrugged. She would think about that later. First she would cheer herself by hanging the new painting. She tried it against the living-room wall, then against the violet-flowered wallpaper of the hall. Dissatisfied with the effect, she bounded upstairs and settled for placing the painting by the side of Hans's bed. How beautiful it was, how merry and colorful. When the war was over she would enjoy picnics again in the countryside near Versailles, relaxing in fields of fragile red poppies and dreaming of future happiness. Suzanne closed her mind to the vexing question of the man who would accompany her on this idyllic outing, contenting herself with the idea that it would be either David or Hans, whichever survived the holocaust. She wondered curiously where David was and how he managed to know so efficiently what was happening in the house in the avenue Foch.

On the other side of the city, Slagel was pacing the floor of his office. For forty-eight hours Standartenfuhrer Gunther had not been seen. For two days officers of the SS had been combing the city center trying to find him, but they had found no clue to his whereabouts. Slagel had searched the files in the cabinet of his superior's office and had also found nothing relevant to the situation. Gunther, it appeared, had simply vanished. Slagel sat with his head sunk on his chest. Had Gunther been killed? Had he had a heart attack? Was he lying in some shabby French hospital unable to communicate? Slagel felt light-headed with rage. If Gunther were replaced by a rigorously disciplined officer sent from Berlin, the joy would vanish from his life. He would return to being a faceless, powerless nobody, without the means to fulfill the compulsions that drove him. He thought with respect and gratitude of his superior, remembering the day when he had first shown Gunther what he could do in the interrogation rooms and the promotions that had followed. At each posting Gunther had requested him as interrogation officer, and Slagel was fiercely proud of his relationship with the omnipotent officer. He decided, despite the risk of disciplinary action if he were discovered, not to report Gunther missing. In the meantime he would sift through lists of every known contact, every collaborator who had reported direct to the Standartenfuhrer, every place Gunther had visited during the past week, and every establishment that had been under surveillance at any time during the previous six months within a reasonable radius of the spot where Gunther had told his driver to leave him.

Two things came to light after a sleepless night of examining relevant information. Gunther had had two invaluable spies within a few hundred meters of the spot where he had stepped down from his car. They were a French schoolmaster, Raoul Dufferre, and Violet St. Claire, a whore working in a house in the rue Pigalle. Slagel sent for both. Within the hour Dufferre was in his office, but of Violet St. Claire there was no trace. When a Gestapo officer reported the address to have been false or incorrect, Slagel screamed abuse at him.

"Are you suggesting that Standartenfuhrer Gunther did not know the whereabouts of his informers?"

"No, sir, only that the address you gave me is now part of a convent. It has been taken over by nuns from an order in the next street."

"Did you question them?"

"I did, sir. They said the house was once occupied by a woman and some girls but that they had left long ago."

"Did the woman leave a forwarding address?"

"Yes, sir, she did."

"Give it to me."

Slagel read the address and tore it to pieces. Nine rue des Saussaies was a Gestapo interrogation center, guarded by the SS and full of suspected résistants. Slagel dismissed the officer and, after ascertaining that Dufferre had not seen Gunther for weeks, allowed the schoolmaster to return home. Then he continued to sift through files, dossiers, and folders, without finding anything that would help him locate his superior. Each time the phone rang he flinched in case Berlin High Command was calling Gunther. But his unease was unnecessary. No one tried to contact the Standartenfuhrer.

Dusk was falling, turning the stone buildings of the avenue Foch pink in the sunset. Slagel saw nothing of the beauty of his surroundings because his mind had wandered back to thoughts of Armand Lognon, the Jew who had eluded them after exhausting weeks of pursuit. Lognon had lived in the rue Pigalle, spied on by Violet St. Claire and cosseted by Francine Dubois. Slagel left the office and ordered a car to take him to the house in the rue Pigalle. As he stared up at its façade he cursed the futility of his inquiries. What was to be done? Could he authorize a house-to-house search of the area without arousing suspicion on the part of Gunther's superiors? He shook his head, knowing he had not the authority for such drastic action. He went home and lay on his bed reading the dossier on the woman who had befriended Armand Lognon. It told him nothing. Francine Dubois had been born Francine Aperovicci, in Sicily. She had been educated on the streets, married once to a Frenchman and divorced at the age of thirty. She had lived in Paris since the spring of 1935. There were no details on Madame's friends, contacts, relatives, or social life. Slagel paced his room, appalled to have been outwitted by a whore.

Mme. Francine had been keeping Gunther prisoner in a house in the suburb of Chantilly. He had been tied to a bed and for two weeks injected at six-hour intervals with heroin. Addiction established, it was part of Madame's plan to set him free. She inspected a dinner table set for two with tall green glass goblets, a turkey, and a bottle of Montrachet to lighten the bizarre atmosphere that would prevail between them. Gunther was wheeled in a chair to her presence, his feet still bound. His uniform, which had been cleaned and pressed, hung on him like a coat from a hanger. His bloodshot eyes surveyed the room, which was empty, as was the rest of the house, but for the table, chairs, and luxurious meal. It was nearing the time for Gunther's evening injection, and his hands were beginning to tremble. He could barely concentrate, and had no appetite for the meal, so he sat vacantly watching Madame and wondering where such a creature had managed to obtain such splendid food. After a while Francine spoke.

"Do you know why I brought you here, Standartenfuhrer Gunther?"

The prisoner shook his head.

"I thought that a villain of your reputation should know how it feels to be at the mercy of another human being. Today I am going to release you, and from this moment you will be at the mercy only of yourself and your craving for heroin."

"I shall overcome it. I am an officer of the SS."

"Perhaps you will, perhaps not."

Gunther looked around in vain for the white-coated attendant who had looked after him during his stay. And as Madame enjoyed a hearty meal he began to scratch his arms and his hands and to twitch in an agony of uncertainty. His mouth felt dry and putrid; his skin had a pricking, tingling itch. His breath was coming in short painful stabs that made him wince, and he wondered if he was going to collapse.

Mme. Francine rose and took a hypodermic from the tray at her side, along with a piece of rubber tubing and a packet of white, water-soluble powder.

"You must learn how to do this before you leave us, Standartenfuhrer. Go ahead, you've seen Jacquot do it enough times."

Gunther fumbled to tie the band around his arm, tightening it so the veins stood out like raised blue rivers on a salt-white plain. Madame watched as he prepared the injection, clearing air from the syringe with a squirt of liquid toward the ceiling. Then he hesitated, unable to pierce his own flesh despite the craving he felt. Madame waited without pity. She was remembering the substances with which the Standartenfuhrer's prisoners were injected in the house in the avenue Foch. Their screams kept neighbors awake for hours, and many Parisians in the area had been compelled to sell their mansions for a pittance rather than listen to the horrendous sounds of the interrogation prisoners.

At last Gunther inserted the needle, and Madame heard a sigh of relief as torment turned to rapture. How quickly it acted, how fast the liquid gold spread its reassuring rays around his body. Madame put the pieces of the kit in a leather pouch and handed it to her prisoner.

"Keep this safe, and these also. You'll need them until you can establish your own connection."

Gunther pocketed the small white packets and the leather

purse. Then he toyed with the turkey, barely touching the elegant wine. At this moment he felt omnipotent and above the minor worry of his future. He was thinking a thousand jumbled thoughts, each connected with his plans for the résistants imprisoned in the cellar of the avenue Foch. He felt certain that once he returned to his office he would be twice the man he had been before because he had survived everything that had been done to him during his captivity. The white powder reassured and deluded, and Gunther felt absurdly content. From time to time he consulted his watch as though late for an appointment. Madame drank her coffee, and when the meal was over called a car to take her prisoner back to Paris.

"Do you wish to go to your office or to your home?"

"To my office."

Nothing more was said, and within minutes Gunther was on his way to the city center. He held his head high, his arrogant attitude amusing Madame's driver, who knew from past experience what agonies the German had in store. Gunther clutched the leather pouch, from time to time checking the contents before relaxing as the car sped on. The driver insisted on dropping Gunther at the Rond Point of the Champs-Elysées instead of involving himself with certain pursuit from the avenue Foch. The Standartenfuhrer glowered, making a note of the number and thinking vindictively that Madame's driver would not go far before he was arrested. Hailing a passing German patrol car, Gunther ordered the driver to take him to his office in the avenue Foch. Mme. Francine's driver watched until the Standartenfuhrer disappeared. Then he turned the car, parked it where he had stolen it a few hours previously, from the curbside of the Elysée Palace, and returned home on the Métro.

Gunther walked smartly to his private office, disdaining the startled looks of clerks and secretaries working late. A low buzz of comment filled the room, but he felt above it, so overjoyed was he to be alive and back in the place where he was king. Slagel was at his desk, poring over dossiers. When Gunther appeared he leaped joyously to his feet and saluted. Then his expression froze and his body faltered. His superior was immeasurably changed. The pristine uniform hung loosely from his shoulders; the pudgy hands were covered with bruises and sores. The jovial face seemed hypomanic and moving out of synchronization with Gunther's words.

Gunther leafed through papers on his assistant's desk and asked, as though nothing untoward had happened, "Anything interesting today, Tristan?"

Slagel struggled to control his rising panic.

"Sir, you have been absent for two and a half weeks. May I ask where you have been?"

Gunther frowned in confusion. Two and a half weeks! Had he really been away so long? As though remembering something he had forgotten, he picked up the telephone and ordered the arrest of the driver of the blue Renault 751033 PE. Far away in the city center, a Gestapo officer tried to arrest the driver, only to discover that the man was one of his own superiors. Slagel poured himself a brandy and handed another to Gunther.

"I reported that you were sick with scarlet fever, sir. I thought it best to take time to find you, but I had almost given up hope."

Gunther laughed delightedly, making Slagel wince. The laugh was too loud, the movements disjointed. And what was the bag the Standartenfuhrer was clutching so desperately? Slagel watched as Gunther sipped his drink. Then he asked gently, "May I ask where you have been, sir?"

"I was abducted by Francine Dubois. She murdered our informant Violet St. Claire and locked me in a house God knows where. I believe I was in the Chantilly area, but I cannot be sure."

"But why did she do this? She made no demands for your release. I received no communication of any kind as to your wherabouts."

"No doubt Madame had her reasons."

Gunther looked at the man across the desk, the silver hair damp with sweat, the empty blue eyes that were suddenly desperately concerned. Although Slagel had been his protégé for the past four years, Gunther could not bring himself to describe the indignities he had suffered. He rose, put down the glass, and gave Slagel his first order.

"Find her, Tristan. Her house is in the rue Pigalle."

"The house is empty, sir. Madame vanished shortly after you did."

"And the place in Chantilly?"

"We'll go together and search the area."

Slagel spoke to the Standartenfuhrer's driver and arranged a motorcycle escort. The two men departed minutes later. In the car Slagel broke the news of the death of SS Oberst-Gruppen-fuhrer Reinhard Heydritch. "The hangman" had been ambushed in a grenade attack in Czechoslovakia and had died despite the frantic efforts of German doctors in a military hospital in Prague. Thirty thousand Czechs had been killed in reprisal for the murder of one of the Fuhrer's favorite Reichsprotektors. Slagel explained with relish that in addition the entire village of Lidice had been razed to the ground as a punishment for the crime.

"The men and boys of the village were shot, of course. The women went to the medical experimental block at Auschwitz. There, at least, they will be useful. The children were put into the gas ovens of Ravensbruck to avoid unnecessary expenditure on food. It will be many years before the birds sing again in Lidice."

As he listened, Gunther had the sudden premonition that the tide which had run for so long in their favor was turning like the wrath of God to drown them all. For a brief moment he remembered the old church where he had been taken to worship when young, and the words of the priest as he recited the commandments. Then he gritted his teeth and forced such unrewarding thoughts from his mind as he watched the road ahead.

They drove around Chantilly for over an hour before finding the house where Gunther had been imprisoned. The place was deserted, and there were no near neighbors, so the two men could question no one as to the whereabouts of Mme. Francine. Slagel walked from room to room, examining doors, walls, stairways, and finding only a vast emptiness. He was about to return to the car when he saw a cellophane strip wedged between the first and second stair. Bending to pick it up, he noticed a trace of white powder on the fragment and, tasting it, knew that it was heroin. He returned to the car and was driven back to the city. At his side the Standartenfuhrer was silent. In the hours since his return, the euphoria of the injection had worn off, replaced by sudden feelings of emptiness and insecurity. He clutched the black leather purse to his chest and kept looking at his watch. It was ten forty. At midnight he would relieve his pain with a shot of liquid life. Out of the corner of his eye Slagel observed his superior and asked himself how he was going to keep the Standartenfuhrer's enforced addiction secret. He dropped Gunther at his house near the Tuileries, dismissing the driver and walking home alone through the fear-ridden streets of Paris. For the first time, as he thought of Gunther's decline, Slagel was moved to question the future. Fear made him vicious, and as panic returned like a wraith to its murderer, he locked himself in his lonely room and made plans that would annihilate all opposition in the city.

The following afternoon Suzanne paused to speak with Mme. Crystalle in the rue Gabrielle. She had decided it would be best to tell the opera singer that she was being followed by the Gestapo so Madame could pass on the message to everyone in the street.

"Madame Crystalle, I'm being followed by the Gestapo. If you or any of the neighbors come to my house they'll be under suspicion, so I would be very grateful if you would tell Vivienne and the Rogers and Monsieur Corbeil and everyone else not to acknowledge me when they see me."

Madame beamed as though she had received good news. Then she flounced back to her house and called, "Thanks for the lettuce, Zizi. In about two weeks I shall have some pickled walnuts and I'll let you have some."

The surveillance officer scowled at the flamboyant redhead who spent the early mornings warbling scales till his ears protested. Then he followed Suzanne to the shops, making a note of everyone to whom she spoke, every gamin who bounced a ball in her direction, every little girl who said hello. As usual, there was nothing suspicious about Suzanne's behavior, and the officer felt bored and frustrated. Suzanne Castel was without doubt the dullest subject he had ever been instructed to observe.

In the rue St.-Rustique Suzanne looked in the window of the pest-control shop, remembering how her mother had shuddered each time they passed its gruesome window. The dead rats

were gathering dust, the traps had gone rusty, and the door
was padlocked because the owner had died on hearing that his
only child had been shot in a reprisal raid. Next door was M.
Rosenberg's shop, also padlocked, the dark red blinds drawn and
faded to bois-de-rose. Suzanne looked sadly at the discolored
brass doorbell, startled to see a shadow passing behind the blind.
She hurried on, praying the man following her had not seen
the change in her expression. Was Rosenberg still in the shop,
hiding out until the day when someone would come to tell him
the Germans had gone? Suzanne saw two housewives arguing
violently over an oxtail in the butcher's shop. With the wisdom
of Solomon, the butcher cut the tail in half and handed each
her bony share. On his window a printed notice stated, THERE
WILL BE NO MORE MEAT UNTIL THE 1ST OF THE MONTH. She walked
on to the builder's yard, her brain buzzing with conjecture.

Later, on her way home, Suzanne paused to look through the
wrought-iron railings of the old manor house at the corner of the
rue Norvins. Since the days of early childhood she had dreamed
of living in the house, though she knew she might never have
the means to do so. She looked admiringly at the magnificent
cedars in the garden, at the orangerie and the potager and the
wisteria trailing along the façade. As she looked she was imagining
names for the long-empty property—la maison du Lierre, le clos
Montmartre—but none seemed to fit, and most made the dignified
property sound like a restaurant. Reluctantly Suzanne passed
by toward the rue Gabrielle. When she was almost home she saw
a young man rushing toward her from the steps of the rue
Foyatier. There were two Gestapo officers behind him in hot
pursuit. Leaping aside, Suzanne almost collided with the surveillance officer who was following her. As she did so, she was horrified to see him draw a revolver and take aim at the fugitive.
Suzanne pushed his arm aside, roaring in simulated fury, "Don't
think I don't know you've been following me all afternoon. Go
away at once or I call the gendarme."

The officer returned his gun to its holster, cursing as the
handsome young résistant disappeared into the rabbit warren
of steep streets and crowded squares. Suzanne entered the garden
of la maison Fleuri, still looking as indignant as she could. Behind her the surveillance officer was debating whether Suzanne

Castel had saved the résistant deliberately. Instinct told him she had, but he had no proof, and her outburst could have been genuine, because he had been following her for days. For a moment he hesitated. Then he returned to his vantage point in the alleyway, resolved to watch his subject more closely in the future. He made a note on his sheet of the incident and advised the relief officer to watch closely because Castel had suddenly become a more likely suspect.

Hans was painting the walls of the living room when Suzanne arrived home. The pale sand-color wash he was using made the room seem full of sun, and he sounded cheerful as he called down from the ladder, "How did you get on at the shops? Was there any oil?"

"One small bottle, and this is the last."

"Did you get anything from the butcher?"

"Nothing. There was a notice saying there'd be no meat until the first of the month."

"Perhaps I should go out hunting. What do you think, Suzanne?"

She looked up in surprise. Was it safe to go to the forests and woodlands of Paris with a rifle and without a permit?

"Where would you go?"

"I don't know, anywhere where there's some open ground. A few rabbits would be very welcome at the moment. I feel as if my stomach has shrunk to the size of a pea. Did the Gestapo officer follow you again?"

"He did, and I had a problem while I was out."

"Tell me about it."

Hans climbed down the ladder, listening as Suzanne explained what had happened. He was troubled that she so constantly seemed to attract attention, unintentionally, by doing something on the spur of the moment that was dangerous. But there was no point in chiding Suzanne. She was a creature of impulse, and she would never change. Hans filled his jacket pockets with cartridges and took his rifle from the cloakroom, picking it up and looking down the barrel as Suzanne stood anxiously by.

"I shall cycle toward Versailles. If I am very late, you must go to bed."

Hans kneeled to light the fire to warm the room in the chill that would come with the night. Suzanne kissed him tenderly, reluctant to be left alone.

"Take care not to trespass, Hans. A farmer in Fontainebleau shot a man who was hunting on his land last week."

When Hans had gone, Suzanne went upstairs and looked out on the steps of the rue Foyatier. One surveillance officer was leaning against a lamppost reading a racing paper. No doubt the other was in the alleyway, waiting for her to do something he could report. She returned to the living room and read through the help-wanted column of the newspaper. It was months since she had worked, and the next show was not scheduled to open until December. She thought of her depleted money supply and the extent of her dependence on Hans. Then she touched the wall and, finding it dry, began to rehang the paintings and replace the books. As she worked she thought of the fruit she was going to bottle over the weekend. In the garden the trees were heavy with plums and pears. The greenhouse was still full of tomatoes, and Hans had grown some peppers specially to please her. When the room was tidy again, Suzanne went to the kitchen to warm some cabbage and potato stew. Her mind dwelled on the thought of steak, and she felt sick at the smell of the boiling cabbage.

By eight it was chilly. By nine it was dark. Suzanne threw acorns and pine cones on the fire with some willow twigs gathered during a visit to the park.

At ten thirty there was a knock at the door. Suzanne froze in fear. Who could be calling at such a late hour? She ran to the door and asked who was there. Hans replied that he could not reach his keys. Suzanne opened the door and let him in, exclaiming gleefully when she saw a fat hare tucked under one arm and a pair of pigeons in the other. Hans handed her a letter.

"As I was coming through the gate a young girl gave me this and then ran away."

Hans took the hare to the outhouse and hung it from a hook in the ceiling. In the kitchen, Suzanne was reading the note that had just been delivered.

Dear Suzanne,
    You will not have heard of me, but David has often shown me your photograph, so I recognized you at once when you

saved my life this afternoon. If you ever need help come to
the Cimetière de Montmartre any evening around seven and
I shall return the favor by helping as best I can.

Yours,

Alexander Esterhazy

Suzanne thought of the young adventurer who had escaped
from the Gestapo. Even in such hard times, he had worn an
elegant white silk shirt, and his body had been tanned and lean,
not pale and flabby, like most of her friends' in Paris. She began
to toast stale bread over the embers, spreading the slices thickly
with mashed courgette and anchovy paste—all she had in the
larder. Hans grimaced when he tasted the concoction.

"Maybe I should go and shoot a few animals in the zoo?"

They both laughed, recalling David's Christmas menu, and
Suzanne was to remember the evening as the last happy moment
for many enervating months. Unaware of the storm clouds
gathering, the lovers retired to bed and loved the night away.


In a Gestapo interrogation room in the avenue Foch, a young
girl was talking as she had never talked before. She told of the
messages she often delivered to Suzanne Castel and of her own
boy friend, Alexander Esterhazy. Though she forgot to mention
Esterhazy's habit of visiting the cemetery of Montmartre to
rendezvous with friends, she gave his address and the address of his
married sister, Natasha Rollet. Confident that the information
had won her a reprieve from execution, the frightened girl looked
up at her interrogator and flinched. The icy blue eyes wanted
more, the skeletal face demanded everything. The girl racked
her brain for something to say, someone important to incriminate.
Exhaustedly she babbled on, a modern Scheherezade waiting for
the respite that would come with the dawn.

When Gunther was satisfied that the girl could tell them no
more, he had her shot in the courtyard outside his office. As he
looked down on men removing her body and cleaners swabbing
the cobblestones, he mulled over one curious piece of information
the girl had given him. That small piece of the puzzling jigsaw
which had been eluding him for months could now give him David

Chambord. Gunther went home to change and shave, informing his assistant that he would be back in the office by eight thirty.

Gunther's elation contrasted strangely with Slagel's perplexity as he stood at the window apprehensively looking out on autumn leaves swirling around the path below. What had the girl meant by her incriminating statement? If he had not known that she was too afraid to lie, he would have disbelieved what she had revealed. He sat at his desk, waiting for the dawn, unable to reconcile his personal feelings with the unacceptable task ahead.

Suzanne was wakened by a hammering at the door. She got up, put on a robe, and called in a loud voice, "I'm coming, just a moment." Hans looked out from the landing window, paling at the sight of a low black car and two men in leather overcoats. He dressed as quickly as he could, smoothing the bed and forcing himself to work out how he could bargain for Suzanne's release from Standartenfuhrer Gunther. Below, in the hall, a gruff voice was questioning Suzanne.

"You are Suzanne Jacqueline Castel?"

"I am."

"How many persons are living in this house?"

"Just myself and Major von Heinkel."

Hans appeared on the stairs, his face commanding and stern.

"What is the meaning of this? Why have you disturbed Mademoiselle Castel at such an early hour? It's barely half past seven."

"We are here on the orders of Standartenfuhrer Gunther."

M. Corbeil's cockerel crowed, heralding the morning, and on the other side of the road Suzanne heard the screeching ring of a neighbor's alarm clock. She waited for the Gestapo officer to explain what he wanted, but he was rummaging in his pocket to find a typed official notice. When he had the card in his hand, he stood to attention and recited, "Major Hans Pieter von Heinkel, in the name of the Fuhrer I arrest you for treason. You will hand over your service revolver and accompany me at once to the interrogation center in the avenue Foch. Heil Hitler!"

Suzanne stood quite still, her eyes filling with tears, her hands gripping the stair rail to keep from falling. Hans looked bemused for a moment. Then his eyes met Suzanne's, and they both knew there had been no mistake. Suddenly Hans felt a profound sense of sadness, a bitter regret that could never be put into words. He returned to his bedroom, followed by the two men, who waited until he had dressed. His dignity and autocratic presence impressed them, and neither dared tell him to hurry. When the three came downstairs into the hall, Suzanne placed herself between Hans and the door.

"What does this mean? How *can* they arrest you?"

"I don't know, Suzanne, but I shall soon find out. If I am not back by this evening you may need money. Here is my bankbook, I have signed all the checks. My gold watch and chain and my cigarette case are on the dresser, don't hesitate to sell them if you need cash. The only other money I have in Paris is lodged with General-Oberst Funnen at Wehrmacht headquarters. He is a friend of my father's and he will help you. If you are in trouble, give him this and tell him I asked him to give you every assistance."

Tears began to pour down Suzanne's face as Hans handed her his Iron Cross.

"What are you trying to say, Hans?"

"I am saying au revoir, my darling, till soon."

Suzanne kissed him, sniffing the country smell that had first drawn her to him. Then Hans was gone, pushed into the back of the ugly black car like a common criminal. Suzanne stood at the gate, watching until the car disappeared from sight. And from their windows neighbors also observed, pitying Suzanne's white, anguished face and wishing they could help. Hans had kept Suzanne alive wth food brought from all over Paris. He had also been generous with her friends and neighbors, and many thought him more a Frenchman than some they knew. As the clock struck eight Vivienne appeared with a cup of real coffee and a sachet of brown sugar. Ten minutes later Mme. Crystalle arrived with some small pies made of liver and potatoes. Suzanne kissed them both gratefully and excused herself, disappearing to the bedroom to stare at the yellow roses Hans had picked the day before and the painting of the red poppy field he had bought on their trip to the city center. Why? she asked herself. Why Hans? But there was no answer. Hans had been taken by Gunther, who was known to be obsessed with the idea of pursuing anything that might lead him to the resistance leaders he longed to capture. Hans's downfall had been accomplished through *her* and because of his tenuous link with David. Suzanne wondered grimly who had talked, who had told of Hans's meeting with David and the happy, forbidden Christmas they had all spent together. Unable to cope with the agony that clawed at her mind, she sat looking out on the distant city. She was still there at nightfall, still waiting for the sound of Hans's key in the door, but the only sounds were from an owl hooting in the distant vineyard. Suzanne looked at the gold-and-ebony watch on the dressing table, the wristband on which Hans's name and serial number had been etched, and the cigarette case he had offered at their first meeting. She wrapped them carefully in tissue paper and hid them in her drawer. She would never sell them, never, no matter how hungry she became. They would be waiting for Hans's return, however long it took.

# CHAPTER NINE

*January, 1943*

Suzanne crossed out the fourth of January on her calendar and began to count. Minutes later she knew that it was just fourteen weeks since she had last seen Hans. She rose unsteadily and went to the kitchen to make a drink, knowing she was ill and accepting the idea that she would have to visit the doctor. A new man had just set up in practice in the place Emile-Goudeau, near Picasso's former studio in the Bateau Lavoir. Suzanne wondered if he would tell her she was not eating enough or her problems were in the mind. Of late her thoughts had darted like butterflies from one subject to the next, never lingering on any one because each seemed more uncomfortable than the last. She wondered why David had so determinedly refrained from making contact with her and if he was still alive. If so, did he still love her? And Hans, had he been sent back to Germany for court-martial or was he too gone forever from her life? Suzanne had tried by every means she knew to find out what had happened to Hans, but her inquiries had been totally fruitless.

The doctor wrote out notes in a stylish script on a card he would occasionally mislay because he was distressed and disturbed by Suzanne's condition. Now and then he looked to the corner of the room where Suzanne was dressing behind a screen. The old man thought how beautiful the girl was, how hauntingly innocent

and untouched by the blackest aspects of war. It was sad to have
to tell her such unfortunate news.

As she dressed, Suzanne's mind was racing. Dr. Merimée had
been very thorough in his examination and noncommittal on its
completion. For the first time that she could recall, she was terrified by the possibility of pregnancy. In the past few months,
starvation, lack of the basic necessities of life, and constant
tension had wrought havoc with the feminine cycles of most of the
women she knew. Suzanne had therefore found it easy to discount
her own departure from normality. But in the light of the doctor's
gentle probing she emerged from behind the screen, her face
pale with apprehension. She walked slowly to where Merimée
was sitting on his mahogany chair and asked timidly, "What's
wrong with me, Doctor? Am I suffering from malnutrition?"

"You are indeed, Mademoiselle Castel."

Suzanne breathed a sigh of relief, closing her eyes briefly to
thank God the news was no worse. Her prayer was interrupted by
the doctor's voice.

"You are also fourteen to sixteen weeks pregnant."

Seeing her color change, Merimée rose and poured brandy into
a medicine glass. Suzanne gulped the fiery liquid, a hundred
urgent questions leaping into her mind. But she said nothing
and sat, her hands fluttering, her mouth forming words that
never reached completion. The doctor did his best to sound
encouraging.

"I shall give you vitamin pills to supplement your diet, and you
need have no worries about my fees. I made my money a long time
ago, before this dreadful war came to try us."

Suzanne smiled shakily. She was pregnant, pregnant, pregnant.
Dazed, she mumbled inaudibly, "The father of my child has
been arrested."

"Where did they take him?"

"To the avenue Foch."

Merimée turned away so Suzanne would not see his unease.
As he looked through the window at a gray wintry sky, he thought
that few ever returned from the interrogation center, and those
who did were damaged in mind or body.

Suzanne was remembering with horror that Hans's arrest had
been because of her, because his love had not allowed him to

betray David at their Christmas meeting. She looked at the doctor's shiny morning coat, the gray-striped trousers, and old-fashioned pince-nez above the snow-white beard. As she watched, Merimée handed her two slips of paper. Then he led her to the door.

"I would like to see you again in one month. In the meantime, I am always here if you need me. If there's no reply to the surgery door, ring the bell to my private apartment upstairs."

"You've been very kind, Doctor."

They shook hands, and Suzanne stepped out into the street. Pale sunlight was shining on leafless trees in the square, dappling pink and yellow houses and the ivy-covered bar on the corner. Suzanne sat on a bench, staring at her surroundings. Tourists in lederhosen were taking pictures indiscriminately of even the most mundane things. Frenchmen were scurrying past, scowling at their unwelcome visitors, and children in the schoolyard were singing rude songs about German stupidity.

Suzanne read the prescriptions without understanding them. In her pocket she had the last of the money drawn with the checks Hans had signed and left with her. It was not enough to buy food *and* expensive medicine. Opening her hand, she let the prescriptions blow away with dead leaves and some paper doilies from the bakery at the corner.

As she walked home Suzanne struggled to take in the news she had just been given, but her mind would not accept it. Her first thought was to search for Mme. Francine so she could find out how to obtain an abortion. Then she shook her head resignedly. Abortion was out of the question, against her religion, her conscience, and her longing for peace of mind. The child was hers and Hans's, conceived of their love in the midst of squalid disorder. She could not murder it before it saw the light of day. Hunger made her stumble, and she shivered violently in the icy wind as she turned the corner into the rue Gabrielle.

The young man who had been watching Suzanne from the bar window frowned. Why was she so distraught? Why had she thrown away her prescriptions? And why had Suzanne's face had the blank look of a sleepwalker? Alexander Esterhazy frowned into his glass of ersatz beer. Then he paid for his drink, went to the phone and spoke urgently with his contact.

Inside la maison Fleuri, Suzanne was rummaging in the storeroom for cabbage, beans, and lentils to make a pan of soup.
The soup cooked, she thought that only a few months previously
she had been sure the Allies were coming to set Paris free. In
August they had heard via the BBC broadcasts that the British
had landed in Dieppe. Then there had been an ominous silence
and a news blackout that heralded the failure of the raid. Every
man and woman in Paris had been downcast, and the streets had
been silent with resignation. To add to the depression they felt,
the Propagandastaffel had circulated the story that the Fuhrer had
ordered prisoners of war from Dieppe to be released as a reward
to the citizens of that town for their good behavior in refusing
to assist the invaders. Parisians with relatives in Dieppe shunned
them. Letters were returned unopened. Only later would the
truth be established. Suzanne went to the living room and poked
the fire, wondering, as she looked into the flames, if the Allies
would return with the Americans to add strength to a new in-
vasion. She had faith that they would, and it was this slender
hope that made her go on.

Hans was alone in a cell that measured six feet by four feet
by seven feet. There was no window in the box, and the air stank
of excrement and vomit. For a hundred days he had been imprisoned without light, heat, exercise, or human companionship.
Twice a day water and stale black bread were put under the door.
Once a week maggot-ridden cabbage soup was given in addition
to the bread, and occasionally he had been dragged out so the
cell could be hosed down. Certain that Standartenfuhrer Gunther
was softening him for the interrogation that would decide his
fate, Hans had done his utmost to keep from going mad. Every
day he exercised by pressing his tall frame against the ceiling
and flexing his legs against the cell door. He knew it was important to remain lucid, so he counted and remembered poems,
military orders, and even the letters of the alphabet. In the second
month of his imprisonment, Hans took to singing the words of
favorite songs and then to composing a history of the Heinkel
family from the fourteenth century to the present. But gradually

the assault on his senses began to tell, and he repeated himself
often and forgot the names of even the closest members of his
family. As he did not know night from day, he slept whenever
he felt tired, ignoring the hammering on the cell door intended
to prevent him from resting. What he was unable to ignore
were the festering rat bites on his body and the screams of agony
from other prisoners, which gave him nightmares as he slumped
uncomfortably against the wall. Sometimes, for hours on end, he
thought of Suzanne, dreaming of loving her again, of visiting
favorite places in the city with her, and of remaining for the
rest of his life at her side. Every day he willed the purgatory to
end. But the torment dragged inexorably on.

Hans had no knowledge of the war that would help him bear
his detention more easily. There were those in Paris who knew
that since the British raid on Dieppe there had been a lull in the
advance of German might. The Fuhrer's forces had been stopped
by the Russians before Stalingrad. Rommel had been halted by
the British at El Alamein. The blitz on London had failed because Cockney resilience and English sangfroid had refused to be
intimidated. America was well and truly involved in the war, and
the might of Uncle Sam had begun to erode the hitherto un-
checked strength of the Fatherland. In Paris people were whispering for the first time that the Germans could be defeated. But
for the prisoners in the avenue Foch there was only pain, fear, and
the hope of a quick death by firing squad.

When he was near collapse, Hans heard the key grating in his
door. The officer on duty called him out, and he staggered like
a drunk to a barred room near the interrogation hall. Hans looked
around, his eyes watering painfully in the unaccustomed light.
Were the walls swaying to and fro? Was the window coming
nearer and then receding? Was this yet another of Slagel's
ingenious ways of reducing his prey to idiocy? Within minutes
a tin bath was brought in with green soap and dressings for the
suppurating sores on his festering body. Hans wondered if
this was the show of kindness that often prefaced interrogation. He washed as best he was able, drying his body on a
rough gray towel. Often he fell to the ground because he
was weak and his balance had become faulty. His hands were
so covered with boils and bites that he could not fasten the

buttons of the clean clothing put out for him, so he called for the warder's assistance. Then, leaning cautiously forward, he looked in the mirror, starting violently at his reflection. He had lost fifty pounds and resembled a walking skeleton. The sun-tanned face was chalky white, the eyes scarlet-rimmed, the skin covered with crusty scabs. For a moment Hans tried to collect his thoughts. But before he could work out what had happened to him, he was ordered to follow the orderly to a room on the other side of the corridor.

Behind a gray steel desk Hauptsturmfuhrer Slagel was pouring cream into a large cup of coffee. Hans lurched into the room, clutching the bureau to steady himself and rubbing his eyes as he tried to clear the mists of confusion from his mind. Slagel motioned for him to sit, and, when he had added two heaped tea-spoons of sugar to the coffee, handed the cup to his prisoner. Hans resisted the urge to grasp it like an animal. Aware that his eyes could not focus, he balanced the cup on his knee, holding it with both bands, fiercely determined that Slagel would not have the pleasure of seeing him spill the precious liquid on the floor. Slagel's pale face flushed with emotion. This, surely, was the moment. Standartenfuhrer Gunther had ordered special treat-ment for Hans von Heinkel. He had therefore been kept for one hundred and two days in total sensory deprivation. Slagel grimaced at the putrid skin and leaking lesions that had already bloodied the clean clothes. When Hans returned the cup to the table Slagel spoke.

"I wish to know everything of your relationship with David Chambord, known also by the code name Dakota Chanson and as Charles Latour. I have decided to question you alone in order to warn you, Major von Heinkel, that the next interrogation will be before Standartenfuhrer Gunther. I shall then be ordered to force you to give the information he requires. Do you under-stand?"

Hans nodded wearily.

"Now please tell me what you know. Start with David Chambord and leave out nothing."

"I know very little of Chambord."

"I also wish to know every detail of Suzanne Castel's involve-ment in resistance work. I know of your own personal relationship with her and I know you have condoned her seeing Chambord in the house."

Hans looked at his hands and waited, his mind fighting to take in what was being said. Slagel motioned him to speak, and after a while Hans replied.

"I first met Mademoiselle Castel when she came to the office to obtain a work permit. I was later billeted at her home."

"At your own request."

"Yes."

"Why was that?"

Hans's eyes lit with pleasure.

"I had fallen in love with her. I wanted to be near her."

Slagel motioned him to continue, but Hans was not concentrating. He was looking outside toward the boulevard, his eyes filled with longing.

Slagel snapped at him, "Continue, Major von Heinkel."

"After the death of Suzanne's father, who was shot by a reprisal squad, and that of her mother, who died of a heart attack . . ."

Hans's voice trailed off, and his eyes closed. Slagel tapped the desk with a ruler.

"Please try to concentrate, Major von Heinkel."

"After the deaths of Suzanne's parents we became lovers. As far as I know, Suzanne never received any communication from her fiancée. She told me David Chambord was engaged to her, and I know she had seen the wanted notices. I think she had the affair with me because she was sure her fiancé would never return to Paris alive."

"We intend that he does not."

Hans thought of David, whose strength and determination had so impressed him. Then, looking down at the pus-stained shirt, he sighed. If Suzanne were to see him now she would weep that he had been unable to triumph over the adversity of imprisonment. He wondered what David would have done in similar circumstances, rousing himself when Slagel shouted for him to continue. Where to start? And what to tell, when there was little to say except that he loved Suzanne and always would? Slagel began to pace the office as Hans stumbled to marshal his thoughts.

"At Christmas . . ."

"The Christmas of last year, Major von Heinkel?"

"Yes."

"Yes *sir.*"

Hans frowned, continuing as though unaware of the Hauptsturmfuhrer's presence.

"At Christmas I went back to Germany for domestic reasons."

"And Chambord came to see your lover? Did it not strike you as strange that he knew the precise dates of your absence?"

Hans considered this interminably. Then he looked at Slagel, narrowing his eyes so he could focus and catching something in the cold blue eyes that chilled him. When he was able, he continued his story.

"David knew nothing of my presence in the house, because Suzanne had not been in contact with him."

Slagel drew a letter from a folder at his side and Hans winced as the sibilant voice read: " 'My dear David, How are you? Yesterday I saw your face on a wanted poster in the rue Gabrielle. I stole it, of course, and gave it to Carrie, but not until I had carried it everywhere with me for a few weeks. . . .' "

Slagel handed the note to Hans, who returned it unread.

"I'm sorry, I cannot focus my eyes to read."

"This is a letter from Castel to her fiancé. It was sent in the middle of last year via a courier. We intercepted it, copied the letter, and then sent the messenger on her way."

Hans wondered what else Slagel had in his folder. What next was going to be thrust upon him? He thought of Suzanne, wondering why she had not told him she was writing to her fiancé. Now her impetuousness would be the death of them both. Hans was silent for a moment. Then, as he began to think of their Christmas meeting with David, he seemed momentarily to savor the happy memory.

"After Christmas, when I returned to Paris, I found David Chambord with Suzanne."

"And you failed to report this?"

"I did."

"You realize the penalty for treason?"

"I do."

"Continue, Major von Heinkel."

Slagel admired his prisoner's self-control and the dignity he retained despite his appalling injuries. At no time had the gallant major asked for leniency for himself or his lover. This troubled Slagel, who looked uncertainly at the prisoner, shocked by the realization that he still did not feel in complete control of the situation. He listened as the deep voice continued, angry with himself for admiring Hans.

"David Chambord left that same day, the day I arrived back in Paris. He gave me to understand he was going back to the South of France."

"Where in the South of France?"

"Chambord never mentioned his whereabouts in my presence. As I remember, he spoke only of the lack of gas in the area and of the high price of food. He also gave Suzanne a menu from the Restaurant Voison in 1870, when Parisians ate the animals from the zoo. We laughed at the picturesque dishes that were described."

Hans paused to enjoy again the memory of the moment when uproarious laughter had echoed in la maison Fleuri. Slagel made notes and continued relentlessly with his questions.

"Did Chambord ask you for information on German plans for Paris?"

"Never at any time."

"Did you hear him ask Castel to ascertain such information?"

"I did not."

"Did he ask her to meet with Alexander Esterhazy, whose life she saved, or with Armand Lognon, who was her lover?"

Hans willed himself not to scream abuse at his interrogator.

"Lognon was not Suzanne's lover. He was a young lad who stole a photograph of her from the showcase outside the Bal Tabarin. I believe he was infatuated with Suzanne. As for Esterhazy, Suzanne had never met or heard of him until the day she saved his life."

"What did you do when she told you what she had done?"

"I did nothing. I am not a security officer. That is your job, Hauptsturmfuhrer, and the job of the Gestapo."

Slagel poured more coffee and handed it to Hans. His eyes were intent, his thoughts racing. He felt sure Hans was telling the truth, but perhaps not the whole truth. He watched as Hans tried to balance the coffee cup on his knee, and when he spoke again his voice was gentle.

"Please continue, Major von Heinkel."

"A few days before my arrest, a young girl delivered a note

to Suzanne. I took it from the girl as I was returning from a hunting trip. After we collided at the front door, the girl ran away."

"Did you recognize her?"

"I had never seen her before."

"Are you sure?"

Hans nodded wearily. Exhaustion was overwhelming him, and it was all he could do to keep from falling to the ground. He drank the coffee quickly and made the decision to tell nothing of the note Esterhazy had sent Suzanne.

Slagel walked to the window and looked down on the courtyard.

"Do you know what was in the note?"

"I think Suzanne said it was a letter thanking her for saving his life."

"Is that all you have to tell me?"

"I was arrested the day after the note arrived. I don't know if Esterhazy contacted Suzanne again."

Slagel sat facing Hans at the desk.

"Major von Heinkel. I am sure you have told the truth to a point. I am also sure you have condoned Castel's participation in resistance work and the company of her fiancé, David Chambord. But what I want is *facts*. Standartenfuhrer Gunther wants to capture Chambord, and nothing will stop him. He also wants Chambord's group alive. We know their names and their addresses. But in the case of Esterhazy and his sister, neither has returned home since you were arrested. I can only assume that this is because they feel you will tell of their involvement with Chambord."

Hans struggled to follow Slagel's reasoning. It was true. Why *had* Esterhazy and his sister disappeared at the same time he had been arrested? After a long pause he asked Slagel, "May I ask, sir, if I am the only person connected with Chambord who has been arrested during this period?"

"I had the girl, the one who delivered the messages and letters. She told everything before she died, but she knew very little of importance. But you, Major, you will tell me what I need to know. You *must* tell me, or you will die in an interrogation room, like all the rest."

Hans wondered why Slagel should falter at the prospect of killing him when he had killed so many others. Then, when he had summoned all his strength, he rose and stood to attention.

"It is well known that you have at your disposal the means to make people talk. When you have used all those means on me, Hauptsturmfuhrer Slagel, you will be forced to admit that I have spoken the truth. With your experience of such matters I should have thought my innocence and my ignorance of Chambord's business obvious."

Stung by the reprimanding tone of Hans's voice and the disdain in the damaged face, Slagel had him taken away to the cells. For a moment he sat at his desk, knowing that Hans had spoken the truth. But would the Standartenfuhrer believe he was innocent? Slagel knew he would not and that he would insist on the use of every last means of eliciting information the major did not know. Trapped by fear and the inevitability of Gunther's obsession, Slagel decided to send for Suzanne Castel. The girl could verify Hans's answers, of that he was certain, and perhaps this would save the major from Gunther's ruthlessness.

Hans was taken to a green-painted cell on the ground floor The cell had one small barred window and a pallet bed in the corner. Hans lay on it, trying to stop his head from spinning in shock at being released from the black hole where he had been kept for so long. He slept fitfully until the early hours of the morning. Then he lay awake thinking of Suzanne. At around 4:00 A.M. the occupant of the next cell began to tap on the wall and Hans realized he was tapping a message. *What . . . is . . . your . . . name?* Hans replied that he was *Hans . . . von . . . Heinkel.* The tapping ceased, replaced by noises that seemed to be coming from the outer wall of the building. Hans climbed unsteadily onto his bed and stared out into the darkness. A shaft of moonlight caught the slim figure of a man who had successfully eluded the SS guards around the building. As Hans watched, the shadowy figure disappeared over the wall into the avenue Foch. Hans's heart leaped with joy, and for the first time in weeks he dared hope. Was it possible David Chambord was coming to rescue him?

The next morning Suzanne was brought to the house in the avenue Foch, to be questioned by Haupsturmfuhrer Slagel. She was led down a corridor and through a room full of typists and messengers who ignored her presence. Suzanne's heart was pounding with terror, but she hardened her face, determined not to show fear as she came face to face with the man she had always dreaded meeting.

"I am Haupsturmfuhrer Slagel. You may remember we met once before."

"I remember."

"Sit down, please. I have asked you here so you can tell me about Major Hans von Heinkel."

"Is he still here?"

"He is indeed."

"Why is he still a prisoner?"

"Major von Heinkel is to be charged with treason."

"Then why has he not been charged?"

"We have to question him first."

"But Hans has been here for fourteen weeks!"

"Fourteen weeks and three days precisely."

Suzanne breathed deeply, shocked and infuriated by the amused smile on Slagel's face.

"Fourteen weeks is quite long enough for any man to be questioned, Haupsturmfuhrer. Could there be some other reason for Major von Heinkel's long stay?"

Slagel looked suddenly bewildered, and, taking advantage of his silence, Suzanne issued a threat.

"If you do not release Major von Heinkel very soon, I intend to go to the commander of Gross Paris and tell him that you have been indulging in sadistic games with a German officer who received the Iron Cross from the Fuhrer."

Slagel leaped to his feet, his voice shrill with fury.

"How dare you threaten *me!*"

"I am not threatening you, Haupsturmfuhrer. I am simply stating a fact. If you do not release Major von Heinkel, I shall report you to the commander of Gross Paris."

"You have been brought here to answer certain questions. You will answer them without further comment. Please be sure to tell me the whole truth, as I shall know at once if you are lying."

The door opened, and Standartenfuhrer Gunther entered. For a moment the two men conferred. Then Gunther sat in the chair next to his assistant, listening to the interrogation. Suzanne looked in surprise at Gunther's twitching face and the hands that fumbled constantly up and down his jacket. Was the notorious Standartenfuhrer ill or losing his nerve? Had the vitriol of war corroded even his sureness of purpose? Suzanne's deliberations were interrupted by Slagel.

"We know how you met Major von Heinkel and how you admitted your fiancé into the house during the major's absence. We also know you have been corresponding with Chambord for some months."

Suzanne chose her words with great care.

"While Major von Heinkel was away in Germany I was attacked by the Gestapo agent Claude Laval. I don't know who killed Monsieur Laval, but everyone hated him, and I survived his attack only because of the arrival of my fiancé, David. You have been having me watched, so you'll know that I had no idea David was coming to Paris, and you'll also know that I haven't written to my fiancé since October."

"Are you suggesting that Chambord had nothing to do with the death of Claude Laval?"

"Of course I am. A man like Monsieur Laval must have lived in constant fear that someone would take revenge on him for all the people he had betrayed."

Slagel cursed the insanity of Laval and the fearless defiance of the girl on the other side of the desk. As he examined her, Suzanne wondered if Slagel hated her because she was French and a patriot or because she was loved by Hans von Heinkel. Slagel resumed the questioning.

"I also know about the day you and your fiancé spent with Major von Heinkel, about the things they discussed like gas prices and food prices and the menu Chambord gave you."

A flicker of a smile lit Suzanne's face. Then she was serious, afraid when Slagel spat out his comments.

"I wish to know what Chambord discussed with the major. I wish to know what Chambord discussed with you and what he asked you to do."

"Hans and David talked about Hans's visit to Germany. His father was ill, his brother had just been killed, and Marguerite was suffering from consumption. Hans needed to talk of the people he loves."

"And when you were alone with Chambord?"

Suzanne's face became dreamy, and Slagel felt suddenly uncomfortable.

"David and I made love and talked of our future. He never discussed his work with me, and during the time we had together we were too involved with each other to talk about the war."

Slagel was silent. The Castel girl was a temptress who had ensnared Hans von Heinkel and then betrayed him with the resistance leader. He looked at her with disgust.

"Is promiscuity your habit, Mademoiselle Castel?"

"I have only ever been loved by two men."

"And which one do you love? From your attitude I must assume that it is Major von Heinkel. I also assume that you wish the major to return to you, so perhaps we can make an agreement. I will tell you what I wish to know and you can decide if you can assist me. If you can, I shall release Major von Heinkel. If you refuse to cooperate, the consequences will be very serious."

Suzanne remained impassive, waiting for the conditions that would secure Hans's release. Slagel's voice hissed menacingly.

"First, I wish to know the location of the Chambord cell in southern France. Two, I wish to know when next he will be in Paris. Three, I wish to know the whereabouts of the Esterhazys. Four, I wish you to write a note to your fiancé indicating that you will meet him at a location I will tell you. That is all, Mademoiselle Castel."

Suzanne took a deep breath and replied, "I can answer certain of those questions, but I cannot tell you what I do not know, Hauptsturmfuhrer."

Slagel examined the expressionless face and was unable to fathom what Suzanne was thinking. His deliberations were interrupted by Gunther's flat, insistent voice.

"Mademoiselle Castel, I am convinced that you are lying and that you have the information we require. I am also convinced that you have had the assistance of Major von Heinkel in your endeavors."

Slagel stared uncomprehendingly at his superior, and Suzanne wondered why he seemed so fearful. Gunther continued calmly, without emotion, though his words shocked Suzanne to the core.

"If you do not give me the information I require, Major von Heinkel will be shot, while you watch, five minutes from now. Make your decision, Mademoiselle Castel."

Slagel rose and hastened to the Standartenfuhrer's side. "Sir, may I speak with you?"

"Not now, Tristan. It's important I resolve this matter."

Suzanne was thinking of the questions and the threat so surely made. Then her mind turned to thoughts of Hans, who was locked away somewhere in this morbid building. She knew where David and his group were in southern France, but she had no idea of the whereabouts of Alexander Esterhazy and she had never met his sister Natasha. She would be willing to write a letter to David telling him to meet her in the place of Slagel's choice *if* she could be sure that he would release her so she could warn her fiancé of the danger. But nothing was sure, not even Slagel's promise to release Hans. In the silence of the stark white office, Suzanne became aware that for her the moment of decision had come. Should she save Hans's life and betray David? Or should she condemn her lover and secure for herself and David whatever future the war would permit? She thought of the happy times she and Hans had had together, the picnics, outings, and sightseeing trips in the still of the night. She remembered the cornfields where they had kissed and the flower markets and cafés where they had spent their money. But overpowering their brief happiness was the weight of the past. She remembered David's first meeting with her, their first kiss, and the togetherness of many years that bound them inextricably together. Closing her eyes, she thought of the night when David had loved her for the first time, and suddenly everything was clear and simple. Suzanne accepted that she would suffer for the rest of her life for what she was about to do, but she answered without further hesitation.

"David Chambord has *never* told me his whereabouts in the Midi. He thinks I'm too young and silly to be involved in such important work. With regard to the Esterhazys, I never saw Alexander before the day I saved his life and I have no idea of his whereabouts. As for writing to my fiancé, well, I have been *longing* to write to David, but he told me he could not arrange any more deliveries or pickups of mail through his courier. So I am afraid I cannot help you."

Slagel watched Suzanne disbelievingly. He had been so sure she would break under pressure. Gunther's face was impassive, but his eyes contained such hatred Suzanne looked away. To Slagel's surprise, the Standartenfuhrer rose and drew back the blinds of the window that overlooked the courtyard. When Slagel looked out he saw Hans standing against the gray stone wall. Suzanne went to the window, as instructed, and looked down, her heart leaping in pity and admiration because she had never loved Hans as much as at that unforgettable moment. A sickening revulsion filled her mind as Slagel hissed his last command.

"Don't be a fool, the Standartenfuhrer is not bluffing! Do as he says or Major von Heinkel will be shot. If you do what you have been asked to do, I give you my word the major will be released. I *promise*."

Suzanne flinched at the sores covering Hans's emaciated body and the bloodstained clothing that hung from his once strong frame. Tears of anguish fell down her cheeks, and she began to pray for his ordeal to be over. Gunther called to the officers below to be ready, and Suzanne heard the crisp metallic click of rifle bolts. Hans mouthed *I love you* and briefly touched his fingers to his lips in a final kiss. Suzanne wept bitterly, hiding her face in her hands so she would not see her lover die. Slagel was watching Gunther with all the fascination of a snake for a mongoose. Sweat had soaked Slagel's jacket, and he was desperately alarmed because the situation had passed suddenly out of his control. His voice was unsteady as he spoke.

"I will give you one last chance, Mademoiselle Castel. Tell us what we want to know and no harm will come to Major von Heinkel."

"I cannot help you, Hauptsturmfuhrer."

Slagel turned to his superior in a final attempt to postpone the inevitable.

"Give me one more chance, sir. I assure you I shall obtain the information you require."

Gunther appeared not to hear the request, and as he lowered his arm a hail of bullets spat in the courtyard below. Then there was silence. One bullet had pierced Hans's forehead, another had lodged in his throat, and he lay facedown on the wet stones, his hands stretched out in mute appeal. Suzanne cried in agony, her head whirling, her chest tightening in shock and contrition. It was over. Hans was dead, a victim of her love for David.

When she opened her eyes, orderlies were removing the body and a cleaner was mopping the courtyard floor. Gunther had disappeared to his office, and Slagel was staring into the courtyard, his body taut with unreleased tension. Suddenly he began to scream like a madman, terrifying Suzanne with his threats.

"Get out of here! I don't need you, I shall find Chambord without you, I promise. I shall see him dead as you have seen Major von Heinkel. *Then* and only then will you understand what you have done today."

Suzanne walked dazedly from the room as Slagel slumped in his chair.

In his private office, Standartenfuhrer Gunther was filling the syringe with heroin bought from a new dealer in the sixteenth district. For a moment he hesitated. Then he pushed the needle into his arm and waited for the contentment he craved.

Suzanne's head was aching, and she had sickening pains in her back and stomach. When she reached the front door of the building, there was an animal howl of excruciating agony followed by a crescendo of horrifying calls for help. Near breaking point, Suzanne ran to the boulevard beyond, pausing at the gate to catch her breath and willing herself on despite the pain because she wanted only to put distance between herself and Hans's murderers.

Slagel rushed to Gunther's office and found his superior suffocating. He called for a doctor and medical orderlies from the torture rooms, but it was too late. Hurriedly Slagel pocketed the needle, the tubing, and the white paper sachet that had been specially prepared for the commander of the interrogation squad. Gunther's face was purple and contorted with agony, his body blotchy and red, his arms spread stiffly over the table. The inside of his nose and mouth was pouring blood, and Slagel realized, with something of a shock, that Gunther had been poisoned by the very substance he had so often ordered injected into the prisoners. Leaving the doctor alone with Gunther, Slagel went to the dispatch area and stood looking down on the body of Hans von Heinkel. For a brief moment he touched the fair hair with the tips of his fingers, lightly, as though still unable to believe what had happened. He had had no intention of ordering Hans to be shot. Indeed, his plan had been based on the assumption that kindness after deprivation bred a familiarity and loyalty otherwise impossible to achieve. Slagel covered the body with a sheet and returned to his office, his face a pallid caricature of sorrow. Everything was going wrong—first Gunther's disintegration, now the calamity of his death and that of Hans von Heinkel. The news from Berlin was troubling, and the Fuhrer had become erratic and uncertain in his ways. Orders were changed daily, and no one knew whether they would be able to keep Hitler's most prized possession, the city of Paris. Slagel sat staring out the window, wondering where the downslide would end.

Hours later, Slagel was still alone in his office. His shock had turned to fury, and he vowed to seek out and destroy every résistant in the city. For a moment, on his way out of the office, he looked down on the courtyard. Then he slammed the window, shattering the glass. Tomorrow he would demand a new office. Tomorrow he would arrest every known résistant and the wives and children of them all. He would have Suzanne Castel watched by a special new squad of French criminals who could infiltrate the Montmartre area and hopefully insinuate themselves into the confidence of those who lived in the rue Gabrielle. Slagel gave orders that Gunther's body be returned to his mother, in Dresden. Then he walked aimlessly home through the silent streets of the sixteenth arrondissement. The man who had posed as a heroin dealer watched triumphantly from his window. Mme. Francine's plan had worked perfectly, ridding Paris of the notorious Gunther without the possibility of reprisal. The "suicide" would be kept quiet. No Frenchman would have to die for the murder.

As Slagel walked home, folk turned their backs and a young boy threw a tomato at him. Slagel appeared not to notice. He was thinking that the people would not look so defiant once he had arrested their sons and their fathers. His mind turned to thoughts of Hans and, straightening his shoulders, he unconsciously aped the aristocratic bearing he had so admired. As he thought of Hans's bravery, rage screamed through his mind and he became obsessed with the thought of killing David Chambord. In allowing Hans to die, Suzanne had chosen Chambord as her future partner.

Slagel thought grimly that he would make sure Chambord never lived to enjoy his fiancée's body.

When Suzanne reached the Rond Point of the Champs-Elysées, a strange weakness swept over her and she wondered why her clothes were wet with sweat when the day was dull and chilly. Suddenly warm liquid gushed down her legs and she realized that she was bleeding profusely. Desperate to get home, she ran on but when she reached the forecourt of the Théâtre Marigny she collapsed, her face ashen, her body twisted in pain. The young man who had been observing her on David's orders stopped his car and, after looking around cautiously, ran to her side with his companion.

"God, what a sight! Suzanne's miscarrying, what shall we do?"

"We'll take her to Merimée, he'll know what's needed."

"Hurry, Alexander, the patrols are due."

Merimée looked down on the unconscious girl. Suzanne had lost a lot of blood and was going to need a transfusion. He consulted the card made on her last visit, sighing with relief that her blood group was a common one.

"What is your blood group, André?"

"Rh. Negative A, I have to carry a card."

"And yours, Alexander?"

"Mine is O positive."

"Roll up your sleeve, please."

Suzanne woke in a darkened room. She was burning hot and yet shivering. At the window she could see two shadowy figures, and at her side Merimée was reading a novel by Proust. As she remembered the events of the morning, she began to weep.

"Have I lost the baby?"

"I'm afraid so, my dear."

"Standartenfuhrer Gunther is going to get someone to write to David so he will come to Paris and meet them in a spot where the Gestapo will be waiting. He said *I* should write the letter, but I refused. Then he said he would shoot Hans if I didn't answer his questions, but I couldn't betray David. I'm responsible for Hans's death, just as if I had shot him myself."

Merimée injected a sedative, and soon Suzanne's eyelids flickered and she fell asleep. André and Alexander withdrew from the apartment, leaving the doctor alone to watch his patient. Merimée was pensive. He had just received an urgent letter from David telling him that Slagel was planning to plant French criminals from a special squad in areas of high resistance. In return for information given on leading résistants, the men would be released from jail, where they had been serving time for capital offenses. Merimée sighed wearily, wondering how much longer the fear and uncertainty would go on. David's contact in the avenue Foch had just been shot, so there would be no more firsthand information. He thought again of the warning—*Take care of any new faces in the area*—and made a note that he must telephone Mme. Crystalle so she could warn all the members of the Free Paris Association of the latest development.

A few days later Suzanne arrived home on a sharply cold winter morning. Denuded trees formed lattice patterns against a pale gray sky, and the house already felt musty and damp. There was no wood, no coal, no fuel of any kind, and the only thing that provided color in the house was the painting of the red poppy field, which she moved to her own bedroom. Suzanne wanted to cry, but shock and pain choked emotions at birth, and she walked like a wraith around the silent house. In the pantry there was a stale loaf, six eggs given her by Vivienne, and a fancily decorated cabbage pie from Mme. Crystalle. Suzanne looked at the yellow roses Hans had picked for her and touched them gently. Long dead, their brown petals fell soundlessly to the floor, and a sharp thorn pricked her. Suzanne squeezed a drop of blood from her finger, remembering the emaciated body in the courtyard and knowing that she must throw the roses away. For a moment she hated herself for what she had done. Then she began to hate David because he seemed responsible for all her troubles.

Late that night Suzanne sat in bed trying to work out her future. How long would it be before she stopped thinking of Hans? How long before she could prevent herself from wanting to die? The real murderer of Hans von Heinkel was war, but it was impossible to hate a word, however evocative of suffering. At 3:00 A.M. Suzanne went downstairs and looked at her collection of photographs. Lovingly she touched the one of Hans in his "French" outfit, standing by the Pont Neuf, looking down on the Seine. How handsome he looked, how happy his smile. Suzanne remembered again the bruised and bleeding man who had, with his last words, told her that he loved her. At last tears came and she wept for love lost and for the child who had never been born. In the early morning, as the sun rose, Suzanne was still there. But now she was calmer, older, and irrevocably changed. Gone was the romantic young girl who had dreamed of passion. Gone were the plans for an idyllic future that had kept her alive. From this day Suzanne resolved to live by the hour, praying for guilt and the desire for punishment to vanish and for the sunlight to return to her mind.

After breakfast, Suzanne put Hans's things in a suitcase that she locked in her bedroom cupboard. Then she sawed up an old chair for firewood and cleaned every room in the house, trying in vain to remove reminders of Hans's presence. But still the elusive image lingered, and she wondered if the ghosts of the past would ever bid good-bye. Exhausted by her efforts, she went upstairs to rest, and her eyes lingered on the poppy painting. She touched it gently, knowing she could never remove it. The sunlit field would remain forever a pleasure, a punishment, and a reminder of what might have been. Tears coursed down her cheeks, and she rose and looked out the window, because she could not bear to remain in one place for more than a few minutes. Fine rain was falling, dampening the dark buildings like a melancholy shroud. Suzanne looked blindly out over the rooftops, unaware that she was being watched.

# PART III

# CHAPTER TEN

## *October, 1943*

It was nine months since Hans's death. At first Suzanne had walked around Paris like a woman who has just heard she is dying. Every street seemed full of unforgettable memories, and often she thought to herself, There's the cafe where Hans and I used to have lunch . . . there's the bridge where I took his photograph . . . and the Ritz Hotel, where we slept in the bridal suite. It had been six months before she could pass such familiar landmarks without weeping. The period of extreme distress had been followed by one of self-loathing and recrimination, then by a hectic phase of involving herself in suicidal risk, when for weeks Suzanne had delivered messages to résistants all over the city at the instigation of Alexander Esterhazy. Each time she had heard a car siren wailing she had wondered if the Gestapo was coming to arrest her. And each time she returned home safely she wondered if God's punishment upon her was going to be a long life plagued by images of the past.

Suzanne was sitting on the terrace overlooking the garden. The leaves of trees in the rue Foyatier were turning gold, scarlet, and sepia, scratching underfoot as locals toiled up the steps and swirling like angry waves in the autumn breeze. Everything was fading, dying, going to seed. Suzanne touched a swollen poppy pod that burst in her hand, spewing its seeds on the soil. The cabbages were turning yellow, and she had cut the last of the lettuce. Suzanne thought that everything was changing, and so was she. With the end of summer she was feeling the snail-slow return of normality. She still often thought of Hans, but gradually the agony was fading, and often she imagined the affair to have been a brief interlude of perfection in the perpetual tension of war. In the last few weeks she had allowed her mind to dwell on thoughts of David and how she longed to see him. Alexander had told her that David was alive and well but that he had decided to stay out of her life until she was sure of her feelings. Suzanne wondered if David no longer wanted her, if he had found another woman to love. Doubts entered her mind, disrupting the days, and often she stared longingly into space, exhausted by speculation.

Since the end of the show at the Bal Tabarin a month previously, Suzanne had been dangerously short of money. Hungry and painfully thin, she debated whether to call on General-Oberst Funnen to collect the money Hans had mentioned. But the idea of approaching a German after all that had happened was distasteful, and Suzanne thought fiercely that she would rather starve. With each passing week her hunger increased, and she wondered if she was going to collapse from malnutrition. Was the solution in her own hands? She could not prostitute herself for food, as some women did when they were desperate. She would not inform on friends and neighbors in return for payment from the Germans, and she could not grow enough to feed herself now the summer was over. In a few weeks' time the winter cabbages would be large enough to cut and there would be potatoes to be dug from the lower end of the garden. The apple tree had had the blight, so there were no apples, and the pear crop was very small. There was nothing left in the larder but a crust of stale bread, a packet of lentils, and a box of matches. Suzanne wondered what her mother would have done in such a situation. Within minutes she had decided to rob the garden of a well-known collaborator in Pigalle. The man was on holiday in Brittany. He would not return for at least another week.

When it was dark, Suzanne trudged down the hill and across the boulevard to the rue Pigalle. She entered the side gate of the house and made her way to the garden. In the unfamiliar surroundings she fell over a refuse bin, freezing in fear at the metallic clang as it rolled down the paved alleyway. The collaborator's garden was almost as empty as her own, but in the shed she found an oak-smoked ham hanging from a hook in the ceiling. She grasped it eagerly, her mouth watering at the salty smell of its outer rind. On the other side of the shed there were apples in crates, and on the shelves she found beans preserved in salt and potatoes by the score. Suzanne filled her shopping bags with everything she could carry and then rushed home, not caring who saw her. Once inside la maison Fleuri, she put the potatoes, beans, and fruit in the storeroom and hung the ham from the hook in the pantry. A sense of achievement made her cheeks glow, and she wondered why she had not thought of stealing as a means of salvation before.

Father Valery was overworked. At sixty he was still strong and willing, but the privations of war were sapping his energy, and often he longed to sit in the garden doing nothing at all. Worried about his health, Mme. Bettine scolded him.

"Do try to rest, father, or you'll be useless to your friends in the resistance."

"Will you stop telling me off as if I were a lad, madame? Anyway, what do you know of my constitution?"

"I know you're up for mass at six every day and still traipsing around Paris at midnight, meeting folk who daren't come out in the daylight."

"Get on with your work, will you, the new Father's due and all we can do is argue."

The new Father created a good impression. He was tall and thin and prison pale, but his table manners were impeccable and often he closed his eyes to pray in gratitude for the comfortable post he had been given. All would have gone smoothly for him had not one of Mme. Crystalle's more persistent girl messengers arrived to check on the new arrival. Claudine le Marchet was twelve, intelligent, and impressed by her responsibility to the Free Paris Association. She had been told that the Gestapo might plant criminals on the Butte to spy on them all, and had worked meticulously gathering information for the Association about every new arrival. She approached Mme. Bettine in the kitchen of the presbytery.

"Can you tell me the new Father's name, madame? I need it for my information list."

"He's Father Robert Jacques Farrier."

"Which parish did he come from?"

"I haven't had a chance to talk with him yet."

"How old is he?"

"I think he's twenty-nine."

"Was he ever in the war?"

Mme. Bettine promised to find out the information for the following day, and Claudine returned home. The new priest watched from his window, disturbed by what he had overheard. That evening, as he expected, Mme. Bettine questioned him.

"Tell us about your last parish, father."

"I was assistant priest at St. Marc, eight kilometers from St. Nazaire, madame."

"I hear the Germans are using St. Nazaire as a submarine base."

"That's true, madame. However, everything has been very quiet since they arrived. We expected trouble, but it never materialized."

Father Valery, who was eating a rabbit leg, looked up in surprise. In March of the previous year British commandos had raided St. Nazaire. It was incorrect to say that all had been quiet and peaceful. Forewarned by Mme. Bettine of the Association's interest in the new Father, the old man spoke cheerfully.

"This is a fine rabbit, isn't it, father? We buy them from a poacher, you know."

"It's very tasty, sir."

Father Valery continued in his jocular way.

"Did the English ship *Triumph* do much harm when she exploded in the dock of St. Nazaire, father?"

The new priest hesitated momentarily.

"The Germans soon had the fire under control, father. No one was killed, as far as I recall."

Valery looked at his dinner and knew he had lost his appetite. The English ship had been the *Campbeltown*, and the fighting around St. Nazaire had lasted for two days, with considerable loss of life. He continued to make polite conversation for a while. Then he retired exhausted to his room. In the privacy of his quarters, Valery struggled to decide what to do. If he made the new Father aware that he knew he was a Gestapo plant, Farrier would be replaced by another infiltrator, one they did not know. If he did not get rid of Farrier, he would place himself in great danger. Every week Father Valery collected messages and information from outlying resistance groups and delivered this to résistants in the city center. How could he continue to operate whilst being observed round the clock by Haupsturmfuhrer Slagel's spy? Unable to sleep, the old man rose and looked out on the night. There was light in the new priest's bedroom and, looking down, Valery saw Farrier trying on his vestments, back to front. He sighed wearily and returned to bed.

In the darkness, Slagel stood at the window of his office. He had just received a message from one of the agents on the Butte Montmartre. Slagel read it again, smiling delightedly.

> Castel still alone in her home. No messages or instructions received from Chambord, who is confirmed to be arriving November. Priest Valery visiting resistance cells in Barbès, Rochechouart, St.-Denis, St.-Ouen, and Clichy. Require instruction on extent of pressure to be put on neighbors of Castel for further information about Chambord's arrival. Children still being used by members of the Free Paris Association as messengers. Am unable to observe these adequately without reinforcements.

Slagel put the paper down and considered the implications of the message. For months his spies had had nothing to report from Montmartre. All contact between Castel and Chambord seemed to have ended, and Slagel had thought the revenge he craved a lost cause. But now Castel was without food and desperately short of money. She had been buying barely enough food to keep a child from starving, and no doubt her fiancé felt obliged to come to her rescue. Slagel rose and looked at the wall map of the hill of Montmartre. For weeks he had been studying how to cut off escape routes that David Chambord might use. He had learned by heart reams of information about residents of the warrenlike area and whole sections of a guidebook on the topography of the quarter. Other work had, of necessity, been neglected, but Slagel did not care, too obsessed was he with the idea of realizing his dream.


Inside the priest's house, Farrier was watching impatiently from the window. Father Valery had gone out at three thirty and still had not returned. Had someone warned him the Gestapo was coming to apprehend him on his return, when he would be carrying important papers from outlying resistance cells? Farrier paced the room, his eyes constantly looking to the window and the view from the steps. He was desperately anxious that Mme. Bettine should not know he had betrayed Father Valery, and his nervousness increased when she appeared with a tray of tea and some ginger biscuits. Madame wondered why Farrier seemed so agitated and why he kept looking out of the window. Was he waiting for someone to arrive? Farrier sat in Father Valery's armchair, sipping his tea and enjoying the rare luxury of biscuits.

"These are very good, madame. Where did you buy them?"

"David sent them for Father Valery. I suppose he steals them from black marketeers."

"David Chambord?"

"Yes, father."

"Where is Chambord?"

"He's in the Alpes Maritime, but he wouldn't thank me for telling you where."

Unable to control his tension, Farrier rose again and looked apprehensively down to the place St.-Pierre. Madame felt suddenly terrified that the spy had already reported Father Valery to the Gestapo. She looked uneasily at Farrier as he began again to pace the room.

"Are you waiting for someone, father?"

"I was wondering where Father Valery was."

"I get the impression that you're watching the square. Is someone waiting there for Father Valery?"

Farrier looked searchingly into Madame's eyes, his face turning pale because he knew from her attitude that she suspected him.

"You know about me, don't you, madame?"

"I think you're working for the Gestapo, monsieur."

"Where did I go wrong?"

"You couldn't tell us anything about St. Nazaire and you were obviously not familiar with the mass. As a matter of interest, who are you, where do you come from, and where have you been during the war?"

"I'm an actor and I have been incarcerated in the Salinières prison in Bordeaux since 1939."

"What did you do?"

"I killed my fiancée, madame."

"Whatever made you agree to work for the Gestapo?"

"They offered me my freedom if I would come to Paris to infiltrate the Montmartre area. Other men from the same prison have been sent to areas of equally active resistance."

The statement chilled, but Mme. Bettine remained calm. Farrier finished the last of the tea and went upstairs to pack, returning minutes later with his suitcase.

"I'm leaving, madame, don't try to follow me."

"I wouldn't dream of following you, monsieur."

Farrier's sudden departure confirmed what Madame had suspected, that he had already denounced Father Valery to the Gestapo. Madame watched as he made his way toward the steps and his harshly earned freedom. Disillusioned by Farrier's behavior, Madame found it impossible not to hate him.

Farrier was furious at having been discovered. As an actor he had relished the part he had been asked to play, but he had not been given sufficient time to study the background of the character, and life in the presbytery had often mystified him. About halfway down the steps, he threw away the restricting white collar. Suddenly he was happy the masquerade was over. When Haupsturmfuhrer Slagel saw the documents Valery was carrying he would forget his annoyance that one of his agents had been unmasked. Farrier hoped fervently that he would not be sent back to prison. He paused for a moment to change hands with the heavy suitcase. Then he walked on, down the steep steps toward the place St.-Pierre.

Mme. Bettine crept forward on slippered feet. When she was close behind Farrier, she gave him a massive push with all the force she could muster. Farrier dropped the suitcase as he hurtled forward, and a gendarme standing below heard the sound of a body crashing down the steps. Over and over the man rolled, his head bouncing with sickening thuds against the sharp stone of the stairway. The gendarme ran forward to examine the motionless form, shaking his head in resignation because he knew it was too late. As he blew his whistle, Madame removed the incriminating suitcase Farrier had been carrying and the clerical collar he had thrown away. Then she ran swiftly, silently back to the presbytery and made two urgent telephone calls.

Half an hour later, when Father Valery arrived in the place St.-Pierre, he saw a Gestapo squad car at the foot of the steps. He thought fearfully of the documents he was carrying, slowing his pace as two men emerged from the car. Suddenly there was a fearful commotion on the upper part of the steps. A gang of boys was fighting, and somewhere a woman was screaming wildly. The two Gestapo officers turned and called for order. When the fracas continued, one of them ran up the steps, only to find that the boys had scattered over the walls of neighboring gardens. Cursing, the officer returned to his colleague, and together they turned to watch the approach of Father Valery. They were shocked to find the street empty. There was no sign of the priest. The two searched every house at the foot of the steps and found nothing. The Germaine family was eating dinner. The widow Marignon was in bed with her lodger, and next door the dancer from the Folies Bergères was having a row with her boy friend. The Pastel children were waiting for their father to arrive home from the factory, and the only other householder who could possibly have helped Father Valery was in his garden, cursing the slugs that had eaten the cabbages. The leather-coated men turned to the avenue Foch, unable to work out what had happened.

When their car had disappeared, Father Valery stepped out of the widow Marignon's bed and thanked her for saving his life.

"I'm grateful to you, madame. Thank God they didn't ask us to get out of bed, or I would have been discovered to be fully dressed and with a briefcase!"

The widow laughed delightedly.

"I received a phone call, father, warning me that you would be passing and that you might be in danger."

Father Valery rubbed his chin in puzzlement as the widow led him to her front door.

"You know, father, this is the first time I've been in bed with a man for fifteen years, and it was nice, very nice."

Blushing furiously, Father Valery made his way home, arriving at the presbytery panting with embarrassment and exhaustion. When the documents had been safely hidden, Mme. Bettine brought him a glass of port and a piece of cheese.

"Your face is very flushed, father."

"I'm not answering any of your questions, madame."

"Where did you hide when the Gestapo came?"

Father Valery bit his lip.

"Sometimes, madame, I believe you know what I'm doing even when I'm miles away."

Mme. Bettine smiled gently. She had telephoned her young nephews in the rue Gabrielle and asked them to create the disturbance on the steps that had saved Father Valery's life. She had joined them, screaming as if she were an actress at the Comédie-Française. Now she almost burst into peals of laughter at the Father's puzzled face. Unaware of his housekeeper's secret, Father Valery savored his port, relieved the ordeal was over.


The following morning was clear and sunny. Suzanne was in the garden picking the last of the pears when she heard shouts in the street below: "The Gestapo has caught Claudine le Marchet!" Suzanne put down her basket and ran to the gate, where she met Vivienne.

"Zizi, they've taken Claudine to be executed in the place des Abbesses."

"What happened?"

"She was on her way to deliver a note from David to Natasha, when Slagel's men caught her."

"Is Natasha dead?"

"No, she got away. But you realize, Suzanne, if Claudine talks they will arrest Esterhazy and torture him until he tells where David is."

The two women ran to where Claudine was standing, white-faced, against the wall of the square. Her braids had come untied in the struggle, her skirt was torn, but her face was livid with determination, and she was calling to her mother, in the crowd, "Don't cry, maman, please don't cry."

A profound silence fell on the crowd, and many kneeled to pray as four young soldiers formed a makeshift execution squad. When Slagel arrived he stepped out of his car and stood for a moment looking down on the child.

"You are Claudine le Marchet?"

"Yes."

"You carry messages for the Free Paris Association?"

"I do."

"This morning, when you were on your way to deliver a message from David Chambord to Natasha Rollet, my men caught you. Are you aware that Chambord and Rollet are both wanted by the Gestapo?"

"Yes."

"Where is Natasha Rollet?"

"I don't know."

"I shall have you shot if you do not tell me."

"I don't know where she is."

Women in the crowd began to weep. Some wondered if they could attack Slagel and the soldiers, even though they were unarmed. Slagel tried again to force Claudine to speak.

"If you do not know where Rollet is, how did you hope to deliver the message?"

Madame le Marchet ran forward, her eyes full of tears.

"Please, Claudine, tell him what he wants to know."

"I can't, maman."

"Why not?"

"Because when I have told he will shoot me."

In the silence that followed this exchange, Slagel heard the metallic rattle of gun bolts and, looking up, saw Esterhazy and his sister on the roof of a nearby building. He stepped back, narrowing his eyes in the sunlight, uncertain what to do. He was alone with a driver and a squad of youthful SS recruits. There were at least sixty angry people in the square and two well-armed résistants on the roof.

Before he could make a decision, pandemonium broke out. Natasha and Alexander fired, and Slagel's execution squad fell to the ground. Another burst of gunfire echoed and people scattered, carrying Claudine with them. Slagel made a dash for his car, horrified to find the driver slumped dead over the wheel. He looked up to the roof, but the Esterhazys had disappeared, and he knew they would be on their way down to kill him. Frantically he dragged the driver's body from the car. Then he leaped inside and drove away toward the rue Houdon. Suddenly he could go no farther because of steps ahead. He ran from the car to the corner of the street. Soon he had disappeared into the labyrinthine alleyways.

For a while he hid in a chapel. Then, as he regained his composure, he struggled to remember the plan of Montmartre on his office wall. Nothing seemed as it had appeared on the map. Streets that had looked wide and free were encumbered with nooks and crannies, steps and fountains. Eventually Slagel worked out where he was, and when he emerged he was sure which way he must go. He had reached the steps leading to the safety of the busy thoroughfare below when the fishmonger's wife saw him. Carmencita ran outside the shop and fired her husband's gun once at the Hauptsturmfuhrer's head. Slagel fell headlong down the steps, coming to rest on the pavement of the boulevard de Clichy. Within minutes he was taken to the military hospital in Neuilly.

Slagel woke in the intensive care unit. The bullet had hit him in the face, to the side of the nose. Another centimeter and it would have lodged in his brain or severed his spinal column. Only the strong white teeth had saved his life. As he lay half conscious, half awake, he wondered what was going to happen to him. He was unaware that his left eye had been removed along with some of his teeth and a section of the jawbone. Then he heard a nurse talking and realized that he had little hope of survival. In the darkness of his mind Slagel willed himself to live. Hate made him strong, and he tried to concentrate on thinking only of David Chambord. He would enjoy killing Chambord, and he would never forget the look that would come to Suzanne Castel's face as she watched her fiancé suffer. Slagel bore his pain bravely, and eventually, to the surprise of those who had operated on him, his condition began to stabilize. In a few weeks he would be taught to walk again. And if he was lucky, in a few months he would be discharged. Slagel listened to the comments of those who attended him, grimly determined to get well.

By nightfall it was very cold. Suzanne put a blanket around her shoulders and sat in the living room reading one of her father's books. But she could not concentrate. She kept thinking how quiet it was and how she longed to hear M. Corbeil playing the waltz from *Carnet du Bal*. But Corbeil had refused absolutely to play his violin from the day the Germans arrived in Paris. As she sat, alone and lonely, images of David kept filtering into Suzanne's mind and she longed for him to return to Paris. Sometimes when she thought of marrying David she still felt unfaithful to Hans. But gradually his image was receding, secure on the pedestal of happy memory, intangible and untarnished by time. Shivering, Suzanne decided to sleep on the sofa in front of the fire. In the darkness she tossed and turned, resolving to keep busy so she would not keep wondering with whom David was spending his days.

Alexander and his sister were walking home together after celebrating Natasha's thirtieth birthday at the Petite Chouette, a hole-in-the-wall bistro near les Halles. Natasha loved the place because the rough clientele talked of nothing but annihilating Germans. As they reached Montmartre Natasha looked at the iron lamp-posts outlined against the sky and thought how lovely it would be when the lights of Paris were lit again. Someday it would happen, but not until every German had been driven from the city. Then silver lights would shimmer on the boulevards, ancient gas lamps would glow green in the Marais, and on the bridges of the Seine torches would cast golden reflections on the water.

Suddenly a shot rang out, shattering the peaceful silence of the night. Natasha fell forward, her white dress bloodied and soiled. Wounded, Alexander staggered to her side and held her in his arms, crying softly because he knew she was dead. Two little girls returning home from their piano lesson appeared at the corner, their white blouses shimmering in the moonlight. As they drew near, Alexander called frantically to them, "Hide in a doorway, someone is shooting at me!"

But as another volley rang out the children froze in fear. Then, like tiny marionettes, they fell without a whimper. Alexander dragged himself to a nearby house, hammering at the door until a boy appeared.

"I've been shot, let me in."

"Go away! We don't want any trouble here."

The boy slammed the door in his face, and Alexander knew he was at the mercy of the gunman. His eyes searched the darkness, trying to assess where the sniper was hiding. Then, when he had almost given up hope, he found himself lifted in the strong arms of Pasquale the fishmonger.

"Where are you hurt, Alex?"

"In my right arm and both legs."

"Your sister's dead, and so are the children. I heard the shots as I was coming up the hill."

"Did you see the sniper?"

"I chased him, but he got away."

"Did you recognize him?"

"No, but I'm sure he was German. I marked him with my knife so we'll know when we go to search for him. I reckon he went up that street toward the convent."

Hours later, when Alexander was sleeping under sedation in the attic of Merimée's house, Natasha was buried in an unmarked grave in the cemetery on the hill. The children's bodies had been handed over to their grief-stricken parents, and it had been agreed at a meeting of the Free Paris Association that there would be a house-to-house search of every street in the Montmartre area. Mme. Argentine, who had owned a hotel in the place des Abbesses for forty years, would be accompanied by three gendarmes in her search of the properties on the lower slopes of the hill. Corbeil would search the streets of the upper hill, also with a party of gendarmes. Pasquale was congratulated for his bravery, and the residents were hopeful that they would catch the unknown assailant.

At nightfall thirty-six hours later, Corbeille and Madame reported their findings. Only two householders in the area had refused them entry. After obtaining warrants, they had dis-

covered that one woman was hiding her son, a deserter from
the army. The other had an illegal radio set in her kitchen.
When they had called at the convent on the hill they had been
told by a surly "gardener" that they would not be admitted. It
was Corbeil's opinion that the place had been taken over by
German intelligence. The archbishop of Paris was consulted and
an order sent direct to the convent that would open it to the
scrutiny of those who sought the sniper. A committee of residents
then went to view the occupants within the cloistered walls. On
ringing the bell, they were greeted by silence. When they tried
to enter, they found the doors unlocked and the building deserted.
Filing cabinets in the downstairs rooms were empty, and there
was evidence of the hurried removal of radio equipment. Corbeil
had been right. Like the British, the Germans had been using a
convent as a base for intelligence operations. Unlike the British,
they had done so without the concurrence of the sisters. Corbeil
imagined the nuns had all been shot or sent away to concentra-
tion camps.

In the military hospital, Tristan Slagel was learning to walk. Day
after day he tried to regain his equilibrium, but the bullet had
done extensive damage and his balance would forever be defec-
tive. Despite everything, he believed implicitly that determination would be enough to overcome the monstrous disability of his
imbalance. A black patch covered the empty eye socket, a grim
smile curled the thin lips, and nurses scurrying by were afraid
despite their respect for the Haupsturmfuhrer's courage. Slagel
had just been informed that he would be invalided out of the SS.
The news had shattered what remained of his confidence, and his
expression was alternately vacant, defiant, angry. After hours of
deliberation he resolved to defy the German authorities by staying on in Paris, as a civilian, in order to have his way. Nothing
mattered anymore but finding an opportunity to kill David
Chambord. Slagel looked longingly at the searchlights in the
night sky, longing to be free.

On the night of November fourth, David arrived at la maison
Fleuri. Suzanne ran to him, throwing herself into his arms, piti-

fully relieved to be reunited. For a moment they clung to each other in silence. Then David ruffled her hair, and Suzanne cried from sheer joy that he still loved her.

"You came back to me. I thought you'd gone forever, David."

"Kiss me, Zizi, I've been so lonely without you."

# CHAPTER ELEVEN

*June, 1944*

David's hideout was in the ancient village of Cagnes. Summer was idyllic on the Côte d'Azur, and the house was full of the scent of wild lavender and honeysuckle. The surrounding Cézanne landscape was covered with German bunkers and tank traps of fortified concrete, every field, hill, and wood disfigured with barbed wire. Still the place was beautiful, and as David touched a frond of powdery mimosa he wished Suzanne could be there to share its magic. He poured another cup of chickpea coffee and looked through his binoculars to the distant palm-lined promenade where bull-necked officers sat drinking real coffee procured for them by black marketeers. David frowned into the bitter dregs of his cup, hating those who had bled the area dry. Lately, even the casinos had been taken over by high-rolling enemy officers determined to enjoy one last fling before the Gottedammerung. Nothing seemed to belong to the French anymore, though there were a few local businessmen who had grown rich on the wild spending spree.

David went to the table and read again the message he had just received from Paris. Tristan Slagel had been released from the military hospital two months previously and was now said to be prowling the streets of Montmartre intent on revenge. During the same period, David knew, four of his contacts in the area had been murdered, including Claudine le Marchet and Pasquale's wife, Carmencita. Now, surely, Suzanne was in danger.

Slagel had been invalided out of the service but he had remained
in Paris, ignoring orders to return to Germany. David could
only assume that his reason for staying was to complete the un-
finished business of destroying those he loathed. He tried to think
why Slagel hated Suzanne so insanely, but he found it impossible
to think like a man deranged.

The note also said that as Pierre Lefaucheux had been arrested
by the Gestapo along with most of his resistance group, David
should return as quickly as possible to the capital. The people
of Paris were preparing for the uprising they hoped would liberate their city. Armbands printed with the slogan "Live free or
die" had been issued, and "live free or die" were the words in
every patriotic mind. David thought of his friend Lefaucheux,
lying tortured in a prison cell in Fresnes. If Lefaucheux were
shot, what would happen to his wife? And what would happen to
Suzanne if *he* fell into the Gestapo's hands? David sat mulling
over the irony of his situation. He was an American, not a Frenchman bound by patriotism to fight for his country. He could be
leading a peaceful life in New England, not risking everything
in a fight for a country that was not his own. But his love for
Suzanne had made him want to stay in France, and often
she joked that his only ambition was to end the autumn of
his days in a black beret, drinking pastis under the apple tree
like any other venerable Gallic gentleman. David looked down at
an old man sitting at a twirled-iron table outside the Bar
Jean-Pierre. As there were no waiters, the man enjoyed a moment
in the sun before serving himself with a demitasse of coffee.
David thought wryly that the pensioner was the picture of himself
in forty years' time.

Anya was walking up the street with the local washerwoman,
helping carry the basket piled with towels and sheets from the
local inn. A little girl called shrilly to her cat, "Where are you,
Pistachio? Where are you?" And everywhere there were the
sounds of folk working in the blacksmith's forge, in the bakery,
and in the fields. Anya set her shopping down in the garden and
lit a fire in the makeshift barbecue David had built. She unwrapped the unappetizing sausages she had bought and kissed
David when he came to join her.

"When must we leave for Paris, David?"

"We'll go on the eleven-thirty goods train tonight."

"I hate the idea of going there! Why can't we stay here, where we're needed?"

Though they had not been lovers for over a year, Anya was still violently jealous of Suzanne. When David did not reply to her outburst, Anya began to feel sorry for what she had said.

"I'm sorry to be so bad-tempered, David. When we first met I wanted to be your friend. Then I wanted to be your lover. Then I fell in love with you and became a pest!"

"You're not a pest, Anya, you've always been my right hand."

"Say it again, David, I love to pretend that you need me."

That night, as they were traveling toward Paris, Anya began to feel hungry. She thought longingly of the olives and stolen pastis she and David enjoyed in the dusk of evening, the new-laid eggs and lime-blossom tisane they had for breakfast, and the small treats he brought home after a hunting trip. Once they were in Paris it would be the end of her relationship with David, and Anya admitted to herself that it would be best to go away in order to try to forget him. She wondered if she would be able to get a pass to visit Vichy. From there she could travel by night to Bordeaux and then through the Aquitaine region to Spain. She stole a glance at David, wondering what he was thinking.

David was making plans to marry Suzanne, somehow, some-where, probably with the connivance of his friend Father Valery. His face lit with pleasure as he remembered their November re-union. After Hans's death he had stayed away from Suzanne, knowing that the shock would have shattered her. But when they had met again it was obvious that she loved him as she had always loved him, completely, touchingly, with absolute trust. It had been one of the happiest days of his life. David felt the ring in his pocket and was impatient to put it on Suzanne's finger.

David had decided that as Slagel was prowling the Montmartre area he would not stay at Suzanne's house. Instead he would share the attic of Merimée's house with Alexander Esterhazy. Anya registered at Ottoline's and they met again over dinner at the doctor's home. As Anya looked down at black country snails and potatoes covered with heavy cornstarch gravy, she thought sadly that there seemed already to be a distance between herself

and David. The food was tasteless and heavy, and she kept
thinking of the game David had shot on the estate of an absent
millionaire, the scented green grapes growing on the terrace of
the house in Cagnes, the silver-wrapped oreillettes they had
given each other for Christmas. Now and then she stole a glance
at David, but he seemed to have forgotten that she was present.
When he began to question Merimée about Suzanne, Anya excused herself and hurried back to Ottoline's. She was greatly distressed and in the darkness of her room wept bitterly because she
felt alone and lonely. She could not sleep, so she paced the room
until the small hours, looking down from time to time on the
empty streets of Montmartre. At 3:00 A.M. she noticed a dark-
clad figure walking past Ottoline's. Anya pulled the curtains aside
and examined the man's face. He was German, of that she felt
sure. But who was he, and why was he out at such a late hour,
staring fixedly at the bar and then at Merimée's house across
the square?

When David thought it was safe, he sent a messenger to
Suzanne, telling her to meet him at the crémerie belonging to
Mère Gil. Alexander, Merimée, and Anya were present as they
ate lunch. Anya looked often at Suzanne, thinking resignedly
how vibrant David's fiancée was, how gypsy wild and intriguing,
with her tawny eyes and long black hair. No wonder David
adored her. Unaware of the relationship there had been between David and Anya, Suzanne chatted happily about her
new job at the Club de Paris.

"We start work at three each afternoon and finish at dusk.
The money's terrible, but I'm happy to be working. When
I'm short of food I steal from black market restaurants or I take
a part-time job in one of the German houses."

"Tell them about that suitcase of food General-Oberst von
Boineburg-Lengsfeld gave you!"

Alexander laughed out loud at the memory of the salmon and
turkey the commander of Gross Paris had encouraged his maid
to accept. Amid joyous laughter, Suzanne left for the club. Anya
sat looking across the table to where David was pensively frowning. Sensing that they had much to discuss, Alexander and Merimée withdrew, leaving the couple alone. Impulsively, Anya leaned
across the table and kissed David.

"I've decided to leave France and go to Spain. Will you help me get a pass to Vichy?"

"I had no idea you were thinking of going away, Anya."

"I only decided last night over dinner. I'm in love with you, David, and you are in love with Suzanne. I can't blame you, but I don't want only to be your right hand, and I realize that I shall never be anything else."

"When do you want to go?"

"As soon as I can."

"Right now you'd be best staying in your room at Ottoline's. They say Slagel's still searching for me in Montmartre. I don't know him and I've no idea how he found out I'd arrived, but I'm sure he'll be as dangerous as a rattlesnake."

"Probably he was having the stations watched. Last night there was a man watching Ottoline's. I wonder if it was Slagel."

"Did he just stay outside?"

"No, first he watched Ottoline's, then he went across the square and looked up at Dr. Merimée's house. Then he wandered around the streets. I had the impression he was searching for someone."

"Slagel's been invalided out of the SS. He should have gone back to Germany with the other wounded, but he stayed, God knows why."

"Perhaps to kill you?"

In the afternoon, David went to meet Suzanne. He had told her to wait for him on the steps of Sacré-Coeur. As he drew near he paused among the surrounding trees to check the open area before the cathedral. Nothing suspicious caught his eye, but David continued to watch and wait. The steps were dusty in the sunlight, and the only sounds were the cooing of pigeons and the panting of old ladies toiling upward for the five o'clock mass.

Relieved that the afternoon air-raid warning was over, Suzanne sat reading a pamphlet picked up in the rue du Cavalaire: "PREPARE THE BARRICADES." She felt joyful at the thought of fighting for Paris, and proud that the people had taken the initiative. She rose as David ran toward her, clasping him to her chest, happy to be alone at last.

"Where are we going, David?"

"I want to see Father Valery."

"Why?"

"I'm going to ask if he'll marry us this evening."

"You haven't proposed to me!"

"I asked you to marry me a long time ago, in the orchard near the Montmartre vineyard."

Suzanne smiled a secret smile, touched by the memory of the excitement she had felt.

"Ask me again, David."

"I sure as hell won't—you might turn me down."

"No I won't, I'll say Yes, Yes, *Yes*."

At dusk, Suzanne and David stood before Father Valery at the altar of St. Pierre. Vivienne and M. Corbeil had been summoned as witnesses, and Mme. Crystalle appeared, regally dressed in her best blue faille, to sing a lilting song of love as the two repeated the responses. Suzanne looked wonderingly around the ancient chapel, at the pale tallow candles and glowing crucifix above the altar. Then she gazed at David as he kneeled at her side and knew beyond doubt that she would always love him and that she always had. Her hand trembled as David put on the ring, and she closed her eyes, praying fervently that they would be lucky enough to see Paris in the springtime together. When Valery had pronounced them man and wife, Mme. Bettine invited everyone to a celebratory drink. Suzanne followed Madame past the flickering candles and stern-faced saints on the windows, pausing to inhale the incense-laden air before leaving the chapel for the presbytery.

Father Valery whispered in David's ear, "If you'll take my advice, David, you'll not go back to Suzanne's home tonight. Madame Bettine tells me that Hauptsturmfuhrer Slagel is still around. He has been for weeks, and in my opinion he'll not rest until he's shot every résistant in Montmartre."

"Where could we go, father?"

Mme. Bettine served glasses of port as Father Valery considered the question.

"There's the Hôtel de la Paix. It's been empty for a long time."

"Zizi wouldn't like to spend her wedding night on bare boards, father."

"It's empty of people, David, but there are still bottles in the cellar and beds in the rooms. No one will search the place—why should they?"

They were all talking animatedly when they heard the creak of the presbytery gate. Mme. Bettine snuffed the candles, thankful for once that there had been a power cut. Then she whispered to Father Valery, "There's someone in the garden, father."

"You'd best show our guests to the passage in the cellar, madame."

Madame Bettine led them from the sitting room to the wine cellar, helping them as they stumbled in the darkness to an outer door used by routiers when making wine deliveries.

"You'll know where you are when you get outside, won't you, Zizi?"

"Thank you for everything, madame."

Suzanne kissed the housekeeper's cheek and passed through to the street. Then, like phantoms, they all vanished into the darkness, Corbeil, Vivienne, and Mme. Crystalle to the rue Gabrielle, David and Suzanne to the Hôtel de la Paix.


Mme. Bettine locked the cellar door and returned with a bottle of wine to the parlor of the presbytery. Almost at once there was a knock at the door, and Slagel entered the house. Madame listened fearfully as he urged Father Valery to tell him where David and Suzanne had gone.

"Castel and Chambord were seen entering the chapel not more than thirty minutes ago."

"I just married Suzanne and David."

"And where have they gone?"

"I suppose they went back to Suzanne's home."

"They have not gone back there. I have been watching the rue Gabrielle for the last hour."

"Then I don't know where they are, Haupsturmfuhrer."

"I think you do, Father Valery."

Madame began to fear that Father Valery's life was in danger. She was wondering how to get her gun from the kitchen drawer when Slagel herded her and the Father into the garden. When he had placed them against the wall, he spoke again.

"I will give you one more chance, father. Where have David Chambord and Suzanne Castel gone?"

Father Valery remained silent, and Madame wished she dared tell him how much she had loved and respected him in the thirty years of their association. She edged closer to Valery's side and slid her hand in his.

"Is he going to shoot us, father?"

"Don't be afraid, madame."

"I hope it will be quick."

Valery took the work-worn hand in his own and kissed it tenderly.

"Of course it will, and at least we're going together. Imagine how upset we'd have been to be parted."

Two shots rang out in the night. Two bodies slid down the garden wall of the presbytery.

Slagel returned to the rue Gabrielle. As he expected, Suzanne's house was empty. The priest had lied to the end. Slagel walked unsteadily to the corner of the street and sat on the steps of the rue Foyatier. His head was throbbing, and waves of nausea engulfed his body. Somewhere, he was thinking savagely, Suzanne Castel is happy with the man of her choice. He remembered the moment when she had denied all knowledge of David Chambord, and the gallant way Hans von Heinkel had died. Loathing made him go on and slowly, painfully, he climbed the steps. He would not leave Montmartre until Chambord was dead. He must be strong, however bad the pain. As he walked dazedly back and forth through the deserted streets, Slagel reasoned that the couple could not have gone far. With a curfew in operation, the streets of the city center would be far more dangerous than the unpatrolled lanes of Montmartre. With luck he might yet catch them.

Suzanne was in the bridal suite, lying under clean pink sheets. She was drinking champagne and eating beef from a can because David could not find any plates. As she watched her new husband, her eyes shone with happiness.

"This is the nicest meal I've ever had."

"When we tell our kids we spent our wedding night in an empty hotel drinking champagne and eating beef loaf from a can, they won't believe us."

"And we made love as the bombs dropped on Paris."

"Is it always this bad, Zizi?"

"It's been worse lately. The American planes come in the day-time and the British at night. They're bombing the railway lines all around the city so the Germans can't get out."

"Or in."

They lay in the darkness in the ancient four-poster bed, watching as the sky turned red, yellow, and smoky gray. The suburbs were burning, the train tracks shattering, and the once impregnable German camp on the outskirts falling to the Allied bombers. In a house nearby they heard someone playing an elusive melody on the piano, faltering, altering, and replaying a dozen times, as though the composer were not yet satisfied with the piece. Then, as the melody emerged, a voice sang the first line: "Take me to your heart again, let's make a start again, forgiving and forgetting . . ." David knew that the message was prophetic. Tonight was the beginning of a new life, the life they had both longed for, the togetherness they had always craved. He turned to Suzanne, kissing her tenderly as they made plans for the future.

Anya scrambled over the wall of Vivienne's house and tapped gently on the door. Vivienne was in the kitchen, drinking a cup of weak tea.

"What are you doing here, Anya?"

"I just heard that Father Valery and Madame Bettine have been shot."

Vivienne's eyes were wide with shock.

"Father Valery married David and Suzanne last evening."

For a brief moment Anya's shoulders drooped despairingly, and Vivienne realized that she was in love with David, as Suzanne had been in love with Hans. She poured Anya a glass of elder-berry wine.

"If you're thinking of warning David, I'd say you shouldn't interrupt their honeymoon."

"Would it be better to let them think themselves safe? What if they go out to buy food, madame?"

Anya left the Marchand house, having ascertained that David was at the Hôtel de la Paix. As she neared the hotel, she paused to be sure no one was following. Then she entered by the back door and ran upstairs, seeking some sign of David's presence. The ground-floor rooms were empty, but on the mezzanine she found a pink door leading to the bridal suite. Suddenly nervous, Anya crept inside and looked wistfully down on the sleeping couple. When she shook David's shoulder, he leaped up, rubbing his eyes.

"Anya! What's happening, what are you doing here?"

"Father Valery and Madame Bettine were shot last night. I think Slagel killed them and he's still wandering about. I thought you should know."

David buried his face in his hands. Valery had been his friend since he first came to Paris at the age of twelve. It was almost like losing a father.

"I thought there was trouble last night. After we were married, I heard gunshots coming from the direction of the presbytery. Dear God, when's all this going to end?"

"Shall I go out to buy something for you and Suzanne to eat for breakfast? Tell me what can I do for you, David."

"Go right back to Ottoline's and stay there until you hear from me. You're in as much danger as I am, Anya."

"What are you going to do?"

"When it's dark I'll move with Zizi to the barn in the vineyard."

"And if Slagel starts a search?"

"I don't think he has the power to order a search. But if he does, we'll get out over the rooftops."

"Shall I tell Dr. Merimée where you are?"

"Yes, and tell him to let the rest of the group know when they arrive."

"I'll do my best, David."

Suzanne turned sleepily, murmuring as she woke. Anya ran from the room, tears streaming from her eyes, because she felt like an intruder where once she had been a welcome friend. She wiped her eyes and tried to think how good it would be to leave Paris so she could start forgetting the past. But the thought of freedom and a new life in Spain did little to cheer her, and she sobbed inconsolably.

David looked out the hotel window on the scene below. Before breakfast he would buy Suzanne some flowers and a loaf of new bread, if there was any to be had, from the bakery on the corner. He watched a song thrush trilling on the bough of a chestnut tree, its throat upstretched, its feathers puffed out by the breeze. As he dressed, he heard the sound of a shot. He ran outside, stunned when he reached the corner of the rue Cortot to see Anya lying in a pool of blood. Her eyes were still open, and as he approached she tried to smile.

"I was praying you'd come, David."

"What happened? For Christ's sake, what happened?"

"I was crying, so I didn't see the man until it was too late."

"Who was it? Was it Slagel? Anya!"

She tried to speak, but she felt weightless and light-headed, as though part of her body were already dead. David saw a man approaching, a skeletal-thin stranger dressed in black, with a patch over one eye and a hideously deformed face. He thought of the descriptions he had been given in the early days of Tristan Slagel, and this man did not match them. Then he saw the man drawing a gun, and leaped to save his own life, crashing his fist into the stranger's face again and again. Slagel's gun rolled along the dusty ground and fell with a watery plop into an open sewer. David returned to Anya's side, gathering her into his arms because he feared she was dying.

"I'll take you to Merimée."

"There's no point. Please go back to the hotel, David. I'm dying, there's nothing to be done."

A little girl skipped from a nearby house to the bakery on the corner, and the sounds of morning began to fill the air. Women appeared to brush their steps, and the postman's bicycle creaked along the cobblestones. At this last moment of her life, Anya was content because David had left his bridal bed to be with her. She clutched his hand with all her remaining strength.

"We had good times, didn't we, David . . . and I was your right hand . . . to the very end."

David felt the moment of death, the shudder that emptied the life from her lungs. Stung by the loss, he carried Anya down the street to the pharmacist's house and left her there while he telephoned Merimée with instructions to pick up the body. In his distress, David forgot the unconscious man on the pavement of the rue Cortot. He was thinking how Anya had loved him and how needlessly she had died.

Suzanne was in the hotel kitchen making coffee on a primitive burner. When she saw David's shirt covered with blood, she thought he had been shot.

"What happened, where are you hurt?"

"I'm not injured, Zizi. But Anya's dead, she was shot by a man I didn't recognize."

"Did she say who he was?"

"I don't think she could see him."

"See him! Did he come back after he'd killed her!"

Suzanne put a cup of coffee before David.

"I don't know what happened, Zizi. Anya said she'd been shot by Slagel. Then this man appeared and drew a gun on me. He had one eye and his face was badly scarred. The description I have of Slagel didn't fit him."

"What did you do?"

"I knocked the hell out of him. I'd have killed him if I could have been sure it was Slagel, but I couldn't."

"Where is he now?"

"I left him in the rue Cortot."

"We'd better leave here."

"We'll go tonight. In the meantime, you'd best pack as much of the food as you can find. We'll need it when we get to the barn."

Suzanne forced herself to eat, but she had lost her appetite. David's stricken face had answered the question she had been wanting to ask, whether he and Anya had been lovers. She told herself that as David had tolerated her own affair with Hans, she must say nothing of her chagrin at the realization of his association with Anya. But she was hurt and disappointed. She wished that she could be home in la maison Fleuri, tending the garden and sitting by the fire. There would be no light, no heat, nowhere to cook once they went to the barn. She wondered how long they would have to stay there. Then she admitted to herself that Slagel would never cease his vendetta against David until one of them was dead.


Slagel was bleeding from the mouth as he staggered down the hill. He felt the bruise on his chin and closed his mind to the agony. Chambord had not killed him because he was unsure of his identity. The American would never get a second chance. Slagel made his way to Suzanne's house. When he had finished what he had to do there went home. On arrival he noticed that there was no sound from the white bird that usually trilled to welcome him. Puzzled, he walked to the cage and peered in. The bird's body was rigid in death, its yellow beak tightly closed, its legs like small claws, curved and stiff. For days he had known the bird was ill; now it was gone. He sat by the empty fire grate and held his head, desperately trying to stop the screeching noises in his mind. Was there really a hell and was hell a part of life to be suffered without complaint? The pain was so appalling, he knew he was going to have to get help. By mid-morning Slagel was back in the military hospital.

The barn where Suzanne and David were hiding was surrounded by ripening vines. Crickets chirruped in the undergrowth, and friendly sparrows begged crumbs at the door. Suzanne was covered with a blanket because the night air was chilly. She was making an al fresco dinner from the contents of the cans. David was looking out at the vines and wondering how to tell Suzanne the appalling news he had just received from Alexander Esterhazy.

"Zizi, I have something awful to tell you."

"Say it quickly."

"La maison Fleuri has been burned down."

Suzanne was so shocked she did not cry. She just sat staring at the stars as David's words reeled around in her mind. David tried to speak reassuringly.

"The house is badly damaged, but some of your things are safe. Vivienne's taken everything that's left to her house, and I told her to keep it till you can collect it."

Overhead, the night bombers appeared and antiaircraft searchlights crisscrossed the sky. Suzanne watched lightning flashes mingling with the lights and listened as thunder roared with the bedlam of destruction. She told herself she must be grateful that she and David were still alive. But she had to force herself not to scream abuse, because the news had hurt every nerve in her body. That night she could not sleep. La maison Fleuri had been tradition and security, a place where family memories fought the paralyzing traumas of war. She kept thinking of something M. Corbeil had once said: *We're not fighting just for France, we're fighting for our home, our family, and our little piece of garden.* . . . Without her home and garden Suzanne felt suddenly beaten. She crept to David's side, and together they watched the sky turning red as houses in the suburbs began to burn.

As the sun rose, David lit a fire and brewed tea for them. He had decided what to do and was confident that he could turn Suzanne's distress to delight.

"Don't think about the fire, Zizi. I'll soon find you another house."

"I don't want another house! I could never like it at all."

"You're wrong, you know. You'll love the one I'm going to buy you."

"Are Americans always so confident, David?"

"Sure we are. We never admit that anything's impossible!"

# CHAPTER TWELVE

## August, 1944

On the first of August the French 2nd Division under Philippe Leclerc went ashore at Utah Beach. Eisenhower was still camped in Granville and the people of the Cotentin Peninsula were agog at the prospect of the coming liberation. On the third of August General von Boineburg-Lengsfeld was suspended as military commander of Paris. A few days later his replacement arrived in the city. Von Boineburg-Lengsfeld was appalled to hear that this was to be General Dietrich von Choltitz, a Prussian aristocrat descended from generations of military men. Von Choltitz was loyal without question to the Third Reich, an officer whose pedigree included the destruction of Rotterdam and participation in the devasting siege of Sevastapol. The new commander was known as the officer often designated by the Fuhrer to cover retreating German armies. In twenty-nine years he had never disobeyed an order. On the ninth of August, as von Boineburg-Lengsfeld waited in his elegant mansion for von Choltitz to arrive for dinner, he and his colleagues were unhappy, apprehensive men.

General von Choltitz wore a monocle. He was short, heavy, and pudgy-faced. His manners were impeccable, his devotion to the Fatherland unquestioned. His home life was idyllic, and it was of his family and in particular of his new son that the commander was thinking as he drove down the tree-lined boulevard skirting the Bois de Boulogne. Pretty suntanned women in

flowered turbans were walking with their children in the sunlight of evening. The general smiled briefly, though his mind was
in a turmoil. For the first time in his entire military career he
was reluctantly facing the fact that his superior was mad, a
yellow-toothed, palsied maniac, not the goose-stepping almighty
he had once revered. Von Choltitz was aware that he had been
sent to Paris to destroy the city. As a dedicated fighting officer
he found the task offensive. Any fool could destroy, but it took
a strategist to defend. Deep inside, Dietrich von Choltitz knew
that he would shortly be ordered to commence the systematic
destruction of the city's main buildings because the Fuhrer
could not countenance losing them to the Allies. A light breeze
rippled the chestnut trees, and the scent of magnolia was
everywhere. The general looked up at fine stone houses with
elaborate chimneys, elegant town residences of the nobility and
the diplomatic corps. On a corner, near the gates of the
Bois, there was one small, green-shuttered cottage that was the
home of the park keeper. Von Choltitz thought the cottage a
dignified midget among an assembly of giants. He sighed wearily
because he too felt dwarfed by circumstance. Whenever he tried
to steel himself for a task that he knew to be empty of military
merit, whispering voices in his soul told him he must strive to
die like a soldier, not as the fatuous puppet of a lunatic. He
wiped sweat from his brow as the driver turned into the
driveway of von Boineburg-Lengsfeld's house. The general was
waiting to greet his guest on the steps.

During dinner von Choltitz barely spoke. He was shocked by
the lavish food and disgusted by the women who kept offering
him favors. Puzzled by the nervousness of his host, he wondered
just how lax discipline had become in Gross Paris. Faisan à
l'alsacienne with a Gewurtztraminer was followed by veal in
tarragon sauce, a Pinot Noir by a Champagne Grand Cru, luscious
profiteroles by perfect black coffee. Von Choltitz remembered
how hungry his wife and daughters had been on his last visit
home and how the baby had cried when he left. He looked
around the sparkling gold-mirrored room with its gilded pillars
and Galérie de Glace chandeliers and thought the whole house a
bizarre seraglio unsuited to the ascetic necessities of the military
mind. He was and would always be a soldier. He wondered

earnestly if the Fuhrer realized the situation. As soon as dinner
was over, von Choltitz made excuses to leave. There was an embarrassed silence as he walked through the door. Those present
felt they had just met the man appointed by the Fuhrer as exe-
cutioner-in-chief of Paris.

On the tenth of August the railwaymen went on strike. On the
twelfth of August von Choltitz ordered the twenty thousand
members of the Paris police force to be disarmed. Five thousand
weapons were seized. Then, suddenly, the men vanished from
the streets. Rather than give up the rest of the ammunition and
the guns they knew they would soon be needing, they too had gone
on strike. Many joined the résistants; others waited eagerly to be
told what to do. Law and order vanished from the streets, and
French snipers took to the rooftops, forcing German patrols to
take shelter in armored trucks and tanks. Molotov-cocktail-
making became the work of Parisian women of all ages. No one
questioned whether they would succeed, because to think of
failure was to contemplate annihilation. At this moment the
French resistance had no tanks and no large arms, only one
thousand light arms, and an archaic fortified vehicle fit for a mu-
seum, for which they had no shells. General von Choltitz had five
thousand men, one company of tanks from the Panzer Lehr
Division, machine guns, and sixty Luftwaffe aircraft at le Bourget
airport. After the police had gone on strike, the Bank of France
followed suit. Then the Métro ceased running, and in quick
succession the telegraph, post, and grave-digging workers went
on strike. All over Paris corpses were put in cold storage or
burned on funeral pyres. Gas and electricity services were almost
at a standstill, and still the strikes escalated.

On the fifteenth of August General von Choltitz ordered the
Gestapo, the Allgemeinen SS, the Devisenschutzkommand, and
members of the Propagandastaffel to leave Paris. If he must
fight for the city, he planned to do so with the Wehrmacht and
the elite Waffen SS. Those who were leaving took suitcases
crammed with the spoils of war, but when they reached the
devastated stations they found no trains to take them home to
Germany. Striking railmen had pulled up miles of track, sabotaged
points, and wrecked engines. Even with replacement drivers to
take over from those on strike, it would be impossible to leave

Paris. The German queues grew longer and longer, and the railmen congratulated each other on having successfully cut off the enemy retreat. Small branch lines became busy with desperate officers commandeering rerouted trains. Those who waited in the boiling heat of August wondered fretfully if they were ever going to see Germany again.

Von Choltitz pushed aside his dinner and retired to his room in the Hôtel Meurice. That day he had been shown plans that would enable him to destroy the aqueducts supplying Paris. He had also received blueprints for industrial sabotage that would render the factories of the city unworkable for months or even years. A mine plan guaranteed to destroy all the great monuments had been submitted for his approval, and von Choltitz had given permission for the mines to be laid, though he had been careful to retain personal control of their detonation. Daily, sometimes hourly, he was receiving frantic calls from General-Oberst Jodl in Berlin: "Is the destruction of Paris yet arranged?" Von Choltitz lay on his bed, staring at the ceiling. The Allies were grouping in Normandy. Common sense told him he would eventually be forced to surrender Paris. If he surrendered a city in ruins, he would undoubtedly be shot. In addition, history would remember him as a moron who had blindly obeyed the Fuhrer. If he surrendered Paris whole, there was a chance of survival, with a place in history as the savior of the most beautiful city in Europe. He looked at the photograph of his wife holding the son they had longed for for so long. And in the warmth of a summer evening he prayed that Jodl would not call him again.

At dawn on the nineteenth of August, résistants gathered in front of the Cathedral of Notre Dame before surging toward the Préfecture, where they raised the French flag and destroyed the German one. By nightfall, gunfire could be heard all over the city, and many householders took the risk of copying the résistants by flying the tricolor from their bedroom windows. Taking advantage of this new mood of hostility, the Swedish consul-general visited von Choltitz and suggested a truce. The commander agreed with alacrity, abandoning his plan to recapture the Préfecture the following morning. At all costs he knew he must avoid destroying the city. At all costs he must hold on until the Allies arrived. The Americans were one hundred and seventy-five miles from Paris. Surely, soon they would come to liberate it.

The next day was Sunday, a peaceful green and yellow summer morning. Elderly gentlemen went for a walk in the Bois. Young women took their poodles to be clipped near the Ile de la Cité, and small boys were fishing on the banks of the Seine. Old ladies sat in their gardens sewing new dresses from long-hoarded material in case the Americans arrived to free them. And at the Hôtel Meurice, General von Choltitz had just been told that demolition experts specially sent by the Fuhrer from Berlin had finished laying the explosives. With increasing desperation von Choltitz was lying to his superiors about the situation in Paris. He had not even informed Jodl that there was an insurrection. He paced the room, his pale face taut with anxiety. Where *were* the Americans? Why hadn't they made their move?

Far away from Paris, in a sunlit suburb of Algiers, Charles de Gaulle was plotting the liberation of Paris. Sick of his grandiose plans for France and his patriotic desire to fight for the capital, the British had ordered him out of London. The Americans agreed with the British, determined not to let the Frenchman's personal ambition involve them in the loss of more men than was necessary. And so de Gaulle sat alone, under virtual house arrest, in the pink dusk of an African evening. He was listening to the reverberating prayers of a distant muezzin and perfecting his strategy. Fireflies danced on the lawn, emerald lizards scurried up the wall, and waves lapped a white sand beach. The autocratic man smoking a cigar saw nothing of his surroundings. He was preparing to defy those who had banished him and planning the greatest coup of his life. He would return to France, keeping his promise to the people of Paris. When he walked inside to dinner, he felt that destiny was his companion.

When de Gaulle landed in Normandy he was taken at once to meet General Eisenhower. De Gaulle made his plea for Paris, but the general demurred. The Allies would *not* fight for Paris. From a military point of view, they could well free France of the Germans without losing precious manpower by fighting for the capital. Paris was important to the French, but it was not a strategic necessity. Eisenhower would not be tempted to give in to sentimentality. De Gaulle felt instinctively that the American agreed with him but that he would not be allowed to squander resources by departing from the plan agreed on by the Allies. Downcast but not defeated, the Frenchman made his way to the Château de Rambouillet, thirty miles from Paris.

Unaware of de Gaulle's intentions and ignorant of the insurrection planned by the résistants of Paris, Eisenhower completed his preparations for freeing the French people of their German occupiers. Once he reached the Seine he would be able to proceed to the rest of the country, emptying every town and village of the Germans and capturing any who remained to fight. A young French girl arrived with the general's lunch. Politely he thanked her, shocked when she slammed down the tray and burst into tears. Eisenhower looked sympathetically at the shuddering body.

"What's wrong, honey?"

"I know what you're doing! You've made a plan that will enable you to avoid fighting for Paris!"

Eisenhower sat at his desk, wondering how she had acquired her information. The girl wiped her eyes and looked derisively down at him.

"The resistance has its plans and Frenchmen are going to fight for our city. They'll be killed, of course, and you, my fine American general, will be remembered with your British friends for letting our brave men die."

The girl rushed away, leaving Eisenhower to ponder her outburst. He thought of the SHAEF report that had first made him aware of the true cost of liberating Paris, the cost in food for the starving, in gas, in medical supplies, and, most important of all, in American soldiers. He looked stubbornly out the window at the green fields of Normandy, but the girl's words remained in his mind, and he wondered if the right decision had been made.

That same day, von Choltitz's truce crumbled. One hundred and six résistants died, and four hundred were wounded as the fighting increased. Hospitals were commandeered by the resistance, and soup kitchens set up for those who had no food. Young girls and students were enlisted as stretcher bearers, and there were first aid posts in most of the principal squares.

The following day resistance newspapers gave the order everyone had been waiting for—"To the barricades!"—and the people
of Paris came out of the darkness to fight their way to the light.
Suzanne and David joined neighbors from the Montmartre
area as they ran down the hill to the boulevard Rochechouart.
Signboards were torn down, to be used as roadblocks, with sewer
gratings, shutters, paving stones, and hoardings for extra weight.
Eager hands pushed the heavy blocks into place, and everyone was
delighted that at last the moment had arrived when they could do
something active about their loathing of the Germans. By noon,
thirty streets of the quarter had been blocked. Within forty-eight
hours, four hundred city roads would be impassable.

Suzanne sat eating an apple, happy to be out in the open again
and joyful to be preparing for the end. She watched admiringly as
David and Alexander tore down a pissoir from the place d'Anvers,
adding its iron weight to the high-piled obstruction. When they
could find nothing else in the streets with which to fortify the
blockade, householders came out and offered pianos, beds, chairs
and tables, anything that would prevent the tanks from advancing.
Women delved into their larders and gardens, and herb soup was
passed around every hour to keep the hungry workers from
collapsing. As they worked in the hot sunlight, the people were
ecstatic to be in charge, at last, of their own destiny.


General von Choltitz had just received a suggestion that Luft-
flotte III should bomb to the ground a section to the northeast of
Paris as a reprisal for the disobedience of the population. The area
would include Montmartre, Pantin, La Villette, and the Buttes-
Chaumont. At least eight hundred thousand people would be
killed in the raid. Von Choltitz had agreed to think about this,
though he had no intention of committing such a futile act of
revenge. His eyes searched the distant horizon and he wondered
desperately when the Allies would arrive. After lunch the telephone rang, and Jodl's shrill voice echoed in the stillness of the
room.

"Choltitz, what is happening? Why has Paris not been destroyed?"

The commander rose to his full height, took a deep breath, and for the first time told the General-Oberst in Berlin what was happening.

"I have been unable to supervise the destruction as you instructed because there is an insurrection and I need my men to quell it. Also, I am in need of reinforcements. Please see that these are sent at once, General-Oberst."

At 9:00 P.M. Choltitz received another harrying phone call. He pacified Berlin and retired, exhausted, to bed. News had just come that the Americans were in Rambouillet, thirty miles from Paris. Tense and impatient, von Choltitz could not sleep. He had disobeyed every order the Fuhrer had given him. It was more than likely that he would be hanged ignominiously for treason within the next forty-eight hours. Where *were* the Americans? In the small hours he rose and looked out the bedroom window at the graceful arches of the rue de Rivoli and the Tuileries beyond. The alluring presence of Paris cast her spell, and von Choltitz knew he could not ignore his instincts. But how to walk the tightrope of treason and defiance, how to hold on until the Allies came? Suddenly the military mind ticked, and he realized that there was only one way to avoid certain arrest and the total destruction of the city. At dawn he sent for the Swedish consul-general, who had arranged the truce, and over breakfast confided his true position. He was under orders direct from the Fuhrer to destroy Paris. He had defied those orders for many days. Now, because of the increasing fighting, he could defy them no longer. He did *not* wish to raze the city to the ground. Would the consul make contact with the Americans on his behalf? He handed the consul a pass and a map of the suburbs of the city and then ate a hearty breakfast.

On the barricades men and women were dying, ammunition was running out, and attacking German tank crews were being roasted to death, victims of well-aimed gas bombs. On the morning of the twenty-third, the Americans dropped arms on the city. Within minutes people ran outside to collect what they could find. The people of Montmartre were shocked to see German tanks approaching to demolish the barricades they had built far below their homes on the boulevard de Rochechouart. For a moment they stood in stunned silence. Then someone shouted, "De Gaulle is in Rambouillet!" and a great cheer rang out that resounded from the ancient walls. The tanks began to pepper apartment houses of the quarter with shells. Children were thrown from upstairs windows into the arms of waiting civilians. A young résistant leaped onto the leading tank and lobbed a grenade into the turret. Then, leaping down, he raised his arms in a triumphant cheer as the tank exploded. Within seconds he was shot by an SS sniper on the roof of a nearby building. Corbeil was looking after a young boy who had just seen his mother killed. Mme. Crystalle was making soup for those who were fighting. Suzanne was acting as a stretcher bearer for the wounded. David crept up on the SS sniper on the roof and broke his neck. When he returned, Suzanne called to him, "Where are the Americans? Why don't they come?"

David shrugged helplessly; there was no answer to her appeal. The noise of the fighting was deafening, and soon whole streets were demolished by the advancing tanks. The numbers of homeless increased with alarming speed, and casualties were laid in church halls and even on the streets because the hospitals were full to overflowing.

When he realized the implications of what was happening in Paris, General Eisenhower gave orders for the Leclerc Division to advance. The Leclerc Division was followed by the 4th U.S. Infantry, the 4th Engineers Combat Division, the 22nd Infantry, and the 20th Field Artillery.

Unaware that rescue was at hand, the people of Paris fought on. Mass burials were arranged for those who had died, and the distribution of the remaining ammunition took place at dawn. They would fight to the last shell and the last man able to hold a rifle. There was nothing more to be done.

At dusk the Leclerc Division reached Paris. Résistants hidden around the city center heard the rumble of tank treads, a sound synonymous with disaster. Was this the sound of the tanks of the crack SS 26th Division? With heads bowed they waited. Then someone noticed white stars on the sides of the tanks, and they knew that these were no enemy monsters come to destroy them. Loud cries of "Long live America! Long live France!" rang out, and men who had fought like tigers cried like children. They ran to the courtyard and swarmed like ants over the newcomers, and a great shout went up, a cheer, a howl, a voice-breaking, adulating homage that would soon be echoed in every street in Paris.

General von Choltitz had retired early. Now he stood at his bedroom window looking out at a sea of tricolor flags flying from every building. French radio programs were interrupted without warning for the statement that Paris had been relieved. The "Marseillaise" was played, and householders all over the city opened their windows and turned up the volume of their forbidden radios so neighbors could hear the good news. Wearily von Choltitz accepted that for him the war was over. There remained only the uncertainty of the future and the ignominy of surrender. Deep in his heart he knew he had done the right thing.

Suzanne and David joined the congregation at the Cathedral of Sacré-Coeur in a service of thanksgiving. And all over the hill friends were celebrating because the occupation was over. At Ottoline's, long-hidden bottles reappeared, and two Englishmen who had been hiding in her cellar were brought out and roundly kissed by all the customers. For the first time in four years the great bell of the Sacré-Coeur boomed, and soon church bells all over Paris were sounding rippling arpeggios of triumph. There would be fighting the next day, and many would die, but tonight the bells of Paris were ringing and it was time to celebrate.

The twenty-fifth of August was a day of death and defiance. Fighting raged until evening, and many brave men and women died. The city suffered in expelling those who had occupied her. But at last the pangs of rebirth were over and all but a few stubborn SS officers were gone.

To celebrate the victory, Mme. Crystalle threw a party for her friends. After beer and stolen chicken, Madame sang an aria from Puccini, Mme. Roger did a conjuring trick, and M. Corbeil took out his violin and played the haunting waltz from *Carnet du Bal.* Suzanne felt tears running down her cheeks as she listened to the old man playing. For a moment memories filtered through her mind, making her think of her parents, of Hans, and of times long past when she had still been young and foolish.

At midnight everyone adjourned to the terrace, where Alexander had arrived with a case of champagne. They were sipping the luxurious liquid when an enchanting scene unfolded far below. First the Eiffel Tower appeared like a longed-for vision, then the Palais Royale, les Invalides, and the Arc de Triomphe. The lights of Paris had been lit to herald a new, free day. Everyone cheered, and Mme. Crystalle led them in a chorus of the "Marseillaise." No one felt like sleeping, so the party went on until 5:00 A.M. Mme. Crystalle said a prayer: "Dear God, thank you for keeping us safe. Please care for those who will never see Paris again." Then everyone went home to prepare for the victory parade.

After the party, Suzanne and David went for a stroll on the hill. Here and there they paused so Suzanne could point out a favorite spot or a house with which she was in love. David kissed her tenderly and hugged her close to his heart. The occupation was over! He could barely believe their good fortune. In the rue St.-Rustique they paused outside La Bonne Franquette, the restaurant immortalized by van Gogh. Soon the owner would be serving his famous hare pâté again and the delicious soupe aux poissons. In the rue Ravignan the lace maker's shop stood forlornly barred. It too would come to life now the Germans had gone. In the rue Norvins Suzanne looked through the railings of the house she had always loved.

"This is my very favorite house."

"I know, you told me so when you were fifteen, and sixteen and seventeen and forever!"

"If we were rich we could buy it."

"I *have* bought it, Zizi."

Suzanne threw her arms around her husband's shoulders and kissed him delightedly. Then, suddenly, they realized that they were not alone. A white shirt gleamed in the moonlight, and as Tristan Slagel walked toward them an exultant smile lit his face. They rushed away toward the place du Tertre, hiding in a doorway as Slagel passed by. They watched in horror as he went slowly, methodically around the square, searching every archway in the ancient cobbled arena. When Slagel's back was turned, David led Suzanne back to the rue Norvins and fumbled to open the padlock so they could hide inside the grounds.

Realizing that his prey had eluded him, Slagel reasoned that he would have heard if the Chambords had gone by the rue du Cavalaire or the rue du Mont-Cenis. They must have backtracked down the rue Norvins. He walked slowly, cautiously after them, looking right and left into doorways and culs-de-sac until he came to the handsome manor in which Suzanne and David were hiding. For what seemed like an age he stood puzzling where the couple could have gone. Then he made his way up the hill in the direction of the Chat Noir.

As dawn lit the sky with the pale yellow of a summer morning, Suzanne and David emerged from the house and ran down the hill. Slagel stepped from the doorway where he had been hiding and followed them. His patience had been rewarded. The Chambords had been very, very close. Now and then he paused in a desperate effort to still the pounding pains in his head. But he did not give up, and doggedly, inexorably, he began to close the gap between them.

Suzanne and David were passing the stalls of a street market when they realized Slagel was behind them. They rushed to the crowded boulevard, joining people on their way to watch the parade. Slagel followed, gradually pushing his way toward them.

Suddenly David pulled Suzanne into a crowded café. Slagel passed by, and they breathed a sigh of relief that they had eluded him. They waited until they were sure he had gone. Then they ran toward the Champs-Elysées to watch the march of the victors.

Slagel was not far away, resting on the steps of an old fountain. Pale with exhaustion and sick with pain, he saw David and Suzanne as they ran by. He rose to follow them, guessing they were going to the Champs-Elysées. Slagel took a black beret from his pocket and tied a kerchief around his neck in the hope that he would more easily blend in with the crowds.

In the wide, tree-lined boulevard, bands were playing the "Marseillaise." Men had decked their tanks with flowers, and women of all ages were kissing soldiers of all nationalities. Now and then there was gunfire from SS officers sniping from the rooftops. But the people took their lead from de Gaulle, who marched unarmed and unprotected toward the Etoile. The scene was an undulating mass of flags and flowers. Paris had never been so happy.

Slagel continued to stalk the unwary couple as they crossed the road near the Rond Point. He was enjoying the scent of victory and the certain knowledge that he was going to have his revenge. Chambord would die at the moment of the city's triumph—the ultimate irony for one who had survived so long. Steadying himself, the German checked his gun and circled behind the couple. As he took aim, a bullet hit Slagel in the back of the head, and he fell to the ground, blood surging through his mouth. An SS sniper on a nearby roof ran away, elated to have killed what he thought was another Frenchman.

Unaware of the drama behind them, Suzanne and David walked hand in hand to the parade.

In the gutter Slagel lay dead, his face upturned toward a triumphant flyby of Allied planes.